By the same author

Historical Fiction

Where Seagulls Fly (2013 Edition)
Song of the Sea
The Hanging Tree

Selected Other Fiction

The Black Rose (short stories)
Eve White
For Love or Money
The Magical Isles Trilogy (Compendium Edition)
Quiddity
The Red Brick Road
Synergy

Mind Body Spirit

The Empty Cup
Enlightenment: One Man's Search for the Truth of Existence
Everyday Magic
Intuition: A User's Guide
Live Your Bliss
Reality Perception
There is Only Now

The Shepherd of St Just

By Edwin Page

Curved Brick

First published to Kindle & paperback in 2016
by Curved Brick, UK

No.63

1

He was cast in the light of the pale moon rising as he stood ankle-deep in the waters, his feet numbed by the chill. Keeping his breathing steady, Wynfred adjusted the grip on his spear, its point bloodied by the demise of the pack. Only one lone female remained, lurking somewhere in the darkness which cloaked the marshland on the border between England and Wales.

The high reeds to his left rustled as the breeze sighed across the waters and the moon's reflection was splintered by ripples. There was a faint sound from the copse of trees on the far side of the stretch, fifty yards ahead.

Caspian let out a low growl.

'She will soon be ours,' he reassured calmly, glancing sideways at his faithful wolfhound, its muzzle stained by the gore of the night's hunt.

Wynfred slowly began to stalk towards the stunted and twisted trees. The edges of his wolf-skin cloak stirred in the wind, its head covering his unruly dark hair. His gaze remained fixed on the shadows beneath the moss-hung branches, searching for any sign of his quarry.

Caspian made his way through the waters beside him, the sound of his passage giving Wynfred a sense of certainty. The outcome of the hunt was not in doubt. The she-wolf would soon succumb to the steel of his spear and the bite of his hound.

Discerning more evidence of movement within the copse, they fell still barely ten yards from the low trees.

The huntsman could feel his heart beating hard, its rhythm given greater vigour by the thrill of the pursuit.

Wynfred drew into the shadows cast by the reeds in the hope his approach would be masked. Angling his back towards them, he tightened his grip on the spear in readiness.

Sounds of hasty departure arose in the hush and Caspian immediately gave chase. Wynfred watched as the wolfhound bounded from the waters. Arcs of spray were loosed from his shaggy grey coat as he set off into the copse and vanished into the darkness beneath the boughs.

The huntsman took a steadying breath as he listened to the undergrowth whispering in disturbance. He tried to spy evidence of his hound's whereabouts, seeing nothing but moonlit boughs and the indistinct shapes of high grasses and ferns.

The wolf leapt from the reeds at his shoulder, its dark shape looming in his peripheral vision.

Wynfred barely had time to turn before it was upon him. Its weight sent him tumbling backward, the waters washing over his hide clothing with the splash of his entry and caressing his bearded face with cold lips.

The beast raked a paw across his right cheek, claws ripping his skin. It bit down upon his left shoulder and he let out a scream.

Pushing fiercely up with the length of the spear trapped between them, he yowled in pain as its teeth were torn from his flesh by the strength of the action. The wolf was thrown into the marsh beside him. Regaining its footing, cascades of spray glittered in the moonlight as it made to bite his neck.

Suddenly stopping, the wolf looked over its shoulder towards the copse. Turning to him once again, it barred its teeth and let out a deep growl before setting off in the opposite direction from the trees, passing swiftly through the marsh.

Wynfred struggled to his feet, clothes and dark curls dripping, face tight with pain. He stared after the beast, feeling the warmth of blood mingling with the water upon his right cheek and drawing down into his beard.

Raising his hand, he tentatively touched the wounds as Caspian appeared from the trees, a fox hanging from his mouth. The cuts were deep, his flesh brutally torn by the passing of the wolf's claws.

The wolfhound moved to his master and studied him a moment before letting the limp corpse drop to the waters. It raised its muzzle to Wynfred's cheek and sniffed at the blood, nostrils flaring as it caught the vague scent of the wolf arising from his master's clothes.

Caspian let out a growl and looked about the marshes for any sign of the beast.

With a wince of pain, Wynfred reached out and rested his hand upon the wolfhound's shoulder. 'Do not fret, Caspian. She will not escape us.'

Jaw set against the pain in his cheek and shoulder, he blinked water from his vision. 'No, she will not escape us,' he reiterated as he stared in the direction the wolf had fled, his eyes narrowed and smouldering with hatred.

2

Kerra stepped out of the stone-built cottage and into the sunshine which bathed the far reaches of south-west Cornwall. It was a mild day in October, the nine year old barefoot and robed in a simple dress of washed-out nettle green. The breeze wafted the long waves of golden hair that framed her face, her skin as pale as a winter moon.

Taking the left-hand path through her mother's beds of medicinal plants, she passed around the side of the low building. A dimpled smile graced her lips as a pair of white butterflies flitted before her, dancing about each other playfully.

Kerra made her way towards the woods that rose to the rear of the cottage, the march of trees stretching away to the north-west as they clung to the upper slopes of Nancherrow Hill. Looking up, she saw a seagull hovering high above and came to a halt. She closed her blue eyes and imagined her wings outspread, the wind ruffling her feathers as she surveyed the rolling countryside beneath her lofty position.

Her eyes opening, she watched the bird for a while longer and then continued towards the woods. Entering their shadows, she moved with practiced ease through clusters of bracken and began to scout out edible fungi for the cooking pot.

As she neared the Sacred Oak, Kerra spied a herd of roe deer grazing on the long grasses beneath its spreading boughs. She paused, noting their white rumps as they remained oblivious to her presence and she watched with a sense of joy.

Moving away so as not to disturb them, she came upon ox tongue fungi growing on a rotting tree trunk, their large brown caps gathered in a mossy crevice. Crouching, she gathered the front of her dress into a makeshift pouch and began to pick some, taking hold of their slimy stalks and careful to leave a few in order that they should spore new growth.

Pleased with her find, she moved on through the stillness, meandering between the widely spaced trees. She passed through a glade and began to hum contentedly, raising her face to the sun as cool blades of grass whispered against her legs.

Kerra passed through a strand of ferns and found herself at the edge of the woodland midway down the slope of the hill, her humming coming to an end. Remaining in the wan shadows beneath the boughs, she looked north-west, following the path of the stream that ran the length of the vale and flowed into the sea a little to the north. The crooked head of the valley was thick with trees that broke two hundred yards away, a small croft in their final embrace as it squatted on the far side of the stream.

'Estren Onan,' she murmured, narrowing her eyes and seeking any sign of activity at the croft. She had been warned on many an occasion not to go near the strange shepherd who lived there and had heard tell that he dwelt with spirits.

A shiver passed through her as Kerra turned her attention to the nearby grassland and warily broke from the tree-line. Bending, she took up a few mushrooms and then saw a circle of toadstools a few yards ahead. A thin smile deepened the dimples upon her cheeks as she recalled what her mother had told her about fairies dancing above such rings when the full moon paled the night sky.

Movement drew Kerra's attention down the slope to where the foot of the valley broke into rolling countryside. Half a dozen sheep were grazing on the far side of the stream, a pair of goats accompanying them.

'He will not be far away,' she mumbled, scanning the area near the flock, their fleeces gathering their winter thickness.

Her gaze suddenly stilled and her chest tightened. Beyond the flock sat Estren Onan, his eyes holding her in their dark aspect. He sat against a solitary apple tree growing at the foot of the far slope and marking the end of the vale.

Kerra caught her breath, pulse brisk and powerful. She swallowed hard, continuing to stare at him without daring to blink. Her grasp on the front of her dress tightened, body beginning to tremble with tension as the urge to take flight grew.

A small and shaggy black hound raised itself from its stomach as it lay beside the shepherd, looking up the slope at her. Estren Onan patted the dog without turning to it and smiled softly.

Reaching to a woven basket brimming with apples that rested by the dog, he took one and held it out towards her.

Kerra turned and ran, releasing the grip on her dress. Fungi tumbled about her feet as she made for the concealment of the woods, listening intently for sounds of pursuit.

Reaching the trees, she did not pause or turn, but barrelled through the dappled greens. A blackbird's alarm pierced the woodland and she heard the muffled sound of hooves making haste away from her disturbance, the image of the roe deer coming to mind before her thoughts turned to the safety of home.

3

Kerra breathlessly entered the cottage, quickly shutting the door behind her.

Her mother looked up from where she crouched beside the fire pit dug in the centre of the dwelling's earthen floor, stilled in the action of placing a new log upon the flames. 'Is all well, Little Bird?' she asked with concern.

Kerra caught her breath. 'I saw Estren Onan. He offered me an apple.'

'You spoke to him!' exclaimed her mother, a look of shock upon her narrow face as she got to her feet, the log still clutched in her hand.

She shook her head, cheeks reddened by the exertion of her flight home. 'He held it out to me.'

'I have told you many a time not to go near the croft.' The reprimand was accompanied by tightness about her mother's eyes, shallow crow's feet at their edges.

'I was collecting mushrooms at the southern end of the vale, away from the croft.'

Her mother studied her expression and saw no trace of a lie.

'I came from the woods to the meadowland beyond and did not see him at first. He was sitting against the apple tree that grows there.'

Kerenza nodded. ''Tis well you heed my warning. Estren Onan is not to be approached.'

'He did not appear strange in any way. He were like an ordinary man by my eyes.'

‘It may be that he appears so, but you have been told before that he is a man who speaks to the spirits. They have been seen wandering with him from time to time. He keeps their company and ‘tis best that you stay away.’ She adjusted the pale blue cloth beneath which her honeyed hair was gathered. She wore a simple woollen dress of the same colour over her short wiry frame, her daughter having inherited her petite stature and a good deal shorter than other children of her age in the settlement.

‘I saw no spirits,’ responded Kerra, ‘only his sheep and a dog at his side.’

‘You cannot always see spirits, Little Bird,’ replied Kerenza, her voice softening in response to her daughter’s innocence. ‘‘Tis in darkness that they likely make themselves known. In daylight their presence is by sensation only. Did you feel a chill and unnatural touch upon your skin?’

Kerra shook her head. ‘Not that I recall.’

‘Then it may be he was without their company this morn.’ She adjusted her head covering once again with her free hand. ‘Now bring me the bunch of nettles from beside the table. I must make a healing tonic for Tetker. She ails with the first of the autumn cold.’

Kerra nodded and moved to stand next to the old oak table on her left, three rough wooden stools stowed beneath. She scanned the array of dried herbs, roots, plants and branches hanging upon the wall beside it.

‘If there be none then take yourself to the garden and cut some more,’ instructed her mother.

Finally spying what had been requested, she took down the nettles and was careful to hold them by the cord tied about their stems. She went over to join her mother at the fireside, Kerenza having crouched once again and the log now upon the flames.

Kerra passed the nettles and settled onto her haunches, finding comfort in the close proximity of her mother. She watched her pluck a few leaves from the bunch, seemingly unaffected by the sting. Kerenza then placed the nettles on the earth beside her and took up a wooden bowl, dropping the leaves within. Taking a length of crystal that had been leant in the vessel, she began to crush the leaves with the flat faces of its point.

Kerra's expression became thoughtful as she turned her attention to her mother's profile, seeing the look of concentration and noting the silent movement of her thin lips as she repeated a special incantation. 'Some would say you are not so different from Estren Onan,' she commented softly.

Kerenza's brow knitted and she slowly turned to her daughter as she finished the incantation. 'Why would you say such a thing?'

She blushed slightly. 'There are those who call you strange,' she replied, looking down at the earth between them, 'because of your potions.'

Kerenza looked upon her daughter for a moment and then nodded. 'Aye, there are some,' she agreed, 'but they still come to me when in need.'

'So it may be that you and he are alike.'

Letting the length of crystal rest in the bowl, Kerenza cupped her daughter's chin and raised her gaze to hers. 'These are not potions that I concoct. They are tonics of nature and natural magic. Abiding with spirits and holding counsel with them is not a natural art. Do you understand?'

Kerra frowned and gave a vague nod.

'You must be wary of him and the vale in which he dwells. Your safety is my concern and I would have my Little Bird stay out of harm's way.'

'What harm could he do?'

Kerenza released her daughter's chin and returned her attention to the medicinal preparation in the bowl, taking up the crystal once again. 'That I do not know,' she admitted as she crushed the leaves, 'but do not wish to discover through hap of chance.'

Kerra remained quiet and stared into the flames. Kerenza stopped her activity and turned, studying her daughter's face, the roundness of youth starting to fall away to reveal the woman she would become.

'I know that look,' she stated.

Kerra turned to her with feigned ignorance. 'What look?'

'One that betrays your curiosity,' she replied. 'You are not to seek out Estren Onan, Little Bird. It may be he could bewitch you or even have you possessed by the spirits with whom he abides.'

There was a moment of thoughtful silence as Kerra toyed with the question that had plagued her during the return home.

'Do you think he is able to speak with Father?'

The weight of the question unbalanced Kerenza, her surprise fleetingly seen in the widening of her eyes. 'I…' She struggled to answer. 'I do not think you should trouble yourself with such thoughts. They can only lead you to distress or danger.'

'But if he is able then we can discover what happened,' responded Kerra with a growing sense of conviction.

'Promise me you will not venture near the croft,' said Kerenza firmly.

Her daughter withered, shoulders slumping.

'Promise me, Kerra.'

'I promise,' she replied sullenly.

Kerenza continued to regard her for a few moments and then returned her attention to crushing the nettle leaves. 'I want you to take this to Tetker when I am done,' she said, changing the topic of conversation.

'What if I catch her cold?'

'The water laced with angelica and honey that we drink every eve guards against such a thing.'

Kerra frowned and reached out, idly taking hold of a small branch protruding from the fire pit. She prodded the burning timbers in front of her with its glowing end as smoke rose to the hole in the thatch above. 'I still may catch it,' she mumbled.

Kerenza chose to ignore the comment. She picked up a skin of water which lay beside her and drew out the stopper with her teeth. Pouring a little of the liquid into the bowl, she secured the stopper back in situ and returned the skin to its resting place. 'Fetch me the Ramsons,' she instructed.

'Be that the wild garlic?' enquired her daughter.

Kerenza nodded.

Kerra stood and walked over to the selection of curatives hanging beside the table.

'What be its use?' asked Kerenza, tutoring her child in knowledge but not in practice until she was of greater age.

Kerra pondered a moment. 'It helps circulation.'

'And is good for the blood,' added her mother as the girl took down a bundle of long and slender leaves.

'These?' She turned and held them up.

'Very good,' nodded Kerenza.

She returned to her mother's side and handed her the Ramsons. Kerenza rested the bowl upon her lap and tore up a couple of the dried leaves, dropping the pieces into the nettled water. She took to crushing them with the crystal, the water tainted green as her lips moved silently and her daughter watched on.

4

Kerra passed along the earthen track between two cottages, high grasses leaning towards her as they grew at the base of the stone walls to either side. She could hear grasshoppers amidst the stalks, stirred by the autumn sun.

She approached the small dwelling beyond, a wooden cup containing the tonic cradled in her hands, a leaf covering its top and secured with cord. The thatch was black with rot beneath the eaves and she caught its pungent smell on the light breeze as she neared the door.

Coming to a halt, she noted dirty cobwebs gathered beneath the overhang of the roof, glistening with night's lingering moisture and hung with the remains of cocooned corpses. She turned her gaze from the macabre decorations and knocked upon the timbers before her.

'Come,' responded Tetker from within, her voice like that of a crow.

Kerra opened the door and entered the gloom. A sneeze arose from the rear and she found the old woman seated upon her cot, dirty fleeces about her hunched shoulders and thin ghosts of hair hanging about her face. Her eyes were red and puffy, mucus glistening on her top lip. Smoke hung thinly in the air, the fire crackling and its light adding to the sickly hue of Tetker's skin.

'Good day, Tetker. How goes it?' greeted Kerra, feeling for the old woman who had been a friend of the family for many years. 'Mamm has made you a healing tonic.' She stepped closer and held out the cup.

'Good day, Young Kerra,' rasped the old woman, coughing briefly. 'I must confess that I have had better days and many of them.' Tetker beckoned her over with a withered hand.

Kerra hesitated a moment and then passed around the left of the fire, feeling its heat against her bare legs. Stopping a few yards shy of the woman, she stretched out her hand.

'Where be thy hug of greeting today?' asked Tetker as she shifted closer on the cot and reached for the cup, the firelight illuminating the white whiskers upon her chin. Her fingers brushed against Kerra's as she took hold, the touch like that of worn leather.

The girl blushed a little and her head hung low. 'I fear catching the cold,' she admitted.

Tetker nodded. 'And I should not wish it upon you,' she said while removing the leaf covering, her hands trembling slightly.

Lifting the cup, she smelt the contents and then dipped in a finger, placing it between her bloodless lips and closing her eyes momentarily as she tasted the tonic. Nodding to herself and setting the cup upon her lap, she looked to the young girl.

'Thy mother is skilled in the ancient arts of healing and magic, for more than just herbs are infused in this potion.' Tetker sniffed and wiped away the mucus beneath her nose with the edge of a fleece, the wool glistening.

'Magic?' Kerra looked at the old woman curiously.

'Aye, magic,' replied the old woman with a nod.

'Tis only nettles and other herbs from the garden.'

Tetker grinned, her crooked and rotting teeth revealed as her lips drew back. 'She has yet to school thee in the ways of old, but thee will learn.'

'Will learn what?'

‘That is not for me to say, but for thy mother to teach when she feels the time has come.’ She lifted the cup and took a sip.

Kerra studied the old woman for a moment as she considered what had been said. The image of her mother’s lips moving as she prepared her medicines came to mind and she wondered at the likelihood that she was weaving spells into the potions. Shaking her head, she turned and made for the door, the fire spitting as she passed and a few embers leaping onto the earth by her feet.

‘Payment is upon the table,’ stated Tetker as the girl passed between the fire and the dilapidated piece of furniture. ‘Please pass on my gratitude to thy mother.’

Kerra’s steps faltered and she turned to scan the chaotic selection of oddments upon the tabletop. Spying the leaf-bound block of honey, she took it up and continued on her way.

A thought came to mind as she reached the door and she turned back to the old woman as she supped her medicine. ‘Do you know aught of Estren Onan?’ she asked, believing that if anyone were to know more about him then it would be one of the village’s oldest inhabitants.

Tetker lowered the cup. ‘Estren Onan,’ she echoed, ‘Strange One.’ She shook her head, wisps of white hair swaying as they hung about her face. ‘His real name is Jacob.’

‘Jacob,’ repeated Kerra, the simplicity of knowing his name serving to dispel some of the mystique surrounding his existence.

‘Aye,’ she nodded. ‘I grew up with his father, Gorlas, and Jeremiah of Goose Back Farm. We were friends long ago. Inseparable, my mother used to say. Then Jeremiah was betrothed at the age of twelve in order to unite two of the farms of the Cape and we barely saw him. Gorlas and I continued to remain close, even after he too was wed, but that closeness came to an end.'

'What happened?'

'He was ne'er the same after his wife passed. The croft became his hermitage, his and his two sons, Jacob and Joseph. He avoided the company of others and the Christianity which he had so embraced was cast aside as he returned to the old ways.'

'The old ways like Mamm follows?' asked Kerra with increasing interest.

Tetker nodded. 'Aye, like thy mother follows.'

Kerra thought for a moment. 'I have not heard mention of his father and brother dwelling at the croft.'

Tetker shook her head and looked to the flames. 'A sad business,' she stated, sniffing and wiping her nose.

Kerra waited for her to continue, but the old woman's gaze seemed lost to the fire. 'What was a sad business?' she prompted.

Tetker raised her gaze and stared across the fire pit, the air hazy and rippled by rising heat. 'They came down with a terrible affliction and were to the grave afore thee were born.'

'Are they the spirits with which he is said to dwell?'

The old woman snorted. 'They say a great many things, do they not? I am sure they say things about thy mother. Ye should not pay heed to loose tongues.'

'Even Mamm says he speaks with the spirits.'

'And what is wrong with that?' asked Tetker, holding the girl's gaze. 'I speak with my husband daily and it has been nigh on ten years since he was lost at sea.'

Kerra looked across the flames thoughtfully. 'Then there is nothing to fear?'

'That is not what I said to thee. I said to pay no heed to loose tongues.'

She nodded as she digested the information that had been imparted. 'I hope you are soon feeling better,' she said in parting.

'Give my regards to Jacob,' responded Tetker with a knowing smile, her crow's feet deepening.

Kerra hesitated, mouth open as if about to protest the old woman's perceptive comment, Tetker clearly in no doubt as to her intention to discover more about the shepherd. Holding her tongue, she exited the cottage and stood on the threshold after shutting the door.

Setting off, she walked briskly between the cottages set before Tetker's humble abode. She passed across the Gathering Place encircled by dwellings at the heart of St Just. A small flock of geese hissed and called as they scattered before her. One of the men of the settlement nodded his greeting as he stood on a ladder making repairs to the thatch of his roof but she gave no response, her mind distracted by thoughts of Jacob as she made her way home.

5

Kerra entered the garden, the front gate tapping shut behind her. Bending, she plucked a dandelion head from beside the path. She turned it between her thumb and forefinger, studying its soft fragility.

Taking a deep breath, she raised it to her lips and blew. The seeds were loosed and took gentle flight. She watched as the sunlight leant them a downy glow and they drifted through the air. They were carried above a patch of nettles growing against the fence that ran along the front of the garden and marked its boundary.

Her focus moved from the seeds to the woods rising behind the cottage. She pictured Jacob sitting beneath the crab apple with his hand outstretched in offering. There had seemed no sign of malice in his gesture.

The door opened and her mother's thin form was framed against the gloom within the cottage as she stepped out. She noted her daughter's presence as she moved to the left, a blade in her hand in readiness to take cuttings. 'How was Tetker?' she enquired.

'Full of cold, but grateful for the tonic. I have her payment.' Kerra raised the wrapped block of honey.

Kerenza nodded. ''Tis gratefully received. We will be able to continue taking our angelica and honeyed water well into the winter.'

She stepped to a bed of plants beneath the near window, the shutters open and a thin trail of smoke passing out over the lintel. She crouched and selected a suitable sprig, deftly slicing it from the stalk.

‘Is there need of more firewood?’ Kerra asked as she wandered along the path towards the door, trying to inject her question with nonchalance.

Kerenza looked over her shoulder knowingly, aware that her daughter wished to visit the wood and most likely look upon the vale beyond. ‘I have need of your assistance in the preparation of Pencast’s curative,’ she stated, wanting to keep her daughter close.

‘He still suffers?’ She came to a halt a few yards from her mother.

‘It takes time for gout to heal.’ The knife sliced through another tender stem. ‘When we are done, I will test you on the healing properties of each plant hanging by the table.’

‘Again?’ Kerra frowned.

‘Aye, again and yet again thereafter until all are known by rote,’ replied Kerenza as she moved past her daughter and went to the door.

Pausing in the entrance, she turned. ‘One day you will take my place as healer and it would go ill if you were not properly schooled in the art. What would happen if you mistakenly used mandrake root or were mistook in your choice of mushroom?’

‘I know which mushrooms are safe to consume.’

‘Indeed, but do you know which can bring on visions and derangement?’

Kerra looked at her mother without answer.

‘You still have much to learn, Little Bird.’

Kerra’s expression fell and she stared down at her feet.

Kerenza looked upon her daughter and softened. Reaching out, she gently ruffled her blonde hair. ‘Do not fret, Little Bird. I do not expect you to be fully skilled in the art as yet. It takes time and you have time aplenty. You are but nine and I did not practice the art without my mother's guidance till fifteen years of age. Even then I still had need to ask her advice from time to time.'

Kerra nodded as a small flock of seagulls passed overhead, calling as they flew west towards Kilgoodh Ust. She looked up and watched them pass over the settlement, wishing to feel the wind beneath her wings.

'If you lend me your assistance, it may be you can take yourself out when we are done,' said Kerenza, ushering her daughter into the cottage and leaving the door open to allow more light into the gloomy confines.

6

Kerra crept barefoot through the woodland on the upper slopes of Nancherrow Hill. Gently rolling waves of mist were gathered between the trunks and marked her passage with swirling disturbance. Night had left a parting chill which raised gooseflesh upon her arms and caused her to shiver. She moved with considered slowness, her presence a mere whisper as dew-dampened fronds drew across her dress and caressed her skin.

It had been four days since last she had found herself in the stretch of trees upon the western side of the vale. Her mother had been watchful, but Kerra had been sure to make no mention of Estren Onan and thereby dowse any concern that she would attempt to seek out the shepherd. The thought that he may be able to speak to her father's spirit and discover what had become of him burned brightly in her mind and it was this idea that bolstered her courage as she walked through the trees.

Passing through a patch of ferns, she began to feel disquieted, certain that she should have reached the edge of the woods. Her skin tingled as crows stirred in the spectral form of the Sacred Oak, their calls subdued and their presence reduced to smears of shadow in the paleness.

A small animal scurrying from her approach gave Kerra a start. She stopped, hand rising to her chest and feeling the pounding of her heart beneath the dress. She took deep breaths and glanced over her shoulder as she considered retreating to the security of the cottage and returning on a clear day.

Shaking her head, Kerra forced her feet to take her onward with greater haste as she sought to be free of the trees. A growing brightness hinted at the woodland's edge and she felt a sense of relief as the mist began to thin.

She halted on the fringes of the wood and peered down the slope. Fingers of mist reached from between the trunks and stroked the grasses of the meadowland as the watery sunlight revealed no sign of Estren Onan or his flock.

Kerra glanced about, getting her bearings and savouring the faint warmth of the day. The chill of the woods began to vacate her, but the chill which had grown within still lingered as she sighted the apple tree at the foot of the slope opposite.

Setting off at a gentle stroll while feigning a search for mushrooms, she veered right and made her way towards the tree. She surreptitiously glanced to either side as she was released by the strands of mist drawing out of the woodland and the wetness of the grasses washed upon her feet.

Her pace was quickened by the last steepness of the incline and she leapt the stream at its base, soon finding herself stood before the crab apple. She looked at the weight of fruit upon its twisted branches as bees and wasps languidly passed amidst those that had fallen, their activity yet to shake off the drowsiness of early morn.

Taken by the urge to touch the rough bark, she stepped forward and placed her palm against it. Closing her eyes, she gave an unspoken greeting, sensing the tree's vitality beneath the press of her hand.

Kerra opened her eyes and withdrew her palm, a soft smile deepening the dimples upon her rounded cheeks. The bleating of a sheep caused her to stiffen and turn to the north-west. She looked up the valley in the direction of the croft, the building hidden from sight as it rested before the woodland that filled the crooked head of the vale. The air was hazy with moisture and at first she could see no sign of approach. Then, some hundred yards away, the vague shapes of the flock became apparent as they emerged from the veil.

Her pulse increasing, Kerra looked around for a place to hide herself. The remains of a dry stone wall rested a short distance beyond the apple tree, a strand of silver birch aglow in the sunshine on the shallow slope beyond.

She quickly made her way past the crab apple. Treading on a rotting fruit in her haste, she felt stinging in the ball of her left foot and winced as she hurried to the small section of wall.

Scrambling behind it, Kerra ducked down and sat upon the earth with her back to the stones. Bringing her sole into view with the assistance of a hand about her ankle, she then plucked the crushed wasp from her skin, redness already spreading from where it had pierced her with its poisoned jab.

She inhaled between her teeth and her eyes watered. Reproaching herself for her carelessness, she tried to block the pain from her mind and turned her attention to the approach of the flock.

Shifting against the stones, she placed her hands upon their coldness, but dare not raise her head above. The sound of the sheep meandering through the grasses became increasingly distinct and she thought she could discern the vague rhythm of Estren Onan's staff as he followed behind.

She swallowed against her rising tension. Her body trembled with nervousness and the possibility of discovery as she heard the shepherd settle against the tree with a groan.

Time slowed. She dare not move for fear the sound would give away her position, her pulse still quickened.

One of the sheep appeared around the right-hand side of the wall, grazing the grass and paying her no heed. She watched it with wide eyes, expectant of a bleat of alarm when it spied her in the lea of the stones.

The beast slowly moved up the slope as the autumn sun climbed higher and the air remained misted by moisture rising from the vale. She shifted her knees upon the earth, a stone beginning to dig into her skin. Wincing at the sound, she glanced at the strand of birch behind her as she wondered at the chance of sneaking away. The lone sheep between the trees and her position acted as a deterrent, Kerra sure that it would alert Estren Onan to her departure.

'There is no need to remain hidden.' The voice was deep and warm.

Kerra stiffened.

'I have bread and cheese enough for the both of us.'

She remained motionless, unsure as to what course of action to take. The muscles in her legs quivered in response to the urge to take flight, her heart turbulent against her ribcage.

The shepherd's hound came around the wall, moving to her without hesitation and sniffing her elbow. With tail wagging, it licked her face and left a trail of saliva across her cheek.

'Bess does not bark and therefore believes you to be no threat, and I am certainly no threat unto you. Will you not make yourself known and join me?'

Kerra slowly got to her feet, her head and shoulders rising above the stone wall. She found Estren Onan still seated beneath the boughs, turned at the waist and looking over with a smile. His pale and crooked walking stick was leant against the tree beside him and he wore a brown cloak with a pale robe tied at the waist beneath. The hood of the cloak was lowered and gathered at the nape of his neck, revealing his thinning mousy hair.

'Ah, there you are,' he said, his dark eyes sparkling. 'I did think to remain quiet, but fresh bread and cheese is best shared in good company.' He glanced at the cloth package tied with cord that rested on his lap.

'My name is Jacob,' he introduced. 'Please, come join me. Neither I nor Bess will bite.' His smile broadened.

Kerra glanced down at the shaggy black hound, who was staring up at her with its tail still wagging enthusiastically. She hesitantly walked around the section of wall and began towards Jacob, the dog following beside her.

'Please sit,' said Jacob softly, holding out his hand to the grass in front of him.

She settled cross legged no more than a couple of yards from the shepherd, filled with tension and stomach churning.

'Do you have a tongue?' he enquired with a jovial tone and a raised eyebrow.

She nodded.

Jacob chuckled as Bess settled herself beside Kerra and rested her chin upon the girl's lap.

'She is in want of a scratch behind the ears,' he stated, glancing at the dog.

She began to scratch the hound, her gaze never leaving the man in front of her. He had a kindly face, jowls belying his age as they began to sag, Kerra guessing him to be a little older than her mother. His eyes echoed the kindliness of his rounded features, the lines at their sides telling of happiness in their upward curve.

'Do you have a name?' He cocked his head to the side a little as he made his enquiry.

'Kerra,' she stated quietly, her pulse beginning to calm. 'My mother calls me Little Bird.'

'Ah, your tongue gains life,' he said jokingly. 'Be you from Lannust?'

She looked at him in momentary confusion and then recalled that her grandmother had referred to the settlement by that old Cornish name. She gave a nod. 'Aye, from just beyond the woods on Nancherrow Hill,' she replied, briefly looking over her shoulder in the direction of home. 'How did you know I was hiding behind the wall?'

'See for yourself,' he replied with a sideways glance.

She turned to the grass between the crab apple and the portion of dry stone wall. Her passage was clear to see, the glinting dew having been taken from the blades by her footsteps.

'I knew where you lay hidden and also knew you to be a child. The imprint left in the crushed apple was not substantial.' His smile faded a little. 'Why did you choose to hide yourself away?'

Kerra's cheeks were touched with a flush of embarrassment and she looked down as she continued to fuss the dog, rubbing beneath its greying muzzle. 'I have heard… things,' she replied.

'Things?'

She nodded, unable to meet his gaze.

Jacob waited for her to expand, but she remained tight-lipped. He could see her discomfort and decided not to pursue the matter further.

‘Would you like to partake of the bread and cheese?’ he asked, taking up the bundle and undoing the knot in the fastening cord.

Kerra looked up with cheeks still reddened and gave a nod. She watched as he pulled aside the cloth to reveal a piece of bread with unborn grains embedded in its softness. Beside it rested goat’s cheese wrapped in leaves which were slowly opening now that their confinement had been removed.

‘Did you make them?’ she asked as her mouth watered in response to the scent of the bread.

There was a slight pause before he nodded his response. ‘Aye.’

She looked at him curiously, detecting that something went unsaid. His eyes were downcast as he tore the bread in two and then his gaze met hers as he held out her share.

‘My thanks,’ stated Kerra as she took the offered sustenance, noting a touch of tension to Jacob’s smile, his eyes a little tighter than they had been.

The shepherd took the soft cheese speckled with herbs and broke it in half, passing her portion upon the leaves in which it had been wrapped. She carefully took it as Bess watched the activity, the hound’s gaze following the cheese as Kerra held it in the air above her head.

‘Here, girl,’ said Jacob, patting his thigh.

Bess looked at him and then rose, moving to sit beside him expectantly.

‘She has a penchant for goat’s cheese,’ he said, the strain vanishing from his expression as he let the dog lick his fingers. ‘It may be what has helped her reach such a grand age.’

‘How old is she?’

‘She will be fourteen when spring draws its breath.’

Kerra looked at the shaggy canine, raising the bread to her mouth and tearing off a bite as the flock grazed around them, one of goats sniffing the back of her head as it meandered by. Chewing for a couple of moments, she broke off some cheese and placed it into her mouth, savouring the creamy taste infused with mild herbs.

They sat in contented silence as they consumed the food, Jacob giving Bess an occasional piece of cheese. Finishing, the shepherd brushed the crumbs that had tumbled to his lap into his hand and placed them on the earth nearby.

'For the insects,' he stated when he noted her curious look. 'We should share nature's bounty for 'tis not ours alone.'

Kerra gave a vague nod of response as she finished the last of the cheese and Jacob got to his feet. He reached up and pulled two apples from the branches before settling back against the trunk.

'My mother was buried beneath this tree,' he said as he stared at the fruit.

Jacob turned his thoughtful gaze to the girl. 'Now she feels the sun, rain and wind through its leaves and branches. She takes flight in the blossom and with the birds and bees that frequent the tree.'

He took a bite of the apple in his right hand. 'She becomes part of my existence…' he said, holding the other out to the girl.

Kerra took it, noting his expectant look and taking a small bite.

'…And she becomes part of yours.'

She studied the apple in her hand and thought on what he had said. There was a depth to the shepherd that she had not expected, a depth that had both warmth and consideration.

‘She lives on as part of the tree and within all things that partake of its life.’ His smile was touched with melancholy. ‘Her life is now truly woven into the life of the vale and beyond.’

There was a momentary silence as he took another bite of his apple.

‘I think I would like to be buried under a fruit tree,’ commented Kerra.

‘Aye, but may that be many years from this day,’ he responded with a thin smile as Bess went to Kerra and let out a little groan. ‘She asks that you put the leaves on the ground so that she may lick them clean.’

Kerra placed the leaves in which the cheese had been wrapped on the grass and Bess looked to her master. Jacob nodded and the hound took them up in her teeth, moving into the shade of the tree before settling and licking them.

They sat for a while, enjoying the satisfied fullness of their stomachs and the gentle warmth of the sun. Kerra lounged on her side, head propped on her hand as she watched insects pass above the grasses and wistfully plucked at the blades in front of her. She could not fathom how the dark stories of the shepherd had arisen. She found him a pleasant man, though was disappointed not to find evidence of his communion with spirits, the hope that she could discover her father’s fate vanishing with the morning mist.

Kerra began to hum to herself as her thoughts turned to the question of whether to inform her mother of Jacob’s true nature. She wanted to reveal what she knew, but to do so would also be to reveal that she had disobeyed the instruction to stay away from the vale.

‘Be that the Lay of Ailla?’ asked Jacob as the tune lifted from her lips.

Her gaze moved to him and she nodded. 'Mamm sings it to me when I cannot sleep.'

'As did mine,' he stated, memories stirring in the depth of his brown eyes. 'Many were the windswept and stormy nights when The Lay was the lullaby that brought me restfulness. Please, continue.'

Kerra began to hum once again and the shepherd listened with a faraway look upon his face. He stared at the woodland upon the higher reaches of the valley's western slope, his focus turned within.

'Her body taken by the sea, her heart forever his to be,' he sung softly as she reached the end, blinking and turning to her. 'A sad tale indeed. As a boy it moved me to sleep, but as a man it has the power to move me to tears.'

Kerra regarded him contemplatively. She had anticipated a hardened man of few words who shunned the world and was without joy. What she had found was an expressive man at one with his surroundings.

'I am not as you expected,' he stated, fathoming her thoughts.

She shook her head.

'I hope that to be a good thing.'

'Aye,' she replied, considering whether to reveal the tales she had heard about him dwelling with spirits, part of her hoping that he would say they were true.

''Tis time I made my way home,' she said after a moment, deciding to broach the subject at another time and sitting up. 'Mamm will soon be wondering where I am to.'

'I am glad to have made your acquaintance, Kerra. Should you wish to visit with me again, you are very welcome,' he stated as she got to her feet and dusted down the back of her dress.

'My thanks,' she replied, 'and for the food. I hope I will pass this way again soon,' she said, knowing full well that she would return at the earliest opportunity.

'Fare ye well, Young Kerra. May Dor Dama's blessing be upon you.'

'Dor Dama?'

'The All-Mother,' he explained with his characteristic smile. 'She nurtures and sustains all things and all things belong to her.'

She gave a nod of understanding, having heard her mother talk of such things on occasion. 'I thought she was called Earth Mother.'

'Like all belief, such terms are just words, but the truth behind them is the same,' he responded.

She regarded him momentarily and then gave a nod. 'Farewell, Jacob,' she said in parting.

'Until next we meet,' he replied.

Kerra turned and began up Nancherrow Hill towards the waiting woods. Jacob watched her departure with a kindly expression, Bess seated beside him as the sheep and goats continued to graze.

Pausing at the tree-line, she glanced back and raised her hand. Jacob lifted his in return and then she passed into the arms of the undergrowth beneath the boughs, disappearing from sight.

7

Kerra parted company with the trees through a dell flanked by hawthorn bushes, their branches laden with berries. A small herd of white cattle with wide horns grazed beyond, a scattering of thistle towers rising about them as they lifted their heads and looked over with temporary interest, their noses and inner ears coloured black.

Gathering her dress into a pouch, she hurriedly plucked the red fruit from the nearest bush. She was made glad by the thought that she would be returning home with something of use to her mother, something that may conceal the true nature of her wanderings.

Once she had gathered what she deemed to be a satisfactory amount, Kerra set off toward the vague traces of smoke rising above the trees and bushes fifty yards to the north. She skirted the fringe of the wood, sensing the vale beyond and the shepherd that dwelt there. She was already eager to return and discover more about him, the possibility that he abided with spirits requiring greater exploration before she was prepared to relinquish all hope of finding answers to the riddle of her father's disappearance.

The rough circle of dwellings about the Gathering Place came into view to the left, her own home still concealed by a cluster of low and twisted trees which marked a sunken area of marshland. She moved between them and the woodland, the shallow pools beneath the marsh trees choked with weeds and grasses.

The rear of the cottage was first revealed and then the rest of the building drew into sight. She spied a horse and cart on the far side of the wattle fence that marked the front boundary. There was firewood piled on the flat bed, the mule standing patiently at the far end as it chewed on grass pulled from beside the fence.

Kerra made her way alongside the cottage, taking the well-worn path between the plant beds. She passed around the corner and Breoc stepped out of the open front door, briefly scratching his narrow beard. A deerskin rested about his shoulders, a leather jerkin beneath which was open on a deep green shirt. His hide leggings were laced at the sides and boots spattered in mud.

'Good day, Miss Kerra,' said the trapper and woodsman as he turned to her approach, touching his forelock as he made his way towards the cart, his hair dark and ragged.

'Breoc,' she replied simply, not having taken to the man who had been visiting regularly since the spring.

Kerra walked into the cottage as the trapper hefted two bundles of branches from his cart. Her mother was attending to her headpiece, straightening the ring of platted wool that held the pale blue material in place over her hair.

'I was beginning to wonder what had become of you,' she said distractedly, taking hold of the bottom of her jerkin and giving it a downward tug so that it displayed her figure more favourably.

'I picked these for you,' replied Kerra, lowering the front of her makeshift pouch.

Kerenza gave the berries a perfunctory glance before checking the lower reaches of her dress, picking off a twig and dropping it onto the fire beside her. 'My thanks, Little Bird.'

‘They are hawthorn berries. Good for the heart and blood.’

‘Aye,’ nodded her mother as Breoc entered. ‘Would you like some mead when you are done?’ she asked the trapper.

‘That would be a welcome reward for my efforts,’ he replied with a broad smile as he crossed to the right and placed the bundles on the already substantial woodpile.

He turned and wiped perspiration from his brow with a forearm. ‘Two more and I think you will be set for the autumn chills,’ he stated before making his way out of the cottage, sunlight slanting in through the doorway and open windows to either side.

‘Where shall I put them?’ asked Kerra.

Her mother made no reply, but stood staring after the roguish man.

‘Mamm?’ she asked with greater volume.

‘What?’ There was irritation in her tone as she turned.

‘The berries,’ stated Kerra, holding up the pouch slightly.

‘Oh, on the table will do.’

Kerra frowned and moved over to the old table, careful that none of the berries should fall to the earth as she emptied her dress. She heard Breoc enter once again and place the last bundles of wood on the opposite side of the interior.

‘There,’ he stated breathlessly.

Kerra stepped beyond the table and went to her cot in the rear corner. She seated herself on the edge, the timbers creaking weakly beneath the fleeces. The sunshine streaming in through the near window warmed her feet, the rest of her cloaked in shadows which were deepened by the presence of the table and curatives hanging on the far side.

‘The mead that you offered would be a welcome refreshment,’ reminded Breoc as he stood beside the woodpile and wiped his brow once again.

‘My apologies,’ said Kerenza with embarrassment as she made her way to the table.

She unstopped an earthenware jug and poured a little of the alcohol contained within into a cup selected from a shelf on the wall behind. Resealing the jug, she took the cup across to him.

‘My thanks,’ he said, taking it from her and their fingers brushing lightly.

Her cheeks became flushed and she looked coyly down at the floor.

‘Will you not be joining me?’ he asked.

‘Mead sets my mind to befuddlement and I must prepare tonics once we have parted company,’ she replied. ‘My ears burn with heat after only a couple of sips,’ she added, nervously raising her eyes to his.

‘Truly?’ His eyebrows rose with amused inquisitiveness.

She nodded. ‘I have been told they glow and can feel the truth of it.’

He held her gaze, trying to find courage enough to voice the words he wished to say. ‘To my mind ‘tis all of you that glows, with or without a sip of mead,’ he stated, taking a drink to bolster himself after his revealing words.

‘My thanks,’ she responded, the flush deepening upon her cheeks.

‘They are heartfelt words,’ he said, the strain in his smile betraying his anxiousness as he continued to hold her gaze meaningfully.

There was an awkward silence and Breoc raised the cup again as he tried to think of something more to say. Kerra sat in the corner watching the interaction with a glum expression, disquieted by the attention paid to her mother by the trapper. She had thought nothing of it when first he had started to visit. His father had been struck down with a fever and his worsening condition brought Breoc to the door one eve in early spring. He had returned thereafter for additional medicine until his father was restored to health.

Kerra had believed that would be the end of it, but the trapper began to arrive with gifts of meat from his snares, timber from the woods and even flowers picked from the fields. His interest was not in doubt, but he had initially been spurned by her mother. Then, as spring became summer, her attitude began to soften towards him until it had now become one of open fondness.

Her frown deepened as she watched Breoc finish the last of his drink and wipe his lips with the back of his hand. He held the cup out to Kerenza and as she took it he gently gripped her wrist and drew her to him.

Kerra felt a sense of alarm and quickly cleared her throat with exaggerated volume. Her mother pulled away from the trapper, his hand falling to his side.

'I had best set to the task of preparing Old Tetker's tonic,' stated Kerenza. 'She suffers greatly with a cold that will not relent.'

'And I must to my snares,' he said, both of them clearly discomforted and feeling unsure of how to part company in the circumstances.

Breoc leant forward and gave her a peck on the cheek. She blushed and bowed her head.

He stepped to the door and turned. 'I will see you anon, my glowing Kerenza,' he said with a tight smile.

'I look forward to receiving you and enjoying your company.'

They stared at each other for a prolonged moment and then he left the cottage, striding to the waiting cart and leading the mule towards the heart of the settlement. Kerenza went to the door and stared out after him, raising her hand in farewell when he glanced back.

'I do not like him,' stated Kerra bluntly.

Her mother turned in the doorway. 'And what reason do you have to make such a judgement?'

She thought briefly. ''Tis a feeling.'

'A feeling? You cannot harbour dislike based on a whim.'

''Tis not a whim. There be something about him that makes me ill at ease.'

Kerenza moved to crouch before her daughter and took Kerra's slender hands in hers. 'Do not fret, Little Bird. No one will ever replace your father,' she said softly.

Kerra shook her head. ''Tis something else that causes me to take against him.'

'A feeling,' said Kerenza with a disapproving shake of her head as she released her daughter's hands. 'Such warrants nothing more than my disregard. Now, if there be naught else, I suggest you take yourself out and leave me in peace,' she stated while straightening.

'He ignores me,' blurted Kerra.

'I know that not to be true,' replied her mother reproachfully. 'Only just today I heard him greet you with cheer.'

'He greets me, but spares no other words for me.'

'It may be he is not used to children and knows not how to act in their company,' countered Kerenza.

'Why is he without children or a wife? Is there not something unusual in that?' Kerra held her mother's gaze. 'I have heard tell that he became obsessed with other women of the village in years passed. He haunted their every step and flew into jealous rages when they spoke to other men.'

Kerenza's eyes narrowed as she stood before her daughter and searched for any trace of a lie. 'Who told you this?' she asked with suspicion.

'Pencast when last he had gout. He had seen Breoc visiting with you and made comment.'

'And why have you held your tongue until now?'

'I did not think you would entertain thoughts of more than friendship with the trapper,' she replied, 'until today.'

'I have seen no sign of obsessive behaviour, only of growing fondness.'

'Nor I in truth,' conceded Kerra, 'but that is not to say 'tis not so.'

'Are we to pass judgement merely based on the words of others? Surely his actions should be taken into account? They speak only of a kindly man,' said Kerenza pointedly, raising an eyebrow.

'We could ask others,' suggested Kerra.

'We could, or we could simply allow our own experience of the man to mould our opinion of him rather than concerning ourselves with the opinions of others,' replied Kerenza, her expression softening when she saw her daughter's dejection.

'Let us strike a bargain,' she said, crouching once more and looking to her daughter's blue eyes. 'If Breoc ever behaves in such a way as to cause concern I will see no more of him, but while he and I remain friends you will make every effort to be gracious.'

Kerra pondered and then nodded. 'Aye,' she agreed softly.

'Good,' said Kerenza with a nod of affirmation. 'Now we must to the preparation of Tetker's tonic,' she stated, rising and turning towards the bunches of plants beyond the far end of the table.

Kerra watched her mother select the required curatives and move to the fireside. Rising from the cot, she made her way over and sat upon the earth next to her. She stared at her mother's hands as she broke leaves from a stalk, signs of age showing in the growing tightness of the skin, veins raised beneath.

'What other ingredients do we need in order to treat her cold?' asked Kerenza, glancing at her daughter.

Kerra did not reply, but simply got to her feet and went to fetch the required herb. As she returned to the fireside she tried not to think of the possibility of a romantic entanglement between her mother and Breoc, but the thought lingered as an insidious whisper at the back of her mind.

8

'Did thee visit with Jacob?' asked Tetker over her shoulder, attentive to the task of moulding a block of honey resting on the table before her, a flat length of wood in each hand.

'Aye, I went only this morning,' replied Kerra as she lingered by the door, which remained open in order to usher away the pungent odours within the cottage.

'What be thy opinion now ye have spent time with him?'

'He seems a kindly man.'

'And what of the spirits he is said to dwell with?' asked the crone as she paused to wipe her nose with a forearm.

'Of them there was no sign,' she replied with a grimace, seeing a trail of mucus glistening upon Tetker's liver-spotted skin.

'I learnt long ago to pay no heed to such tales,' said the old woman with a knowing tone.

'He shared his food with me,' stated Kerra.

'Indeed.' Tetker put the pieces of wood aside and began to wrap the honey in leaves. 'Ye have discovered for thyself that the words falling from loose tongues are oft born of ignorance.'

The old woman turned and walked over to Kerra, her eyes puffy and reddened, as they had been on the previous visit. 'Here.' She held out the honey.

Kerra took it and nodded her thanks.

'Will ye visit with Jacob again?'

'As soon as I am able,' she replied.

Tetker studied her face a moment. 'Something ails thee,' she stated, looking into her eyes.

Kerra shook her head. 'My health is as it should be.'

'I do not talk of thy body, but thy mind.'

She looked to the floor. ''Tis my mother.'

The old woman waited for Kerra to expand, knowing that whatever plagued her needed to find release.

'Breoc has taken an interest in her.'

'And she in him?'

'Aye,' nodded Kerra. 'I have heard tell of Breoc's past and fear it will go ill if she were to take up with him.'

'I thought thee had learnt to pay no heed to loose tongues?' said Tetker pointedly.

'Do you know of his past?' She looked up into the old woman's cold-ridden eyes.

Tetker nodded. 'I have heard things.'

'That he pursues women to the point of obsession?'

The old woman raised an eyebrow. 'Who told thee so?'

'Pencast.'

'Pencast was in competition for one of the women's hearts and did not take kindly to Breoc's involvement. As far as I am aware, there have only been two women that Breoc has pursued and neither has voiced complaint to me in regards his behaviour.'

'But I have a feeling about him, a bad feeling.'

Tetker held her gaze for a while as she considered her response. 'Thy father still resides in thy heart. It may be that his presence makes it ache at the thought of thy mother with another man.'

Kerra sighed. 'It may be,' she conceded with a slight nod, admitting to the old woman what she could not bring herself to admit to her mother. 'I also fear how things may change.'

‘How many precious moments have thee been able to preserve? How many times has the sun remained in the sky when thee have wished it so?’ asked the old woman. ‘Change is a natural part of life, Young Kerra. ‘Tis the only thing on which thee can rely. It comes whether we wish it or not, so ‘tis wise to make the best of it.’

‘The best of it?’

‘Aye,’ said Tetker with a nod. ‘Do not leave thyself at the periphery of their union, but become part of it. Do not distance thyself, but savour the closeness.’

‘But I do not feel close to him.’

‘Only ye can remedy that.’ She held the girl’s gaze meaningfully.

‘I will try,’ responded Kerra after a moment.

‘And ye will try to make thy own judgements rather than paying heed to gossip?’

Kerra nodded. ‘I will.’

‘Good.’ Tetker smiled warmly, the wrinkles upon her face gathering and deepening. ‘Do ye feel better for having spoken of this matter?’

‘Aye.’ Kerra nodded once again. ‘My thanks, Tetker.’

‘I am gladdened to have been of assistance. Dwell on it no more and do not allow it to create distance between thyself and thy mother.’ The old woman rested a withered hand upon her shoulder. ‘I will pray for a favourable outcome for all concerned.’

Kerra looked down at the honey in her hands. ‘I had best be on my way,’ she said softly. ‘My thanks once again.’

Tetker removed her hand and the girl turned, stepping from the house. She watched as Kerra was flanked by the cottages set before her own and then passed into the Gathering Place beyond.

Her smile faded as a black feather floated down before her. The old woman’s gaze followed its pendulum movement until it settled upon the ground at her feet, a tremulous shiver passing through her and causing her shoulders to tremble.

'Be it an omen of ill fortune?' she asked herself in a whisper.

She frowned as she stared at its dark form. 'No, the shiver arises from the cold that grasps me and the feather is merely a crow's castaway,' she stated, her tone without conviction as she closed the door and heavy clouds drew in from the west.

9

Rocks secured the sides and rear of the waxed cowhide as Wynfred sat beneath with his back to the escarpment on the high hill. A stick propped up the front, water dripping from the hide's edge just in front of his nose. Dark curls were stuck to his glistening forehead as he stared out into the night, the fires of Bristol to the north-east, dimmed and drawn out by the rain.

He scratched his beard as his gaze moved to Caspian, the wolfhound seated at the edge of the outcrop, his fur matted. They had been tracking the she-wolf southward for eight days, following the scant evidence of her passage.

Wynfred raised his hand to his cheek and touched the scabbed wounds she had delivered. The wolf would pay for the disfigurement and he would take her head as a prize to be mounted upon his wall. This was his oath, this was his hatred's desire.

A strong gust of wind blew the rain into his face and he looked to the darkened sky. The hide offered only meagre protection in such conditions, but he was prepared to undergo discomfort in order to track down the beast which had wounded both his body and his pride.

Adjusting his position, Wynfred drew into the hide's protection as far as he was able, feeling a rock jutting into his back from the hillside. The cowhide shelter drew in and out with each gust and he imagined himself within in a black heart, his hate and determination the dark blood that caused it to pulse with such vigour.

A sneer arose upon his face as the wind howled against the rocks, imitating the cry of his quarry. 'I will have your head,' he swore, looking westward. The wolf lay somewhere in the darkness below his position and Wynfred felt sure it knew he was hunting it.

He reached for his travelling pack and hauled it onto his lap. Opening it, he delved inside and withdrew a small parcel wrapped in cloth. He pulled back the folds and looked at the dwindling strips of salted pork before taking one.

Closing the cloth and placing the foodstuff into the pack, he began to chew on the piece he had selected, finding little by way of satisfaction from the sustenance. His stomach groaned as he settled, shifting again to find greater comfort.

His gaze turned to Caspian as the hound settled onto the slick rocks, apparently unaffected by the wash of wind and rain. He had been presented to him by King Edward's head wolf hunter, Peter Corbet, in recognition for his services to the crown in helping to eradicate the beasts from the counties bordering Wales. Many were the wolf bounties he had collected, though their kind were so numerous that it would be a long time yet until they were cleared from the wilds of England.

The clatter of a falling rock disturbed Wynfred's thoughts. It smashed upon the outcrop, pieces scittering in every direction.

Caspian rose and turned, growling as he looked up the hillside.

Wynfred scrambled from beneath the shelter, almost knocking the supporting stick loose as he did so. Straightening once free of the confinement, he stared up the escarpment, eyes narrowing as he drew a dagger from his hip.

At first he saw nothing in the darkness. His gaze then settled on the vague silhouette of the she-wolf against the clouds.

There was a brief moment when he swore he spied the red glow of its eyes and then it was gone, vanishing over the far side of the hill's brow.

'You cannot hide from your doom,' he yelled through the squall, raising his fist.

He stood and stared upward, face awash as he lowered his hand. 'I will hunt you to the ends of the earth if need be,' he mumbled. 'This I vow to you, devil.'

Wynfred glanced at the spear lying beneath the cowhide, the tip glinting dully in the deep shadows and promising vengeance. 'No, you cannot hide from your doom, for I carry it with me,' he said with a sneer, glancing to the hilltop one last time before returning to the shelter.

10

The trees bent and leaned in the wind, Kerra's hair tossed and thrown in front of her eyes. She cleared her vision of the golden strands as she made her way through the lively woodland, timbers creaking and the canopy filled with rustling. Leaves tumbled, torn loose from branches that waved a vigorous farewell to the summer that was receding into memory.

She reached the meadowland and looked down the slope at the foot of the vale. Her gaze immediately sought out the apple tree, the grasses on the hillside seeming like waves upon the ocean as the wind passed over them.

Finding that Jacob was not present, she turned to her left and looked north-west along the small valley. The low croft was visible nestled against the woods that loomed beyond, but there was no sign of the shepherd or his flock.

With a touch of disappointment, she began down towards the stream. Jumping its waters, she turned in the direction of the croft and cleared her sight of hair once again, wishing she had tied it back before vacating the house. Her mother believed her to be picking more hawthorn berries and had instructed her to return by late afternoon so that they may attend Mass, having not attended thus far that week.

The wind buffeted and pushed her forward, adding greater haste to her steps as Kerra neared the croft and passed a stretch of corn stubble at the foot of the eastern slope to her right. She stared at the stone building beside the stream. It was long and narrow, its far end in a state of disrepair, the bleating of sheep arising from behind the tumbledown walls. She presumed Jacob to be in residence, spying smoke rising from a hole in the cottage's thatch, the fumes torn to shreds and drawn up the valley. A dry stone wall marked the boundary of the garden and came to an end by the stream to the left, the stretch of water running alongside the abode having been widened beyond the ability for even a man to leap.

She stopped before a small gate of bound branches that had been whittled free of their bark. Placing her hand upon it, she pushed it open and two small bells announced her entry as they hung from the top rung. The sound of barking arose from within the cottage as Kerra glanced at them, their brass tarnished and green in places.

She began towards the door partway along the front, passing along a track of dry earth between the building and the stream. As she neared it, the door opened and Jacob peered out, his gaze immediately settling on her approaching form.

'Good day, Young Kerra,' he stated as he quickly stepped from the cottage and closed the door behind him, the shutters of the window alongside her banging against their fastenings.

'Good day, Jacob,' she replied as he walked to meet her.

'How goes it?' he enquired.

'Well, and with you?'

He nodded, his smile slightly strained.

'Did the bells announce my arrival?'

Jacob gave another nod. 'As they do for all who pass into the garden.'

'Do you have many visitors?' she asked in surprise.

The shepherd chuckled. 'In truth, you be the first.'

Kerra could not help but grin, both with amusement and with a sense of being significant. 'I hope I am not disturbing you.'

'Not in the least. I was about to take Bess out and gather firewood before the rains come,' he said, looking to the threatening clouds, their bellies looming low and darkening the day. 'It would be a pleasure to have your company.'

Kerra's smile widened.

'Wait here and I will fetch her,' he said, turning and making his way back to the door.

Jacob paused and looked over before entering, Kerra sensing he was checking that she had not followed and getting the distinct feeling that he did not wish her to enter. She glanced to the window near to her left as the shutters strained and rattled, trying to find some clue as to what lay beyond, but seeing nothing but darkness in the cracks between.

The shepherd reappeared with his crooked stick in hand and Bess at his heels. He secured the door and went to the girl, the hound trotting over and sniffing Kerra's hand before relieving herself against the wall.

'Here,' he said, holding out a small piece of cord, ''tis for your hair.'

'My thanks.' Kerra took it from him and gathered her windswept locks behind her head. 'Why have you widened the stream alongside the garden?'

'To encourage fish,' he replied as she tied back her hair, a few stray strands still loose about her face. 'Only the other day I caught a pike there.'

She nodded as she lowered her hands. 'Ready,' she stated.

'We must through the gate as there is no other exit from the garden,' he said with a gentle ushering motion.

Kerra glanced at the building and then turned. As she approached the gate, she noted a squat tower of stones rising from the mud and grass to the left, vegetable beds beyond reaching around to the rear of the croft. A flat piece of granite rested atop the structure and scattered upon it were the remains of various foodstuffs, including apples and berries in various states of decay. Scraps lay on the patchy earth about the tower and all showed signs of having been eaten by insects and other animals.

'What is that?' she asked with a nod of indication as she paused in the gateway.

Jacob glanced at the stones. 'There are those that may call it an altar,' he replied, 'but I see it as a table where I share my bounty with others who dwell in the vale.'

'Spirits?' asked Kerra, her eyes widening as she looked back at him and the spectre of her father lifted into mind.

'Not as I am aware,' he said with a smile. 'The vale is not only my home. Many are the creatures who dwell herc and they have as much claim to its fruitfulness as I.'

She looked at the table as she considered his words, feeling slightly disappointed that there had not been a more fantastical explanation of the structure's purpose. Then a thought arose, its genesis being the time they had previously spent at the apple tree.

'Your mother is part of their existence now,' she commented over her shoulder, 'and so even she has eaten from that table in a sense.'

Jacob's expression became one of pleasant surprise. 'Aye, she abides throughout the vale and beyond. She dwells in beetle and bee, rat and raven. That be one of the reasons I respect all life, for she may reside in any creature that I come across.'

Kerra nodded as she stepped through the gateway. 'I understand,' she said as she came to a halt where the path lost definition and became lost to the grass.

'Which way?' she asked as the shepherd drew alongside, Bess remaining close.

Jacob took the lead without replying, walking to the left and following the garden wall to its corner. Passing around it to head north, Kerra increased her pace so that she strode beside him, seeing a vague path through the grasses which hinted at his regular passage to the woods that filled the head of the vale.

Bess trotted ahead now that she was certain of the direction of travel. They moved past the far end of the croft, Kerra peering over the wall and regarding the ruined section of the building with curiosity.

'Why is this end of the cottage in such a state of disrepair?' she asked.

'Have you been told of the fearful trembling of the ground that came upon this land afore you were born?

She shook her head.

'It came upon the vale and Lannust without warning many years ago,' he reminisced, slowing his pace as the wind messed his hair. 'Many were the walls that tumbled as the earth shook with violence. Then, as sudden as it had come, the shaking abated.'

Jacob looked over to the remains of the walls at the north end of the building. 'The croft was built long ago by my grandfather's father, but the section that has fallen into ruin was built by my father in order to house the flock. He only completed the enclosure a few months before the shaking took place.

'I make repairs from time to time in order that the sheep and goats may find at least some shelter there,' he added as they passed beyond the boundary wall and made for the tree-line ten yards ahead, Bess already waiting for them there.

'Why have you not rebuilt the walls and made good the roof?'

'It has character beyond that which it possessed when in good order. Wildflowers rise from between the fallen stones and there is a pair of swallows that nest in the eaves every spring despite the precarious nature of the remaining timbers. As long as the flock does not suffer, I prefer to leave it so.'

Kerra regarded him curiously. Jacob was indeed a strange man, but not in the way that those of St Just believed. How he both viewed and interacted with the world was not something she had come across before. The people of the settlement saw their lives and their relationship with nature in a mainly practical light, whereas there was a romance to the shepherd's perspective, one beyond the everyday existence she was used to. She could not deny that even though this was only their second meeting, she was already very fond of Jacob due to the endearing quality of his unusual and kindly nature.

'What distracts you so?' he asked, seeing the thoughtful expression upon her face as they entered the woodland, the branches and undergrowth alive with the passage of the wind.

'I was just wondering what could cause the earth to tremble,' she said, hiding the true nature of her thoughts.

'Have you heard the tales of Tewal-Tan?'

'Dark Fire.' She nodded. 'He be a dragon who lived hereabouts long, long ago. My father told me of him and of the hero, Bryn.'

'Aye, Tewal-Tan were a black dragon with a throat the colour of the setting sun.'

‘Because of the fire that burned there,’ added Kerra. ‘He laid low the village of Carn Euny with his fierce breath and the might of his tail and claws.’

Jacob gave a nod of response. ‘Do you recall where the sorcerer Meloc imprisoned him?’

‘Beneath St Michael’s Mount,’ replied Kerra. ‘He fooled Tewal-Tan into believing there be a great treasure there. The beast stood at the entrance to a cavern that Meloc had fashioned with magic and saw a golden glow within, thinking it to be gold.’ She paused to push aside fern fronds as they passed through a patch of bracken and made their way deeper into the gloomy woods, the clouds pressing close above.

‘When the dragon went inside he found the light only to be a reflection of his throat upon the slick rocks, but by the time he realised the truth it was too late. Meloc sealed the cavern and Tewal-Tan fell into a deep slumber. There he is said to rest unto this day.’

‘You remember the story of his capture well,’ said Jacob. ‘I believe that the trembling of the earth may have been the dragon moving beneath The Mount.’

‘He is awake?!’ she exclaimed, her expression one of horror.

‘He may have been stretching in his sleep or disturbed by dark dreams that caused him to toss and turn.’

Kerra looked at him worriedly and Jacob brought her to a halt by laying a comforting hand upon her shoulder.

‘Do not worry yourself, Young Kerra,’ he said with a soft smile. ‘If he were awake the ground would have trembled again and again as he tried to escape his imprisonment. You can rest assured that Tewal-Tan sleeps on.’

The tightness of her features softened, the tension easing as she considered his words and accepted their reasoning. 'Some say a giant dwelt upon The Mount not so long ago and that a mermaid came to Zennor and tempted the man who loved her back to the sea,' she said as they stood before each other in the wind-stirred woods.

'I have also heard tell of such,' confirmed Jacob with a nod as he removed his hand from her shoulder.

Kerra hesitated in putting voice to the words that came to the forefront of her mind. 'Some also say that you abide with spirits.'

A look of mild surprise lifted his brow. 'Do they now?'

She nodded, noting that he made no protest of innocence. 'Do you?' she enquired, the vague hope of communicating with her father rising once again.

Jacob laughed, his eyes sparkling. 'Only those of rock and stream, tree and bush,' he replied. 'Come, let us continue or it will be dark before we have even begun to gather wood for the fire.'

He set off and Kerra watched him momentarily, the woodland moving all about him with urgent stirring and waving. Following, she decided to pursue her course of questioning as a fallen elm was revealed between the trees and Jacob made towards it.

'Have you ever talked with the spirits of people?' she asked as she stopped in the high grasses about the sloping trunk, the tree's root bowl rising to the right, torn from the foot of the eastern slope and a hollow left in its wake.

'Not as I recall,' he replied without turning to her, taking a hand axe from beneath his cloak. 'If I chop the branches, it would be appreciated if you could gather the pieces.'

She nodded. 'My father went missing last winter,' she stated, seeing the shepherd stiffen slightly as Bess sniffed the top of the fallen elm and the grasses into which it descended.

'At sea?' he asked as he readied the axe above one of the branches, a number already having been hewn from the trunk upon a previous visit.

She shook her head. 'He went to check his traps in the woods upon Nancherrow Hill one misty morn and ne'er returned. We searched the trees north and south, but found no trace. I hoped you would be able to speak with him and discover his whereabouts.'

The axe swung down and bit into the branch near its join to the trunk, pieces of bark spitting onto the grass below. 'I am sorry to disappoint.' The axe arced downwards a second time and was lifted once again.

'Do you know aught of his disappearance?' she asked, studying his face.

The axe wavered and then sliced through the air, the blade's angle causing it to ricochet along the branch uselessly. Jacob adjusted his grip on the darkly stained handle and glanced at her. 'I have nothing to offer but my condolences.'

'It may be that he is still alive,' she responded without genuine belief.

'Do not cling to such hope, for it can only lead to greater suffering.' He raised the axe and brought it down with vigour, the blade cutting deep. 'He will always be alive in your heart, and that must be enough.'

'You had a father and brother,' she stated.

He nodded as he levered the axe from the branch and lifted it in readiness. 'And I carry them both in my heart,' he replied as he continued to chop, his tone hinting at the pain held within.

It was the first time Kerra had seen evidence of discord in his life and its presence added depth to his existence. His had not been a life merely of ease and harmony, but had been marred by the loss of his family.

Jacob rested the axe in the grass at his feet and took hold of the limb which he had been chopping. The branch came away with a tug and twist, the last fibres tearing loose.

'There,' he stated, dropping it to the grass. 'It may be you can find timbers lying about the nearby trees,' he said, the implication of his words not lost on her.

Kerra nodded and turned away as Jacob began to hew another branch from the elm. She wandered between nearby trunks, scanning the ground and taking up small branches, Bess staying close and eyeing the firewood she collected with a playful look. She did not feel a sense of rejection in response to his thinly veiled wish to be alone, but understood its origin. Many were the times when she had needed to take herself into solitude after her father's disappearance.

Her thoughts turned to the chill winter's day when he had vanished without a trace. The weak sun had shone from behind high cloud, its touch one of vague warmth, its summer heat stored away as the land slumbered. Thick mist had clung to the land and the day had passed in a blaze of orange diffused by the moisture, the long night drawing in from the east and only the brightest stars revealed. Her mother had been increasingly restless, fretfully going to the door to pass outside and around to the rear of the cottage in the hope of happening upon her father as he returned.

As time wore on, her mother's worry was given voice, the pressure within forcing its expulsion through mumblings and questions of his whereabouts. She paced and repeatedly stoked the fire as Kerra sat upon her cot, the hour when she was usually to bed passing without notice as they waited for her father to arrive home.

No longer able to bear the confinement and feeling the need to act, Kerenza had taken off the veil covering her hair and wrapped it about the end of a timber taken from the woodpile. Lighting it above the fire, she had exited the cottage with the torch held aloft, the door left open in her haste.

Kerra had followed, spying the maiden moon between shreds of cloud as she hurried to keep up. They passed into the still woods in the deep of night, the mist cleared by a growing breeze. An owl hooted from amidst the branches, its haunting call seeming ominous in the flickering darkness.

They had searched long after the flames of the torch had gone out, calling out his name and praying to hear a response arising from somewhere in the blackness. No response had come, the chill and lack of light finally forcing them home.

There was no sleep that night. It was longer than any other that she could recall, stretching out to the point when she thought it may never end. When the dawn light first came there was a sense of relief, one soon forgotten as they once more set to searching the woods.

For two days the search had continued. Others from St Just joined with them, her father's name called from every direction as hope of finding him faded like the embers of a fire. Now, nearly a year passed, those embers were all but extinguished.

Kerra bent and picked up a small fallen branch, Bess still lingering close at hand. She looked to the hound and languidly tossed the timber to the side, Bess giving brief chase. She sighed as the sharp sound of the axe regularly cut through the woodland and the stick was dropped at her feet with an eager look.

'Where did you go, Father?' she asked quietly, the question taken by the wind's disturbance as she bent and picked the branch up once again, feeling the dog's saliva against her palm as she threw it with greater effort.

Glancing about, she found that Jacob was no longer in sight. Using the sound of his chopping as guidance, Kerra began to make her way back to him with an armful of timbers. She regularly threw the branch for Bess as her mind remained distracted and she was filled with a melancholia that weighed heavy upon her shoulders.

Passing through a patch of ferns, the shepherd came into sight on the far side of the fallen tree. She approached with heavy steps, the grass waving and washing against her shins. Ducking under the sloping trunk, she moved to where the pile of hewn branches lay and dropped the fruits of her gathering upon them.

'My thanks,' said Jacob as he tore the branch he had been cutting from the elm and placed it atop the pile. 'I think 'tis enough for now.' He wiped his brow with his sleeve, a thin sheen of perspiration glistening upon his face.

Fastening the axe to a strip of leather tied about his waist, he took a length of thick cord from a pouch sewn onto the pale robe that he wore beneath his cloak. Kerra watched as he gathered it about the wood, passing it beneath and then pulling it tight around the branches until he was satisfied that they would remain secure.

Tying the ends, Jacob hefted the bundle onto his shoulder, leaning his head away from the stubs of smaller branches protruding at the sides. 'We should return before the rains come.'

Kerra nodded wordlessly and waited for him to lead the way.

He looked upon her for a moment as Bess waited nearby with the stick clasped in her teeth. 'I did not mean to cause offence,' he stated softly, having noted her slumped demeanour.

‘None was taken,’ she responded, looking into his dark eyes and seeing a touch of regret. ‘Your need for solitude was understood.’

Jacob smiled thinly. ‘You have wisdom and insight beyond your years, Young Kerra.’

He glanced to the sky after feeling a spot of rain upon his cheek. ‘Come, we should be away or there will be no escaping the coming downpour.’

She nodded and they set off in the direction they had come. Bess led the way, vanishing into swathes of bracken to reappear shortly thereafter with a glance to check on their progress, the stick still in her possession. Silence lay between them, one without any awkwardness or the need to be filled with words.

They passed out of the woods and approached the croft, the wind against their faces and the clouds spitting their warning of what was to come. Walking alongside the dry stone wall, Kerra glanced over at the ruined portion of the building. She nodded to herself, finding that it did indeed have more character than the rest of the cottage and knowing it was a place that she would have keenly explored should she have come across its likeness on her wanderings.

Stopping before the gate, Jacob turned to her. ‘There is something I must ask you,’ he stated.

She looked at him curiously.

‘What are your mother’s thoughts on you keeping my company?’

Kerra was surprised by his question, but had no wish to lie. ‘What causes you to ask?’ she said, trying to sidestep the need to answer.

‘You say that those of Lannust believe I abide with spirits. If your mother is of the same belief, then I find it hard to imagine that she would gladly let you spend time in the vale.’

‘She pays no mind to it,’ she responded.

‘She cares not?’

Her cheeks reddened slightly and in so doing revealed the truth.

‘She knows not,’ stated Jacob in realisation.

Kerra turned her gaze to the ground.

‘Do you not think there is need to tell her?’

‘I know what she would say in reply.’ She sighed deeply and scuffed the earth with her foot. ‘She has already instructed me not to pass into the vale or seek out your company.’

He regarded her for a while and she could feel his gaze upon her.

‘You must tell her.’

She looked up at him, her pensiveness softened by the warmth of his eyes.

‘‘Tis for the best, Young Kerra. Remember what I said about having wisdom beyond your years? Put it to good use, tell her of our meetings and let her know the truth; that I do not abide with spirits.’

‘She will not listen,’ she responded as the rain began to fall more heavily.

‘Try,’ he said, smiling thinly.

‘What if she still refuses to see the truth?’

‘Then you have tried.’

‘And I may still visit with you?’ She looked at him hopefully.

Jacob hesitated and then nodded.

Relief showed in her expression.

‘Now you must leave or you will arrive home soaked to the skin,’ he said with a glance at the clouds. ‘Dusk brings a storm.’

Kerra followed his gaze. ‘Is it dusk already?’

‘Aye, though hard to tell on such a day as this.’

‘I am late and have not yet gathered the berries,’ she said, stepping back from him.

‘Berries?’ he asked without comprehension.

‘I told Mamm I was going to collect hawthorn berries.’ She turned and began away from him hastily.

‘I will see you soon, Jacob,’ she called over her shoulder as she leapt the stream and broke into a run, ascending the vale’s western slope towards the march of trees above.

‘Take good care, Young Kerra,’ he replied, ‘and may Dor Dama see you safely home.’ He watched her for a few moments before turning and opening the gate, allowing Bess to pass through as the rain dampened his windswept hair.

11

The rain beat heavily upon the thatch. Gentle hisses arose from the fire pit as drips fell from the hole in the roof above and were consumed by the struggling flames. Kerra stood nearby, savouring the warmth as she donned a green woollen dress and a leather jerkin which she began to tie at the front. Her mother waited impatiently, seated on one of the stools that were usually stowed beneath the table.

Two knocks sounded upon the door.

Kerra fell still. The thought that it could be Jacob coming to speak with her mother came to mind and she tensed, staring at the portal apprehensively.

Kerenza huffed and rose from the stool with exaggerated effort. 'Who would come calling on such a foul evening?'

She opened the door to discover Breoc standing beyond, his hair and beard dripping wet and his clothes slick with rainwater. 'Good evening, Breoc,' she greeted with forced cheer as Kerra breathed a sigh of relief and continued with her task. 'Come in and find shelter from the rain.'

'My thanks, Kerenza,' he responded, touching his forelock as she moved aside and he entered the cottage.

'What brings you to my door in such inclement weather?'

He pulled back his long hide coat to reveal a rabbit hanging at his hip. 'I found three in my traps this day and thought you may be happy to receive one for the cooking pot,' he stated while untying it. 'Here.'

‘‘Tis much appreciated,’ she stated, taking it from him.

‘Are you not going to greet our guest, Kerra?’ she asked pointedly as her daughter finished tying the front of her jerkin.

‘He made no greeting to me,’ she responded rebelliously.

‘Good evening, Miss Kerra,’ said Breoc with a slight bow.

‘Evening,’ she replied simply.

Her mother stared at her with displeasure. ‘My apologies,’ she said after turning to the trapper. ‘She is taken by an irksome mood. I had need to scold her not long past.’

Kerra looked over at her mother with a touch of anger, unhappy that she should share such a thing with Breoc. ‘I am ready,’ she said with a hard edge to her tone.

‘And not before time,’ responded Kerenza with a glance at her daughter. ‘She went out to pick berries and returned late, wet and without naught to show for her wanderings.’

Kerra’s anger grew. ‘Because I was with Jacob,’ she blurted.

‘Jacob?’ Her mother turned with brow creased.

‘Estren Onan,’ she clarified, already regretting her revealing outburst.

Kerenza and Breoc stared at her in shock, both rendered temporarily speechless.

‘I gave you instruction not to seek him out,’ reprimanded her mother. ‘You gave me your word and I am disappointed to find ‘tis not your bond.’

‘Have you not heard that he dwells with spirits?’ asked Breoc.

‘I have heard and know it not to be the truth.’

'You know nothing of the sort,' snapped her mother.

'I have seen him walking with one at his side,' stated the trapper.

Kerra and her mother both looked to him, taken aback by his claim.

'Really?' asked Kerenza.

'Aye,' he replied with a nod. 'Sea mist was upon the land as I checked my traps one morn. I came to the eastern edge of the woodland upon Nancherrow Hill and heard voices in the vale below, though I could not discern the words that were spoken.

'Creeping closer, two figures passed north alongside the stream, no more than vague apparitions. One was Estren Onan, the other a pale spirit, hooded and cloaked.'

'He does not abide with spirits,' protested Kerra.

'The evidence of my eyes is to the contrary,' responded the trapper. 'I tell you, Miss Kerra, he dwells and speaks with the dead. He is an unnatural man.'

''Tis not true,' she insisted with increased volume, glaring at Breoc.

'Calm yourself,' said her mother angrily. 'You will not speak to Breoc in that way.'

'But he is wrong.'

'I said, enough!'

They stared at each other, Kerra's mouth opening to reply, but her words silenced by the sternness of her mother's gaze.

'I am sorry for my daughter's outbursts. I did not bring her up to act in such a way,' said Kerenza as she turned to the trapper.

'She is but young and naïve,' he responded with a disarming smile.

'Will you be attending Mass?'

He shook his head, a couple of drops of water loosed by the action. 'I will attend on the morrow and beg my pardon for my absence today,' he replied, unable to hold her gaze. 'I have an admission to make.'

She looked at him curiously. 'What is it?'

'The gift of the rabbit is not the only reason for my visiting with you,' he revealed, shifting restlessly.

'No?'

'No,' he replied with another shake of his head, looking at her as he nervously scratched his narrow beard. 'I came to ask if you would accompany me to the celebrations at the end of the month.'

'The festival of Kalan Gwav?'

Breoc nodded. 'You would do me a great honour if you were to attend at my side.'

'And it would be an honour to be beside you,' she replied with a flush to her cheeks.

'I will call for you before dusk and we can dowse your fire together.'

Kerenza looked into his eyes a moment and simply nodded, well aware that the act of dowsing the fire in his company would hold great significance. It would announce a union beyond that which they had thus far shared, one that the entire community would witness when they gathered at the bonfire to mark the end of harvest and the beginning of winter.

Kerra looked at them across the fire pit, the ripples of heat in the air reflecting the emotions still smouldering within her, ones stoked by the thought of Breoc helping to dowse the fire. She wanted to voice complaint, but knew her mother would not listen, that she had taken a step too far with her earlier protestations and the admission of visiting Jacob. She would wait for a more opportune time and then broach the subject with measured care.

‘I should take my leave. Father will have skinned one of the conies in readiness for supper and will be waiting for my return.’ Breoc stepped to the door.

‘My thanks for the rabbit,’ said Kerenza. ‘I look forward to seeing you in readiness for the celebrations in four days time.’

‘I am sure I will see you afore then,’ smiled Breoc. ‘Will you be going to the meeting tomorrow at the Gathering Place?’

‘If the weather is more agreeable,’ she replied with a nod.

‘Then I shall see you there.’ He took hold of the handle and opened the door, a curtain of drips falling from the thatch above and the night beyond filled with rain.

‘Fare ye well, Breoc.’

‘Fare ye well,’ he responded before stepping out and closing the door behind him.

12

Wynfred ran through the mizzle in the dawning light. He held his spear in readiness as the spectres of trees drew out of the paleness, only to fade at his back. Caspian had already gone ahead, the wolf's tracks fresh in the mud and the beast somewhere close at hand.

Veering to the left, the huntsman descended a slope into the cool depths of the whiteness. His face glistened with a mixture of perspiration and drizzle, drops falling from his fringe and beard as he made haste across the uneven terrain. He leapt over a rock and drew to a halt, ears pricked as he listened for any sign of his hound or the wolf being pursued.

Silence pressed in upon him.

Wynfred set off once again, making his way around a large rock that materialized before him like a sleeping giant. Passing across a meadow, he jumped over a brook that gurgled softly, his feet sinking deep into the boggy ground on the far side. His expression tightened, pace hampered by the marshland as he fought to pull his calfskins free of the mud with each step.

The hush was broken by the sudden rasping of crows.

Wynfred listened, trying to discern the direction of the alarmed cries, the mist diffusing the sounds and making it difficult to ascertain their origin. He cocked his head to one side as the calls began to die down and then set off to the right.

Mud slurped with every lift of his boots and his brow furrowed in response, the noise accentuated in the stillness. The going was laboured as he struggled towards a strand of trees ahead that were no more than vague shadows. He shivered as the sweat of his body cooled and the dampness of the day leeched into his clothes.

Wynfred thought he spied movement within the trees and went still. His eyes narrowed as he looked for any sign of his quarry and he silently cursed the mizzle that so hampered the hunt.

A shape appeared between two of the nearest trunks. The huntsman stiffened and tightened his grip on the spear. He stared at the beast, its misted silhouette like something from a dream as he willed it to draw closer.

It stepped forward and he charged, splashing through the last of the marshland and letting out a fearsome yell as he levelled the spear with its chest. The sound died away in his throat as Caspian was revealed by the retreating mist, the hound staring at him incredulously.

Wynfred frowned and quickly glanced about, hoping for some fleeting sign of the wolf. He knew that in all likelihood his howl of attack would have set the beast to flight and lowered the tip of his spear after seeing nothing of note within the pale surroundings.

Stepping up onto the solid ground between the trees, he rested his hand upon Caspian's shoulder. 'She alludes us again,' he commented, 'but it will not be long until we pick up her trail again and continue our pursuit.'

The wolfhound let out a groaning yawn, turning its head to briefly lick at his master's hand.

'I know,' replied Wynfred, rubbing Caspian behind his ear. 'My hunger gnaws at me also, but my appetite for the she-devil is far greater, for the time being at least.'

He lowered his hand and looked upward, trying to discern the whereabouts of the sun, but finding the task impossible. Looking at the trees that haunted the nearby landscape with their dark presence, Wynfred then set off deeper into the woodland.

'Come,' he instructed, glancing back at his hound as he moved like a phantom between the trunks.

13

Kerenza tightened the laces of her jerkin and looked to her daughter as Kerra sat upon a stool by the table. 'Are you not coming, Little Bird?'

Kerra shook her head. ''Tis a meeting for the adults, not the children of St Just,' she replied. 'Besides, 'tis still raining.'

Her mother paused in readying herself. 'You are not to venture into the vale while I am absent,' she instructed.

'I will wait here for your return,' replied Kerra, making sure to keep her gaze steady despite the deceit of her words.

'Make sure you do. I will not suffer anymore wayward behaviour.' Kerenza's tone was filled with stern warning.

Kerra nodded.

Her mother pulled on her shoes and then flung a cape of cowhide over her head and shoulders. 'I should not be long,' she stated as she made her way to the door.

Opening it, she lingered upon the threshold, turning to look at her daughter and assessing whether she could be trusted to remain true to her word. With a frown that revealed her doubt, she stepped into the persistent rain and closed the door behind her.

Kerra rose from the stool and hurried to the near window, leaning close and peering with one eye between the shutters. She watched as her mother hurried away in the direction of the Gathering Place. Feeling satisfied that she was beyond sight, she hurriedly dressed for the inclement conditions.

Within a short time she had donned a jerkin and hide cloak over her woollen dress. Slipping on her shoes, she went to her cot and reached beneath the straw-filled pillow. Locating the piece of rabbit meat that she had saved from the previous night's supper, she then made for the door, stopping before it and listening for an instant before exiting the house.

Kerra ran around the cottage and into the woods, grateful for their concealment. Heavy drops pattered upon leaves and earth as she made her way through the march of trees, the ground sloping beneath her quick steps.

She broke from the tree-line without faltering as she moved down into the vale, looking for any sign of Jacob. Spying him by the stream to her left, she made a beeline towards the shepherd.

He looked up, an expression of concern arising in response to her haste. 'Is all well?' he called as she drew within earshot, the flock bleating with mild disturbance at her hurried approach.

Kerra nodded, unable to find breath to answer. She leapt the stream and drew to a halt before him. Doubling over, she placed her hands upon her knees as she filled her lungs with air.

Jacob looked in the direction she had come, seeking any sign of something untoward despite her gesture that all was well.

'I have not long,' she panted as Bess sniffed her legs in greeting and she briefly scratched the hound behind the ears.

'Why such haste?' he asked.

Kerra wiped a drop of rainwater from the end of her nose as the flush of her exertions began to fade from her face. 'I spoke with Mamm, as you asked. She has forbidden me from visiting the vale,' she said between laboured breaths, crouching and slipping the rabbit meat from her jerkin. She let Bess take it from her palm and then gave her an affectionate pat on the head.

'Your words failed to persuade her of my true character?' he asked as she straightened. 'I did not realise my reputation had grown so powerful so as to muddy the minds of even those who are told the truth. I thought the testament of your words would bring clarity and am saddened 'tis not so.'

'The trapper, Breoc, said that he has seen with his own eyes the spirits that dwell with you.'

'Truly?'

'Aye,' she said with a nod. 'He claims to have spied you walking with one of them alongside the stream one misty morn.'

Jacob looked to the woods upon Nancherrow Hill. 'Many have been the times I have seen phantoms in the mists that settle in the vale. Each time I was mistook and the phantoms were but conjurations of my mind.'

'I protested your innocence,' she stated.

He nodded. 'My thanks, Young Kerra.'

'You could return with me and speak with my mother directly,' she suggested with a hopeful tone.

'I fear no words will undo those that have already bound me in dark rumour.'

'There is still hope that they can be undone.'

Jacob reached out and placed a hand upon her shoulder, forcing a smile. 'You know the truth and that will have to be enough for now.'

Kerra frowned. 'I do not know when I will be able to return. Mamm is sure to keep me under her watchful eye for the time being.'

'For my part, I would not have you suffer,' he said. 'I would also not have you deceive those who are only concerned with your welfare.'

'You do not wish for me to visit with you again?' she asked with a hurt tone.

'Those were not my words. I would not wish for you to be punished and neither would I wish for you to lie to your mother.'

'Then I will not lie,' she stated matter-of-factly. 'I will simply omit the truth.'

Jacob could not help but smile. 'You have a judicious mind for one so young.'

'I do not wish to cause my mother distress and yet will not give up my time with you,' she responded.

Jacob nodded. 'For the latter I am grateful and for the former thankful.' He gave her shoulder a gentle squeeze and then removed his hand.

'I better make my way home before Mamm returns from the meeting.'

'Meeting?' asked Jacob.

'The village meets at the Gathering Place to discuss the plen-an-gwary,' she replied.

'Place of the play?'

Kerra nodded. 'Some have put forward a proposition to build an amphitheatre of earth about the Gathering Place. Some of the elders have voiced protest and today's meeting is for these to be heard and argued.'

She retreated a step and frowned. 'I must be away.'

'I hope you will soon find opportunity to return,' said Jacob.

'And I,' she concurred. 'Fare ye well, Jacob.' Kerra turned and leapt the stream, beginning up the slope beyond.

Stopping, she looked back at the shepherd thoughtfully. 'The festival of Kalan-Gwav begins in three days time,' she called. 'If you attend then the rumours of your communion with spirits may start to be undone.'

'I will make no promises, but it may be that I shall come,' replied Jacob, raising his hand in parting.

Kerra continued to stare at him through the falling rain for a moment and then hurried on up the hill as he watched her leave. Bess moved to the bank of the stream and glanced over her shoulder at her master, asking if she had permission to follow with the look in her eyes.

'Triga,' he instructed simply, the hound remaining in place despite her desire to chase playfully after the girl.

His expression thoughtful, Jacob turned his attention to the flock, the oil of their fleeces protecting them from the worst of the weather. He adjusted the grip on his stick and wished human life could be so simple.

With a sigh, he glanced west to see that Kerra had vanished into the trees. 'May Dor Dama's blessing be upon you,' he said softly as rainwater ran down his face.

14

Kerra hastened around the side of the cottage and looked to the door and windows when she reached the front. There was no outward sign of her mother having returned home, only a thin trail of smoke rising from the hole in the thatch.

She paused before the door and tentatively took hold of the handle, glancing towards the heart of the village and grateful not to see her mother's approach. Opening it, she found the interior to be empty and quickly slipped inside.

Taking off her cloak and jerkin, she hid them in the deep shadows beneath her cot and rested her shoes before them. Hurrying over to the other side of the cottage, Kerra selected some slender branches from the woodpile and went to the fire. The flames were low and weak, much of the timber having fallen into the dark ruin of embers.

Putting the branches upon the earth, she crouched and then placed the smallest in the fire pit. She waited for the flames to take hold, drawing her hair over her left shoulder so that it would more easily dry and holding her hands towards the heat.

The hiss of steam turned into the crackle of consumption after only a couple of minutes and Kerra fetched thicker pieces of wood, placing them atop the others. A flurry of sparks lifted to the thatch as she tried to settle herself, feeling increasingly tense as the expectation of her mother's return grew.

It was not long until the door opened and Kerenza hurriedly stepped in out of the rain. Closing it behind her, she looked to her daughter and noted the dampness of her hair. With a surreptitious glance, she spied the shoes beneath the bed and saw the trace of mud at the heels.

'Did the meeting fare well?' greeted Kerra with a light tone and tight smile.

Kerenza stepped to the fire pit, clothes dripping wet. 'Naught has yet to be decided,' she stated, moving to take one of the stools from beneath the table. 'Has all been well here?'

'Aye,' nodded Kerra as her mother removed her cowhide and rested it over the stool, the jerkin soon following.

'Did you have need to go out?' Kerenza removed her headpiece without looking at her daughter and shook her hair free.

Kerra detected the probing nature of the question despite its apparent innocence. 'There was a mouse,' she lied.

'A mouse?' Her mother took another stool and moved it to the fireside, seating herself to Kerra's right and warming her hands over the flames.

'Aye, in the woodpile. I caught it and set it loose in the garden,' she expanded, the guilt of the lie weighing heavy and causing her head to bow.

Kerenza nodded, noting her daughter's posture. She knew Kerra's words to be untrue and was certain of where she had been, but had not the energy to confront her or engage in argument after debating the plen-an-gwary. It had been a quarrelsome meeting, the weather souring people's moods and making them more prone to stubborn disagreement.

‘You should change into some dry clothes,’ suggested Kerra, her mother’s silence making her feel uncomfortable and suspecting that she was aware of the deceit.

Kerenza stared into the flames for a few moments, the chill which had settled still clinging to her bones despite the warmth radiating from the fire. She composed her thoughts, chose her words and then looked over at her daughter.

‘I know you have visited with Estren Onan,’ she stated quietly.

Kerra opened her mouth to speak, but her mother held up her hand to silence the protest.

‘I have not the energy for argument,’ she said, voice and expression filled with sadness. ‘I am disappointed in you, Little Bird. You have broken your promise and lied to cover that fact. More than that, I do not recognise my daughter in such actions and believe it must be Estren Onan’s influence which has guided you to become so contrary to the girl I thought I knew.’

‘‘Tis not his…,’ began Kerra.

‘No,’ stated her mother firmly. ‘I will have no words from you for they cannot be trusted. You are hereby confined to the house and front garden. There will be no wandering. There will be no opportunity for visits to the vale.’

‘What about Kalan-Gwav?’

‘If in three days you have returned to being the child I know, then it may be that you can accompany me.’

‘With Breoc?’

‘With Breoc,’ confirmed Kerenza with a nod.

Kerra’s frown deepened. ‘I do not like him.’

‘He is not of your concern.’

‘And if you marry him?’

‘That is my choice, should he choose to ask.’

‘I will leave home if you wed *that* man.’

Kerenza stared at her daughter and sighed. ‘Do not be so foolish. You will do no such thing. Now, fetch more wood for the fire and think on what I have said and on your behaviour since you began to spend time with Estren Onan. You will see the truth of my words.’

‘’Tis only because you will not let me visit with him openly,’ said Kerra, rising to her feet. ‘If you were to allow it, then there would be no need for deception on my part.’

‘If you were to heed my instructions and remain true to your word there would be no need for deception,’ stated Kerenza pointedly.

Kerra moved to the woodpile with an exaggerated heaviness of step. Grabbing up a few branches, she returned to the fire and threw them down upon the floor, stray pieces of bark scattering about them.

‘You will not listen to me and will not allow me to visit with him despite having come to no harm and seeing no spirits,’ she stated with tears of frustration in her blue eyes.

‘You heard what Breoc said. He saw them with his own eyes.’

‘I do not care what Breoc said,’ she replied, the first tears falling down her cheeks. ‘I have seen with my own eyes that he does not abide with spirits. I have visited with Jacob three times and he only abides with his flock and Bess.’

‘Bess?’ asked Kerenza, trying to soften her tone and aching at the sight of her daughter’s distress despite the disappointment she felt.

‘His dog,’ she replied.

Kerra sniffed and wiped her nose with the back of her hand as she tried to blink away the tears gathered within her eyes. She took a wavering breath to calm herself and then crouched, taking up one of the branches and placing it on the fire.

'I went to him while you were at the meeting, told him that you did not believe my words and that I would not be able to visit with him for a time. I also said he should come to Kalan-Gwav in the hope his presence would dispel the rumours about him.'

Kerra turned to her mother. 'Will you not believe your daughter over a man?' she pleaded. 'Jacob does not abide with spirits, but is a kindly soul.'

Kerenza regarded her daughter thoughtfully, seeing the trails of tears glistening in the firelight. 'It appears to me that I have judged Estren Onan…'

'Jacob,' Kerra cut in.

'Jacob,' nodded her mother. '…On the accounts of others and it may be that I should make my own account of the man. If he attends Kalan-Gwav you can introduce us and if not then I may accompany you to the vale.'

'I can visit with him?' asked Kerra in astonishment.

'That is not what I said. Your behaviour over the next few days will count for much, but I do promise that I will judge Estren… Jacob,' she corrected, '…for myself.'

Kerra looked at her mother for a moment and then went over and flung her arms about her, holding her tight. 'My thanks, Mamm,' she said, the words filled with feeling.

Kerenza hugged her child, feeling the dampness of her blonde locks against her cheek.

'I am sorry,' stated Kerra as they parted, her eyes once again glistening with tears. 'I did not wish to deceive or cause upset.'

'I can see the truth of it,' she responded, a thin smile gracing her lips as she felt relief and a surge of love towards her daughter.

Gathering her into her arms once again, Kerenza gave her a kiss on the cheek. ‘I love you, Little Bird,’ she whispered, ‘and only seek to keep you safe from harm.’

15

Kerra bent to cut a sprig of thyme, the sun's warmth resting upon the back of her head. It was the eve of Kalan-Gwav and the clouds had finally broken early in the morning, the wind moving round to the south-west and bringing blue skies.

She looked about the plant bed before her, trying to locate the next herb that she needed to take a cutting from, the small knife glinting in her hand. Spying the parsley, she carefully stepped over to it, her shoes sinking into the sodden ground.

Crouching, she lay the bundle of sprigs already taken from the garden upon the earth and then selected one from the plant before her, slicing through the stem. The sound of a throat being cleared took her attention and she turned to the front gate, finding Tetker standing beyond.

'Good day, Kerra,' greeted the old woman. 'May I enter?'

'Of course,' she replied as she straightened. 'How goes it?' she asked, making her way out of the bed as the old woman opened the gate and began up the main path.

'It goes well. I am free of the cold that gripped me and think that is deserving of a hug.' She smiled, wrinkles deep and large nose casting a shadow upon her face as the wisps of white hair about her head stirred in the breeze.

Kerra stepped over and placed her arms about the old woman, as was her habit when Tetker was not full of cold. 'I am glad you are better,' she said as they parted.

'Thanks must go to thy mother and the potions she makes. If it were not for her knowledge and talents I would still be ailing or worse,' she replied. 'I would not be the first to succumb to such sickness and pass to the grave.'

'I am happy 'tis not so.'

'Not half as happy as I.' Tetker grinned.

Kerra chuckled.

'Is thy mother home?'

She shook her head. 'She is searching for mushrooms in the wood,' she replied with a nod towards the trees rising behind the cottage.

Tetker held out a block of honey wrapped in leaves. 'This is the last until the spring comes. 'Tis a gift of thanks rather than payment.'

Kerra took it from her heavily veined hand. 'I for one am grateful and am certain Mamm will also appreciate the gift.'

'How go the visits with Jacob? Is he well?'

Kerra glanced over her shoulder, looking to the trees visible beyond the corner of the cottage to her left. Seeing no sign of her mother, she returned her attention to Tetker. 'I have visited with him a few times and find him to be a man like no other,' she revealed, the volume of her voice kept low. 'He is thoughtful and has a depth I did not expect.'

Tetker nodded. 'So it was with his mother.'

'Mamm intends to meet with him.'

'Ye told her?' A look of surprise widened the old woman's deep-set eyes.

Kerra glanced towards the woods again, nervous that her mother may be near the tree-line and able to hear what was passing between them. 'Would you like to come in?' she offered. 'Mamm has made a cordial flavoured with dandelion and burdock and I shall pour you a cup.'

Tetker could see the girl's anxiousness. 'That sounds very agreeable,' she responded with a nod.

Kerra led the way into the cottage, stepping over to the table. Taking one of the stools from beneath, she placed it beside the fire pit, the remains of logs smoking but no flames visible.

'My thanks,' stated the old woman as she seated herself with a soft groan, adjusting the woollen shawl about her bony shoulders and holding her hands out to the vague heat despite the mildness of the day.

Kerra went to the woodpile and selected a few slender pieces which she added to the fire in order to warm her guest. 'I only revealed the truth to Mamm a couple of days ago,' she admitted as she crouched beside the pit. 'We have come to an arrangement.'

'Indeed,' nodded Tetker, 'and what would that be?'

'She will meet with him and judge his character for herself. If she finds him to be as I say, I will be permitted to visit with him,' she replied. 'Breoc claims to have seen him walking with a spirit in the vale and that caused argument at first.'

'It may be that he did.'

'It was a misty day and I think it likely his imagination deceived him.'

'The imagination is indeed a tricky thing and can conjure many a sight that exists only in the mind,' she responded knowingly. 'When will thy mother meet with Jacob?'

'Either at Kalan-Gwav or soon thereafter.'

'He will attend?' For a second time the old woman's expression became one of surprise.

‘It was a suggestion I made to him. Whether he will come…’ Kerra shrugged and let the sentence remain unfinished.

‘He has lived in isolation for many years and so it would be unwise to expect him to brave the stares and whispers of the entire village.’

‘True,’ she replied with a frown, the hope that he would make an appearance receding as a result of Tetker’s words.

‘Fret ye not, Kerra.’ She reached out and took the girl’s hand in hers, giving it a gentle squeeze. ‘When thy mother meets with him she will see the truth of the man and ye will be free to spend time in his company.’

Vague footfalls drew their attention to the view out of the left-hand window. Kerenza passed by and then appeared at the door, the woven basket at her side containing the plentiful fungi she had foraged in the woods.

‘Greetings Tetker,’ she said with mild surprise when she set eyes on the visitor. ‘Tis good to see you risen from your bed. Fare you well?’ she asked as she stepped inside.

The old woman nodded. ‘Ye have my gratitude, Kerenza. If it were not for thy curatives I would still languish beneath my fleeces,’ she replied, rising stiffly as Kerenza went to her and they shared a hug of greeting.

‘‘Tis good to see the light returned to your eyes,’ said Kerenza as they parted.

‘Some say ‘tis the light of wisdom, but I say ‘tis the sparkle of youth still harboured by my mind, a youth that my body has long since forgotten,’ she said with a grin as she seated herself once again.

Kerenza smiled and placed the basket upon the table, glancing at the sprigs that her daughter had collected in her absence. 'I see you have gathered most of what is needed,' she stated as she turned towards the fire pit.

'We are only in need of dandelion,' replied Kerra.

'I interrupted the task and was kindly invited in,' said Tetker, turning to the girl. 'Was there not mention of dandelion and burdock cordial?'

Kerra smiled and nodded, rising to her feet. Her mother handed her the jug as she neared the table and then took three cups down from the shelves on the wall behind.

'My thanks,' said Kerra as she began to pour the flavoured water.

Resting the jug on the tabletop once the cups were filled, she took one to Tetker before returning to fetch her own. Kerenza lifted the last to her lips and took a sip, moving to stand in the sunshine spilling into the cottage through the doorway.

'This is pleasing indeed,' said Tetker with an approving nod after swallowing a mouthful, looking into the cup as she licked her lips.

'I would be happy to instruct you in its preparation.'

The old woman turned to Kerenza and gave another nod. 'That would be kind indeed.'

'Tetker brought us a block of honey as thanks for the curatives,' stated Kerra.

''Tis the last of the year. My bees go to their winter sleep and will not wake again until the spring warmth stirs them from slumber.'

'Are you sure you can spare it?' asked Kerenza.

'I have plenty to see me through the barren months.' The old woman took another sip of her drink.

'My thanks. 'Tis a welcome gift.'

''Tis not I who deserves thy thanks, but my bees and my late husband for tutoring me in the art of keeping them.'

'Where did he learn such an art?' asked Kerra.

Tetker glanced at her and then turned her gaze to the fire as flames consumed the new timbers. ''Tis a story that only one other of St Just is party to,' she said with a touch of melancholy. 'I would have thee both swear it will not be made widely known.'

Kerenza's brow furrowed in curiosity as she regarded the old woman hunched before the fire. 'I shall tell no other,' she stated.

'Nor I,' confirmed Kerra as Tetker glanced at her.

The old woman took a breath as she stared into the flames. 'You knew my husband as Garret of Lostwithiel,' she began, glancing at Kerenza, 'but the name he was born to was Edward. His place of birth was many miles to the east, beyond the river Tamar. He took holy orders at an age too young to truly know his own mind and did not settle into the monastic life. It were during that time that he learnt the art of bee keeping.

'His dalliance with a girl from the local village was discovered and he took flight, fearful of the harsh punishment which was sure to be metered out. My parents had not long passed, a pestilence claiming many in the village that year. He was found half starved and delirious in the woods nestled in the north of the vale where Jacob abides.'

She turned to Kerra. 'It were Jacob's father and I that discovered him there in the days when we still roamed together.'

'You were a friend to Jacob's father?' asked Kerenza with a look of surprise.

'Aye,' said Tetker as she looked to the woman standing in the doorway, 'for many a year. Gorlas were younger than I, but we shared the same imaginings; fighting off goblins with sticks in the woods, stalking unicorns through the trees, making traps by which to capture fairies. In early childhood we were oft joined by Jeremiah of Goose Back Farm, all finding the world to be a place of magic and wonder.'

She returned her attention to the fire, the soft smile which had temporarily appeared fading as her thoughts returned to the tale she was telling. 'I were but fifteen when we happened upon Edward and he almost twice that, but my heart was his with just one look. He were a handsome man in my eyes,' she said, glancing at Kerra.

'We took him to my home and there I nursed him back to health with Gorlas' help. Edward was prone to feverish mumblings during his recovery and I discerned what had befallen him. It was then that my mind fixed upon the idea of hiding his identity.

'When he were recovered enough, we concocted the lie that all of St Just were told; that he were Garret of Lostwithiel and had come west in the hope of better fortune after fire had taken all he had. We claimed to have happened upon each other on the Pendeen road, there striking up a conversation during which I offered lodging at my cottage. We were wed within three months of his presence being revealed.'

'Did anyone ever come looking for him?' asked Kerra.

Tetker shook her head, wisps of hair swaying. 'We lived a peaceful life,' she replied. 'I take ye both into my trust now not only because ye are the most dear to me of all who dwell in St Just,' she stated, looking from one to the other, 'but also so that ye will trust my words regarding Jacob.' She held Kerenza's gaze meaningfully.

'He is a gentle soul that would do no harm to man or beast. He respects the old ways, the gentle ways of living as one with the land. Many could learn much from him, but instead they seek to slight that which they do not know or understand. 'Tis good company with wise counsel that Kerra keeps when visiting with him in the vale.'

'She told you?'

Tetker nodded. 'I did not think it my place to inform thee of her actions, especially as I saw nothing in them other than a young girl's inquisitiveness. Now that I discover ye are aware of her visits to the vale, I feel that I can voice what I know to be true of the man.'

'And I thank you for it,' said Kerenza. 'I will meet with him in person, but am encouraged by your report of his nature.'

'I knew Jacob as a boy and a young man.'

'What brought your bond with Gorlas to an end?'

'The death of his wife. Gorlas kept Jacob and his brother close, unbalanced to the utmost severity by the loss. He became reclusive, his boys forced into seclusion with him. 'Tis an isolation to which he grew accustomed and which became a way of life.'

Tetker looked to Kerra. 'I pray thy meetings with Jacob may return him to us, that he will find the will to be part of the community now that he no longer abides under the yoke of his father's malady.'

'Why do you not visit with him?' asked the girl.

'Many have been the times when I have thought of doing so, but alas my feet have ne'er taken me there. I fear rebuttal and disappointment.'

'Why would he do such a thing after you shared such a bond with his father?' asked Kerenza.

The old woman sighed. 'I abandoned Gorlas in favour of Edward. Many were the times he came calling and on each occasion I gave my excuses and sent him away. Then, after his wife's death, there were no more knocks upon the door and the distance which had been opening between us became so great that I could not find the courage to bridge it and go to the vale. I fear Jacob will have not forgotten this treatment of his father.'

'Surely after all this time…'

Tetker shook her head. 'No. 'Tis better that Kerra goes to him,' she stated. 'I do not believe he will attend the festival on the morrow, but it may be that one day he will wish to visit the village, if only out of curiosity.'

The sound of the gate opening drew the women's gaze out of the door. They found Breoc approaching, a brace of large fish hanging at his side, cord tied about their tails. He strode along the path, a smile dawning when he spied the woman with whom he was besotted standing just inside the doorway.

'Good day, Kerenza. You look radiant in the sunlight,' he complimented as he stopped before her, glancing into the cottage and seeing Tetker and Kerra watching him.

His composure was temporarily lost after discovering their unexpected presence. Cheeks brushed with red, he took an involuntary step back. 'Good day, Tetker. I am gladdened to find you well again.'

'As am I, Breoc,' she said with a thin smile.

'Good day to you also, Miss Kerra.' He touched his forelock.

'Good day,' she replied simply, not attempting to feign cheer.

The trapper returned his attention to Kerenza. 'I…' He cleared his throat, briefly looking at the seated audience and feeling the weight of their watchfulness. 'I exchanged one of my rabbits for some fish and thought you may be happy to receive a couple for your supper. They were caught only this morning.' He held the mackerel out to her.

‘That is very thoughtful of you,’ she said as she took them from him. ‘It has been some time since last we dined on fish. Would you care to join us?’

Kerra’s frown deepened, the trapper catching sight of it as he glanced into the cottage again.

‘I should be on my way.’

‘You can join Kerra and I for supper if it pleases you. It seems only fair that you should partake of your gift,’ she offered, briefly lifting the mackerel.

‘It would please me greatly, but I would not leave my father to eat alone.’

‘He would be welcome also.’

Breoc pondered a moment, sorely tempted by the invitation. ‘Another time maybe,’ he said eventually, backing away as if the pressure of the watching eyes were forcing him into retreat.

‘I shall see you on the morrow to dowse the fire,’ he called before turning and making his way to the gate, passing out of the garden. Closing it behind him, he looked to Kerenza one last time and then set off along the path that followed the fence to the north.

‘Ye will dowse thy fire with him?’ asked Tetker. ‘I did not know thy relationship had grown so strong.’

Kerenza stared after the trapper a moment longer and then turned. ‘In truth, it has yet to do so. You may call the dowsing a statement of intent rather than reality.’ She smiled softly.

‘Be that wise?’

‘Why would it not be so?’

‘Ye are not merely sending a message to the rest of St Just, but to Breoc also. ‘Tis akin to a promise of union, such is the symbolism of the act carried out together.’

‘I do not see it as such. ‘Tis but a declaration of our companionship to others and to Breoc ‘tis a sign of my willingness to entertain courtship.’

‘I think it a bad idea,’ said Kerra.

‘I am well aware of your opinion,’ responded her mother with a hard glance.

‘If ye feel it to be right, then who am I to speak against it?’ said Tetker.

There was a moment of silence and then she rose from her stool with a grunt of effort. ‘‘Tis time for this aging body to return home in order that it may rest a little and continue to an even greater age,’ she said with a smile.

‘Would you care to join us?’ asked Kerenza, holding up the pair of fish.

She shook her head. ‘Though my thanks for the invitation.’

Kerra got up and went to the old woman, hugging her affectionately. ‘Fare ye well, Tetker.’ she said. ‘May Dor Dama bless you,’ she added in a whisper.

Tetker regarded her with amused curiosity as they parted.

‘What did you just say?’ asked her mother.

Kerra’s expression became tense as she turned towards the door. ‘I gave a blessing.’

‘You mentioned Dor Dama,’ stated Kerenza as she studied her daughter.

Kerra gave a nod. ‘Jacob talked of her and I have heard you state her name on occasion.’

Her mother looked to Tetker, worry clear in her eyes.

The old woman raised her hands. ‘I will not tell a soul,’ she stated. ‘Besides, the old ways are not far from my own heart.’

‘You must ne’er say Dor Dama’s name in the company of any from the village,’ said Kerenza with utmost seriousness.

‘Why?’ Kerra looked at her in bewilderment.

‘There are many who would frown upon such and some would even call you ‘witch.’ The flames of the old ways have been smothered by the followers of Christ, but their embers still smoulder in those who have not forsaken them.’

‘Heed thy mother’s advice, Young Kerra. ‘Tis not safe to openly acknowledge Dor Dama these days.’

Kerra looked to Tetker and then to her mother, eventually nodding her confirmation.

The old woman made her way to the door, Kerenza moving aside to allow her exit.

She turned after passing over the threshold, smiling warmly. ‘My thanks once again for the tonics that have seen me back to good health,’ she said. ‘I hope you will both visit with me soon.’

‘You can be certain of it,’ responded Kerra.

She moved to stand beside her mother as Tetker made her way to the gate and then passed beyond. Turning, she raised a hand in parting and then began towards her cottage on the other side of the village to the west.

16

The wind moaned across the moor as Wynfred wandered through the dusk, Caspian at his side. He cursed the failing light as he sought evidence of the she-wolf's passage. The trail had gone cold more than a day passed and his frustration was growing.

Using his spear as a staff, he leant upon it and looked to the west. A band of brightness marked the end of the bank of cloud lingering overhead, one that brought with it occasional drizzle and made the search a miserable endeavour.

Trying to ignore his gnawing hunger, he passed over stunted grasses and glistening rocks. A small wood of ancient and twisted trees came into view, tucked against the side of a hill. They were thick with grey lichen, like old skin peeling and flaking. He frowned at their barren branches and the rocky ground beneath, no sign of the wolf amidst their trunks and little by way of shelter offered by their presence.

He paused and stared at them a while, briefly wondering if they were dead or if the winds had torn away their autumn robes. The scars upon his cheek began to itch, as if to remind him of the task at hand. Nodding in response, Wynfred set off, trudging through the dreary landscape as the light continued to wane and he sought the merest hint of the beast's whereabouts.

Darkness had drawn in by the time he spied a round shack resting within a dell thick with marsh grasses. Its shape was barely discernible, only the firelight from within announcing its presence, glowing through cracks about its door and lending the smoke rising from the hole in its roof a sickly hue.

Caspian growled and he patted the dog's flank.

'There is nothing to fear,' he said, more for his own courage than the hound's, a feeling of unease arising from deep within as he considered what kind of person would choose to live in such a forsaken place, the answers that came to mind filling him with tension.

They moved towards the shack with hesitant steps, the wolfhound also sensing that something was untoward and remaining close to his master's side. Wynfred's boots sank into the waterlogged ground, each footfall giving rise to a squelch that marked his approach to anyone with keen hearing.

He drew to a stop a full ten yards from the door, looking to the light beneath to see if he could discern movement within, but seeing only the vague play of firelight. There were no sounds from inside the hut and the tall grasses that grew against its wattle and daub walls were strangely still.

'Will you be coming in?' The female voice issued from within and had a distinctly nasal quality.

Wynfred's free hand rested on the hilt of the dagger at his hip. Feeling distinctly uneasy, he slowly made his way across the boggy ground towards the door, his hunger and the need for rest driving him forward. He leant heavily on his spear and glanced to his side, discovering that Caspian had remained at a distance.

'Here boy,' he stated.

The wolfhound let out a moan of displeasure and moved towards him with wary slowness, hackles rising along his spine.

Wynfred looked to the ridge of raised hair and felt a shiver of response run down his back, as if some ancient part of him remembered once being able to echo the action. Returning his attention to the door, he drew to a stop before it and reluctantly removed his hand from the dagger. The huntsman reached out and grasped the rough handle, taking a bolstering breath.

Opening it with precautionary slowness, firelight spilled upon his scarred and bearded face, the interior reflected in the aspect of his widened eyes. A mat of cut and dried grasses rested on the far side of the fire pit. Upon it sat an elderly woman of small stature who was wrapped and draped in furs. She was smiling, the gesture disconcerting and accompanied by a strange sparkle in her grey eyes.

'You will have no need of the weapon,' she said, looking to the spear. 'I will do you no harm.'

'Who are you?' His question was a breathless whisper, fingers retaining their tight grip on the spear.

'I am…' She glanced upwards in thought. 'I am different,' she replied, eyes glittering as she stared at the huntsman in the doorway.

'You are hungry and weary from travel. Come in and rest awhile.' The dwarf gestured for him to enter with a wave of her hand.

Wynfred glanced around the hut, seeing cuts of cured mutton hanging from the wall and venison beside, a woodpile beneath spanning the entire left curve. Grasses grew to the right, the marsh reaching into the hut and a bed of turnips sewn into the earth between the boggy ground and door.

''Tis not just strangers that come a wandering,' said the dwarf, looking to the meat, 'and 'tis easier to grow crops in the shelter of my home than in the wilds beyond.

'Please, come sit and you can have your fill before resting the night.' She indicated for Wynfred to seat himself before the fire. 'Your beast can enter too, if it so wishes.'

''Tis a wolfhound.'

'Ah,' nodded the dwarf. 'A creature born of both wolf and dog.'

'No,' said Wynfred with a shake of his head. 'A dog bred for the purpose of hunting wolves.'

'You hunt wolves?' The dwarf studied him closely. 'Nay, you hunt a single wolf, one who has left its mark.' She nodded towards the scars.

'How can you know this?'

''Tis written upon your face and within your eyes. You are driven by the need to take revenge, but are you sure 'tis you that hunts? It may be that you are your own prey.'

Wynfred looked at the diminutive woman, judging her mind to be addled, but that she posed no threat. He stepped into the hut and gave a whistle over his shoulder, not turning from the figure on the far side of the fire. The wolfhound entered, staying close to the doorway as the huntsman shut it.

Stepping towards the pit, he settled on the dry earth before it, resting his spear across his lap and keeping hold of its shaft in readiness. The dwarf looked through the rising heat and then took a dark pouch from her belt. Opening its drawstrings, she tipped a selection of teeth onto her grubby palm.

Wynfred looked at them in mild horror and was certain that they were of human origin, noting that most were discoloured by decay.

'Shall we see where your fate lies?' asked the dwarf rhetorically.

She tossed them to the ground beside her, the teeth chattering briefly as they fell. Wynfred peered over, discerning nothing from the way they had fallen.

The dwarf turned to him. ‘These once belonged to old friends,’ she stated, ‘and they speak to me still.’

‘And what do they say?’ asked Wynfred.

‘Ah, so there is interest after all, but not belief, I fear.’ She held the huntsman’s gaze. ‘They whisper much of interest, though naught that can be shared. Some things are not meant to be known.’ She smiled.

‘Will you sup with me?’ she asked, suddenly rising and revealing her height to be no more than three feet, the teeth left upon the floor and pouch falling from her lap. ‘I will prepare some venison.’

‘Who were your friends?’ asked Wynfred, his lack of belief in the telling of fortunes overcoming his intrigue as to what the teeth had told the strange creature.

‘That is a tale indeed,’ she responded, stretching above the woodpile and finding that she could not reach the venison. ‘There were three who arrived here,’ she said, taking up a thick log that she used as a step.

She removed a cut of meat from where it hung and then went to the rear wall, a selection of wooden bowls and utensils resting at its base in a disorderly clutter. She began to hunt through the bowls, mumbling to herself as she did so, her words unclear.

‘You said there were three of you,’ prompted Wynfred, his nose wrinkling in disgust as the dwarf took up two bowls and stepped over to the marsh grasses, scraping the mouldering contents out with a spoon, a few small flies rising about her.

‘Ah, yes,’ she responded with a nod as she returned to the fireside, the glistening residue of what had been inside the vessels making Wynfred’s stomach tighten as he glanced at them.

‘There were three of us that came upon this place,’ she said as she took up a knife and began to cut slivers of meat into the bowls. ‘It was but a ruin then, those who had once lived here having passed on to greener pastures.'

'Greener pastures?'

'Death or another place to settle far away from here, it matters not. Both are greener pastures,' she replied, glancing up and then looking to a small pile of turnips beside the door.

Wynfred followed her gaze. 'I will be satisfied with meat alone,' he stated, noting the discolouration of the vegetables and turning back to her.

'As you wish,' she said with a nod, continuing to cut slices into his bowl, but leaving hers own only half-full. 'We travelled long and in secret to get here. The nights were our ally.'

'Were your friends…' He sought the right words. '…As you?'

She glanced over the flames and shook her head. 'One was a man with a child's arms and legs, the other with no legs at all, though he had taken to walking on his hands with practiced ease. We were entertainment for those who paid to see us,' she revealed. 'Or it may be that we were horror,' she added after a moment's thought.

'A freak show,' he stated.

Her eyes tightened as she regarded him. 'By hap of chance we were as we were, just as you are as you are.'

'I meant no offence.'

'Then you will be pleased to hear that none was taken,' she replied. 'We were freed from our bonds one night and made good our escape. There was a giant of a man also, one who we tried to track after we decided to remain together rather than take separate paths.'

'You did not find him?'

She shook her head. 'Like you, we found that the track went cold upon the moor. We were weary and hungry and came upon this place built upon a small table of land within the marsh, its roof in a state of collapse. Taking what shelter was afforded by the walls, we decided to remain, concealed from the world and safe from discovery by any but the most hardy traveller.'

'And the giant?'

'I know only what the teeth have told me of his fate and am made glad by what they tell.' She held his bowl out over the fire, showing no concern for the heat rising from the flames.

'My thanks,' said Wynfred as he took the food.

'There is enough there for both you and your hound,' she stated.

He looked at the piled pieces of venison and took a large handful, placing them upon his lap. Turning, he rested the bowl beside him. 'Come, Caspian.'

The wolfhound looked to the food and made his way forward. Sniffing at it, he eagerly tucked into the welcome offering, the huntsman glad he would not have need to eat from the filthy vessel.

The dwarf glanced at the teeth beside her. 'Alas, my companions did not survive the first winter. The journey here and the harshness of those early days in this place made them weak and prone to sickness. I alone endured, but they were returned to me in summer when the marsh retreated and their bones were revealed.'

She nodded to the door and Wynfred looked over his shoulder as he chewed on a piece of meat, his eyes widening when he spied two toothless skulls resting in the eaves above.

'They watch over the entrance and speak to me through the chatter of their teeth,' she stated.

Wynfred looked to the ivories resting upon the earth beside the dwarf and realised that it was their sound and not the way in which they landed that was of importance.

‘How long have you resided here?’ he asked, taking up another piece of venison.

‘The count of years is beyond my reckoning. ‘Tis enough for me to have forgotten my name,’ she replied with a smile. ‘When I arrived my hair was blonde, now ‘tis white. I had youth and now I have old age. I think it will not be long until I am to part this world and then this place will fall into ruin once more. It may be that another will happen upon it and find the life it offers to be suited to their needs.’

A silence drew in about them, hanging heavy in the smoke haze. The woman seemed to have shrunk with the effort of telling her tale, as if the breath expended had caused her to draw into herself like a skin of water drained of its contents. She sat hunched and silent within the furs that had become mountainous upon her small form, the meagre pieces of meat untouched and forgotten within the bowl upon her lap.

Wynfred could think of no words to break the hush as he chewed on his food, his mind still distracted by the past she had revealed. Hers was a life he could barely imagine and he felt blessed not to have been born to such misfortune.

‘You had best get some sleep in order to continue your journey on the morrow.’

The dwarf’s words interrupted his thoughts and he looked over at her. ‘I must wash the sores on my feet before I lay my head to rest.’

‘I have ointment that will help soothe your pains,’ she stated before regarding him with a thoughtful look. ‘If you persist in pursuing the wolf your need for revenge will seal your own fate.’

‘Is that what you were told by the chatter of the teeth?’ he asked dubiously.

‘I know it in my heart.’

‘The only fate to be sealed will be that of the beast,’ he said, patting the spear.

‘Your fates are indeed entwined should you continue, but not in the way you would think.’

‘And yet you will not reveal unto me what was spoken?’

She shook her head. ‘All I can give is my advice to turn back, to return east to your home, for if you venture further into the west there will be no return to the life you knew.’

Wynfred studied her a moment, her words and gaze carrying a weight far beyond the slightness of her physical presence. ‘I cannot turn back,’ he said eventually.

‘This I know in truth, for your eyes burn with the need to take revenge,’ she replied sadly, confirming the words with a nod. ‘I shall discover the whereabouts of the ointment while you cleanse your feet,’ she said, turning to the bowls and cups behind her and beginning to search.

Wynfred continued to watch her for a while and then removed the spear from his lap, taking up the last piece of venison and putting it into his mouth. He reached for a boot, feeling the throb of the sores within its confinement and thoughts turning to the relief that the cold water of the marshes would offer when he passed barefoot into the night in order to cleanse his feet.

17

Wynfred woke with a start, the wolf of his dream howling and snapping through the thick forest in which he was lost and at its mercy. It took a moment for his mind to adjust to the waking scene of a smouldering fire pit, light spilling in from behind him as he lay beneath furs and his nostrils were filled with the scent of earth mingled with damp grass.

He slowly sat up, wiping the dream's residue of perspiration from his forehead and looking across to the vacant mat on the far side of the fire. Glancing about the hut's interior, he found no trace of the dwarf. His gaze came to rest on the pair of skulls above the open door, Caspian seated below facing the marshes outside.

Pain flared in his back as he yawned and stretched. He moaned in response and rubbed just above his waist, gaze falling on two bowls of food which rested to the left of the fire. He leant over and picked one up, raising it to his nose and sniffing tentatively.

'Mutton stew,' he said, dipping a finger into its thickness and tasting it. Despite the stew's coldness, he found it palatable and placed the bowl beside him.

'Caspian,' he called, the dog rising and making his way over.

Taking up the other bowl and raising it to his lips, he tipped it and began to break fast as Caspian lapped up his portion. He noticed that his feet were without discomfort and nodded to himself in appreciation of the dwarf's ointment.

Finishing the food, he set the bowl down and stretched again, the furs falling away from his back. Slowly rising, he moved to stand in the doorway and stared out into the marshy dell. The day was still young, but he was a little perturbed that they had already lost some of the daylight to sleep. The sooner they set off, the sooner they would pick up the she-wolf's trail once again.

The sensations of his dream returned as a vague uneasiness lurking in the shadows of his mind. He felt his jaw tighten and the words of warning uttered by the dwarf came to the fore.

Pondering a moment, he shook his head in dismissal. He would not entertain the idea of giving up and returning east, especially not merely based on the ramblings of someone who was clearly unbalanced after a harsh life and many years spent living alone in the bleak wilderness of the moor.

Glancing to his left when Caspian drew up beside him, Wynfred rested his hand upon the hound's shoulder. He smiled thinly, feeling the tightening of his cheek about the scars that the wolf had given him. His stamina restored by the rest and food, he felt confident that they would rediscover the devil's tracks.

'We shall continue into the west,' stated Wynfred as he and the wolfhound looked out into the bright day, the hazy sunlight turning the marsh waters golden and dew glittering on the bowed grasses of the dell.

18

Kerenza heard the slow beat of hooves and the creak of a wagon. She looked up from where she sat cross-legged before the fire, her hands in a bowl set upon her lap as she kneaded the oats, flour and honey within. 'I think Samuel approaches,' she stated as she peered out of the open door, the new day beyond bathed in sunshine.

Kerra paused in her task of grinding rose petals, a small bowl resting before her on the table as she sat upon one of the stools. She glanced out of the window, the open shutters moving slightly in the light wind. A large black horse came into view, back bent by years of labour. Holding its harness was a short man with wild hair, his nose large and displaying an old break which bent its bridge. Behind was a cart, a pile of sand contained by its low sides.

'Should I go to him?' she asked over her shoulder.

'If you think you can carry the pail,' replied her mother. 'My hands would be in need of a wash before carrying out the task.' She held them up, her fingers covered in the ingredients she was preparing.

Kerra set the crystal in the bowl and rose from the stool. Making her way past her mother, she went to the other side of the cottage and fetched the bucket from beside the woodpile, two others resting nearby, one filled with water, the other containing their morning expulsions.

'Be sure to give my greetings,' instructed her mother as Kerra went to the door and stepped from the house.

‘I will,’ she replied as she made her way along the path and Samuel brought his horse to a halt, having drawn alongside the front fence.

‘Good day, Samuel. How goes it?’ greeted Kerra as she drew up to the gate.

‘Good day to thee, Kerra. All is well, and ye?’ Samuel smiled at her, a scar punctuated by the shadowy hollow of his empty eye socket running down the left side of his face.

She gave a nod of response.

‘Hand me the pail and I shall fill it for ye,’ he stated, reaching over the gate.

Kerra handed it to him and the old farmer moved round to the rear of the cart. ‘I hear thy mother is to dowse thy fire in the company of Breoc.’

‘That she is,’ replied Kerra with a frown and an unenthusiastic tone.

‘News travels fast,’ called Kerenza.

Kerra turned to find her mother standing in the doorway, her hands clasped before her jerkin.

‘Good day, Kerenza,’ said Samuel with a slight bow. ‘It does indeed. I swear the village knew that I had lost my eye afore even I did.’ He smiled, filling the bucket with a practised scoop.

Kerenza chuckled. ‘Kalan-Gwav would not be the same without your delivery before the celebrations.’

‘My thanks,’ he responded with a nod as he handed the pail to Kerra.

Her jaw clenched as she strained under the weight, the bucket’s handle held in both hands and arms pulled straight.

‘What are thee making for the feasting?’ he asked, noting the state of Kerenza’s hands.

‘Oat cakes flavoured with rose petals and a touch of honey.’

‘The perfect farewell to the season of fruitfulness,’ said the farmer as he walked to stand beside the horse.

‘I best be on my way. There be many deliveries to make and old Toby is not as fit as he used to be.’ He patted the horse’s neck affectionately and then took hold of the harness.

‘Our thanks for the sand,’ said Kerenza. ‘We shall see you at the festivities.’

‘Fare ye well.’ He made a clicking sound and gave the harness a tug, Toby snorting and setting off, following the path north alongside the fence.

Kerra began towards the door, glancing down at the damp contents of the pail and seeing a sand hopper crawling across the surface before burying itself out of sight. The faint scent of the sea wafted up to her as she approached her mother, the weight growing with every step as she staggered and the bucket swung gently between her legs.

Kerenza moved back into the cottage and Kerra took the pail to the fireside, gratefully setting it down. Shaking her arms to rid her muscles of tension, she walked back over to the table and seated herself on the stool.

‘How did he lose his eye?’ she asked as she took up the crystal.

‘In all honesty, I do not know,’ replied Kerenza as she settled upon the ground facing the doorway, the fire before her crackling. ‘I have ne’er thought to ask. He has been without it since first I met him, so must have lost it through some mishap when still but a boy.’

Kerra set to her work, her imagination conjuring images of the farmer in his youth armed with a bloodied blade as he fought off invaders from the sea. She smiled to herself, knowing that in truth the injury had probably been sustained in a mundane fashion, but enjoying her flight of fancy, one encouraged by Tetker's words about goblins and fairies the previous day.

19

The gentle ringing of the bells hanging from the top rung of the gate marked Jacob's exit from the croft. He glanced at them, expression filled with apprehension as he moved into the pasture beyond.

Walking south, his crooked stick beat a soft rhythm of departure. He made his way to a tree trunk which he had dragged from the woods upon the eastern slopes and placed across the stream in order that Kerra would not have to leap its waters.

Crossing its mossy span, he felt the night's chill already gathering, the vale in the shadow of Nancherrow Hill just as his mind was in the shadow of the village that rested there. His nervousness increased with every step as he imagined the scene about the bonfire that would soon be lit, the faces all turned to him and displaying naught but displeasure.

Jacob paused and looked back to the low croft building nestled against the dark woodland. His brow became furrowed, the feeling that he had forgotten something arising with the yen to return to the security of his home.

'Bess,' he whispered, the hound's absence keenly felt.

He listened, but heard no whining plea to join him, only the bleat of one of the sheep that were shut in the tumbledown enclosure on the far side. Taking a bolstering breath, he tore his longing gaze from the croft and continued up the hill, the sun's fading light lending a golden hue to the utmost trees on the eastern slope opposite.

His steps faltered as he drew close to the darkness of the woodland above, the settlement lurking beyond. He felt its presence like a slow pulse, throbbing with the canker of rumour and distrust.

'For Kerra,' he stated to himself, his pace renewed by the image of the girl's dimpled face.

He walked into the woods, passing between the trees with care so as to make as little noise as possible. His tension rose concurrent with the shortening of the distance between him and St Just. Each step took him closer to the settlement in which he had not set foot since his boyhood. He had forsaken the community and they had grown wary of his presence in the vale.

Jacob's pace slowed, his conviction wavering. The branches shivered and he looked up, seeing touches of warm light upon the highest boughs as the sun continued its decline. The silhouette of a gull glided overhead, calling out once it had vanished from sight. The smell of wood smoke wove through the trees and he knew the eastern edge of the village was close at hand.

'Soon the fires will be dowsed,' he whispered, brushing by a patch of withering ferns.

His cloak snagged on a low branch and Jacob glanced back as it pulled loose. 'Even the wood conspires to keep me from the village,' he whispered. 'It may be that Dor Dama tries to warn me against attending.'

His pace slowing further, he drew close to the tree-line and spied a cottage beyond. He came to a halt in the deepening shadows and listened. Two voices arose from within and his eyes widened when he discerned that one of them was Kerra. The other was that of a woman, the shepherd presuming it to be the girl's mother.

Jacob slipped out of the woodland's concealment. Remaining in the long shadow cast by the cottage, he quickly covered the ten yards to its rear, skulking beside the stones.

He made his way to the left corner, peering round with heart pounding. A sense of being alien came over him as he spied other cottages set amidst the low trees and shrubs of the village. He felt the presence of others like a hard skin closing about him, suffocating and restricting. The community carried with it expectations of behaviour that moulded and confined. There were preconceptions and opinions in which he would be cast in their minds. Judgements would be made.

Jacob moved back, settling against the cold stones of the wall and momentarily closing his eyes as he tried to calm himself. ''Tis but one visit and then I can return to the vale,' he said under his breath as small sounds of activity arose from within the cottage.

The trees stirred again and the sound of their leaves was like a whisper of warning, one that called him back home. He looked to the woods, the urge to take flight almost overpowering.

Two knocks sounded on the door to the cottage and he stiffened. Listening, he heard a man's voice give greetings to Kerra and her mother, revealing her name to be Kerenza. The tone of the girl's response left him in no doubt that she did not welcome the guest, but her mother's voice was filled with cheer.

Jacob listened a moment longer and then began towards the trees, unwilling and unable to go to the door now that one of the men folk had arrived. He passed into the cover of the woodland and paused, turning to look at the cottage with a hint of regret.

Continuing into the deep shadows, he made his way back to the vale. The pressure he had felt due to the close proximity of others began to fade and the freedom of solitude took its place. A sense of calm returned as the distance between him and the settlement grew, the voices of the trees replacing those he had heard within the cottage as they watched his passage without judgement or expectation.

20

‘‘Twill be a cold night,’ said Breoc as he moved to stand before the fire and held his hands towards the meagre flames. ‘A chill settles and there is no cloud.’

‘You had best take a fleece from your cot.’

Kerra nodded as she looked to her mother, the two of them seated upon the earth beside the pit, watching as the fire was purposefully left to dwindle.

The trapper settled on his haunches. ‘If my nose does not deceive me, you have made more than oat cakes for the festivities.’

Kerenza glanced over her shoulder at a wooden platter arrayed with food that rested upon the tabletop. ‘Aye, I have made flatbread seasoned with herbs from the garden.’

Breoc breathed deeply. ‘‘Tis a good smell, one to bring warmth even on an evening such as this.’

‘You may try a piece if it pleases you,’ she offered with a smile.

He returned the gesture and straightened, stepping over and taking one of the small round breads from the platter. Returning to his former position, the trapper made a show of sniffing the food, closing his eyes and letting his breath out with a sigh of satisfaction.

Taking a bite, he chewed slowly and nodded to Kerenza. ‘This is good indeed.’

‘My thanks. I will have to make some for you and your father in gratitude for all you have given Kerra and I.’

‘I have another gift for you,’ he stated, reaching inside his cloak with his free hand and withdrawing a pale comb which he held out to her.

She stared at it a moment.

‘Take it,’ he prompted.

Kerenza took the gift and turned it to the firelight. Two rows of thin teeth ran along the top and bottom, three missing from the upper left. On the grip between was carved a vine interspersed with flowers.

‘‘Tis beautiful,’ she commented as she ran her thumb over the floral design, feeling the smoothness of the material from which it had been carved.

‘It was passed from mother to daughter for many an age, but, alas, I was the only child and so it made its way into my keeping. My mother used to say it was made before the time of Tewal Tan.’

‘From what is it carved?’ she asked, returning her gaze to the trapper.

‘Bone or ivory, which I do not know.’

‘I cannot accept such an heirloom when you have already given us so much,’ she said, holding it out to him.

He gently closed her fingers about the comb, pushing her hand away. ‘This gift and those given before were an expression of what lies in my heart,’ said Breoc, holding her gaze meaningfully and Kerenza blushing in response. ‘They require no payment in kind.’

‘Then I shall make bread for you and your father as an expression of what lies in mine,’ she said, reaching out and placing her hand upon his knee.

The trapper glanced down at the contact, the affectionate touch feeding the flames of his desire and filling him with longing. Lifting his gaze, they stared into each other’s eyes and he began to lean towards her, her eyes becoming lidded.

‘We should dowse the fire,’ stated Kerra with exaggerated volume.

The adults turned to her as if in a daze, taking a moment to break from the spell which had been cast by the light in their eyes.

‘The sun is nearly gone,’ said the girl, glancing to the open shutters of the left-hand window, a faint touch of sunlight resting upon the edge of the lintel.

Kerenza removed her hand from Breoc’s knee. Carefully tucking the comb into her tunic, she then moved the pail closer to the fire, resting it between her and the trapper.

‘I think Breoc should but watch,’ stated Kerra. ‘After all, ‘tis not he who lives here, but us.’

‘We will *all* dowse the fire,’ responded Kerenza, giving her daughter a hard look.

The heat of his passion finally subsiding, the trapper ate the last of the bread, remaining silent but aware of what passed between mother and child.

‘Here,’ said Kerenza, holding the bucket out towards Kerra, ‘take a handful.’

‘A handful!’ she exclaimed, frowning at her mother. ‘We usually tip the pail together.’

‘You will take a handful or you will watch as Breoc and I perform the ritual. ‘Tis your choice.’

Kerra glared at her a moment and then turned her gaze to the embers of the fire, all flames now extinguished. ‘I will take a handful,’ she conceded, the wish to spite her mother by refusing to partake outweighed by the wish not to have Breoc take her place.

She gathered sand between her cupped hands and lifted it from the bucket, a spill of grains tumbling to the floor as she carefully settled back.

‘You and I could tip the pail together,’ suggested Breoc, ‘now that Kerra has some sand.’

Kerenza glanced at her daughter and saw her tight expression. ‘I think it best if we all take a handful,’ she replied.

‘I am not sure that will be enough to dowse the fire.’ He looked to the embers. ‘Best we tip the pail in order to extinguish it.’

Kerenza looked at the remains of the branches and sighed, knowing that he was right but that Kerra would likely take greater offence. ‘What Breoc says is true,’ she said, turning to her daughter. ‘Dowsing the fire will be quicker if we tip the pail.’

Kerra stared at the embers, refusing to look at her mother, her eyes burning with greater intensity than the fire.

Kerenza felt the weight of the pail shift and turned to find that Breoc had taken hold. He smiled at her reassuringly, sidling closer as she adjusted her grip on the handle.

Feeling something move against her palm, Kerra recalled seeing the sand hopper when Samuel had made his delivery earlier that day. ‘Wait!’ she said, looking to her hands and trying to open them without dropping their contents, unwilling to throw the creature to its death.

Unable to see it, she parted her palms a little and the sand drained from between them, the hopper quickly burying itself in the small pile upon the floor. She looked up in order to stop the proceedings and request more sand, her expression becoming one of open-mouthed horror as Breoc tipped the bucket over the fire.

‘What did you do that for?’ she asked, staring at the trapper unkindly.

‘I thought we were all ready,’ he replied.

‘It was not Breoc’s fault,’ stated Kerenza in his defence.

‘But he tipped the pail,’ protested Kerra.

'*We* tipped the pail,' corrected her mother despite the fact that she had been an innocent party to the action.

Kerra glared at her, knowing that she was concealing the truth. 'You would lie to your own daughter?' she said with heated accusation.

'You will not speak to your mother in such a way,' said Breoc, receiving a glance from Kerenza that warned him not to enter the disagreement any further.

'I am not lying,' she responded to the girl, taking the pail from the trapper's loosening grasp.

'You are, and 'tis for *his* sake that you do so,' she replied, her reference to Breoc filled with distaste.

'I am not!' exclaimed Kerenza, slamming the bucket to the floor to punctuate her words. 'We tipped the pail and you had already gathered sand to help with the dowsing. Do not blame us for letting it fall from your hands.'

Kerra looked at her mother for a few moments, her expression downcast. 'There was a sand hopper,' she said miserably.

'What?' Kerenza's brow creased in confusion.

'I felt it against my hand and had not the heart to throw it to its death. I was trying to find it and the sand fell from my grasp.' There were tears in her eyes. 'You should have waited for me.'

Kerenza softened upon hearing her daughter's words and took a calming breath. 'It will not survive away from the beach,' she stated, the volume of her words much reduced.

'But I could not be the one to bring about its end.' A tear fell upon her cheek, its path lit by the orange sunset which crept softly through the open door of the cottage, the distant sound of gulls settling for the night carried with it.

‘We should make our way to the Gathering Place,’ said Breoc with a glance over his shoulder. ‘The bonfire will already be lit.’

Kerenza reached out and wiped the tear away from her daughter’s face before rising. ‘Come, Little Bird,’ she said, holding out her hand, ‘we should join the festivities.’

Kerra stared at her hand for a moment and then took it, Kerenza helping her to her feet.

‘Would you like to carry the platter?’

She nodded.

Her mother went to the table and took up the foodstuff that had been specially prepared, turning and holding it out to the girl. Kerra took the platter and held it securely before her as the trapper stepped to the door.

They exited the cottage, leaving the door open to the coming night, the first stars making their presence known in the heavens. Breoc opened the garden gate and let Kerenza and Kerra exit before passing through. Picking up his pace temporarily, he moved past the girl and began to walk beside her mother.

Her pace slow, Kerra fell back from the adults and heard whispered words passing between them. Breoc looked over his shoulder at her and she discerned a hushed reprimand from her mother, the trapper quickly turning away. She knew they were talking about her and wondered at what was being said, staring at their backs as they made their way along the path.

The sounds of mingling voices and the crackle of burning timbers could be heard before the heart of the settlement came into view. The bonfire rested in the centre of the Gathering Place, its flames already licking high into the darkening heavens as it cast its light onto the throng of people gathered about it. The shadows of the villagers were thrown onto the huts encircling the space, like the ghosts of their ancestors called forth by the heat of the fire.

There were spoken greetings and nods as she followed behind her mother and Breoc, the pair receiving knowing glances as they arrived together after dowsing her fire. Their actions were a statement made to all, an open acknowledgement of their involvement.

Kerra's frown deepened as she walked over to the nearest table, the surrounding cottages having brought theirs out so that food could be placed upon them by those attending. She used the edge of the platter to push a jug of mead aside and then set it down on the corner. Taking one of the oat cakes as reward for delivering them safely to the celebrations, she then turned and took in the scene with little interest.

Her gaze settled on Tetker, who was stationed at a table on the other side of the fire to the right. Making her way through the villagers, a few greeting her as she passed, Kerra went to the old woman, seeing her as an island where she could take refuge.

'Good evening to thee, Young Kerra,' said Tetker with her characteristic smile, the firelight illuminating the whiskers upon her chin.

'Good evening, Tetker. How goes it?'

'It goes well now the fire be lit and can take away the chill that tries to cling to my bones,' she replied. 'I may even join the dancing when 'tis begun. That would show there still be life in the old bird yet, ay?'

'That it would,' she agreed with a nod.

'Did the fire dowsing fare well?'

Kerra frowned and shook her head, though did not put words to the gestures. Tetker studied her expression and decided not to pursue the matter further.

'Be that one of thy mother's oat cakes?'

‘Aye, flavoured with rose petals and honey from your bees.’

‘Then they must be delicious,’ she said with a wink.

Kerra chuckled softly as she pushed the last of the moist food into her mouth, her cheeks bulging as she began to chew and scanned the crowd. ‘Even the Jago’s are here,’ she commented through the mouthful, the family of five gathered to the left after having made the journey from Cape Cornwall, which lay a mile to the west.

‘Jeremiah would not miss such a gathering,’ responded Tetker, looking to the stout farmer as he stood with his wife and children. ‘None of Lannust will be absent this night. The starlight has called them all to the celebrations.’

Rhythmic clapping arose from those watching as a ring of people formed about the bonfire. They linked hands and began to circle the flames, the women’s headpieces fluttering as they skipped and pranced. Morwennol, the carter’s wife, began to sing an old Cornish folksong as a second ring wheeled in the opposite direction to the first, both changing course with each new verse.

‘Do ye think I should show them how ‘tis done?’ grinned Tetker, stepping towards the dance.

‘That would be a sight to see,’ replied Kerra with a grin.

The circles broke into pairs that leapt and turned. Tetker moved forward to join them, One-Eyed Samuel moving to take her hands as she entered the spirit of the festivities. Kerra watched, laughing as the old woman looked over with a smile and passed about the bonfire with a spring in her step, the dancing pairs circling its flames.

She saw movement in her peripheral vision and turned to her left. Her expression fell when she discovered Breoc approaching, the trapper moving to stand beside her as she looked back to the dancing throng. He slowly crouched, a forced smile fixed upon his rugged face.

'I understand that you hold no favour with me,' he said under his breath, the words only just audible.

He placed his arm about her shoulders and her tension rose. 'If you speak one more word against me to your mother,' he began, grip tightening and smile still on show, 'I will take you from your bed one starless night and throw you to the rocks of Kilgoodh Ust, your broken body to be claimed by the sea and eaten by the fishes.'

Kerra spied her mother in the dance, Kerenza giving a brief wave and showing pleasure at the sight of her daughter and the trapper in apparent closeness.

'Do you understand?' hissed Breoc, his lips barely moving.

She nodded, picturing him tossing her from Cape Cornwall, the sea raging against the rocks as she plummeted towards them.

'Do not test the metal of my words, for they are as iron,' he stated, 'and if you whisper one word of this to another I shall know it. There be no secrets in St Just, only loose tongues, and if yours be a loose one I shall cut it out before casting you to the rocks.'

Kerra's eyes glistened with tears and her body trembled in his unkind embrace.

'Do we have an understanding?'

She nodded again.

'Mark my words, Miss Kerra, for they hold no lie.' He leant forward and turned to look at her face. His gaze was hard and cold, causing her spine to tingle with a fearful chill.

After a few moments, Breoc released her and straightened. He lingered beside her, his presence looming over Kerra as her body quaked, feeling small and vulnerable.

'Enjoy the festivities,' he said in parting, walking forward to join the dance.

He linked hands with her mother, who smiled over warmly. A fleeting look of concern passed across her face when she noted Kerra's expression, the trapper distracting her with a whoop of celebration as they passed around the other side of the fire and out of sight.

21

Kerra stared up at the rafters as she lay on her cot, a small spider dangling above on a thread that was invisible in the dawn light. Breoc's threat had allowed her no rest and she had suffered a sleepless night, the whispers of its passing collected like soot beneath her eyes.

She shifted beneath the fleeces, straw scraping gently within her hide pillow as the heralding call of a cockerel arose in the distance. The end of her nose ached with a chill that had settled upon her at the festivities and her thoughts turned to the return home.

Her mother had made comment on her silence and she had excused her subdued behaviour with a claim of tiredness. Breoc had carried the lit branch removed from the bonfire, each household taking a flaming brand by which to relight their fires as a mark of the transition into winter. Despite the resurgence of the flames in the fire pit, the chill had not been chased away and she feared it rested deeper than any of a natural origin.

She watched as the spider was caught in a draft and swung in gentle circles a couple of feet above her head. 'Helpless in the changing wind,' she mumbled as the cockerel crowed again and its call was joined by the lowing of cattle to the south of St Just.

Kerra yawned and blinked away tears of tiredness. She dare not tell her mother of what had transpired, was certain that she would seek out the trapper so as to ascertain the truth and he would thereby know of her loose tongue.

She shivered at the thought of a blade passing into her mouth, Breoc grinning wickedly as he wielded the knife. Trying to dispel the image, she wished that she could go to Jacob and seek his counsel, but did not want to break the promise she had made to her mother. She had already undermined Kerenza's trust in her when visiting with him previously and would not sully her character further.

'Tetker,' she whispered in realisation as she tried to discern the whereabouts of the spider hanging above, its vague presence blending into the shadows of the eaves.

She would visit with Tetker and tell her what had happened at the celebration. The old woman would be sure to offer wise words and it may be she would find some solution which would reveal the truth of Breoc's nature to her mother.

Kerra turned and looked to the cot in the gloom of the opposite corner. She was unable to make out her mother beneath the fleeces, but heard the gentle snore which indicated that she still slept.

Straining her neck, she looked to the crack beneath the door to try and discern if the sun had risen. There was no indication and she settled back, knowing that in truth it was too early to visit with the old woman. She did not want to pass through the heart of St Just at a time that would arouse curiosity and cause tongues to wag. Breoc would be sure to hear of her activity and guess at her purpose.

Seeking out the spider, she discovered its whereabouts and watched as it moved up its delicate thread, returning to the timbers supporting the thatch. 'It may be there is shelter from the wind after all,' she whispered as the cock crowed for a third time, some of her tension slipping away at the thought of visiting Tetker, certain that she would not tell another soul of what passed between them.

The day slowly brightened to the sounds of livestock calling and scant birdsong. She heard her mother stir with a snort and the smack of lips. The cot on the far side of the interior creaked and she looked over to see Kerenza sitting up, bare feet to the earth as she rubbed her eyes, a fleece draped over her shoulders.

Kerra watched as her mother got up and stepped to the woodpile, selecting slender branches suitable for kindling and renewing the flames. Moving to the fire pit, she crouched and used the end of one of the branches to sift the ashes, revealing the embers still glowing beneath.

Breaking a few twigs from the bundle held against her chest, she threw them down, yawning and sitting upon the earth as she waited for them to catch light. There was a flare of flame and crackle of consumption shortly after and Kerra sat up, her cot announcing the movement.

'Good morning, Little Bird,' stated her mother with a glance before placing the smallest branches on the meagre flames.

'Good morning, Mamm.' She rubbed the cold tip of her nose. 'May I visit with Tetker today?'

Kerenza nodded. 'It was a joy to see her dancing last night.'

Kerra wrapped a fleece about her shoulders and made her way to the fireside, seating herself to the left of her mother. Kerenza turned to her and gently swept strands of blonde hair from her face.

'You look tired,' she commented.

'I did not sleep well.'

'The excitement of the festival,' stated Kerenza mistakenly, nodding her head.

Kerra made no attempt to correct her mother's assumption but stared at the growing flames, hoping their warmth would soon vanquish the cold.

22

Jacob walked alongside the wall surrounding the croft, making his way towards the woodland gathered in the head of the small valley. The breaking day was diffused by mist, Bess barely visible as she trotted ahead, her coat already dampened by the moisture in the air and hung upon the grass.

The sound of gulls waking to the dawn came haunting and distant as his walking stick marked his passage with dull thuds. His axe was clasped in the other hand, its newly sharpened blade glinting in readiness. A piece of cord hung from the strap of leather fastened about his waist, its end trailing out of his brown cloak.

He passed into the trees to find the mist thinning within the woods. Slowing, he sought the evidence of passage, scanning the ground directly before him with narrowed eyes.

Spying what he was looking for, he followed the vague path of grasses darkened by bruising that marked the direction he and Kerra had taken upon their recent visit. A diminutive wren flitted from one trunk to another as if keeping a watchful eye on his progress.

'Little Bird,' he whispered, smiling as it clung to the bark and moved with quick agility, the calls of other birds arsing within the woodland, subdued and without lustre.

His smile faded, a feeling of disquiet coming upon him as he moved through the widely spaced trees. The mist was gathered in pools between and stirred with his passing, like spirits becoming restless and trying to cling onto his vital essence.

Jacob felt the hairs on his arms rise in response to the sensation and his pace slowed. He looked to the hound as she paused and raised her nose in the air, sniffing and looking about with a snarl of warning.

'What is it, girl?' he asked, scanning the veiled woodland, but seeing nothing untoward.

His grip on the axe grew tighter as he made his way with measured steps. The shadowy form of the fallen elm drew into sight, gaining in definition as he neared with Bess close at his side.

The dog suddenly fell still, nostrils flaring as she looked around. Her gaze settled on something to the right and her hackles rose, a low growl lifting from the depth of her throat.

Jacob looked to the dark and ragged root bowl. Seeing nothing of note, his gaze moved to the indent in the eastern slope where the earth had been rent from the ground. Thick grass grew upon the upper edge of the hole, blades and seed heads drooping over the side. Roots like ghostly fingers hung beneath and created the likeness of a shallow cave behind.

He inhaled sharply and his eyes widened as he looked to the hollow. Within lay a wolf. It was watching him, unblinking and unmoving as Bess continued to growl.

His heart pounded as the beast lifted its head slightly, the movement slow and laboured. It looked to the hound, lips drawing back to reveal its teeth. The creature's activity was filled with weariness and its eyes lacked vigour. Its grey-white coat was dishevelled, the skin of its face tight over bone.

'Shhh,' said Jacob, slowly lowering onto his haunches and placing his hand upon Bess' head.

The dog's growls died away and it looked to him questioningly.

'She will not harm you. At least, not unless you give her cause,' he stated quietly, his pulse beginning to calm.

It was clear that the wolf was in no condition to fight. She barely had the strength to move and her last reserves would only be used in defence.

Bess growled again and the wolf tried to rise on her forelegs, the strain clear as the top of her head brushed against the overhanging earth. Jacob looked to her sorry form as he pondered a moment.

Rising with care, he began to back away, Bess looking over her shoulder. He patted his legs and she withdrew after a hesitation, regularly looking to the beast as the mist increased her concealment. She became a vague figure behind the curtain of roots, like an impression from a dream.

Jacob stopped and stared for a moment. The occasion felt unreal and the thought that he may still be sleeping upon his cot briefly flitted through his mind.

Turning, he made his way towards the croft with Bess behind. 'I will return,' he mumbled to himself as he walked through ferns and grasses.

23

Wynfred walked through the thick mud, the ruts created by wagons marking the boundaries of the track that he and Caspian were following. His spear once more used as a staff, he made his way up a gentle slope, feet aching and the effects of the ointment given by the dwarf wearing thin.

He looked to the trees on either side of the track, their branches dripping after heavy rainfall during the night. The patter of drops falling upon rock and leaf intensified as the wind stirred the forest and he turned his gaze to the dark clouds resting low over the undulating landscape.

His frown deepened as he estimated that there would be more rain to come, rain that would wash away any trace of the she-wolf's passing. They had discovered her trail after long hours of skirting the western edge of the moor where they had happened upon the dwarf. Caspian had brought it to his attention with a bark, the hound's keen sense of smell having detected the wolf's passage through high grasses. They had tracked it for the rest of the day and half the night, Wynfred finally giving in to the need to rest when the rain came, the darkness hampering their efforts.

He shook his head, frustrated that the beast's trail had yet again been lost. Boots slipping in the mud, he steadied himself with the butt of the spear and looked up the incline, seeing a bend around which the track vanished into the gathered trees.

The sharp sound of a smith's hammer began to beat time and Wynfred's gaze moved to the trees ahead and to the right, trying to discern the whereabouts of the forge. The clash of metal upon metal was close at hand and he spied smoke rising beyond the treetops.

Setting off once again, he and Caspian made their way around the bend. The trees retreated to reveal a wattle and daub building, its near end only a few yards from the track. There was a cottage set further back with woodland rising beyond, linens swaying upon a line strung between the house and a nearby trunk.

Wynfred made his way towards the open door of the forge with his hound at his side. Passing across flattened and muddied grass, he slowed his steps as he neared the entrance along its northern side, peering in as the strike of the hammer continued to rise into the morning air. He spied a man with black curls and broad shoulders standing before an anvil. His woollen shirt was rolled to the elbows, forearms thick and scarred by his labours. A fire pot rested beside him, the heart of the coals within glowing with heat.

The smith looked up with his hammer raised as Wynfred neared the door, the tongs in his other hand gripping the metal which he was working. He glanced from the huntsman to his hound, a fleeting look of mild horror passing across his angular features.

'Good day to you,' greeted Wynfred as he drew to a halt in the doorway.

'Good day,' nodded the smith, lowering his hammer.

'My name is Wynfred of Wales, though I am also known as Wynfred Wolf's Bane.'

'You are a long way from home,' commented the smith as he regarded the stranger coldly. 'What manner of creature stands at your side?'

Wynfred glanced at Caspian. 'This is a wolfhound, bred for the purpose to which I hold true. I am a huntsman in service of the crown and I track a wolf westward. Have you heard tell of such a beast in these parts?'

The smith stared at Caspian a moment longer and then looked to Wynfred, shaking his head in response to the enquiry. Glancing at the piece of metal on the anvil, he took it up in the tongs and placed its end in the fire pot.

'What is the name of this place?'

'Bodmin,' replied the smith curtly.

'And your name?'

He stared at Wynfred a moment before answering, assessing the truth of the huntsman's words. 'Gerens,' he answered.

The sound of activity drew Wynfred's gaze to the cottage and he spied a woman standing in the doorway. She was studying him and the hound closely, a teenage boy peering over her shoulder, his eyes wide as he regarded Caspian's giant form.

'Your wife and son?'

'That is not of your concern,' said Gerens guardedly.

'You have nothing to fear from me.'

'I do not fear you,' stated the smith with self-assurance as he held Wynfred's gaze.

There was a brief silence, the sound of the cottage door closing drifting over to the forge. Caspian let out a groan and Wynfred patted his shoulder.

'Could we purchase some food? We have been travelling many days and the supplies with which we began have long been exhausted.'

Gerens considered for a moment and then nodded. 'There be broth enough left from last night's feasting,' he responded. 'You may have your fill at no cost.'

'Feasting?'

'Aye, 'tis Kalan-Gwav.'

Wynfred looked at the smith without comprehension.

'You may know it by the name of Samhain.'

'The first day of winter,' stated the huntsman with a nod.

'My wife made plenty and we returned with a goodly amount uneaten.' He briefly turned, hanging the hammer and tongs amongst other tools resting upon the wall behind him. 'I shall instruct her to fetch it for you.'

'You have my gratitude.' Wynfred bowed his head.

'That is all I require on this festive day,' responded Gerens as he moved to the door and the huntsman stepped aside.

'Nonna!' he called to the cottage, waiting until the woman appeared in the doorway once again, hair uncovered and tumbling about her shoulders. 'Would you bring the broth that remains from the feast?'

'Could my hound taste the generosity of your offer?'

'Bring two bowls,' added Gerens.

She glanced at Wynfred and his hound and then nodded, vanishing into the darkened confines of the cottage. Reappearing shortly thereafter, she carried a metal cauldron in one hand and wooden bowls in the other. She made her way along a muddied path, her approach growing hesitant as she neared the forge, gaze fixed on the wolfhound.

'He will not harm you,' stated Wynfred.

Nonna gave a nod and then looked to the smith. 'Where shall I put these?'

'Bring them into the forge,' he replied, retreating into the gloom of the establishment.

She walked past the huntsman, keeping as much distance as she could between herself and the giant hound, warily eyeing the creature as she went into the building. Gerens cleared a space upon a table cluttered with oddments at the far end and she walked over to him, hearing the stranger enter behind and tensing at the thought of the creature blocking her exit.

Placing the cooking pot and bowls on the tabletop, she glanced at Gerens questioningly.

'He hunts a wolf,' he stated under his breath before turning to Wynfred. 'Please, help yourself,' he instructed, holding his hand out to indicate the huntsman should come forward.

Nonna moved aside, stepping as close to the rear wall as she could, a broken cart wheel hampering her efforts to stay well clear of the beast. She began to make her way to the door as Wynfred leant his spear against the table and took up a ladle from within the cauldron, serving broth into one of the bowls.

'I do not suppose you have heard rumours of a wolf passing this way?' he asked without turning.

She stopped in the doorway, longingly glancing over to the refuge of the cottage before looking to the wolf skin upon the huntsman's back. 'There was something that may be of note,' she conceded, Gerens turning to her in surprise. 'My son came upon tracks the likes of which he had ne'er seen before when visiting the stream.'

'You did not mention this to me,' said the smith.

'You have been busy and it slipped my mind, is all.'

Wynfred placed the first bowl upon the floor. 'Caspian,' he said, his hound stepping forward and beginning to feast on the contents. 'When did he spy these tracks?'

'Yesterday,' she replied, 'or may be it was the day before.'

'And where is this stream of which you talk?'

'Did you come from the south?' she asked.

Wynfred nodded.

'Then you crossed the ford where the path and stream meet,' said Nonna. 'If you follow it north a little you will find an old tree trunk spanning the waters. It were there that Daveth saw the prints, though I cannot say whether they still remain.'

'That they were there is enough,' replied Wynfred as he began to serve himself.

'They may as yet not be those of a wolf,' said Nonna.

'I shall soon discover their truth for myself. My thanks for the food,' he responded dismissively.

Nonna looked at Gerens meaningfully. He nodded in acquiescence, comprehending her silent request to return home. She gratefully stepped out of the forge and hurriedly made her way along the path to the cottage.

'Was it this wolf that scarred your cheek?' asked the smith as he returned to the anvil, seating himself on the far side.

Wynfred turned from the table, nodding as he raised his bowl and supped the broth. 'We have been tracking the devil for a long count of days, all the way from the Welsh border.'

Gerens looked to the beast lapping the last of its food. 'And you say this creature is merely a hound?'

The huntsman nodded again.

'It appears more like some beast of legend, risen from the darkness of bygone times.'

The wolfhound raised its head and looked to its master. Wynfred placed his bowl upon the table and then picked up the other, refilling it with broth before placing it back on the floor.

'And I see his appetite matches his size,' observed the smith.

'I can pay you for the food,' stated Wynfred flatly as he retrieved his bowl.

Gerens held up his hand. 'Not on Kalan-Gwav.'

'As you will.'

Wynfred ate the rest of his broth in silence, Caspian soon finishing his second portion, but not requesting more. Raising the bowl at a steep angle, the huntsman drained the last and wiped his lips with a sleeve while placing the vessel upon the table.

'Your hospitality is much appreciated,' he stated, 'though your wife's cooking could do with more seasoning,' he added under his breath as he took up his spear.

'What was that?' asked Gerens accusingly, brow furrowing as his eyes narrowed.

'I said, your wife's cooking is the perfect way to begin the new season,' replied Wynfred, his hound eyeing the smith.

Gerens stared at him a moment, unconvinced by the deception.

'We must adjourn to the stream in the hope the tracks your son discovered are indeed those of the she-wolf,' said the huntsman as he made his way towards the door with Caspian behind.

Wynfred stepped out and paused. He looked over his shoulder, gaze briefly lingering on a sprig of green oak leaves above the door. 'My thanks,' he said as Caspian passed behind him.

Gerens simply nodded his response, his expression distinctly cold.

Wynfred walked away and the wolfhound drew up alongside him. Rejoining the rutted and muddy path, they headed the way they had come, the sound of the smith's hammer soon beating out its rhythm, as if encouraging the departure of their steps.

24

Kerra walked along the track leading towards the heart of St Just. A wind was gathering from the west and had dispersed the mist of earlier that day. Her hair was blown back, eyes narrowed against the growing gusts as she looked to the dark clouds moving in from the ocean.

She halted as a herd of white horn crossed the path ahead, the pale cattle lowing as they were brought in from out-lying fields to the south. They jostled against each other as they made their way to Gwynsek Farm, where the selection of those to be slaughtered for the winter would be made. They were being driven by a group of villagers bearing sticks, tapping the beast's hind quarters or the backs of their legs if they threatened to stray. Their calls contained a tone of distress that was not usually evident and Kerra wondered at the possibility that they knew what lay ahead for some of their number.

'Miss Kerra,' nodded Samuel as he walked at the rear, mud spattered upon his hide britches.

She responded in kind and continued to watch the herd diminish for a while, feeling saddened by the thought that those of ill fortune were being led to their end. Her frown deepened as her mind turned to the reason for her journey and she was chilled by the recollection of what had happened the previous night.

Setting off again, the worried lows of the cattle sounding in her ears, she made her way across the Gathering Place. The charred remains of the bonfire still smouldered at its centre, smoke swirling into her face before being torn away by the wind. She coughed and blinked away the stinging in her eyes, increasing her pace so as to pass to the far side.

Moving between the cottages that flanked the path to Tetker's, the tail of her hide cloak whipped and snapped behind her, chasing Kerra to the door. She drew up before it and knocked three times in quick succession, catching the scent of the rotting thatch above her head.

'Come in.' The rasping words were followed by coughing.

She opened the door to find the old woman beneath her bed covers, face drawn and eyes thick with mucus as she lay upon her side facing the fire pit.

'Thy expression tells me that I look as bad as I feel.' Tetker smiled thinly.

Kerra shut the door, her hair settling to stillness. 'I will light the fire for you.'

'That would be kind indeed,' she responded as the girl moved to the woodpile and selected pieces suitable for kindling.

'I did not think to see thee so soon after the celebrations. It seems the heat of the bonfire was not enough to ward off the chill of the night.' Tetker coughed again. 'I was not fully recovered and it may be I was a little foolish to expend my energy in the dance.'

'It was not foolishness,' said Kerra as she crouched before the fire pit, 'but the youthfulness that still resides in your mind.'

'Alas, it does not reside in my body also,' she grinned before falling into a coughing fit, eyes closing and the tendons in her neck protruding.

Kerra looked to her with concern. 'Should I to my mother for more of the tonic?'

Tetker raised her hand and shook her head. 'It will pass,' she rasped.

She looked at the old woman for a little longer and then glanced about for the tinderbox. Spying a small tin by the foot of the bed, she reached over and picked it up. Opening the lid, she discovered a pair of flints lying upon a folded strip of deep blue material, a knotted Celtic band stitched in white thread down its centre.

'That be…' Tetker cleared her throat, the strain clear in her face. 'That be the material that was passed about our hands when I were wed to my husband.'

Kerra glanced over to the old woman and nodded before taking out the flints and placing the tin on the ground beside her.

'Here,' said Tetker, struggling to reach beneath her and retrieving a handful of hay from her bedding.

Kerra took the hay with a nod of thanks and placed it in the fire pit, moving some of the sticks so that they rested near the dried grass in readiness for the bite of flame. She began to strike the flints, brief sparks springing forth, but none taking hold.

'Closer,' stated Tetker.

She moved the flints nearer and continued with her efforts. After a few minutes a weak flame sprang to life, smoke gathering within the bundle of hay and escaping in thin tendrils before the fire grew more vigorous, consuming the grass and eagerly taking to the bark of the kindling.

Kerra put the flints away and placed the box where she had found it. Rising, she returned to the woodpile and selected larger timbers for the fire. Placing a few of them in the pit, she was careful not to extinguish the fragile flames.

Tetker turned her sickened gaze to the girl, studying her with affection. 'Thy mother and thyself are the closest to family I have,' she commented.

Kerra turned her gaze to the old woman, finding her eyes glistening with emotion.

'I told thee that Edward and I lived a peaceful life together,' she began softly. 'What I did not tell thee is that we longed to have that peace broken by the cries of a babe. Try as we might, I ne'er took with child. Edward came to believe it was God's punishment for his betrayal of holy vows and the lies I told in order to keep his true identity secret.

'The latter years of our union were tainted by a growing melancholy, darkness gathering within his soul. He became silent and estranged from me, increasingly keeping his own counsel and company. They were sad years indeed.' She wiped a stray tear from her cheek and coughed momentarily.

'I tell thee this because I have left instruction with Reverend Catlin.'

'Instruction?' Kerra looked at her curiously, wishing to dispel the old woman's distress with a hug, but wary of catching the illness that had returned.

'This cottage is to be thine when I pass.'

Her expression became one of shock. 'You are giving it to me?'

'Indeed. Ye are the closest to being kin of all those in St Just.'

'I…' Kerra struggled to find words, the fire crackling as the wind tried to gain entry through the door and shutters.

'Thee are welcome,' smiled Tetker, falling into a coughing fit once again.

Kerra rose and went to the table, taking up a cup and filling it from the pail on the floor beside. She hurried over to the old woman as her affliction gripped her.

'Here,' she stated, kneeling beside the cot.

Tetker tried to calm herself, fighting against the irritation that inflamed her throat. Kerra helped the old woman raise her head, lifting it from the darkly stained hide of the pillow, pale strands of hair hanging lank over her fingers. She raised the cup to Tetker's cracked lips and she tentatively sipped the cool liquid, holding up her hand when she had had her fill.

'My thanks,' she said, clearing her throat as her head was allowed its rest once more.

'I shall leave it here for you,' said Kerra, placing the cup on the ground beside the cot.

Tetker regarded her fondly. 'Thy name is befitting,' she stated with a thin smile.

'Dearest,' responded Kerra, aware of her name's meaning.

'Indeed.' The old woman licked her dry lips as she nodded. 'Indeed,' she repeated wearily.

'You should rest. I will go home and fetch some tonic. It will not take Mamm long to prepare it.' She rose and stepped to the far side of the fire.

'Wait,' said Tetker, looking to her questioningly. 'What was the reason for thy visit?'

Kerra's expression fell. 'It may be better that we speak when you are rested and returned to health.'

'Nonsense,' she replied, the gravity of what disturbed the girl evident within her eyes. 'I am not so sickly that I cannot listen. Come, sit and tell me,' she added, weakly patting the fleece beside her.

Kerra looked to the door and then went back to the cot, seating herself beside the old woman. She composed herself, the door and shutters rattling as the events of the previous night drew menacingly to the forefront of her mind.

'Did you see Breoc standing with me as you danced?' Kerra glanced at Tetker, who gave a nod as her head lay heavy upon the pillow.

The girl turned her gaze to the fire before her. The flames writhed like the tongues of demons, speaking in crackles and snaps, spitting sparks into the air as they turned all to ruin.

'Kerra?'

She blinked and looked to the old woman. 'Sorry,' she said, taking a deep breath.

'What troubles ye so?' Tetker studied the girl, unsettled by the expression upon her face and concerned for her welfare.

'Breoc threatened me.'

'Threatened ye?' Tetker's yellowed eyes widened.

Kerra nodded. 'He said he would take me to Cape Cornwall and throw me to the rocks if I were to speak ill of him to my mother. He also said that if I revealed this threat to any other he would cut out my tongue.'

'Surely there must be some misunderstanding,' said Tetker, barely able to believe the child's tale, but certain there was no lie in Kerra's telling.

'There is no misunderstanding to be had.'

The old woman had to concede that this was true. Such a threat could not be misconstrued.

'What am I to do?' Kerra looked at her with a pleading gaze.

'Water,' requested Tetker as she felt the onset of another coughing fit.

The girl reached down and picked up the cup, passing it to Tetker's waiting hand. The old woman raised her head a little and took a soothing drink, pondering as she did so.

'Though I am loathe to admit it, I have no advice to offer,' she said, retaining the cup and taking another sip before letting her head rest. ‘Would thy mother believe thy words?’

‘I do not know, but if I were to tell her Breoc would be aware of my loose tongue and I would be upon the rocks.’

‘Once others are aware of his threat he would not dare carry it out,’ stated Tetker.

‘I am not so sure. There was steel in both his words and his eyes.’

‘Steel enough to face the noose and become sport for crows?’ asked the old woman with eyebrows raised. ‘For that would be his fate if he should cause thee harm.’

Kerra looked back to the fire. ‘I do not know.’

‘Tell thy mother, Kerra. It be the only real choice. Ye cannot let her remain ignorant of what Breoc had said to thee.’ She reached out and took the girl’s hand in hers, giving it a feeble squeeze.

‘Do not let the fear he has planted take root and spread its dark vines through thy mind, for this is a creeping darkness which shall enslave thee to its will.’ The old woman coughed, her grip on Kerra’s hand tightening with the strain. ‘Will ye tell her?’

Kerra shrugged.

‘Go fetch the tonic and tell her when home. Then ye can tell me what she says upon thy return,’ she suggested.

The girl gave a half-hearted nod.

‘Good,’ said Tetker, giving her hand a final squeeze before releasing it.

Kerra rose and made her way to the door without urgency. The thought of telling her mother about what had transpired filled her with dread. She did not relish the idea of Breoc knowing or of causing hurt. Kerenza was clearly besotted with the man and the discovery of the threat made upon her daughter's life would be sure to put an end to the relationship.

'Do not worry, Young Kerra, for ye do the right thing,' encouraged Tetker as she watched the girl take the handle. 'I will see thee shortly.'

Opening the door, Kerra turned and nodded. 'Take some rest,' she said, 'I will soon return.' She stepped out and closed the portal. Setting off for home, her steps were heavy and shoulders sunken, gaze to the ground as she passed across the Gathering Place lost to thought.

25

Kerra entered the cottage with her head hung low. Kerenza looked over from where she stood by the table and immediately noted her daughter's demeanour.

'What is wrong?' she asked, a bowl in one hand and stems of nettles partially stripped of their leaves in the other.

'Tetker ails again,' said Kerra as she shut the door and moved to the fire, the wind angrily shaking the window shutters. 'It seems that last night's chill has seen the return of her sickness with renewed vigour. I told her I would return with a tonic.'

'I shall make it now,' said Kerenza, turning to the table and setting to the task.

Kerra watched her mother move to the curatives hanging upon the wall. She stood before them and selected a few stems and roots, ones which would make the concoction more potent than had previously been the case.

'There is something else.' The words were forced out, throat constricted and pulse elevated.

'What?' asked her mother over her shoulder as she set her selections upon the tabletop and pulled out a stool on which to seat herself.

'Breoc…' Kerra hesitated. 'He threatened my life at the celebrations last night.'

Kerenza turned sharply. 'What did you say?' she asked in shock, hardly believing what she had heard.

'It was when he crouched beside me. You were dancing and saw us together. He told me that if I said one word against him he would throw me from Cape Cornwall.'

Kerenza studied her daughter for a moment and then shook her head as she tried to come to terms with what had been said. 'You lie,' she stated. 'Your words cannot be true.'

'No,' she replied with regretful conviction, seeing the disbelief and hurt in her mother's expression.

'He was smiling,' said Kerenza as she glanced to the fire, recalling seeing her daughter and the trapper together. 'He was smiling and his arm was about your shoulders,' she said, looking back to her.

'A show for those who could see us,' responded Kerra.

Kerenza stared at her, the wind continuing to be frustrated by the barriers of the shutters and door. Her eyes narrowed and her expression suddenly became hard. 'This is a scheme.'

'A scheme?' Kerra looked to her mother questioningly.

'You have ne'er taken to Breoc and now seek to undo him in my eyes. You fear for what will happen if we are to be wed and long for your father's return,' she said. 'He is gone, Kerra, and Breoc now has my heart.'

Kerra shook her head vigorously. ''Tis no scheme, but the truth. He even threatened to cut out my tongue if…'

'Enough!' snapped Kerenza, holding up her hand to silence her child. 'I will hear no more of it. I know Breoc as well as any and I know such threats would ne'er issue from his lips.'

'But…'

'I said, enough!'

Kerra stood with her mouth open, eyes glistening as she stared at her mother, seeing the anger growing in her expression.

Kerenza studied her daughter a moment with open suspicion. 'You told Tetker of this,' she stated in realisation.

Kerra nodded sorrowfully.

'Then I shall return to her and inform her of the truth when the tonic is done.'

'What I have told you is the truth,' protested Kerra.

'No, 'tis a deceit to serve your purpose. You have tried lesser means by which to end our union and their failure has led you to this,' she responded. 'Did you truly think I would believe Breoc would threaten the life of a child? And not just any child, but that of the woman he professes to love?'

'He loves you?' asked Kerra, her expression filled with torment.

Her mother nodded. 'He told me so last night as we danced about the fire. What is more, I told him that I love him too.'

'But can you not see why he happened to tell you last night? He did so because of his threat to me, as a guard against me telling you.'

'Only you could think in such a way,' said her mother cuttingly. 'You have a sly mind and 'tis a shame you put it to such foul purpose.' Kerenza shook her head and looked at Kerra with disappointment.

'Will you tell Breoc of what I have said?'

'I think it only fair that he know the ills you speak against him.'

'Please do not tell him,' begged Kerra, stepping forward and wringing her hands in nervous agitation as she looked at her mother with tearful eyes.

Kerenza regarded her for a while. ‘I will not tell him all,’ she conceded, ‘for I fear that to hear your accusations would bring him great hurt. I will only reveal that you are still in need of persuasion in regards our union.’

‘Need you tell him aught?’

Kerenza raised her eyebrow in reply.

‘But he will…’

‘You would be best served by making silence your ally for the rest of the morning,’ interrupted her mother. ‘I will prepare Tetker’s tonic and take it to her while you remain here and think on your actions. There has been much to disappoint of late on your part.’

Kerra’s head bowed and she stared at the earth. Her thoughts wheeled and turned. Breoc would be made aware that she had spoken of him and even though he would not be told the whole truth, he would guess at the looseness of her tongue. The threat he had made grew more real and her tongue tingled in response to the imagined blade that would be put to it before she was thrown to the whim of the sea.

She looked to her mother, finding that she had turned her back and was engaged in the preparations of the curative. She stared at her while wishing there were some way to undo what had been said, to unravel the bonds of time and return to only a few minutes before.

With shoulders slumped, she crouched and held out her hands. The heat of the flames could not penetrate the chill which had settled deep within, one which haunted her with thoughts of being taken in the depths of night, of being carried to her doom, one which had been sealed by her own words.

Kerra began to quietly sob, tears rolling down her cheeks and then falling from her chin, their damp touch darkening the ground. She wrapped her arms about herself, but found no solace in the embrace.

Her mother's arm passed about her quaking shoulders and she turned to find her crouching beside her.

'He is a good man,' said Kerenza softly. 'You will come to see it in time, Little Bird.'

She wanted to protest, to try and persuade her mother of the truth, but knew it would be a fruitless task. Instead, she simply nodded, hoping that Breoc would somehow reveal his true nature.

26

Jacob snuck through the trees, the undergrowth animated by the strengthening wind. He had left Bess at the croft, knowing that her presence was unwise. His stick in one hand, he carried a small cloth-wrapped package in the other.

His sense of expectation grew when he sighted the fallen elm through the trees. Looking to its rising bowl, the shadow beyond hinted at the hollow on the climb of the eastern slope.

His steps slowed as the ferns and grasses moved in agitation about him. The branches above rustled as the wind attempted to tear away the browned leaves of autumn, as if knowing it was the first day of winter and seeking to bring about the barrenness of the season.

The indent slowly came into view. He considered skirting to the left and making for the head of the fallen tree, there passing along its length so his approach would be hidden by the root bowl. Discarding the idea, worried that his sudden appearance from behind the concealment would frighten the beast and cause it to fight or flee, he decided upon a direct route which would keep him in clear sight of the hole.

He paused, unwrapping the fish which he had caught in the stream so that the wolf would be able to see the offering. Tucking the cloth into the belt of his robe, he continued with care.

The wolf's presence beyond the thin curtain of roots became increasingly clear as they stirred in the wind. She was watching him warily as she rested upon her stomach beneath the shallow overhang of earth. She raised her head as he drew within ten yards, snarling briefly.

'I will do you no harm,' said Jacob softly as he came to a halt. 'I bring food.' He held out the fish and she sniffed the air.

He threw it underarm and it flopped in the middle of the indent with a vague thud, rolling a few times before settling. He watched expectantly, the wolf shifting her front legs and looking to the food before turning back to him.

Jacob nodded and indicated with his hand for the beast to help herself. ''Tis yours,' he stated simply.

With the laboured slowness of her condition, the wolf lifted herself first on her forelegs and then the hind, muscles quivering beneath her fur. Her snout and head pushed between the roots and she sniffed again, watching him intently.

The wolf moved from her concealment, her steps uncharacteristically cumbersome. Finally turning her gaze from the shepherd, she lowered her head and smelt the fish. She took the food between her teeth and Jacob noted that the fur of her front right paw was pure as snow.

'White Paw,' he whispered, smiling to himself.

The wolf looked to him and growled, her head hanging low as she made her way back into the shallow cave, passing behind the roots and settling upon the earth. She laid her white paw upon the fish's tail and began to eat, tearing at the meal.

Jacob listened to the crunch of bone as the beast ate the head. He had already set a net across the stream before the croft and hoped for another catch later in the day.

‘I will bring more,’ he stated as the last of the food was quickly devoured.

Licking her lips, the wolf returned her attention to him. She stared awhile, assessing him with golden eyes that whispered of the wild. She yawned, lowering herself onto her belly and leaning against the earth at the rear of the hollow.

Jacob backed away, the wolf resting her head on her front paws, but remaining ever watchful as the wind rippled the roots hanging above her. Pausing, he took one last look at the impressive creature before turning and making his way back to the croft through the windblown woods.

27

Kerenza entered hurriedly and moved to the fire. Her face and clothes were awash with the rain that lashed against the front of the cottage, seeping in beneath the door and between the shutters as it was driven west by high winds. 'Fetch a stool,' she instructed her daughter.

Kerra rose from beside the pit and did as she was told, placing it beside her mother before sitting by the flames once again. Kerenza removed the sodden cloth covering her head and draped it over the stool, shaking loose her hair before taking off the rest of her garments and crouching, letting the heat of the fire dry her damp skin.

'Did you speak with Tetker?' asked Kerra with an apprehensive glance.

She nodded, sniffing and wiping a drop of water from the end of her nose. 'I did. She asks that you visit with her on the morrow so that she may speak with you.'

Kerra turned to the fire in thoughtfulness. 'Will you still visit Jacob with me?'

Her mother considered a moment. 'Aye,' she said, nodding again.

'On the morrow?'

'After you have seen Tetker.'

'You will find him to be a good man,' stated her daughter. 'I think you will become friends.'

Two knocks sounded in quick succession and they both turned to the door in surprise.

'You had better answer it,' stated Kerenza as she rose and made for her cot.

Kerra got up and stepped over, taking the handle and looking to her mother. She was still naked, dragging a wooden box from beneath her bed and flinging open the lid. Rummaging through the sparse selection of clothing within, she took out a tatty and faded green dress before lifting it and letting it tumble over her head. She nodded to her daughter as she put her arms through and bent to fetch up a stained jerkin.

Kerra opened the door and her heart skipped a beat when she laid eyes on Breoc. The wind pushed against her, as if his presence sought to force her into retreat. She could hear the rain pattering against the back of his hide cloak as he nodded and touched his wet forelock in greeting.

'Good day, Miss Kerra,' he stated, 'may I come in?'

She moved back as if in a daze, pulse racing at the sight of the man who had threatened her life. The trapper stepped inside, gaze seeking out the woman he professed to love.

'Shut the door, Kerra, or we shall all be drowned,' stated Kerenza with a touch of agitation.

She did as instructed before moving to her cot beyond the table, seeking out its limited security and wishing she could place greater distance between herself and the trapper.

'Good day to you, my love,' said Breoc, touching his forelock once again as he regarded Kerenza's dishevelled appearance. 'Did you have need to venture out?'

She gave a nod. 'Tetker was in need of medicine. She labours under a cold once again.'

'I am sorry to hear 'tis so. The first taste of her honey is one of the joys of spring.'

'Aye, on that we can agree,' she responded, returning to the fireside. 'Come, dry yourself.'

He stepped over and removed his cloak, looking about the interior for somewhere to hang it.

'Here.' She took it from him and went to the wall where the curative plants hung, placing the garment on a free hook to the left.

'My thanks,' he said as she returned and they crouched side by side.

'What brings you to my door on this day?' she asked.

'I need no other reason than to see you,' he replied with a smile, his face glistening with moisture as he leant in towards her and they shared their first tentative kiss.

He lifted his hand to the side of her face. 'This be the first time I have seen your hair loose. It compliments your beauty well.'

Kerenza smiled with mild embarrassment. 'My thanks,' she said, blushing beneath his scrutiny and looking down with a touch of discomfort. 'Will you not join us, Kerra?' she asked, turning to her daughter.

'It would be good to have your company,' said Breoc with a smile.

She looked at them both, seeing only malice in the trapper's gesture. Her stomach churned as she slowly rose from the cot, its creaking ominous. Stepping over, she went to seat herself on the opposite side of the fire.

'Could you fetch more wood before you make yourself comfortable?'

She nodded to her mother and went to the woodpile, taking an armful of timbers.

'Winter announces its arrival,' stated Breoc with a glance over his shoulder, the door and shutters battered by the worsening conditions, the noise persistent and serving to raise Kerra's tension as she returned to the fire.

'Aye, and with a loud voice,' replied Kerenza, the wind howling against the stones of the front wall from time to time, as if frustrated by their immutable presence.

Kerra settled after placing the branches on the fire and stared at the flames before her.

'Did you have a pleasant time last night?' asked Breoc.

She nodded her response without looking up at him.

'What did we say this morning?' asked Kerenza.

Kerra stiffened at the reference and immediately looked to the trapper, finding him regarding her closely and coolly. She was certain he knew.

'I…' She struggled to speak, throat constricting as she fought a wave of nausea. 'I enjoyed the festivities,' she managed, swallowing hard and taking a deep breath, her palms becoming clammy as she clasped her hands together tightly.

'I am glad to hear it,' he replied, Kerra noting a slight change of tone. 'Let us hope we last out until next year so we may enjoy another evening of celebration.' Breoc held her gaze meaningfully and then glanced at the door. 'For if the weather gets much worse we may well be blown away,' he added, turning to Kerenza with a smile.

''Tis not the first nor the last time we shall suffer such conditions,' she responded. 'There will be little sleep tonight.'

'Aye, even the spirits will be wakened by this racket,' nodded Breoc.

'Would you care to stay for supper?'

Kerra looked at her mother with unconcealed alarm, quickly bowing her head again while keeping a surreptitious eye on the trapper as she waited for his reply.

Breoc idly picked up a flaming brand and used it to stoke the fire as he pondered a while. ''Tis an invitation I find myself hard put to decline. I will stay if you can spare a portion for my father. I shall take it to him when I return home.'

'We have plenty,' said Kerenza. 'Talvennor the cordwainer gave me cuts of pork in exchange for the medicine I made for his wife. It was the food or an offer of new shoes.' She smiled at the trapper.

'That is a choice not easily made. Talvennor works his leather well.' He looked to his boots. 'Not a stitch out of place or loosened by wear.'

'He also cures his pork with the same care,' responded Kerenza. 'Let us hope that when you taste it you will agree I chose wisely.'

'Of that I have no doubt.' He looked into her eyes and they fell still and silent for a short time.

Kerra cleared her throat as they began to lean towards each other once again, not wishing to witness another sickening kiss, one that contained the trapper's deceit and vile intentions. They turned to her, Breoc's gaze touched with a flare of anger which he fought to keep in check so as not to reveal the truth of his villainous soul.

'It may be I have caught a touch of the sickness which ails Tetker,' she said, forcing out a cough before clearing her throat again and sniffing.

Her mother rose and stepped around the fire pit before placing the back of her hand to Kerra's forehead. 'You do not seem to be running a fever,' she stated.

'I warrant it be nothing more than a chill that has settled upon you,' added Breoc. 'I can take it to task.' He pulled his cloak back and slipped the dagger from his hip, looking at the sharp blade before holding the girl's gaze.

'My mother always swore by a warm blade held to the temples,' he said, holding the knife to the flames.

'I have a tonic much better suited to fight the onset of such illness,' said Kerenza, moving to the table, 'but she is in no need of it as yet. If there be more signs of sickness, then I will make some. It may be some food is all she needs.'

Kerenza began to gather up what was needed for the preparation of supper, placing plates and a knife before her. Breoc continued to warm the blade for a few moments, his gaze intent upon it and aware that the girl watched his every move.

He took it from the flames, touching its edge before glancing towards the door. 'Night draws in,' he commented, fixing his gaze on Kerra.

'The first night of winter,' said Kerenza without turning, her back to the scene at the fireside.

'Aye,' said the trapper, 'and winter nights are long indeed.' He grinned at the girl and she was chilled by the gesture, shrinking back and her nausea renewed.

Breoc looked his last upon the blade and then slipped it into its scabbard. 'May I be of some assistance?' he asked, rising and making his way over to Kerenza, briefly slipping his arm about her waist and giving her an affection squeeze, glancing at the girl with a malevolent glint in his eyes.

Kerra sat in silence as her mother and the trapper prepared the food. She made no show of being ill, the pretence forgotten as she thought on the blade that he had held above the fire. There was no doubting in her mind as to his intention to carry out his threat. As winter drew out she would find little rest, but would wait for him to come lurking out of the deep shadows of a moonless night.

28

The storm had blown itself out in the early hours, but the wind still blustered and billowed with failing gusts. They pushed at Kerra with unseen hands, as if trying to hamper her progress, to stop her visiting with Tetker. She laboured on, cloak twisting and straining at her heels each time the wind got up, her hair messed and unruly.

Her steps were tempered with trepidation, expecting the trapper to appear from behind every tree and bush. She had found no rest for the second night in a row and the lack of sleep showed ever more clearly about her eyes. Thoughts had become elusive, passing into mind and then slipping away like ghosts. She could not concentrate, the image of her mother and Breoc engaged in a kiss returning again and again.

Chickens scattered before her with clucks of disturbance, but she barely noticed their presence as she crossed the sodden Gathering Place. She glanced to her right, spying the site of the bonfire. It was the blackened core at the heart of St Just, the ash turned to thick sludge by the heavy rainfall.

'Like his heart,' she mumbled to herself as her eyes narrowed against the next gust, steps temporarily faltering and cloak snapping.

Reaching the door to the old woman's cottage, she heard coughing from within. She raised her hand to knock and then took hold of the handle instead as the fit became worse.

Opening the portal, she found Tetker sunk to her knees and doubled over at the foot of her cot, eyes tightly shut as the rasping gripped her. She rushed over, passing the fire pit and quickly taking an upset cup from the floor near the old woman before filling it at the water pail by the wall.

She returned and crouched, holding out the cup. 'Here,' she said.

Tetker was startled by the unexpected voice, eyes snapping open to reveal that they were thick with mucus and glistening with tears. She peered at the girl as if not certain of her reality, coughs still forced from her frailty by the dry irritation of her throat.

'Drink.' Kerra raised the cup towards the old woman's lips encouragingly.

Tetker tried to control the coughing and raised a hand to support the cup, guiding it and managing a brief sip. She struggled against the onset of another fit, the tendons in her neck jolting with the strain. Taking a second sip, she removed her hand and nodded her thanks.

'Have you any of the tonic Mamm brought yesterday?' asked Kerra.

The old woman pointed to the head of the cot.

Setting the cup on the floor, she passed behind Tetker and made her way alongside the bed. She spied the bowl by the pillow and took it up, gently swirling the liquid to ensure the contents had not separated.

Making her way back, she lowered herself onto her haunches. Holding the vessel with a steady hand before the old woman's cracked lips, she waited to receive a nod of readiness and then tipped it, allowing only a small amount of the curative to pass into Tetker's mouth. Kerra watched as she struggled to swallow and then prepared to tip the bowl once again.

The old woman shook her head and gently pushed it away from her face. 'Enough,' she whispered hoarsely.

'But you will not return to good health without it.'

'Enough,' she repeated, swallowing against the urge to cough.

Kerra sighed and lowered the bowl, setting it down beside the cup. She looked on Tetker with concern, seeing the yellowness of her skin as it drew tight over her cheekbones and sank into hollows beneath.

The old woman turned to her and saw the worry apparent in the girl's expression. She raised a tremulous hand and cupped Kerra's cheek. Forcing a smile, she held her gaze, her eyes communicating great affection. 'Do not fret,' she whispered.

Kerra tried to return the gesture, but her lips soon sank into a frown once again. She put her hand to Tetker's as it continued to rest upon her face. 'Fretting cannot be helped when I find you in such distress,' she responded. 'I would that I could make you better and take away your suffering.'

'I know.' The old woman nodded, the pale shadows of her hair stirring.

She took her hand from the girl's cheek and their contact was ended. Taking up the bowl, she cradled it and took another drink of the contents, wishing to ease Kerra's concern. She closed her eyes as she swallowed against the irritation of her throat. Spluttering, her chest tightened as she battled against the urge to cough, the tension easing after a few moments.

'Mamm said you wish to speak with me,' said Kerra as Tetker put down the bowl, 'but we had best wait until you are better and in truth I know what you would say unto me.'

The old woman looked to her and shook her head. 'I am thy ally.'

Kerra regarded her questioningly.

‘I believe thee.’ She swallowed in order to refrain from coughing again.

‘You do?’

Tetker nodded. ‘Indeed.’ She paused as she waited for an opportune moment to speak again, taking up the water and sipping, frustrated by her inability to converse in the usual manner.

She held the cup upon her lap and placed her other hand upon the girl’s knee in a gesture of comfort. ‘There was no lie in thy words to me.’

Kerra felt an immense sense of relief and gratitude. She took the old woman’s hand into her own and held it tightly. ‘My thanks,’ she said, tears gathering in her eyes. ‘I am in your debt.’

‘No,’ responded Tetker. ‘True friends have no debts to one other.’

She felt the sudden tension in the old woman’s hand and saw the strain about her eyes. Tetker was gripped by coughing that forced itself from her hunched form, her mouth wide and tongue protruding as she gagged due to the constriction of her throat.

Kerra gripped her hand with greater strength, hoping the action would offer some support. She waited long moments for the fit to subside and then placed her right arm about the old woman’s shoulders.

Helping her to her feet, she guided Tetker to her cot and moved aside the fleeces to reveal the mat of hay beneath. The old woman sat and then lay down with laboured effort. Kerra placed the covers over her and then went to the woodpile.

Going to the fire with an armful of branches, she placed a few on the flames. They spat and crackled, peeling bark flaring with brightness. ‘That should bring you warmth for the time being,’ she said, turning to place the other timbers by the bed so that they could be added without need of the old woman leaving her rest.

Tetker nodded after turning upon her side to face the fire. 'My thanks.'

Kerra picked up the cup and bowl, taking them to the head of the bed and placing them by the wood. 'I shall call on you again later today and bring more of the medicine,' she stated, wishing to leave the old woman to rest.

'I will speak with Brecca.'

'You are not…'

Tetker weakly held up her hand to silence the girl. 'When I am well enough,' she added, clearing her throat. 'She was once the object of Breoc's affection and it may be she has secrets to tell.'

Kerra regarded her a moment. 'Until then you must rest so that you are restored to full health in good time,' she said. 'I will make you some supper upon my return so that you have the strength to fight the illness.'

'Dearest,' said Tetker with a faint smile as she looked up at the girl fondly.

Kerra took her hand again and gave it a squeeze. 'I will see you again before night falls,' she reassured before releasing her grip and moving to the door.

'Make sure to heed my instruction and remain in your bed,' she said after stepping out of the cottage, turning and finding the old woman no more than a shrunken figure beneath the covers, the illness sucking the vitality from her body. 'Take good care, Tetker, and may Dor Dama see fit to bring you relief.'

'Fare ye well, Young Kerra.'

She shut the door, hearing coughing arise from within and her hand remaining upon the handle as she considered going back inside. The sight of the old woman so gripped by sickness was a weight within her heart and she yearned to bring greater relief than she was able.

With a saddened shake of her head, Kerra released the handle and began to walk away. The wind had died to barely a breath and she heard the call of gulls carried from the coast. The image of Cape Cornwall arose unbidden and a chill caused her to shiver, Breoc's threat a dark presence that lurked in the corridors of her mind.

29

They walked through the woodland towards the vale. Kerra was anxious to get there, to see Jacob and spend time in his company, her mother's lack of urgency causing her some frustration. Kerenza picked fungi from the grasses at the base of a tree, the front of her dress gathered into a pouch that was already half-full.

'You could pick them on the way back,' suggested her daughter, shifting from one foot to the other as she waited ten yards down the incline of Nancherrow Hill.

'There be no rush and I may miss them on the way home. Besides, you are lucky that I agreed to meet with him and so should be thankful rather than impatient.'

'I am thankful.'

'Then have some grace and help me with these,' replied Kerenza, nodding towards the toadstools.

Kerra looked through the trees down the slope with longing and then went to her mother's side. She crouched and began to take the fungi by their stems, dropping them into her mother's dress with those already collected.

'These will serve to make a warming broth.'

'May I take some to Tetker later this day?'

Her mother gave a nod. 'It would do her good.' She shuffled around the trunk, spying another growth to the left.

Kerra's frown deepened, but she made no comment, instead moving to rejoin her in order that the fungi would be picked as quickly as possible. She brushed aside tall grass stems and gathered, hands moving with haste.

'There,' she stated, depositing the last into the makeshift pouch and standing. 'We can be on our way.'

Kerenza looked up at her and shook her head, a rye smile upon her face. She stood and indicated for her daughter to lead the way with an outstretched hand.

They moved through the whispering foliage and passed the Sacred Oak, where rites of old had once been practiced and where Kerra had sometimes discovered offerings made to the spirits of the land. She peered over, gaze seeking out such an offering, but saw no flowers bound with grass or small fruit cupped within a leaf and fastened with strips of bark, such as she had found before.

They reached the tree-line, moving out of the woods and into the grassland. The foot of the vale lay forty yards to the right, the countryside beyond misted in partial concealment. The apple tree stood on the far side of the stream below, the eastern side of the valley rising beyond and crowned with trees.

Kerra looked for the shepherd with eagerness, seeking any sign of the man or his flock, but finding none. 'I do not see him,' she commented over her shoulder as her pace drew her away from her mother's measured steps.

'There be no need to hurry, Little Bird,' called Kerenza. 'I am sure he will not be far.'

She did not slow, but made her way down to the stream, spying the tree trunk that had been placed over it to serve as a bridge. She veered to the left and made for its ease of passage, the grasses swishing against her shins as she hastened through them.

Crossing, Kerra stopped and looked along the vale, gaze moving to the croft seated before the thick woodland to the north. Smoke rose from the hole in its thatch, but she could see no other sign of life. 'He must be inside,' she stated, setting off towards the building as her mother reached the bridging trunk.

Kerenza stopped, staring dubiously at the mossy timber as she clutched the front of her dress and the earthy scent of the fungi wafted to her. Looking to her daughter, she found her rapidly diminishing, having covered almost half the distance to the croft.

She shook her head and sighed, smile still upon her lips despite her slight reservations about visiting with Estren Onan. She walked the length of the trunk and then moved through the shorter grass of the eastern banks where the shepherd's flock clearly spent much time grazing.

Kerra neared the gate, looking back to see her mother nearly a hundred yards behind. She considered waiting, but wanted to surprise Jacob and knew the longer she lingered outside the greater the chance of discovery.

With a growing smile, she opened the gate, careful not to sound the bells hanging from the top rung. She hurried along the path to the front door, pulse elevated with excitement as she trod as softly as she was able.

Kerra glanced towards her mother once again as she grasped the handle and took a breath. Flinging the door open, her expression abruptly fell.

Jacob was seated beside the fire. A pale figure stood beyond his shoulder, turning to the disturbance.

She screamed as she set eyes upon its face, her horrified cry resounding throughout the vale. Birds took to the wing from the nearby woodland, their calls of alarm echoing Kerra's distress.

30

Breoc knocked on the door and waited. No response came from within and he leant his ear to the wood, hearing no evidence of occupation.

Taking the handle, he opened it and peered into the cottage, finding no sign of Kerenza or her foul brat. He frowned and wondered at there whereabouts. He had seen the girl come and go from Tetker's home and thought that maybe they had taken the old woman more of the curative.

The trapper shut the door and briefly considered heading across the settlement to Tetker's cottage. Unable to contrive an excuse that would pardon his being there, he chose to continue with what he had intended after visiting with Kerenza.

He set off towards the woods, passing around the side of the cottage. Walking beneath the boughs, he went north through the strand of trees, seeking out the first of his traps.

Spying the hazel bush beneath which the snare was set, he pushed through a thick growth of ferns and made his way over. He saw the still form of a strangulated rabbit and smiled thinly. Coming to a stop, he crouched and took the catgut from around the creature's neck, resetting the trap before tying the rabbit to his belt.

Moving on, he made for the rotting trunk of an elm which stood in a small clearing, fingers of moss growing up the folds in the base its trunk. There was a hollow on the far side that he knew to be frequented by the wildlife of the woods. A snare had been set in a shrub nearby,

Breoc hoping to catch one of the creatures that came and went from the dank remains of the tree.

His smile grew as he spied a squirrel caught in the trap, the russet of its fur apparent through the veiling grasses. The creature squirmed at the sound of his approach, turning its painfully bulging eyes towards him and staring with both fear and innocence.

'There be life in this one yet,' Breoc murmured to himself as he drew near and bent closer in readiness.

His left hand shot forth, pinning the red squirrel by the shoulders as it squealed in alarm. His right quickly seized its head, giving it a quick twist and feeling the neck snap in his grip.

Remaining still for a moment, he savoured the feeling of power as the squirrel's body twitched in his hands. 'This is what I shall do to the girl when the time is right,' he stated with a sneer of satisfaction.

Taking the cord from about the squirrel's neck, Breoc added the creature to the dead weight at his hip. He reset the snare and straightened, continuing north to check his other traps.

A high scream pieced the woodland and he became still. It was that of a girl and he detected a familiar tone mixed with the fear that was so apparent.

'Kerra!' exclaimed Breoc, looking down the sloping woods towards the vale.

The trapper set off at a brisk pace, eager to discover both the source and reason for the terrified sound.

31

Kerra turned and fled from the fearful sight, urine running down the inside of her legs. Eyes wide and face drained of colour, she passed out of the garden to the wild jingling of the bells hung upon the gate. She ran for the security of her mother's presence, the image of the hideous face beneath the hood filling her mind and driving her on, its demonic features lit by firelight.

Kerenza ran to meet her, the fungi which had been gathered in her dress having been dropped at the sound of her daughter's fearful cry. Kerra flung her arms about her mother's midriff and buried her tearful face into her chest as barking arose from the croft at her back.

'What is wrong?' asked Kerenza worriedly, looking to the building in trepidation.

'A demon!' exclaimed Kerra breathlessly, her body trembling as she sobbed into her mother's dress.

'What?' Kerenza looked down at her in astonishment.

'He does not abide with spirits, but with demons of terrifying appearance,' replied the girl, her face remaining hidden.

'Kerra!' Jacob's voice was accompanied by the dog's continued barking.

'We must go,' she said with panicked urgency, drawing her glistening cheeks from the wool of the dress and looking pleadingly up at her mother.

'Kerra, please,' called the shepherd.

She took Kerenza's hand and began to pull her away, unable to bring herself to turn for fear of what she may see. 'We must leave, now!'

They began to hasten back to the trunk, their pace increasing until they broke into a run, fright propelling them onward.

'He is my brother,' called Jacob after them.

Kerra's brow became furrowed as she rushed across the makeshift bridge and Tetker's words relating to Jacob's kin came to mind. His father and brother had been struck down by a terrible illness. It had claimed their lives and she wondered at the possibility that they now dwelt with him, their spirits still bearing the signs of the disease?

'He is a leper.'

Her pace faltered in response to Jacob's words and Kerra drew to a halt on the lower reaches of Nancherrow Hill. Turning, she found the shepherd stood upon the near bank of the stream, having leapt across beside the dry stone wall that bordered the garden. He held Bess by the scruff of her neck, the hound's tail wagging as she looked up the slope. Peering past him, she saw that the door to the croft was open, but could not see the interior due to the angle of her view.

'The bells on the gate,' called Jacob, 'they belonged to my father and brother.'

'Be it their spirits that dwell with you?' she asked.

'This be unnatural and we should not linger,' stated Kerenza, waving her daughter to follow as she continued up the hill and made for the trees.

'Joseph is no spirit.'

Kerenza glanced back to see that her daughter remained in situ. She stopped and stared in alarm as a pale figure walked from the croft. 'Kerra!' she called.

A chill settled on Kerra as she stared at the robed form, rooted to the spot and her mother twenty yards beyond her position. The figure slowly lifted its hands, drawing the hood back from its dark and ragged hair.

Revealed was a face disfigured and discoloured by countless growths, its nose lost to the lesions.

'I am Joseph,' he announced.

Kerra slowly turned to look up the slope at her mother. 'Be he a spirit?'

'I do not know,' admitted Kerenza, her words and expression filled with trepidation.

'Come, meet him and decide for yourselves,' said Jacob, beckoning for them to return with his free hand as he retained his grip on Bess. 'Keep your distance if you must, but do not let fear or the words of others be your judge in this matter.'

Kerra awaited her mother's guidance, unsure as to what course of action to take and made hesitant by her previous distress. Kerenza pondered and then gave a vague nod, moving back down the slope to her daughter's side.

'We will speak with you both, but only if you withdraw to the far side of the stream,' she stated.

Jacob nodded his agreement and looked to Kerra. 'Bess wishes to greet you. May I release her so that she can satisfy her wish?'

Kerra gave a nod and the shepherd let go of the hound, straightening as she bounded across the grassland. She jumped up, front paws leaving muddied marks on the faded green of the girl's dress. With regular glances towards the croft, she fussed the dog, Bess licking at her hands in enthusiastic greeting.

Jacob leapt back across the stream as the dog went to Kerenza and sniffed the hem of her dress. She looked down, but kept her hands withdrawn, fearful of the hound's possible contamination.

Bess returned to Kerra, the girl having noted her mother's reticence to engage with the hound and following suit. Jacob made his way into the enclosure of the croft and moved to stand by his brother as Bess stared pleadingly up at her.

Kerenza and Kerra looked at each other, both trying to glean courage from the other's presence. They linked hands before walking northward, the dog parting company with them and trotting down the slope.

Bess leapt over the waters and vaulted the gate, joining her master as mother and daughter drew level with the croft. They hesitantly moved nearer to the stream and came to a halt a few yards from the section which had been widened, the grip of their hands tightening.

'I thought your father and brother to have been taken from this world,' stated Kerra, the words addressed to Jacob, her gaze unable to endure the sight of his brother's face.

'Our father passed three years hence when gangrene spread and eventually took his life. My brother, as you can see, still abides with me.'

'Why do you choose to hide him away?' asked Kerenza.

'Your reaction to my presence is answer enough to that enquiry,' said Joseph, pulling his hood back over his head, the deformity of his features hidden in the shadows.

'Why did you not tell me?' asked Kerra.

'I would have revealed the truth in time,' he replied, 'and am sorry it has been discovered in such a way.'

'Be he the spirit of which rumours speak?'

Jacob nodded. 'We oft walk together at night or when the sea mist rolls in and conceals all within its veil. I was not aware that we had been seen and ne'er suspected such stories were being told until you spoke of them.'

'Will you speak of me when you return to Lannust?'

Kerra forced herself to look at Jacob's brother, glad that his face was all but concealed beneath the hood. 'I will not tell a soul, if that be your wish.'

Joseph nodded. 'Aye, that it be.'

There was a temporary silence, the waters of the stream burbling as they passed between them.

'Please, come and join us,' said Jacob. 'We were about to have bread and cheese, and there is enough for all.'

Kerra looked to her mother and Kerenza nodded in response.

''Tis only fair that we hear them out, but we must be careful not to touch anything or venture too close,' she said quietly.

Kerra thought for a moment. 'Jacob remains free of sickness,' she observed.

'We do not yet know if that be by luck or judgement. 'Tis best to err on the side of caution.'

'You need stay no longer than you see fit,' called Jacob. 'There are apples aplenty too,' he encouraged.

'We will sup with you,' stated Kerenza.

'I am glad,' he responded with a weak smile. 'I shall ready the food.'

Jacob turned and walked to the croft, his brother at his side with head bowed. They disappeared from sight and Kerra began towards the stream, moving to the right beyond its artificially widened banks.

'I must wash myself before going in,' she stated, bending to remove her shoes and holding their roughly stitched leather in her hand.

Kerenza made her way to the bank as her daughter lifted the hem of her dress and stepped into the waters, jaw clenching in response to the cold embrace. Kerra proceeded to rinse her shoes and then threw them onto the cropped grass on the far side. She raised the hem of her dress further and squatted to clean away the residue of her fright.

Climbing out, she looked to her mother while picking up the shoes. ‘Do you think Jacob’s brother to be real?’ she asked, still not fully convinced.

‘As real as you or I,’ replied Kerenza before leaping the waters.

‘It must have been he that Breoc spied in the mist.’ She bent and slipped on her damp shoes.

Her mother nodded. ‘Aye, that it must.’

They began to the croft without eagerness, passing through the gate. The bells chimed, their sound making Kerra stiffen and the tightness of her expression belying her nervousness.

‘What is that?’ asked her mother.

Kerra followed her gaze and looked to the right. ‘A table where Jacob shares his food with the creatures of the vale,’ she replied.

They drew near to the door, steps faltering and both having to fight the urge to turn away. Their knowledge of the monstrous face beneath the hood was like an enchantment of repulsion, creating an invisible barrier about the croft through which only the stout hearted could pass.

Kerenza halted just beyond sight of the interior, her gaze fixed on the doorway. Kerra glanced over her shoulder and drew up a couple of yards shy of the entrance, needing her mother’s presence in order to break the spell.

‘Come, the food is waiting,’ said Jacob as he reappeared and waved them in.

Kerenza broke through the barrier created by her mind and moved to her daughter’s side. They made the final approach with uneasy steps, Jacob retreating into the confines before they entered.

Joseph was seated upon a stool to the right of the fire pit, purposefully keeping his head bowed so that his face would not be seen as he scratched Bess behind the ears, the hound lounging at his feet. Jacob made his way to the stool placed on the far side of the flames from the door, a table behind with a row of four wooden plates resting on the near edge, each bearing a flatbread and portion of goat's cheese specked with herbs.

Kerenza hesitantly closed the door, in truth wishing to leave it open should they need to exit in haste. She turned as her daughter moved to the seat on the left, only one remaining vacant, its back to the entrance and located nearest the hooded figure. She stared at it anxiously, its proximity to the leper causing her to remain in place.

'Please, sit,' said Jacob, indicating the empty stool with an outstretched hand before reaching round and taking one of the plates from the tabletop.

Kerenza forced herself to step forward, surreptitiously shifting the stool closer to her daughter as she sat. The shepherd passed the plate across the fire pit and then took another which he gave to Kerra.

'My thanks,' said the girl with a glance across at the bowed figure.

''Tis our pleasure. It has been long indeed since we entertained guests.' Jacob took the third plate and handed it to his brother before taking the last for himself.

The brothers began to eat as Kerra looked to the food, finding no appetite in the presence of the leper, her concern relating to contracting his disease binding her hands in place and tightening her stomach. She glanced at her mother and saw that she too was struggling to bring herself to partake.

'It was I that prepared the food,' stated Jacob through a mouthful of bread. 'You have no need of concern.'

‘In truth, I am not hungry,’ said Kerenza. ‘We ate heartily when we broke fast this morn.’

Jacob looked from Kerenza to Kerra, fully aware of what truly stayed their hands. ‘Would you care to hear the tale of how this came to pass?’ he asked, hoping that words may distract them from thoughts of infection.

Kerra nodded, pushing the plate of food down her lap until it rested precariously upon her knees. Bess looked over from the far side of the pit, licking her lips in anticipation.

‘You would be too young to remember, but a ship carrying pilgrims to Carrack Looz En Cooz was wrecked upon The Wra seven years hence,’ began Jacob.

‘How had they strayed so far from The Mount?’ asked Kerra, imagining a ship crashing into the three rocks that lay off the mainland a little to the east, huge waves heaving against its broken hull.

‘There was a mighty storm and it became lost, passing about The Cape. Wreckage was washed all along the northern shore from here to Zennor.’

‘We heard tell of booty to be found,’ said Joseph, keeping his head low as he picked up the tale. ‘Our father and I went north to where the stream empties into the ocean at Kenidjack. Jacob remained with the flock, such was his good fortune that day.

‘Amidst the bodies and shattered timbers we found clothing and food. Eating our fill, we gathered all we could into the remains of a sail in order to drag it to the croft. ‘Tis there that the disease took hold, as if in punishment for leaving the dead to rot without burial.’

Joseph sighed and his shoulders sagged. ‘Three bodies there were and we thought all to be dead, but as we gathered the booty there came a spluttering. It was a monk, or so we thought from the manner of his dress. He was near death and barely drawing breath.

‘Our father and I pulled him from the surf and tried to lend him our breath in order that he may live. Alas, he passed with his head cradled in the crook of my arm. That is when the truth became known to us.’

‘The truth?’ asked Kerra as she looked across the flames at Joseph.

‘The fingers of his hand released a bell that he had been holding and we realised that he was no monk, but a leper. He must have made the pilgrimage in the hope of being healed. He were dressed as I, though his face had yet to become the dominion of the disease.’

‘Months passed before we recognised the signs of infection,’ said Jacob. ‘Our father sought out Old Tetker for advice and it was upon her words that he and Joseph set off on a journey to find aid.’

‘We were given places in the leper house at St Keverne,’ said Joseph, ‘but we did not stay. Much of each day was spent praying and singing to the glories of God in the small chapel there. Our father’s faith had been lost with the passing of our mother, our contraction of the disease serving to strengthen his return to the old ways of natural law.

‘The nuns tried to persuade him to embrace Christ once again, told him that our suffering was akin to his, that we were enduring purgatory on earth and would go directly to heaven when we passed from this world. He would not listen.’

‘They returned to the croft and we kept their presence secret,’ stated Jacob. ‘At least, we thought that their occupation was unknown,’ he corrected.

‘Whilst travelling they had encountered some that believed their sickness to be a mark of great sin. Because of this, we thought it wisest that they remain hidden from the eyes and minds of those in Lannust for fear of persecution.’

‘This I understand,’ nodded Kerenza. ‘I have suffered accusations merely from the making of curatives.’

‘Witch?’ asked Jacob, looking across at her.

She gave another nod. ‘On occasion.’

Kerra looked to her mother, knowing there were those in the village that thought she wove magic into her medicines, but unaware that she had been accused of being a practitioner of witchcraft. ‘You have ne’er told me of this.’

‘It has been a long time since anyone has openly put voice to such and I did not wish to cause you undue concern.’

‘But we attend Mass almost daily,’ responded Kerra. ‘How then can they believe you to be a… witch?’ she said, struggling to speak the word.

‘They can believe so quite easily. Fear and ignorance stir the mind and are forces of great illusion. They can cause even the most hard minded to believe fanciful things.’

‘Then you understand our need for secrecy.’

Kerenza looked to the shepherd. ‘I do,’ she replied. ‘Not a word will pass my lips.’

‘Nor mine,’ stated Kerra.

Jacob smiled at them. ‘Our thanks,’ he said with a nod. ‘Please eat.’

They both looked to their food and Kerra slowly moved the plate towards her.

‘Jacob prepares all the food,’ reassured Joseph from the concealment of the hood’s shadows.

Kerra picked up her flatbread and took a tentative bite. Her mother watched a moment and then followed suit. Jacob finished the last of his lunch and placed his plate back upon the table, rising and fetching branches from the woodpile against the wall behind Kerra.

Putting them on the flames, there was a hiss of steam as the damp timbers were seared by the heat. He seated himself and took the empty plate from his brother, resting it on his. One of the sheep bleated and the shepherd looked to the door beside the woodpile.

'They ask to graze,' he commented. 'Would you care to accompany me after you have finished your food?'

Kerra swallowed a mouthful of bread and cheese. 'I promised to visit with Tetker before the day is through,' she replied.

'You are friends with her?'

'Aye, and more. She regards us as her family,' she said with a nod towards her mother. 'She ails with a cold and we assist her return to health.'

'As I recall, she is a good woman, one in whom secrets can be entrusted and wisdom can be sought.'

'That she is,' said Kerra before taking another bite of her bread.

There was a brief silence, Kerenza eating the last of her lunch and then looking over to Jacob. 'I must make an apology,' she stated.

He looked across at her curiously, Joseph's head turning as he regarded her from beneath the hood, both she and Kerra keeping their eyes averted.

'I sorely misjudged you and paid too much heed to the words of others. I am glad my daughter has helped me see the truth for myself, for I find you not as expected, but surrounded by a kindly light.'

'My thanks,' he replied.

'My name is Kerenza. Should either of you ever have need of my curatives, I will be happy to oblige. You need only ask Kerra or call at the cottage. 'Tis the first beyond the woodland upon Nancherrow Hill.'

Jacob gave a nod. 'Your offer is most kind.'

'With your good will, I would accompany my daughter here and visit on occasion.'

Kerra looked at her mother in surprise as she chewed on the last of her food.

'Your company would be welcome at any time,' responded Jacob warmly.

They looked across the renewed flames and held each other's gaze, finding the same kindly nature in evidence. Kerenza felt drawn in by his bright eyes, as if a spell were being cast upon her.

She blinked to release herself from the growing mesmerism. 'We should take our leave,' she stated, holding the plate out to the shepherd and her cheeks slightly blushed.

He stood and took it from her. 'I am glad that the secret of my brother's presence is now known to you both and to have spent time in your company.'

'I hope my presence will not be an impediment to future visits with my brother,' stated Joseph, his bowed head towards Kerra.

'It will not,' she stated, her tone firm despite her continuing reservations, the leper giving rise to considerable uneasiness.

Kerra got to her feet and passed Jacob her plate. Gathering it to her mother's, he briefly turned to place them on the table.

'Fare ye well,' said Kerenza, looking from Jacob to the hooded figure who rose from his stool as she spoke.

'My Dor Dama bless thee,' said Jacob.

She smiled in response. Many such words were said by rote, but his tone and the look in his eyes communicated the genuine nature of his blessing. 'And may Dor Dama bless you too,' she replied, feeling a sense of release. She had not been able to openly acknowledge her beliefs for many years and the freedom to do so leant itself to a profound relief. She did not have to hide herself, but could be true to all she was in the company of this man, one whom she had long maligned and avoided.

She frowned and shook her head, staring down at the flames.

'Be there something wrong?'

She looked back to Jacob. 'I feel foolish and saddened. So many years we have abided close at hand and yet I let rumour bar me from the vale and the possibility of our friendship.'

'Do not hold on to regret. Everything has its season and ours has just begun. Dor Dama does not ask our leave or beg our pardon. She knows when things should blossom and when they should fade, and acts for the harmony of all.'

'Such were the words of my mother upon her death bed,' she responded, 'though our season was reaching its end.' She blinked away gathering tears, pushing the sorrowful memories from her mind.

'She is with my mother also and they abide in all things,' he said with a smile of reassurance.

'Jacob's mother is buried beneath the apple tree at the foot of the vale,' commented Kerra.

Kerenza looked to her daughter.

'We ate its fruit together and now she is part of our existence.' Kerra smiled. 'It may be we should plant an apple tree where Grandmother lies.'

'It may be we should,' she responded before looking to Jacob. 'My thanks again for your kindness and your words.'

Kerenza turned and stepped to the door, opening it and glancing over her shoulder. 'Until next time,' she stated, her smile returning.

32

Breoc lay hidden in a patch of bracken at the edge of the woods and stared down the slope to the croft. He resisted the urge to break cover and make for the building despite his belief that Kerenza and her brat had been spellbound. He had caught a glimpse of the spirit entering the building upon his arrival and had seen Kerenza and the girl enter the cottage as if taken by some charm, their movements dreamlike and unnatural.

A murder of crows swooped past his position, calling out as they flew north and rose over the trees where the woodland marched down into the head of the vale. Their cries rang out as he waited, the thought that the dark birds were informing Estren Onan of his presence passing fleetingly through his mind.

The door opened and Kerenza exited with the brat on her heels. Estren Onan appeared in the entrance as they walked to the gate and there were waves of departure accompanied with words that the trapper could not discern.

Mother and daughter passed through the gate and Breoc's brow creased as he thought he heard the faint sound of bells chiming.

''Tis the spell,' he murmured with a scowl, believing the croft to be protected by a charm, one that was broken when passing beyond its boundary, the chimes the sound of the magic falling away.

Breoc watched as Kerenza walked alongside the strip of stubble on the far side of the stream. She stopped and crouched, gathering up her dress as her daughter joined her. They picked at the ground and he could make out faint paleness in their hands.

'Mushrooms?' he asked himself in a whisper, seeing them place the items in the makeshift pouch.

They straightened and followed the stream, making their way to a tree trunk before crossing. He shifted slightly within the browning leaves as they moved up the slope to his right, steadily making their way towards the woods.

As quietly as he could, Breoc retreated and slipped from the bracken. Staying low, he moved deeper into the woodland, making fleet footed towards their route. The sound of their voices drifted to him as he drew closer and spied the Sacred Oak.

Sprinting across the grasses beneath its boughs, he climbed up its substantial trunk until he found a suitable limb on which to crouch. Making sure his cloak hid the squirrel's conspicuous fur, he gripped the tree and drew himself up to the bark for want of concealment.

Glancing down, he looked to the base of the tree where he had spied Estren Onan leaving offerings in accordance with the old ways, but saw no evidence of recent visitation. His gaze moved to the right as Kerenza walked into view below, the brat beside her.

'I knew you would like him,' commented the girl as they skirted the clearing in which the oak rested.

'And you were right,' replied Kerenza. 'There can be no doubting he is a good man.'

'So I may visit with him?' asked Kerra hopefully.

'I see no harm in it.'

The girl smiled brightly. 'Will you visit with him too?' she asked.

Kerenza glanced at the girl. 'Aye, that I will.'

Breoc's brow furrowed as he watched them depart the clearing, passing through ferns and moving away amidst the trees. They were enraptured by a foul conjuration of Estren Onan's making, of this he was sure.

He climbed down the oak and swiftly made his way after them. Catching sight of them ahead, he moved from trunk to trunk, hoping to hear any further words which may be spoken, but Kerenza and the brat falling into silence.

They reached the edge of the woods and passed beyond, the cottage visible to the right. He drew up to the tree-line, staying hidden as he watched them pass around to the front of the building.

Crouching, he deliberated for a while, unsure as to whether he should approach the cottage or continue to check his traps. Deciding upon the latter course of action, unwilling to give the crows a chance to feast on anything that may be caught, Breoc backed away. He would call on Kerenza after the task was completed and see if she would volunteer the truth of her visit to the croft.

33

Jacob stood before the table and took two small fish from the smoking frame which had been placed above the hole in the thatch during the morning. He rested them upon the piece of cloth he had used the previous day and began to wrap them as his brother sat beside the fire.

They had remained silent since their guests had departed, but he knew that Joseph was disturbed by the visit. The secret of his presence at the croft was undone, even if only in part. It had offered protection, allowing them to exist beyond the bounds of the settlement and giving them security in their isolation. Now that sense of security had tumbled down like the walls of the flock's enclosure, Kerra and Kerenza's arrival shaking the foundations of their existence.

'Do you trust them?' asked Joseph eventually.

'Aye,' said Jacob as he finished wrapping the fish. 'You do not?'

'I think they intend to stay true to their word, but I have a…' He paused a moment. '…A feeling.'

Jacob turned to him with the parcel of fish in hand and a curious expression upon his face. 'A feeling?'

'Aye,' nodded Joseph. 'Change is coming.'

'Be that not a good thing? Too long have you been a ghost, living a half-life as you haunt the croft. Now you are known as a man, by the girl and her mother at least, and it may be others will come to know you as such.'

'They see me as no such thing,' he said with bitterness. 'I am but a demon to their eyes. The girl said so herself.'

‘Surely you understand why she reacted in such a way?’

Joseph nodded, the hood moving faintly. ‘Aye,’ he replied, raising his hand to his face and touching the growths where once had been a nose. ‘I understand it well.’

‘It may be that given time they will see beyond the disease to the man within.’

‘I fear that time may not be upon our side.’

Jacob looked at his brother in confusion. ‘What mean you by that?’

Joseph raised his head, turning his face to his brother, the firelight illuminating his disfigurement. ‘Ill fortune comes to our door. This is my feeling, my intuition,’ he revealed

‘Do you speak of Kerra and her mother?’

‘Not directly, but their arrival has set things in motion that cannot be undone,’ he said gravely. ‘Our future stirs in these moments. I heard it whispering in the shadows during their stay and those whispers shall grow into a roaring wind.’

‘You speak like a soothsayer,’ commented Jacob, feeling discomforted by his brother’s manner.

‘I put words to the sensations within, is all,’ replied Joseph. ‘It may be that I should leave and seek out a leper house.’ He returned his gaze to the flames.

‘And what if you be mistaken? You may only be disturbed by the change they have wrought. Long have we remained hidden and cautious, and it may be time this way of life was brought to an end.’

‘But to what end?’ asked Joseph darkly.

Jacob stared at the hunched figure for a while before shaking his head. ‘I will speak no more on this matter now,’ he stated, turning back to the table and taking up a piece of bread.

He stepped around the fire pit and went to the door. 'I hope that you will be in lighter spirits upon my return, Brother,' he said as he took hold of the handle.

There was no response as Bess rose from beside Joseph's feet and began towards him.

'Triga,' he instructed firmly, holding up his hand, Bess looking at him in disappointment.

'I will return shortly to let the sheep graze as I milk the goats,' he said.

Still there was no reply, his brother sitting motionless as he stared at the flickering light before him.

Jacob frowned and stepped out, closing the door behind. The sky was thick with grey cloud and a light breeze came down the vale, the trees and grasses whispering.

He hesitated, sighing and glancing over his shoulder at the door. The clouds in Joseph's mind had long been present, dark and looming. He yearned for a kind wind to usher them away and wished there were something he could do to alleviate his brother's anguish.

With a sad shake of his head, Jacob walked away from the door and went to the rough stone table. Crouching, he broke the bread and placed the pieces upon it.

'Blessed be,' he whispered with a brief bow of his head.

Rising, he walked to the gate and passed beyond, striding alongside the boundary wall. He turned the corner and looked across the vegetable beds at the back of the cottage as he walked parallel with its length. The concern that his brother would not be present upon his return came to mind. He discarded the thought, believing Joseph would not be able to find it in himself to depart without a farewell.

Jacob made for the trees gathered in the head of the vale and moved into their seclusion as his thoughts turned to White Paw. He caught the scent of the fish within his hand and wondered if the wolf would be in want of something to drink.

'I should have brought a bowl of water,' he chastised, seeing the fallen elm through the trees and undergrowth ahead.

The shepherd slowed his pace, moving through the high grasses and looking to the root bowl, as yet unable to see the hollow. He crept closer and spied the wolf lying beyond the sparse roots. She was already aware of his approach and watching attentively.

'I have more food,' he said softly as he drew within ten yards.

She rose on her forelegs, still showing signs of weakness. Jacob lowered onto his haunches and continued forward.

White Paw's lips drew back to reveal her teeth. He slowed further, taking a couple more awkward steps.

A low growl of warning brought Jacob to a standstill only five yards from the hollow. With considered movements, he unwrapped the food. He tucked the cloth into his robes and let the fish lie upon his palm, showing them to her.

'For you,' he stated with a nod towards the offerings.

He threw them underarm into the hollow, unable to see them land from his position, but hearing the gentle thuds. White Paw held him in her captivating gaze for a moment and then raised her rear, loping from the shallow cover and picking up the first of the fish.

Lifting it into view, the wolf kept a watchful eye on him as she ate the tail. Tossing her head back sharply, she took the rest of the fish into her mouth and swallowed it down. The second was also quickly disposed of, White Paw licking her lips and resting upon her haunches, facing the shepherd as she sat in the indent with an expectant look.

Jacob held up his hands. 'There are no more fishes, but I will bring more food on the morrow.'

She looked into his eyes and he saw both longing and distrust in her gaze.

'If only you could tell me your story,' he said.

White Paw suddenly turned, staring intently beyond the far edge of the root bowl. Jacob lifted himself a little and looked into the woodland beyond the elm, seeing nothing untoward.

'What is it?' he whispered, the wolf rising and turning her back to him, ears forward as she listened to something beyond his hearing.

Jacob narrowed his eyes and scanned the undergrowth, still spying naught of concern. Glancing at the wolf, he found her returning to the cover of the overhanging roots. Circling once in the shadows before settling on the earth, she faced the direction from which she had detected a disturbance and continued to watch the woodland.

Backing away slowly, he made his way along the length of the elm, using it to shield his movements from whatever lay within the trees beyond. Reaching a point low enough for him to step over, Jacob did so, bent at the waist and staying low.

A twig snapped to the left and he turned his gaze to a strand of bracken twenty yards away. He caught a glimpse of something dark in retreat, his heart beating like a smith's hammer.

A chill settled upon him as he slunk towards the strand of ferns and wished he had brought his stick. His body was filled with tension as he stared unblinking, waiting to see further movement within the browning plants as their earthy scent drifted to him.

Reaching their ranks, Jacob peered within and saw nothing of note. The shepherd took a steadying breath and glanced over his shoulder. He was given a start by the sight of White Paw only a few yards away, her gaze upon the bracken.

She moved forward and he remained motionless as she passed close.

With a sudden leap, she was within the undergrowth. He watched her move with surprising quickness towards the heart of the strand and heard a high squeal of demise.

The wolf drew out of the ferns with a rabbit hanging from her mouth. Jacob's brow furrowed as he looked to the kill. A thin cord hung from its neck and was tied about a small wooden stake.

'A snare,' he said under his breath, White Paw taking a wide berth as she passed by on her return to the dell.

'You will choke,' warned Jacob, reaching for the stake.

The wolf turned and growled fiercely, bloodied teeth barred in warning.

He retreated with hands raised.

White Paw continued to the dell and passed over its rim, moving behind the roots and resting on her stomach before beginning to eat the rabbit. Jacob moved back over the elm and walked along its length to his previous position, expecting to find the creature choking on the catgut of the trap in which its prey had been caught. Instead, he heard the crunch of wood as he moved about the root bowl and the wolf came into view, her lower jaw smeared with blood and intestines hanging from her chin.

Jacob crouched as she licked the gore away and rested her head on her forelegs. She watched him, all trepidation having vanished from her eyes. The wolf no longer feared him, but was merely wary of his presence.

'Your strength is recovering,' he commented thoughtfully, wondering whether he should keep the goats and sheep in the cottage at night for the sake of their own safety.

White Paw yawned and stretched.

Jacob remained in her company for a few minutes. He had heard many tales of wolves and their deeds, of flocks slaughtered and babies stolen, of men who were changed into their likeness on nights of the full moon and of witches who took on their form. They were a symbol of the wilderness and solitude, one with which he had long identified, but he had never heard tell of any wandering so far west.

'You have come a fair distance I warrant,' he mumbled as he studied her paling coat, her fur cleaner and in better order than when first he had come across her within the dell. She was indeed an impressive sight, one which could instil both awe and fear.

With a last look into the creature's eyes, Jacob saw the untamed spirit within. 'You truly belong to Dor Dama.' He briefly bowed his head in reverence.

Backing away, the shepherd rose when he reached a distance of ten yards. 'Until the morrow,' he said in parting.

She appeared to give a vague nod of response and a look of surprise arose upon his face. Stories of shape changers drew to the fore of his mind.

'Could it be you are not as you seem?' he whispered, holding her gaze, but finding no evidence of anything other than the raw and unbroken will of the wild.

Jacob shook his head. 'No, you are of a singular nature,' he stated, lingering a little longer.

‘My blessings.’ The shepherd gave another bow before setting off in the direction of the croft.

His thoughts turned to his brother. When night came he would walk with him to their mother’s tree in the hope that the freedom from confinement and fresh air would lift his darkness.

‘And it may be we will pass to the trees of the fathers,’ Jacob murmured as he walked out of the woods and heard the sheep bleating, his mind briefly turning to Kerra as he made his way towards the wall in order to climb over and go to the flock’s tumbledown enclosure.

34

Breoc moved through the trees that marched up the western slope of the vale, the rabbit and squirrel hanging from his hip. 'So, the spirit can change its appearance and become a wolf,' he said to himself. 'It must be his guardian.'

He bore a look of distaste as he pushed aside the branches of a bush and continued on. ''Tis unnatural beyond imagining.'

He stepped over a rock and his expression softened, becoming more thoughtful. 'But it may be I can turn this day of discovery to my advantage.'

The trapper's lips curled into a sneer as a blackbird sounded its piercing alarm. 'Aye, I will bide my time.'

He broke from the trees and spied Kerenza's cottage to the left. He made for the building without breaking his stride, wishing to visit with her and find if she would keep her secrets from him.

Breoc passed around the side of the cottage and walked to the front door. Halting, he paused a moment and donned a friendly smile of greeting, though there was a sparkle in his dark eyes that revealed its falsehood.

Knocking twice in close succession, he waited and heard sounds of movement within.

The door opened and Kerenza stood before him.

'Good day, Kerenza,' he greeted as he touched his forelock. 'How goes it?'

'Good day, Breoc,' she replied with a forced smile. 'It goes well, and you?'

The trapper pulled aside his cloak to reveal the animals at his hip. 'Fruitful,' he stated. 'May I come in?'

She hesitated and the brief pause was not lost on him.

'Of course,' she replied, stepping back.

Breoc walked into the cottage and spied Kerra seated on the far side of the fire pit. 'Good day, Miss Kerra.' He touched his forelock once again.

'Breoc,' she replied with a nod, but without any hint of warmth.

He moved to the table and took a stool from beneath. He could feel their discomfort and was happy to increase their unease by implying a prolonged stay as he seated himself by the flames.

'What news?' he asked over his shoulder.

'Nothing of note,' replied Kerenza, moving from the door to the woodpile and taking up a few branches. 'Tetker still suffers with the cold and I am preparing a tonic while Kerra makes a broth with mushrooms we picked in the woods.'

Kerenza placed the timbers upon the flames, crouching beside her daughter across from the trapper. He stared at her over the pit, noting the distance she kept between them.

'Is aught wrong?'

'No,' she replied with a shake of her head, smile remaining fixed and firm. 'All is well. My mind is occupied by thoughts of what is needed for Tetker's curative, is all.' She tried to hold his investigating gaze, but was unable and turned her eyes to the flames.

He rose and moved around the fire as mother and daughter watched him. Stepping to Kerenza, Breoc was certain he detected unease in her expression as he drew close.

He crouched and leant towards her, lips puckering. Turning her head to the side, his kiss was set upon her cheek.

'Not in front of Kerra,' she said to excuse her action.

'You had no shame in doing so before.'

''Tis not shame, but good grace. Kerra has let it be known that she feels uncomfortable with such displays of affection.'

'Has she,' he said coldly, looking around Kerenza to the girl.

Kerra kept her gaze averted, secretly pleased with her mother's words and actions. She concentrated on slicing the mushrooms lying on a board upon her lap and feigned disinterest.

'Aye, and I would not have her discomforted in such a way if it can be helped.'

'Then I shall wait until she takes the tonic to Tetker.'

Kerenza glanced at him and he thought he detected worry in her eyes. 'I would that could be so, but I am to accompany her.'

'Why is there need for you both to go? Surely the girl can carry the tonic alone, or be there discomfort in that also?' he asked with a touch of sarcasm.

She turned to him. 'There is no need for such comment.'

'Is there not? I find I am being treated beyond reason in light of our recent union.'

Kerenza softened, knowing that she was treating him unfairly. 'I am sorry,' she said, forcing a hand to his cheek in reconciliation. 'I have things on my mind.'

'If you share them with me, I may be of some help.'

She shook her head. 'I will talk with you when the time is right.'

Breoc looked into her eyes and eventually nodded. 'If that is your wish, I can do naught but accept it.'

‘‘Tis,’ she confirmed.

The trapper glanced over at Kerra, sure the brat had played no small part in the newfound coldness that had settled between them. ‘I will take my leave,’ he stated, quickly rising as his anger flared.

‘I truly am sorry for my reticence,’ she said, looking up at him.

Breoc moved to the door without turning or deigning to answer. ‘I will visit with you on the morrow and hope to find you more receptive to my presence,’ he said hotly before opening it and stepping out, certain that the meddling girl and the enchantment under which Kerenza had been placed at the croft were responsible for her distance.

‘Fare well, Breoc,’ called Kerenza after him.

He looked to her, but gave no parting words before closing the door.

She listened as he walked away, his steps made heavy by the weight of his anger. Turning from the door, she looked at the flames as the new branches hissed like agitated snakes.

‘Mamm?’

Kerenza turned to her daughter.

‘Have you changed your mind in regards Breoc?’

She pondered before making her reply. ‘No, ‘tis not changed, merely considering.’

‘Considering what?’ Kerra cocked her head to the side curiously.

Her mother sighed, looking to the fire once again and watching the flames writhe. ‘The visit with Jacob,’ she began, ‘it gave me a sense of peace that I have not felt in the presence of another since the passing of your father.’

‘Truly?’ asked Kerra in surprise.

Kerenza nodded. ‘Peace with myself.’

Her daughter’s expression became confused.

'Long have I needed to hide the truth of who I am from others, to conceal part of me which lies at the core of my being, but in Jacob's company that was not so. I could accept myself and reveal all without fear of persecution. The same cannot be said in relation to Breoc.'

'And so you doubt the wisdom of your union?'

'I do,' she confirmed, Kerra having to fight the urge to smile. 'He is not a bad man, but the essence of who I am would have to remain hidden, and that is not the path to contentment. Nor is it the basis of a healthy and nurturing union.'

'Will you tell him so?'

Kerenza's expression stiffened. 'I cannot,' she replied. 'To do so would reveal our visit to the vale and my adherence to the old ways.'

'What will you tell him?' asked Kerra, feeling anxious at the thought of the trapper blaming her for the demise of the relationship.

She pondered for a moment and then fixed her gaze on her daughter's. 'If I have your pardon, I will use your father as an excuse,' she stated. 'I will tell Breoc that his disappearance is too close and my heart still belongs to him, that I was not aware of it at first, but now that we stand on the brink of making our union more steadfast, this truth has made itself known to me.'

Kerra nodded. 'You have my pardon,' she said, hoping that her mother's words would deflect any blame from being laid at her feet.

'It does, you know,' said Kerenza meaningfully.

She looked over in puzzlement.

'My heart. It still belongs to your father, but it has been nearly a year and I must accept he will not return and be open to loving another.'

'I understand,' said Kerra softly.

She studied her daughter for a while, still certain that her dislike of the trapper was rooted in her wish to cling onto the hope of her father's return. 'If you spend the morrow with Jacob, then I may speak freely with Breoc when he visits.'

Kerra nodded and turned her gaze to the fire, feeling a sense of dread despite her wish being granted in regards the demise of the relationship. The trapper's threat came to the fore of her mind and she worried about his apportioning of blame. Breoc was sure to believe she had played some part in it and in a sense this was true. She had taken her mother to visit with Jacob and it was during this visit that her eyes had been opened to the limitations of their union.

Kerenza reached out and placed a hand upon her shoulder, mistaking her daughter's expression and lack of words for a silence of mourning. 'Your father loved you dearly, Little Bird,' she stated with a melancholy smile, 'as do I.'

'And I you,' responded Kerra, placing her hand upon her mother's as spent branches collapsed within the fire pit and sent a darkening flurry of embers towards the hole in the thatch.

35

Kerra arrived at the old woman's cottage as the rain began to fall, its patter accompanied by a rising wind that stirred the tails of her cloak. She knocked and waited, two bowls balanced upon her left hand and wrist.

Hearing no sound from within, she took hold of the handle and entered. The interior was made gloomy by the darkening clouds as night drew in. The fire pit was filled with nothing but ash covering a few smouldering embers, the branches she had left beside the bed still in place. Tetker was motionless beneath the fleeces of her cot, eyes closed and face ashen.

'Tetker?' she asked softly, narrowing her eyes as she sought some sign that life still occupied the old woman's frail body.

There was no response.

With her pulse increasing, she stepped over the threshold, leaving the door open for the light it afforded her. Setting the bowls down beside the pit, she moved to the head of the cot and crouched, her nose wrinkling in response to the sight of thick mucus gathered within the old woman's lashes.

Kerra placed the back of her hand to Tetker's forehead. A tremendous heat emanated from the old woman's skin, which was slick with perspiration.

She stirred, groaning and bursting into a fit of coughing. Her eyes pulled open a little, the mucus allowing no greater parting. Taking a few moments to focus, her gaze finally settled upon the girl's face as her body convulsed and her neck strained.

Kerra glanced down for the cup of water and took it up hurriedly, taking it to the old woman's lips and tipping it. Tetker spluttered and choked, the liquid spilling upon the pale hairs of her chin.

She tipped it again as the coughing calmed and the old woman managed to take a soothing sip. Brushing ghostly strands of hair from Tetker's glistening forehead, she looked upon her with concern. There was no attempt at a smile from the old woman, no strength by which to try and create the illusion that she was not seriously ill.

'You rest. I will get the fire going,' stated Kerra, turning her back and facing the pit.

Taking up the most slender of the branches she had left by the cot, she used its end to reveal the few embers remaining. She snapped it, the sound causing her to wince and glance back, finding that Tetker's eyes had closed once again. She placed the pieces onto the embers and then rose, making her way to the woodpile in order to find suitable kindling.

Returning, Kerra set the small bundle upon the embers. She leant closer, pursing her lips and blowing softly. The smoke increased and wafted away from her with each breath, the wind taking it out of the front door in dirty clouds that were drawn into the east.

Flames sprang to life with a crackle of consumption and she rested back. Watching a while, she set larger branches in place and then went to the door, closing it on the gathering dark.

She paused after turning back to the interior. Her heart ached at the sight of Tetker in the grip of the sickness and she feared the worst as its fingers tightened.

Kerra picked up the bowls from beside the pit and returned to the head of the cot. Setting them down on the compacted earth, she knelt and took up the mushroom soup. 'You must eat,' she stated softly, feeling the fading warmth of the bowl's contents against her palm.

Tetker opened her eyes a little and took great effort to turn upon her back beneath the covers. Kerra slipped her free hand beneath the old woman's head and raised it from the pillow, taking the bowl to her lips. Tipping it, she let a small portion pass into Tetker's mouth and then waited for her to swallow, the insistence of her cough trying to undo her need for sustenance as she spluttered and nearly ejected the food.

After another mouthful the old woman pushed the bowl away, hand falling to the fleeces and her energy spent. Kerra frowned, the soup she had consumed barely diminishing the contents of the bowl.

'You should eat more. It will help you fight the cold.'

Tetker managed to move her head side to side as she closed her eyes. 'No more,' she croaked hoarsely.

'Then you must take some of the tonic Mamm prepared for you.'

Tetker shook her head again, the strain evident in the knots of her brow, the skin gathered in deep wrinkles between her eyes.

Kerra looked upon the old woman fretfully, feeling both frustrated and helpless in the face of her condition. There was little more she could do other than force the medicine upon her and risk it causing her to choke.

'I will stay to tend both you and the fire,' she stated.

'No need,' breathed Tetker without opening her eyes.

'There is every need,' she responded softly, stroking the burning skin of the old woman's cheek, her own concern of catching the illness outweighed by the severity of Tetker's condition. 'I will not leave until you have had more food and at least some of the curative, until I am satisfied that I have done all I can so you are best able to fight the fever.'

‘Dearest,’ whispered Tetker, the faintest trace of a smile lifting her lips.

‘Rest now,’ she responded, continuing to stroke her cheek for a few moments.

Taking up the last of the branches from beside the bed, she placed them on the fire. She reclined against the side of the cot, clasping her legs to her chest and feeling the warmth of the flames upon her shins. ‘You have no need to speak with Brecca,’ she said without turning to the old woman. ‘Mamm has had a change of heart and will be bringing her union with Breoc to an end on the morrow, though it was not my words that swayed her.’

She paused to watch a harvest spider pass over her shoes, its thin legs carrying it towards the woodpile. ‘We visited with Jacob today and she found him to be a goodly man. She has permitted me to return to the vale when I so choose.

‘It be no spirit with whom he abides, but his brother,’ she revealed.

Tetker’s hand settled upon her shoulder and Kerra turned to find the old woman looking at her in questioning surprise, her eyes barely open.

‘‘Tis true,’ she said. ‘At first I thought him a demon, such is the fearfulness of his countenance. The disease has ravaged him and he is disfigured beyond the appearance of a man.’ A shiver caused her shoulders to tremble as she recalled first setting eyes on Joseph.

‘Mamm and Jacob spoke openly of Dor Dama and it was this that changed her mind in regards Breoc. She did not want to enter into a union in which she would have to keep her beliefs secret and so will tell him on the morrow that they will go no further.’

Understanding showed in Tetker’s pallid face. Her hand fell away from the girl’s shoulder and she settled restfully upon the cot, eyes closing once again.

Kerra looked upon her and longed to see improvement. Glancing down at the bowls, she considered trying to feed the old woman more of the soup, but instead decided to let her rest.

'Later,' she said to herself, turning to the flames and shifting on the earth in the hope of finding greater comfort, the edge of the cot pressing hard against her back.

36

Jacob entered the cottage through the door to the enclosure that was located beside the woodpile. Joseph looked up from his stool at the fireside, hood lowered and dark hair framing his disfigurement.

'Greetings, Brother,' said Jacob with a nod, a pail containing goat's milk held in his hand.

He turned back to the open doorway, the night darkening the enclosure as it seeped through gaps in the ramshackle walls. Letting out a sharp whistle, the flock was ushered in with Bess at the rear. They bleated and gathered about the woodpile, trying to keep their distance from the fire and pale figure seated on the far side.

'Are we to sleep with the flock tonight?' asked Joseph without humour as his brother closed the adjoining door.

'Aye. The wolf regains her strength and I would keep them safe until she moves on,' replied Jacob as he placed the pail upon the table and seated himself, Bess trotting over and the shepherd bending to scratch behind her ears. 'How is your mood?'

'Unchanged.'

'I had hoped you would have warmed to the presence of Kerra and her mother on this day and the possibility of their return in days to come.'

'I warm to nothing. A chill has settled upon my soul and 'tis not of winter's making.'

'No, 'tis of your mind,' stated Jacob. 'You think on how you appear to them, believing yourself a monster.

You would rather remain hidden for the rest of your days than suffer the unkind looks of others. I understand this well, Brother, but it may be they will see beyond the affliction.'

He reached out and set his hand upon Joseph's shoulder, holding it firmly. 'I would that others see the truth of your heart for 'tis good and strong, one that should be shown and not hidden beneath the mask of your disease.'

Jacob held his brother's gaze to reinforce the honesty of his words and then removed his hand. 'Let them discover the nature of the man that lies behind the misfortune of your appearance,' he said softly.

Joseph sighed. 'I know well the chill conjured by my mind,' he said, turning to the fire. 'Long have I suffered under its tyranny, but this is something different and rises from the depth of my being. Its icy fingers clasp bone and sinew, heart and mind. It be a portent, an omen of evil tidings.'

'And yet I feel nothing of the like,' said Jacob, looking at the growths upon his brother's face and a swell of pity arising in response. 'Nothing can take the disease from you, but it may be that acceptance on the part of Kerra and her mother can cause you to forget its presence.'

Joseph nodded. 'It may be, but I tell you again, that is not what troubles me, Brother.'

Jacob sighed and turned to the flames, sitting thoughtfully for a while. He could think of no other words by which to alleviate his brother's concerns and worried that he would depart should the fear take greater hold. He felt certain the chill was caused by Joseph's own thoughts, that the reactions of Kerra and her mother were bitter reminders of his unsightly features that he did not wish to endure.

‘I shall prepare a broth,’ he stated, knowing that to dwell on his brother’s condition would do naught to change it.

Jacob rose from his stool, the flock gathered before the door to the enclosure and eyeing his movement. Bess watched as he collected two bowls, wiping out the remains of the morning’s food over the fire.

Setting them upon the tabletop, he picked up the battered cooking pot to the rear and placed it before him. Glancing at the cuts of meat hung above the vegetable sacks to the right, he leant over and selected a piece of cured venison.

Jacob took up a knife and began to slice the meat into slivers, the leg bone already revealed where he had cut the meat for previous meals. ‘Do you still entertain the thought of leaving?’ he asked over his shoulder, trying not to lend the question the weight it truly carried as he glanced down at Bess, who had settled on her haunches and watched with pleading eyes.

There was a short pause before Joseph replied, one of the sheep bleating as the goats settled before the fire.

‘Aye.’

The knife wavered in Jacob’s hand. ‘And where does this thought take you?’

‘This I do not know. All I know is that I think it best that I am away from here. I fear for your safety.’

Jacob looked back in surprise, finding Joseph’s gaze upon him. ‘My safety?’

‘If my presence were revealed things could go ill with the villagers. I fear what they may do, that they may cause us harm or even bring about our demise, such is the strength of the chill upon me. For me this would be a release from suffering, but for you…’ He shook his head. ‘I would not bring such ruin upon you.’

'You do not know how they would react, but only guess with a dark bent. It may be your presence will not be discovered and all these thoughts are naught but sombre imaginings,' replied Jacob.

'As things stand, there are but two who know and they are two I would trust to keep our secret,' he added, crouching to give Bess a slice of the venison, rubbing her head briefly as she let the offering drop to the floor, sniffing it before taking it into her mouth.

Joseph gave no reply, but rose and moved around the pit, stepping by the goats and collecting an armful of branches from the woodpile. Jacob watched and then returned to the preparation of supper, listening as a sheep bleated and his brother placed the timbers upon the fire so that there would be heat aplenty for the cooking pot.

'My thanks,' he stated, their living relationship like a dovetail joint after so many years.

He reached for some turnips and wild onions, taking them to the knife after placing the strips of venison into the cooking pot. Joseph stepped over without saying a word, taking the pot and passing out of the cottage in order to add water from the stream.

Jacob felt his tension rise at the sound of the door closing. He listened intently, his brother's steps soon disguised by the patter of rain. He chopped the vegetables with agitated thrusts, worried that his brother would wander off into the night and never return.

The regular squeak of the cooking pot's handle sounded as it swung by Joseph's side, the additional weight of the water always giving rise to the telltale sound. Jacob felt relief and took a breath before the door opened and his brother entered.

The pot was placed back upon the table and Jacob glanced at his brother, noting that his hair glistened with rainwater. 'You should have pulled up your hood,' he commented as Joseph returned to his seat.

'I wanted to feel the rain,' he replied sullenly as the window shutters muttered against their fastenings.

Jacob could feel his brother's sadness. It lay like a thick cloak about his shoulders and the long winter nights always drew it tighter about him. 'It may be that this is the cause of the chill,' he mumbled to himself.

'What is the cause?' asked Joseph.

He turned to his brother. 'Your anguish grows with the lengthening of the nights. I have seen it before and think it may be the source of the feeling you have.'

'You think it nothing more than the melancholy of the season?' Joseph's eyes and tone revealed his annoyance. 'After what I have said to you, how can you dismiss it so lightly?'

'I do not dismiss it. I try and reason out its origin is all, for I will not believe that our doom lies close at hand.'

'I did not ask you to believe,' replied Joseph with a hard edge, returning his gaze to the fire. 'I believe and that is enough.'

Jacob took a breath as he looked upon his brother, sympathetic to his torment. 'I seek an answer so that you will have doubt enough to stay at the croft,' he admitted. 'I do not wish you to take to the road on the strength of a feeling, but wish you here at my side.'

'When 'tis misty or dark,' responded Joseph with a shake of his head. 'There is something you said earlier that has stayed with me, Brother.'

He fixed his gaze on Jacob. 'That I live a half-life,' he stated coldly, 'and this is true. It may be 'tis time I left in order to gain a greater fullness of life, feeling or no feeling.'

'I did not mean to cause offence.'

'You caused none, merely thoughtfulness,' responded Joseph, his tone softening.

'But where would you go to find such an existence?'

'A leper house would at least allow me the freedom to be seen. I would be in the company of others who suffer in the same way and who would accept me as I am.'

'You and Father returned before and who is to say that you would not do so again?'

'At least I would have tried. If prayer and song be what is required to lead a more normal life, then those I will suffer with greater willing than the enclosure of this place.' He glanced about the interior. 'The flock find release from their enclosure and may wander freely while I am left to linger in the shadows.'

'So you have made up your mind in truth?' Jacob felt a pang of deep sadness.

Joseph nodded. 'Aye.'

'When will you leave?'

'Within the next couple of days. I do not wish to hesitate too long. The feeling grows strong and I would leave before its promise of hardship can come to pass.'

Joseph saw the look in his brother's eyes and rose from the stool. 'Do not worry, Brother,' he said, putting his hands on Jacob's shoulders. 'With my passing from the croft you will be safe and I will be following my own destiny. It may be we both discover richer lives.' His gaze and his words were filled with firm conviction.

'Let us not argue further, but instead savour these last times together.' He smiled, the expression almost lost within the growths upon his face.

Jacob stood a moment as they continued to hold each other's gaze. He took his brother to him and they held each other in an embrace of mutual affection. 'Your company will be sorely missed,' he said through tears.

‘As will yours,’ responded Joseph, his decision to leave almost crushed by the tightness of their hold.

‘I love you, Brother,’ he said, holding the back of Jacob’s head and pulling it to his. ‘I love you dearly.’

‘And I you,’ replied Jacob, his voice cracking with emotion.

They stood together until Bess put her front paws upon their legs in want of attention. They parted and Jacob smiled sadly as he crouched and wiped away a tear before fussing the hound.

‘I will ready our supper,’ he stated, rising and turning to the table as he bit back the urge to weep.

37

Kerra skipped along the path that ran between the plant beds beside the cottage. Day had only recently broken, windblown and clear, but she was filled with eagerness at the thought of spending time with Jacob. She had made her mother promise to visit with Tetker that morning and would do so herself before the light fell from the world.

She passed into the green shadows of the woodland and began to hum the Lay of Ailla, her light tone contrary to the sad tale it told. Moving through a cluster of ferns, she breathed deeply their scent and held her hands out to the sides, letting their damp fronds brush against her palms.

Her thoughts turned to the events of the previous day. The figure of Jacob's brother drew into her mind's eye, hooded and brooding. Her steps faltered and the humming became forced, losing its gaiety as the Sacred Oak came into view.

Kerra walked into the clearing, her expression having fallen with the recollection of Joseph's face and the thought of seeing his fearful disfigurement once again.

''Tis unwise to wander the woods alone.' Breoc stepped from behind the thick trunk of the oak.

She halted, startled by his sudden appearance.

'There are many dangers that may be encountered amidst the trees,' he stated with a grin, briefly scratching his dark beard.

'I have ne'er encountered any,' she said nervously, unable to hold his gaze and heart pounding.

‘No?’ He raised an eyebrow and took a step closer.

Kerra retreated.

‘Why do you recoil?’

‘I have not the time to linger,’ she replied, swallowing hard as her stomach churned and her body began to tremble.

‘You have an appointment to keep?’ he asked.

‘I must be on my way.’ Kerra made to leave the clearing, stepping towards the undergrowth on the left.

The trapper moved to intercept her and she stopped once again, her pulse racing and legs feeling weak.

‘I thought you may like to stay awhile and talk with me, while you can, that is.’ His grin widened.

All trace of colour drained from Kerra’s face, the thinly veiled reference to his threat not lost on her. ‘I have naught to say unto you,’ she responded, voice wavering.

‘But plenty to others, it would seem.’ The grin fell away and was replaced by a scowl. ‘What did you tell your mother?’

‘‘Tis not of your concern,’ she said, taking a step back.

‘In that you are greatly mistaken. I warned you of what would happen if your tongue proved loose.’ He closed the distance between them and his hand moved to the knife at his hip.

‘Her actions are not borne of my words, but of her love for my father,’ she said fearfully. ‘The loss is too near and her heart remains his.’

Breoc studied her expression. ‘She said this?’ he asked in disbelief.

Kerra nodded.

‘And what of the changling and its master?’ he asked after a moment of thought.

‘Changling?’ she asked in confusion.

Breoc's eyes narrowed. 'You know of what I speak.'

Kerra was unable to fathom a response, struck dumb by her lack of comprehension.

'A spell was cast upon your mother. I witnessed its effects with my own eyes.' He regarded her closely as he pondered. 'It may be you and he are in league. You spoke of him and voiced protest when I revealed what I had seen.'

The trapper's expression darkened. 'Aye, that be the truth of it. You and he conspire against me.' His grip on the knife tightened and he began to withdraw it from its sheath.

'That is your destination,' he said in realisation, glancing over his shoulder towards the vale.

Kerra sprang into the undergrowth while his head was turned. Her heart raced with urgent abandon as she rushed between the watching trees. Grasses and bracken whispered of her passage as she strained to discern sounds of pursuit, hearing only the rush of her own blood.

She ran on, expecting to feel his hands upon her at any moment. She imagined him closing at her back with knife drawn and a grin of satisfaction upon his vile face, the image chasing her into renewed effort.

Kerra gritted her teeth as she veered to the right. She followed the slope down into the vale, the weakness of fright apparent in her legs forcing her to follow the lay of the land rather than attempt to make for home.

She burst from the woodland breathless and straining. Her face flushed with effort, she barrelled down the slope.

Kerra lost her footing, the speed too great for her legs to endure. She tumbled, rolling over and over as she careened through the tall grasses towards the stream.

Finally coming to a halt only a couple of yards from the bank, she looked up towards the trees. She scanned the edge of the woods and saw no sign of the trapper as she caught her breath, mouth thick with phlegm.

Struggling to her feet, Kerra looked down as she tried to clear her throat. Her dress was stained by dirt and grass, a few torn blades held in place by the dampness that remained after the night's rainfall.

She peered up the slope again and found no trace of the trapper. Her heart began to calm, her body still trembling in the aftermath of the encounter and her escape.

Turning, Kerra made her way to the trunk that served as a bridge over the stream, lacking the strength to make the leap over its narrow flow. She took the crossing slowly and with care, feeling her feet slipping on the vibrant moss that grew upon its bark.

Once safely across, she made for the croft. Her legs began to ache and she set her gaze on the building a hundred yards away, willing herself to the gate.

The bells chimed her arrival and she walked hastily along the path to the front door. Knocking, she looked over her shoulder at the fringe of the woods and was grateful to spy nothing of concern.

The door opened and Jacob stood smiling before her. 'Good day, Kerra,' he greeted, his expression becoming one of concern when he noted her flustered appearance. 'Is all well?'

'Good day, Jacob,' she replied, stepping into the relative safety of the cottage. 'I ran here, is all.'

Breoc watched Estren Onan close the door to the croft as he crouched within the woods. ''Tis without doubt,' he muttered. 'They are in league.'

He lingered a moment longer, feeling gladdened after striking fear into the heart of the brat. Rising, he turned and walked deeper into the trees to check his traps.

'When the time comes to keep my word, it will be swift and silent,' he said to himself, a malign grin upon his face as he passed into a strand of bracken.

38

Kerra moved to the fire, keeping her eyes averted from the hooded figure seated to the right of the pit. Bess went to her, jumping up with an expectant look.

'Good day, Joseph,' she said, taking the seat upon which her mother had sat the previous day and then fussing the dog.

He nodded within the confines of the hood. 'Good day.'

'Are you sure there is naught untoward?' asked Jacob as he moved to the far side of the pit and looked upon her while standing by his stool.

Kerra gave a nod, Breoc's words about loose tongues causing her to remain silent. Though she had seen no sign of the trapper after her flight, she was taken by an irrational fear that he would know if she were to speak of their encounter. 'All is well,' she said, forcing a smile and her eyes betraying its shallowness.

Jacob studied her a little longer and then turned to the table, a leg of venison resting before him. 'I was just preparing to leave. I have something to show you.'

'What is it?' she asked as the dog licked her hands to encourage more attention.

'A surprise,' he responded over his shoulder.

She glanced at Joseph questioningly, his face hidden as he kept his head bowed. 'Must we to the woods?' she asked, turning to the shepherd as she scratched the dog beneath her chin.

'You will discover for yourself when we leave,' he stated, placing a few cuts of venison upon a cloth lying open beside the leg. He wrapped them and then hung the meat that remained on the bone upon the wall beside the table.

'Shall we depart?' he asked, turning to her.

Kerra stood. 'Will you be joining us, Joseph?' She looked to the top of his hood and tried to cast the image of what lay hidden in its shadows from her mind.

'No, I will remain with the flock,' he responded.

She looked over to the corner by the woodpile, the sheep gathered there in restful poise. 'Why are they not in their enclosure?' she asked.

'Ah,' began Jacob, 'to reveal the reason would be to reveal the surprise.'

Kerra's brow furrowed as she tried to unriddle his words. She looked to him in confusion as the shepherd made his way to the front door with a grin, Bess moving to join him.

'Triga!' he instructed, holding his palm up to the dog, who stopped in her tracks and was clearly disappointed by the instruction to remain.

'Come and discover for yourself about that which I speak,' said the shepherd as he opened the door, holding his hand out to indicate that she should exit first.

'I shall see you anon,' she said to Joseph before turning and walking out of the cottage.

She waited as Jacob closed the door and the wind toyed with her hair, its colour beginning to darken in winter's hold. Passing out of the gate, they turned left and walked around the corner of the boundary wall, Kerra surreptitiously glancing to the woods on the far slope of the vale.

They moved beyond the croft and made for the woods ahead, the grasses about them rippling as the wind came down the vale and caressed their faces. She considered enquiring about the surprise that Jacob had in store, but knew he would not reveal more.

'How is your brother?' she asked, looking to his profile and wishing to distract herself from thoughts of the encounter with Breoc as they entered the woods, leaves tumbling about them.

His expression fell. 'He is…' Jacob sought the right words. '…As to be expected.'

Kerra looked at him a while, wondering at his reply. Her gaze was attracted by movement and she looked up to see a gull glide south above the trees, wings outstretched and silent in its passing.

'There!' exclaimed Jacob in a whisper.

She stopped and looked ahead, eyes widening. The fallen elm was in view between the trunks ahead, a wolf resting on its length near the rising root bowl.

With a hand to her shoulder, the shepherd pulled her into a crouch beside him. '*She*,' he said with emphasis and a nod towards the majestic creature, 'is the surprise.'

Kerra sat quietly as she studied the wolf. It was looking towards them, its pale fur ruffled by the wind.

'She is beautiful,' she commented in awe.

'She is wild and pure. I have named her White Paw.'

Kerra nodded to herself. 'White Paw,' she repeated as her gaze remained fixed on the astounding sight.

'The meat is for her,' he stated.

Her brow furrowed. 'You feed her?' she asked without turning.

'Aye. When I first discovered her in the hollow where the tree once stood she was weak and forlorn. She is much improved with rest.'

'But what of your flock?' she tore her eyes from the beast and looked at him.

'What of them?'

‘It may be she will eat them, especially with your encouragement to remain in these woods.’

‘If that should come to pass then so be it. I share from my table with the creatures of the vale, why should she be any different?’

‘The sheep are not from your table.’

‘But one day they will be. They are part of the bounty which I enjoy thanks to Dor Dama’s fruitfulness. If it be the will of the All-Mother that I should share them, then I will gladly do so.’

Jacob turned to her. ‘Come, let us feed her.’

Staying low, he began to make his way forward. Kerra remained a moment and then followed, warily watching the creature that had been the subject of so many childhood tales of magic and mystery.

They drew up within ten yards of the sloping trunk as the wolf sniffed the air, head towards the bowl. She looked down at Kerra and their eyes became locked. Time stood still in that instant of connection, the girl finding herself stolen by the intensity of the wildness within the wolf’s golden eyes, its primal nature clear in their brightness.

‘Kerra?’

She blinked away the mesmerism and turned to the shepherd. He glanced down and she followed his indication to discover that he was holding out a strip of venison.

‘Throw it to her,’ he instructed quietly.

Taking the food, she looked back to the wolf to find she still watched her. ‘Where should I throw it?’ she asked.

‘Into the grass by the tree.’

‘That will bring her close.’

‘Aye,’ he said with a smile. ‘Let us see how daring she is and, in turn, how daring we are.’

Kerra stared at White Paw, feeling her body stiffen. She tossed the sliver and it vanished into the concealment of the tall grasses below the trunk.

The wolf looked over the edge of the elm and then scrutinized the humans for a moment before rising. She leapt down, barely five yards from their position. Letting out a deep growl of warning, she then ducked her head and plucked up the meat.

They watched as the creature loped around the side of the root bowl and entered the indent beyond. Turning so that she faced them, she then ate the morsel, quickly swallowing it down.

'Another,' whispered Jacob, holding out a second piece.

Kerra took it and threw it into the dell, the sliver landing at the wolf's feet.

'A good throw,' commented the shepherd with a nod as White Paw picked it up and consumed it.

'Here.' Jacob held out the cloth, three pieces remaining upon it.

'Will you not throw any?'

'You have far better aim than I,' he replied with a smile.

Kerra took up the pieces and threw them one at a time into the dell. The wolf ate them in haste, clearly enjoying the cured meat and looking to them for more once all had been eaten.

'Have you anything more?' she asked with a glance.

Jacob shook his head. 'Her appetite will encourage her to hunt. There is food aplenty in these woods.'

'Do you think she will linger hereabouts?'

'I cannot say. Ne'er have I heard of a wolf so far west. The limitations of this small land are opposed to their need to roam. 'Tis a small territory for such a beast.'

The wolf snuffled and they turned as she rubbed her nose with her white paw. Licking its fur, she ran it down the side her face and repeated the process a few times as she cleaned herself.

She fell still, ears rotating. The bite of axes drifted through the trees and she retreated behind the roots.

'It must be the miners of Pendeen. They clear the woods to the north-east for the smelting fires,' commented Kerra.

Joseph shook his head sadly.

She looked at him questioningly. 'Why do you frown so?'

'I would not take my blade to a living tree, whether a sapling or an ancient tas.'

'Tas?' she enquired.

'Aye, tas an dwydhek,' he replied, 'father of the woodland.'

She nodded her understanding. 'Surely you have brought them down for the sake of feeding your fire?'

'No, there are enough fallen timbers in the woods to feed the fires of all who live in these parts. Trees tend the soil and are the watchers of the seasons. They provide food, shelter and warmth, not just for our kind, but for all life. They are truly sacred and are deserving of our reverence.'

Kerra studied his downcast expression, once more struck by the depth and thoughtfulness of the man. He was profoundly connected with the world about him and it was a connection that brought great joy in the play of life, but also great pain due to the intrusion of man.

She reached out and took his hand. 'We should leave her in peace,' she stated with a nod towards White Paw.

'Aye,' he conceded with a faraway expression, looking off in the direction of the tree clearing.

‘Come,’ she stated, backing away and drawing him with her.

They moved a good distance from the dell and then straightened, Kerra keeping her grip on his hand. Turning, they made their way to the croft, Jacob lost to a meditative silence.

‘Shall we take the flock to graze in the vale?’ she enquired.

He looked briefly to her as if having forgotten her presence despite the link of their hands. ‘Aye, they will be in need of air and food after being shut in the croft for the night. Bess will also be longing for the freedom to stretch her legs.’

They left the woods and made their way to the far side of the croft, going to the gate. Taking his hand from hers, Jacob opened it and bent down to place a rock against its lower rungs to keep it in place.

‘Will you come inside or will you wait? I shall not be long,’ he said.

‘I will wait,’ she said with a glance to the closed shutters as they chattered, speaking of the figure lurking beyond.

Jacob gave a nod and walked along the path to the door, entering and leaving it open behind him. The sound of low voices grumbled from the cottage, a few brief words being exchanged by the brothers.

Shortly thereafter, the sheep and goats filed out of the door, the last leaping as Bess ushered them out. Kerra moved a few yards from the gate, staying close to the boundary wall. The hound rounded them out into the pasture as Jacob exited the croft with his crooked walking stick in hand. He strode after the flock, removing the stone from the gate and closing it behind him as Kerra moved to his side.

'Do we take them south to the apple tree?' she asked as the dog looked back for instruction.

'We will let them wander of their own accord,' he stated, the dull pad of his stick marking their passage into the grassland, passing the strip of corn stubble to their left as the wind pushed at their backs.

He gave a whistle with a high end note. Bess followed his instruction, returning one of the sheep to the flock as they continued along the vale. Their pace slowed to a meander as they began to chew the tallest of the grasses, cropping them with tugs of hunger as the stream hurried north nearby.

Kerra looked to the narrow waters, her eyes filled with the sun's glinting light caught upon the ripples. It faded and darkened as if a great shadow had fallen over the vale. She looked up to see a bank of thick cloud drawing in, heavy with the promise of rain.

'It will not be a lasting deluge,' stated Jacob as he looked up. 'The wind drives it with haste and I wager it will clear before nightfall.'

The first drops fell upon their upturned faces, carried on the air ahead of the squall.

'Should we seek shelter?'

'You are welcome to return to the cottage,' he replied, pulling up his hood. 'I shall find shelter beneath the trees.' He began towards the eastern slope of the vale, the arm of trees upon its higher reaches echoing those on Nancherrow Hill opposite and the valley embraced by their presence.

Kerra glanced back at the cottage, smoke coiling and torn from the hole in its thatch. 'I will stay in your company,' she said, putting in a short burst of speed so as to catch up with him.

Jacob let out a sharp whistle and Bess began to guide the flock towards the slope so they could remain under his watchful eye. ‘It will not be a lasting deluge,’ he repeated softly to himself, thinking of his brother’s proposed departure as the rain beat with greater insistence upon his hood.

‘I beg your pardon?’ said Kerra, looking to the shepherd’s face.

‘Nothing,’ he replied, glancing at her and forcing a smile as they began up the incline and he leant more heavily upon his walking stick.

They moved into the shelter of the trees and Jacob drew to a halt as the rain was whipped beneath the westerly boughs.

‘Should we not move further into the woods?’ asked Kerra as she continued on.

The shepherd quickly reached out and grabbed her shoulder, stopping her in her tracks. ‘No,’ he said with insistence.

She looked at him in surprise.

Jacob noted her expression. ‘I would not go further into these woods for fear of witnessing the clearing conducted by those from the mines,’ he said, removing his hand from her.

‘But that was to the north of here,’ she replied.

‘We are sheltered enough.’ He moved closer to the trunk of an elm, the rain pattering on the leaves that still clung to its branches as large drops began to gather and fall with greater volume.

Kerra hesitated and then joined him, moving to his side and looking down into the grassland, stray raindrops adorning her cheeks. The sheep seemed oblivious to the downpour as they grazed in the open. The goats moved up the slope and began to pick at the grasses gathered beneath a thin strand of birch to the left, Bess trotting to stand before her master.

The hound circled a few times and then settled on the dampening earth at his feet as he stood motionless and watching. Kerra studied the shepherd's face, seeing the tightness about his eyes and the clench of his jaw. She knew there was more to his refusal to venture further into the trees, but did not put voice to any enquiry.

They stood side by side in the gloom and stared out from beneath the elm. The grassland wore a robe of stone grey, the woodland on the far slope veiled and vague. Kerra looked over to its shadowy presence and wondered at the possibility that Breoc still skulked there. The memory of their earlier encounter stirred and a touch of dread arose at the thought of passing through the trees on her return home later that day.

Jacob leant his walking stick against the tree and settled on the ground. His back against the bark, he rested his hands upon his lap, head slightly bowed as he surveyed the vale. Kerra glanced at him and then seated herself, trying to push thoughts of the trapper from her mind as the woodland was filled with the rush of wind and a confusion of pattering droplets, the sounds filling the silence which had settled between them.

39

Breoc exited the woodland north of St Just, seeing the smoke being driven from the cottages and into the trees as he turned and began towards the settlement. He vaulted a stone wall and passed into an enclosure of large pigs. They were sheltering in a timber sty in the far corner, is slatted walls in disrepair and awash with rainwater.

He traipsed across the mud and thin grass of the small field, making for the gate mid-distance in the wall opposite. His gaze was fixed on the roof of Kerenza's cottage, visible beyond low bushes a hundred yards ahead with the woodland rising close to the left. The trapper considered her treatment of him the previous day and what he had witnessed in the vale. He remained convinced that she was under an enchantment, that either Estren Onan or the changling that abided with him had cast a spell upon her.

'With the encouragement of the girl,' he mumbled with a sneer.

'Breoc!'

He was given a start by the cry and turned his gaze to the gateway, finding One-Eyed Samuel standing on the far side carrying a bulging sack over his shoulder. The hollow of his empty socket stared blindly from the shadows beneath his hood as he took hold of the top bar, the wind disturbing his cloak.

'Samuel,' he greeted, touching his dripping forelock as he approached and the farmer opened the gate.

‘Feed for the pigs,’ stated Samuel with a backward glance as the trapper came to a stop before him and the rain fell relentlessly from low cloud. ‘Nice weather for fish,’ he added with a grin.

‘Aye,’ nodded the trapper without amusement.

The farmer looked around and then stepped closer to Breoc. ‘Has anyone spoken with thee?’

He looked at him in confusion. ‘Spoken with me?’

‘About the meeting,’ said Samuel, lowering his voice.

‘I know naught of a meeting.’

‘Jeremiah holds a meeting at his farm after darkness falls this eve. It may be ‘tis time for Kernow to rise.’

‘The same has been said each and every year. On the last it was his sighting of a hawk with a snake in its talons that set him to thinking we should march on London,’ replied Breoc sarcastically.

‘True,’ conceded the farmer with a nod, water dripping from the edge of his hood, ‘but I hear tell there is news from Scotland.’

‘What news?’

‘Jeremiah has not spoken of it other than to say ‘tis reason enough to call an urgent meeting of those who have a bent towards Cornish independence,’ replied Samuel. ‘Will you attend?’

He pondered and then gave a nod. ‘I will, but I expect to find it arranged on the whim of a fool’s dream.’

‘Ye think our independence foolish?’ Samuel’s eyebrow rose above his hollow socket.

Disconcerted by the expression, Breoc shook his head. ‘Only the man who sees its fruition in every turn of chance,’ he replied. ‘Jeremiah is not a bad man, but I believe him to be a deluded one. While Edward sits on the throne no mercy would be shown to those who seek to rise up against his rule and no quarter given until such a rebellion were crushed.’

''Tis true,' responded the farmer, a frown deepening the lines upon his weathered face. 'He is not a kindly king.'

'I have not heard of such yet,' replied Breoc, moving to pass the farmer.

Samuel stepped into the field and moved aside, adjusting his grip on the sack of rotting vegetables. 'I will see thee upon this eve,' he stated as the trapper passed out of the enclosure, the wind-slanted rain beginning to ease.

'Aye,' responded Breoc as he walked away, expending little thought on the reason for the meeting, but turning his mind to Kerenza as he again set his gaze upon the thatch of her cottage, watching the smoke of her fire being torn away by the high wind.

The sound of Samuel's pigs snorting and squealing arose behind him as he passed around the bushes and joined the track that would lead him to her gate. His boots were slick with mud as the rain became nothing more than spits and he walked beside the fence that fronted the property, looking over to the banging shutters and door.

Walking into the garden, Breoc felt the wind push him along the path to the door, the plants in the beds to either side ruffled and reflecting his growing agitation. He raised his hand and knocked as he recalled the brat's words upon their chance meeting in the woods and his expression soured.

'You may come in,' called Kerenza, the words lacking warmth and filled with nervousness.

Breoc entered and the wind hurried him in, complaining against the timbers and moaning through the cracks when he shut the door. Smoke swirled around the interior and he sought out Kerenza within the shifting scene, her form materialising like a wraith as she sat upon a stool on the far side of the fire pit, clasping the comb upon her lap.

He wiped his brow with a sleeve and stepped up to the flames, regarding her closely. 'Good day, Kerenza,' he greeted.

'Breoc,' she nodded, unable to hold his gaze and turning hers downward.

There was a momentary silence as water dripped from his ragged hair. The flames phutted as fingers of wind reached into the cottage beneath the door and between the shutters, stirring the lingering smoke as it thinned into a golden haze.

'I spoke with your daughter,' he stated coolly.

Kerenza lifted her head, seeing accusations in his dark eyes. She waited for him to expand, but he remained silent and brooding on the other side of the pit.

'And?' she prompted, feeling intimidated and wishing he would take a seat.

'I wait for you to tell me,' he stated, wiping a drop of water from his nose without taking his gaze from her.

She looked down once again, cheeks flushing. ''Tis hard,' she said as she struggled to put voice to what must be said. 'I do not wish to cause you pain.'

She held the comb out towards him. 'You should take this back.'

'It was a gift,' he responded. 'Besides, we are not done as yet,' he added with conviction.

Kerenza lowered her hand and nervously rubbed the floral design of the comb with her thumb, finding little comfort in the repetitive action. A flock of gulls came calling and crying above the cottage, the sounds filling the hush as he stared at her. The edges of her head covering rippled in the periphery of her vision, as if disturbed by the intensity of his gaze, the pressure of the silence between them pressing in on her until it became unbearable.

'I cannot continue with our union,' she announced. 'I still love my husband.'

'He is gone,' stated Breoc simply.

She nodded. 'But a year has not yet passed.'

'Time enough to mourn the dead.' There was no concession in his tone.

'It may be that he still lives,' she said without genuine belief.

'You know that to be untrue. I hear it in your words and see it in your eyes. He has passed from this world and 'tis time for you to release him.'

'To say is easier than to do,' she countered as the gulls continued to call.

'And yet not two days ago we dowsed your fire together.'

Kerenza sighed and stared at the flames. They danced in the circulating winds, a few patches of sand remaining beside the stones about the pit. 'For that I am sorry.'

Breoc suddenly stepped around the fire. Bending, he cupped her chin and brought her fearful gaze to his as he glared down at her. 'I see it in your eyes,' he hissed. 'You are spellbound.'

She drew her head away from his hand and slipped from the stool, straightening on the opposite side from the trapper. 'Spellbound?'

'I saw you,' he said with an accusatory tone. 'I saw you and the girl enter the croft.'

A look of confusion came upon her, brow furrowing. 'And for that you deem me spellbound?'

Breoc snorted and shook his head. 'Your mock innocence does not fool me. I saw with my own eyes the spirit that dwells with Estren Onan. I saw the unnatural way in which you approached the croft and entered its darkness. You are under an enchantment.'

Kerenza looked at him in shock. 'That was no spirit, that was…' She stopped short of revealing the truth, the promise she had made to Jacob coming to the fore of her mind.

'That was what?' he asked, eyes narrowing.

She looked to the stool between them as the cries of the gulls receded into the east.

'I would have you tell me what dwells with the shepherd,' stated Breoc. 'If not a spirit, then be it a demon that resides with him?'

She glanced up at him in alarm, worried that such talk would lead to persecution of the brothers.

'Your reaction reveals much,' he said with an unkind smirk. 'So it be a demon that dwells with Estren Onan, a demon that can change its form.'

'There be no such demon at the croft.'

He shook his head. 'Much is revealed beyond the words that spill from tongues,' he said, 'tongues which oft put voice to lies.

'You have told me all I need to know without need of speech. Your heart be mine and this was plain for all to see at the celebrations. 'Tis the enchantment that causes this distance. Estren Onan and the demon with whom he dwells have bound your mind with foul sorcery.'

'That is not so,' she protested, her expression pained.

'I will hear no more,' he said with a dismissive wave of his hand. 'You are spellbound and not of your own mind.'

He moved around the fire pit and stepped to the door. 'I know your heart, Kerenza,' he stated, turning to her after taking hold of the handle. 'You had given it to me for safe keeping and safe I shall keep it,' he said, his voice softening. 'I will rid you of this accursed sorcery and in so doing will rid St Just of the evil that lies at its border.'

Breoc opened the door and stepped out into the light rain, looking back at her a moment before closing it behind him. Kerenza stared at the timbers, her heart pounding as his last words sank in. She wondered at his intentions and whether she should have revealed the truth about Joseph's presence at the croft.

She shook her head. To have disclosed such would have been to break her word and the trust that the brother's had in it. Their secret had to be protected, as did her secret of adhering to the old ways. She had heard stories of the ill fortune visited upon those who had been found to follow the Pagan traditions. Theirs had not been a kindly demise, but one of pain and suffering. The followers of Christ, those who looked to his suffering upon the cross, put those who would not bend to their ways through similar suffering without compassion.

With a sigh, Kerenza returned to her stool and glanced at the bowl resting on the table. She had prepared Tetker's tonic upon waking, but had postponed her visit, deciding to wait until she had seen Breoc. Now that the trapper had left, she felt disinclined to leave the confines of the cottage, her mood not suited to the company of others.

She turned her gaze downward and stared at the comb in her hand. Rubbing the design resting between the rows of teeth, her thoughts were occupied by the trapper's last words and a growing chill settled upon her.

40

Breoc stepped through the gate and glanced back at the cottage as he closed it. He turned his gaze to the woodland behind and was momentarily overcome by indecision, standing motionless as the wind messed his damp hair. The passion of his anger urged him to the croft, to exact vengeance on Estren Onan and break the spell, but something held him in place.

He searched his feelings, wondering at the weight in his gut that kept him at the gate. Digging deep, its source was rooted out and he sensed that the time had not yet come to face the shepherd and his changling. Prudence rather than rash action was called for, though to what ends he did not know.

Continuing to struggle against the yearning of his ire, one fuelled by the hurtfulness of Kerenza's distance, he began along the path that led to the heart of St Just. He could sense the croft lurking on the outskirts of the settlement. It was a dark and pulsing presence, an unnatural place both godless and festering.

'We must be rid of it,' he mumbled to himself as he passed the cottage covered in ivy and then moved across the Gathering Place.

Breoc made to the south-west, veering to the left and passing between two of the dwellings that circled the area of grass, the stain of the bonfire's existence still visible at its centre. He walked through a spinney of stunted trees, most of the leaves having been torn from their summer roosts and the branches all but bare. A few stray drops of rain still fell and there was a growing chill as the wind began to shift to the north.

Stepping from the small wood, he walked to the cottage resting beyond, trying to regain his composure before facing his father. He paused at the door, taking a moment to collect himself before entering.

'Good day, Son.' His father sat hunched on his cot, which had been moved close to the right of the fire pit. He was draped in flurs, a cup of brandy cradled in his hands and rough cheeks flushed by his consumption of the drink. His eyes were veiled by hair, but Breoc could see their bloodshot nature beyond the dark waves.

'Is it not a little early to indulge?' he said with a disapproving tone.

''Tis ne'er too early,' replied his father with a slur, lifting the cup and draining it to underline his words.

Breoc went to the fire and crouched, warming his hands. 'Jeremiah calls a meeting.'

His father snorted. 'What be it this time, one of his cattle looks to the east or may it be there is an ache in his little toe that informs him the time has come?' he scoffed, reaching for the earthenware jug resting by his feet.

'There is news from Scotland, though what news I do not know,' replied the trapper as he watched his father refill his cup. 'A meeting is to take place this eve.'

'Is that so?' he responded after setting the jug on the ground. 'Still, I warrant that attending would be a waste of effort.'

Breoc nodded. 'When it has been suggested that we meet at a place more convenient he has raised great objection, stating the need for secrecy.'

'Secrecy,' said his father with a derisive laugh. 'No one should concern themselves with what Jeremiah has to say. He is filled with self-importance and most likely thinks the king himself be keen to know his mind when even those who gather at Goose Back Farm hold little interest in truth.' He drank deeply and wiped his lips with the back of his hand, his beard glistening.

'I say do not attend. 'Tis not worth the walk to Kilgoodh Ust just to hear his foolish words. Better to walk in the opposite direction and go to the woods on Nancherrow Hill so as to check your traps.

'It may be you should set some amongst the rocks of the Cape, then at least when you are called to a meeting you could also check them and kill two birds with one stone,' said his father in jest, shaking his head and taking another drink.

A look of revelation arose in response to his father's last words and he turned to the flames. 'Two birds,' he mumbled as he stared thoughtfully at the writhing tongues and nodded to himself.

'What do you say?' enquired his father, scratching his beard before taking another sip of brandy and wiping his lips again with drunken exaggeration.

'Aye, it may be you are right,' responded Breoc distractedly, a plan beginning to formulate and a grin of satisfaction accompanying its genesis.

The feeling that had held him in place at Kerenza's gate now had its reason. It had not been the time to act, but that time was close at hand. It would see the demise of both Estren Onan and the brat in a way that was gifted by fate's hand and crafted by his own will.

Breoc shook his head in amusement at the workings of fate, laughing briefly. All had fallen into place with only a few words from his father. ''Tis meant to be,' he stated.

'What is meant to be?' asked his father in confusion, his inebriation aiding in muddling his mind. 'I only spoke of setting traps at the Cape in jest.'

‘Do not concern yourself,’ replied the trapper as he got to his feet and stepped to the table at the rear of the cottage, taking up a cup.

He moved to crouch by the head of his father’s cot and took up the jug of brandy, filling his vessel.

‘I thought it too early,’ commented his father with a slanted grin.

‘Today is an exception,’ replied Breoc.

He raised his cup and took a drink of secret celebration, the warmth of the alcohol mingling with the warmth arising from his thoughts of exacting his revenge and breaking the spell under which Kerenza was enchanted. She would be distraught at the loss of her child, but who better to comfort her than the man to whom she had given her heart? His consoling of her grief would bring them closer than ever before and thereby the death of the brat would seal their union.

Breoc nodded to himself and took another sip of the drink, filled with dark joy at the pleasing way in which all had fallen into place.

‘So, will you attend?’ asked his father.

He slowly turned to him, eyes glinting with newfound light. ‘Aye,’ he nodded. ‘That I will,’ he added, the words containing far greater significance than his drunken father could guess at.

41

Jacob and Kerra walked at a leisurely pace, following the flock as they made their way towards the foot of the vale. The rain had ceased, but a biting wind drew down the valley and caused them to huddle into the depths of their clothes, concealing their fingers from exposure.

Kerra watched at Bess kept a close eye on the sheep and goats, holding her cloak tightly about her neck and cheeks beginning to sting. They had spoken little since taking shelter, the shepherd's thoughts elsewhere. She had wanted to ask him about what occupied his mind, but was hesitant to intrude.

'We should sit and eat beneath the crab apple,' stated Jacob, making for the tree at the foot of the eastern slope.

She followed his lead, the shepherd turning and looking to the animals in his charge. He let out two sharp whistles in close succession and Bess quickly moved to the head of the flock, bringing them to a halt before they passed into the open country. The hound lay upon the grass facing them as the sheep and goats began to drift apart and graze.

Jacob looked around and spied the tumbledown section of wall behind which Kerra had hidden herself the first time they had met. 'It may be 'tis best to seek a little shelter,' he stated, nodding towards the stones.

Kerra looked over and gave a nod of response.

They walked over and passed around, settling on the ground in the lea of the wall, the shepherd leaning his stick against the stones. The wind ruffled their hair and a vague moan arose as it found narrow passage through a gap in the stones.

'That is better,' he said, turning to her with a faint smile. ''Tis a shame the barn does not stand here.'

'This was a barn?' asked Kerra.

Jacob shook his head. 'The beginnings only. My father was building it for days such as this, for shelter and for storage if needed. When my mother passed he left what had been done to fall into ruin,' he replied, taking a cloth-wrapped parcel from inside his cloak.

'Will you have bread and cheese?' he asked.

Kerra nodded.

Jacob undid the parcel, removing the folds of cloth from the food resting upon his lap. Taking the bread, he tore it in two and passed one half to the girl. Apportioning the cheese in the same fashion, they began to eat in silence.

He glanced at Kerra as he chewed, her expression downcast and his own mood brought into sharp focus. Jacob was aware that he had said little and could see that his melancholy was infectious, a sense of guilt arising in response.

'When first we met you told me that your mother calls you "Little Bird." Does she call you such because of the high song of your voice?' he asked in the hope of lifting the tone of their time together.

She shook her head. ''Tis because I have always had a love of birds and many are the times I wish I could take to the wing.'

'That would be a fine thing indeed,' he said with a nod.

Finding nothing more to say and seeing that her expression had not changed, Jacob glanced around for something to distract them from the sullenness. He spied a hole at the base of the wall between them, a fallen stone acting as a lintel above the small portal. Tearing off a piece of bread, he placed it on the excavated earth that spilled from the hole like a tongue from a dark mouth.

Kerra glanced down, bending forward slightly in order to see the hole that was angled towards the shepherd. 'A mouse?' she enquired.

'It may be so or it may be that piskies reside here.'

She looked at him doubtfully. 'Piskies?'

'Aye, there are many living hereabouts. Did your mother ne'er tell you of them?'

'They were but children's stories.'

'Were they indeed?' he responded, raising his eyebrows.

She studied his expression for a moment and then leant forward again in order to gain a better view, trying to peer into the hole.

'If you see light flickering from the depths then you can be sure that piskies dwell within.'

'I see nothing but darkness.'

'It may be that they are to their beds after a long night of dancing about rings of toadstools.'

Kerra turned to him, noting a slight grin and seeing a mischievous glint within his eyes. 'You jest,' she stated, an irrepressible smile dawning upon her pale face and dimples deepening.

'Let me take a look,' he responded, placing the cloth containing his food upon the ground.

Jacob got on his hands and knees, moving his face close to the hole. He narrowed his eyes and peered into the darkness. Sniffing deeply, he then nodded and slowly sat up.

'What do you smell?' asked Kerra in a whisper.

'Beef stew, unless I am mistaken.'

She looked at him dubiously as he settled back against the stones.

‘‘Tis a favourite of the piskies and beyond the ability of any mouse to cook,’ he said, enjoying the play of his imagination and the temporary forgetfulness it brought, his brother’s intention to leave pushed to the back of his mind.

Kerra continued to regard him for a while before holding out her bread and cheese. Jacob took it and she put her face to the hole, inhaling deeply.

‘I smell only earth,’ she said as she rested on her haunches, ‘and mice,’ she added in amusement.

He chuckled. ‘But it would have been a wonder indeed to have smelt beef stew.’

‘Aye,’ she giggled, ‘that it would.’

Kerra sat against the wall once again and Jacob passed her the food in his keeping. She bit off some of the bread and then followed it with a little cheese. ‘Do you truly believe that piskies live in these parts?’

‘I have ne’er seen any, but that is not to say ‘tis not so. Many and varied are the faces of Dor Dama and it may be that piskies be one of those faces.’

‘What of spriggans and boekkas?’ she asked.

‘The rock goblins,’ he responded with a nod. ‘Again, I cannot say. My mother told me tales of such creatures and it may be these tales are rooted in some distant past, that these creatures existed long ago, or it may be they exist in a place alongside our own.’

‘Alongside our own?’ she looked at him curiously.

‘Many things are beyond the sight of man and it could be that is where such creatures abide.’

‘So they may one day be seen?’ Kerra’s words carried a hopeful tone.

‘Aye, that may be true,’ he conceded with a nod.

Jacob took a little cheese and placed it by the bread before the hole at the base of the wall as Kerra glanced over. 'So that they can share in the bounty we enjoy,' he stated, 'whether they be mouse or piskie.'

She chuckled, putting the last of her cheese beside the piece he had rested there. Settling back, she finished the bread and felt contented as she huddled into the stowed warmth within her cloak. Bess wandered over sniffing and looking to them in expectation of food.

'I have none left,' said Kerra, holding up her hands and feeling guilty at having not thought of the hound.

'Do not fret. I have brought her a special treat.' Jacob reached inside his brown cloak and took out a small parcel. Opening it, he revealed a few of strips of venison.

'Would you like to feed them to her?' he asked, offering her the meat.

Kerra's smile returned as she slid the cloth across to her palm and then picked up the first sliver, holding it up and watching the dog's gaze followed the venison's every move. She tossed it to her and Bess caught it, barely chewing before swallowing it down.

She threw another, making it a harder catch by aiming higher above the hound's head. Bess leapt and snapped it out of the air, waiting until she landed before eating it.

The rest of the meat was thrown and each strip was caught before being hastily devoured. Kerra folded the cloth and handed it to Jacob, who tucked it back inside his cloak before checking the location of the flock, finding all safely grazing no more than twenty yards from the section of wall.

'The day draws down and 'tis later than I thought,' he commented as he rested against the stones.

Kerra looked to the east, a touch of darkness deepening the cloud cover and creeping westward. 'I will soon take my leave,' she stated. 'I must visit with Tetker to see if her condition improves.'

'Look,' said Jacob, pointing into the sky above the trees on the opposite side of the vale.

A murmuration of around fifty starlings was gathered above the shadows of the woodland. They turned and wheeled in fluid movements, the sound of their many wings audible from where Jacob and Kerra watched transfixed.

'"The black snake be the herald of winter," that is what my father used to tell me. See how it writhes against the chill, casting it off so that it falls upon the land and deepens winter's hold.'

'I see it,' she responded with a nod, awed by the spectacle as the birds prepared to roost in the woods, imagining the thrill of swooping and turning with them.

'The snake will grow as winter takes greater hold, as if its size must be equal to the task of throwing off the chill. I have seen hundreds upon hundreds gathered together in years gone by.'

'I remember seeing the sky thick with them last winter before my father went missing,' she said softly as the starlings continued to coil and turn.

Jacob rose and took up his walking stick. ''Tis time to return the flock to the croft. Night falls thick and fast as the natural turn of the year draws closer.'

Kerra got to her feet. 'The natural turn of the year?' she asked while brushing a few crumbs from the front of her cloak.

'The solstice. 'Tis nature's new year's eve,' he replied, looking to the cloud of starlings as it swooped to the treetops and dispersed.

The chattering and flutter of the birds filled the vale as they settled for the night. Jacob looked to Bess, finding her sitting nearby and staring up expectantly. He nodded to the hound and she moved off at once, herding the flock and beginning to drive them up the vale.

'She acts as if she understands you,' commented Kerra as she watched the dog's practised movements, Bess bringing one of the sheep into the flock from the right.

''Tis no act,' replied Jacob, looking to the girl with his characteristic smile. 'We have developed an understanding that is oft beyond words. When you spend time in the company of another you learn much about their nature and a deep bond is created. You discover that a great many words are not necessary. I share such a bond with my brother also,' he said, the last sentence returning his thoughts to Joseph and his smile fading.

Kerra looked along the vale, barely able to make out the croft against the darkness of the woodland beyond. 'I will accompany you so as to say farewell to him,' she stated, feeling sorry for the man who had dwelt in secret for so long and wishing to overcome the fear that struck at her heart whenever she thought of his disfigurement.

'There be no need. I can pass on your regards,' responded Jacob.

'I would like to,' she said, setting off before her good intentions could succumb to her fear.

They walked up the vale at a pace dictated by the hound, Bess hurrying the flock each time they began to loiter. The growing gloom leant the clouds additional heaviness as their shades of grey darkened. The cold wind tugged at their cloaks as if eager to bite deeper, Kerra's cheeks stinging by the time they neared the croft.

Bess drew the flock to the left, using the barrier of the stream to keep them penned by the wall as Jacob moved to the gate, the girl at his side.

‘Will they spend the night with you and Joseph again?’ she asked as he rested his hand on the gate and began into the garden.

Jacob suddenly fell still, Kerra nearly walking into him and surprised by the unexpected halt. She looked around the shepherd to find him staring at the gate with a haunted expression. Following his gaze, she discovered that only one bell hung from the top rung.

‘He is gone,’ whispered Jacob.

‘Joseph?’

He nodded and turned his gaze to the croft building. He began to approach with slow steps, fearful of the emptiness that lay beyond the door and hoping that he was somehow mistaken, that his brother was still in residence.

Kerra secured the gate open with the rock and followed after him, hastening her steps so that she caught up with Jacob as he reached the door. He opened it and they were greeted by the gloom, a few meagre flames in the fire pit offering little by way of illumination. Looking around the interior, they found only shadows abiding there.

Kerra turned to him. ‘You did not know he was leaving?’

‘He had spoken of his intention to depart,’ replied Jacob without turning to her, gaze fixed upon his brother’s cot in the near right corner.

‘And yet you seem surprised,’ she said, brow furrowing in confusion.

‘He had not said he would leave today and I did not think he would do so without saying farewell.’

Kerra turned to the sound of bleating, finding Bess bringing the flock along the path by the low stone table littered with remains of food. ‘The flock comes,’ she stated.

Jacob did not seem to hear her as he stood in shock.

'Jacob?' She looked to his face, seeing its paleness and the sadness that drew his expression down.

She gave the shepherd a gentle push. He took a step forward, borrowing her will by which to find movement. Turning and blinking away tears, he looked to her and then the flock behind.

The shepherd moved into the cottage and sat heavily upon his cot, glancing at his brother's once again, its head to the foot of his own. Kerra moved to sit beside him, wishing she could find words by which to unburden him of his sorrow.

The sheep and goats filed into the cottage. They moved into the corner opposite, gathering before the door to the enclosure, bleating and bustling as the hound entered behind.

Kerra rose and stepped to the door, closing it on the reaching wind so the flock could not take their leave. She briefly crouched and fussed the dog, Bess raising her chin and her eyes closing in response to the pleasurable attention.

'He has gone,' said Jacob with a disbelieving shake of his head.

'You have lived alone before,' responded Kerra as she straightened and went to the woodpile beside the flock, she sheep bleating and bunching in the corner as she collected up some branches.

'Many years ago,' he responded, 'but I fear that what was once solitude will now be loneliness.'

'What do you mean?' she asked, placing the timbers upon the fire.

'Solitude is the glory of being alone, loneliness the agony.'

Kerra held him in her gaze. 'Jacob,' she said, drawing his eyes to hers, 'you are not alone.'

He looked at her a moment and a melancholy smile arose. ‘You are true to your name,’ he said, his sadness carried in the depth of his eyes.

His comment brought Tetker to mind and Kerra glanced at the gap beneath the door, only a little daylight visible beyond.

‘You should go before night settles.’

Kerra turned back to him. ‘I will stay awhile longer.’

Jacob shook his head. ‘You must go, but your kindness is not lost on me,’ he replied as Bess wandered over to him and rested her chin upon his knee, the shepherd absently rubbing her head.

‘At least you will have her company,’ observed Kerra with a faint smile.

Jacob glanced down. ‘Aye, and ‘tis good company.’

Kerra hesitated a moment and then stepped around the fire pit, going to Jacob and bending to give him a hug. ‘I will return on the morrow,’ she stated as she released him.

‘I will look forward to your visit, as I always do,’ he responded, his eyes glistening after her show of affection, jaw clenched as he fought back the tears.

Kerra went to the door, glancing at the fire and glad to see the new timbers beginning to take. ‘May Dor Dama’s blessings be upon you.’

‘And may she see you home safely,’ he responded.

She took hold of the handle and opened the door, stepping out and the wind immediately messing her hair with chill fingers. ‘Fare ye well, Jacob.’

‘Until the morrow,’ he responded, his voice cracking with emotion as he struggled to stem the tide until the girl had gone.

Kerra closed the door and set off for home. She passed out of the gate and made her way over to the stream, leaping its narrow flow rather than passing further down the vale to the tree trunk. She moved to the slope of Nancherrow Hill, her gaze resting on the woodland above and a shiver coming upon her that was not born of the wind.

Jacob bowed his head, eyes closing and face contorting in misery as his hand stilled upon Bess' head. His shoulders lurched as he began to sob, the vacancy left by his brother's departure pressing close as the night drew in.

42

Wynfred made his way along the track as it climbed a hill north of the fishing village of Penzance, the rainwater of earlier having carved its path through the rocks and mud as it ran down the slope. Caspian walked at his side in the twilight, the hound's steps given additional weight by his weariness.

'We will rest soon,' stated the huntsman, his legs aching and stomach yearning for sustenance with occasional groans.

He leant upon his spear with increasing need, cheeks numbed and nose aching courtesy of the winter chill. His expression was set, hardened by determination and the icy touch of the wind.

They had lost the wolf's trail and he had resorted to questioning all those they came across in the hope of gleaning some clue as to the creature's whereabouts. Little had been learnt, merely rumour and speculation, the people made reticent by the approach of a stranger with such a beast at his side.

'I would have no other beside me during this long march,' stated Wynfred, looking to his companion.

Caspian glanced over as they neared the brow of the hill.

Turning sharply, the wolfhound let out a low growl as he stared along the track. Wynfred looked ahead and saw a figure slowly approaching through the gloom, robed and hooded in pale cloth and carrying a staff. It raised its free hand and the faint tinkle of a bell sounded.

‘A leper,’ stated the huntsman with distaste, moving closer to Caspian as they drew within twenty yards of the figure.

Joseph saw the man move closer to the beast and stepped to the verge on the opposite side of the track to create the greatest distance between them as they approached. He winced with pain, his feet already sore after only a day’s travel, having set off from the croft soon after his brother’s departure with the girl.

‘Alms for a leper,’ he stated, lowering his hand and holding the bell at his side as he kept his head bowed, noting the man’s wolf-skin cloak and warily eyeing the creature loping beside him.

Wynfred drew up ten yards shy of him, Caspian letting out another growl as he stayed at his master’s side. ‘I have a penny, though ‘tis not for your ills, but for your information,’ responded the huntsman, taking a cloth purse from his belt and jangling the contents.

‘Information?’

‘Aye. We seek a she-wolf that may have passed this way.’

Joseph’s head lifted slightly, man and beast little more than silhouettes in the gathering darkness, the vague shape of Carrack Looz en Cooz rising in the wide bay behind them. ‘I have seen no such creature,’ he stated honestly.

‘Have you heard rumour of such in these parts?’

There was a brief hesitation.

‘I cannot say that I have.’

Wynfred’s eyes narrowed. ‘Are you sure of this?’

Joseph nodded. ‘Aye.’

‘I detect there is something you do not reveal.’

‘I speak of what I know. Such creatures do not frequent these lands.’

The huntsman continued to regard the hooded figure for a while and then secured his purse back in place.

'You said there would be a penny in exchange for what I had to tell you,' stated Joseph.

'You told me nothing.'

'I told you all I can. You have had the information and now I would have the penny.'

Wynfred took the spear in both hands and held it at the ready. 'Do you challenge me?'

'I merely remind you of the arrangement that you made.'

'I have unmade it,' stated Wynfred coldly.

Joseph remained silent.

The huntsman waited a moment and then began along the track once again, keeping as much distance between him and the leper as he was able. Caspian walked by his side without taking his gaze from the motionless figure, whose robes were ghostly against the backdrop of the walled field beyond.

Feeling relief at passing the stricken man, Wynfred hastened his steps, glancing back to find that the figure remained in place. He turned his attention to his steps, avoiding the wagon ruts filled with water that captured the faint light of the moon as the clouds above began to break.

Joseph listened to their departure as he thought about his brother and the wolf he had been feeding in the woods north of the croft. His sense of dread was renewed and he stood in contemplation of returning to Jacob's side. It seemed that his feeling of doom was not related to his presence at the croft, but rather to events that would unfold there with or without his attendance.

He turned and looked to the Mount, the ocean surrounding it like polished steel in the light of the moon. Joseph could see the dark landscape stretching away to the east beyond the tidal island. He had thought his fate awaited somewhere within its folds, but it seemed that he had been mistaken.

Looking in the opposite direction, he saw no trace of the man and his beast. ‘I will rest the night and then begin my return,’ he mumbled to himself, looking for suitable shelter somewhere near the track.

43

Kerra knocked and entered without waiting for a response, not wishing Tetker to expend effort in replying and risk a coughing fit. She discovered the fire blazing with stoked vigour and the old woman seated upon her bed on the far side. She was hunched and wrapped in fleeces, the firelight revealing a newfound vitality as it sparkled in her eyes.

'Good evening, Young Kerra,' smiled Tetker, her voice a little husky.

'Good evening, Tetker. I am glad to find you in such a state of recovery,' she replied, unable to hide her surprise.

'It would seem thy mother's tonics have worked their magic.' The old woman grinned.

'Aye, and more,' said Kerra as a smile dawned and she went around the pit, embracing Tetker fondly.

'Sit,' instructed the old woman when they parted, patting the cot beside her.

Kerra seated herself to the creak of timbers and felt the warmth from the fire upon her face, its touch welcome after making her way to the cottage through the cold night.

'How goes it with thee?' asked Tetker.

'It goes well. Mamm has spoken with Breoc and brought their union to an end, though I guess he did not take it well.'

'Ye only guess.'

She nodded. 'Mamm would not speak of it beyond what I have told you, but her manner revealed more than words.'

'Indeed,' responded Tetker, seeing tightness in the girl's expression. 'Do ye still fret over Breoc's threat to thee?'

Kerra nodded. 'Aye.'

'I do not think there is aught to be concerned with now that their union is undone.' The old woman stroked her hair in reassurance.

'You truly believe so?' Kerra turned to the old woman and looked into her eyes, finding them sparkling brighter than they had since Kalan-Gwav.

Tetker nodded. 'What would be gained from such action?' She raised an eyebrow pointedly. 'In all honesty, I still struggle to comprehend why he would make such a threat in the first instance.'

'But he did,' said Kerra a little defensively.

'I do not doubt thy words,' she said firmly, putting her arm about the girl's shoulders. ''Tis just so far removed from the way of my mind. I cannot fathom the cruelty and malice that some are prepared to pour into this world like so much poison.' She sighed and shook her head, the meagre strands of her hair swaying.

They sat in contemplative silence for a while. Tetker drew Kerra closer, cuddling her as she cleared her throat, feeling a slight tickle that lingered after fighting off the worst of the cold.

'Joseph has left the croft,' stated Kerra as the fire crackled and the smoke rose to the thatch with a few glowing embers caught in its greyness, winking out as their warmth was extinguished.

'How is Jacob?'

'I spent the day with him and will call again on the morrow. He was sorely smitten by his brother's departure.'

'He did not know?' asked the old woman in surprise.

'He knew of the intent, but not the time. We arrived at the croft as night fell to find Joseph gone,' she said. 'I think I shall make Jacob a gift so as to bring him some cheer.'

'That sounds like a fine idea. What will ye make him?'

Kerra pondered while looking to the flames. 'A doll,' she replied. 'He can give it my name and then I can be with him in spirit even when not in person.' There was growing enthusiasm in her tone and her straightening posture reflected its emergence.

'It will keep him company now that his brother is not there to do so,' she said, turning to Tetker.

'Indeed, and it will remind him that he is ne'er truly alone.'

Kerra nodded. 'Aye,' she smiled. 'With your leave I will make my way home and create the doll so that I may present it to him in the morning.'

'Of course ye have my leave,' said Tetker, lowering her arm from the girl's shoulders. 'Who am I to delay the making of such a heartfelt gift?' she added with a wide smile.

'My thanks.' Kerra rose from the cot and took a step away.

Stopping, she turned and went back to the old woman, embracing her warmly. ''Tis a joy to find you so well recovered,' she said, before releasing her.

Kerra made her way to the door and took hold of the handle. 'I promise to visit again on the morrow, though when I cannot say. Do you need Mamm to bring more of the tonic?'

‘I think it best she does. I do not wish to suffer another lapse back into ill health.’

Kerra gave a nod. ‘May Dor Dama bless you.’

‘She already has, for without her blessing and the curatives of thy mother’s hand, I would not be speaking with thee now,’ she smiled. ‘Though ye, Young Kerra, are the All-Mother’s greatest blessing,’ she added, holding the girl’s gaze.

‘Ye are truly dearest.’ The old woman’s voice and expression were filled with deep affection.

Kerra blushed with embarrassment and modestly lowered her gaze. ‘My thanks again,’ she said. ‘I would that it were so.’

‘‘Tis so and ye should not doubt it,’ confirmed Tetker.

She looked over to the old woman beyond the flames for a moment and then opened the door. ‘Till the morrow,’ she said in parting, scarcely believing she could be as precious as Tetker said.

44

'Why did you not tell me of Tetker's improved condition?' asked Kerra as she removed her cloak and laid it over the foot of her cot.

'I thought it to be a pleasant surprise,' replied her mother as she sat on a stool before the fire, head covering resting upon her knee as she combed her hair in readiness for evening Mass.

'Indeed it was,' she said with a smile. 'She has made a quicker recovery than I thought possible after seeing how the sickness gripped her last night.'

'She had already fought off its greater strength and this was but its remnants given a foothold by the chill of Kalan-Gwav.'

Kerra nodded as she sat on the edge of her cot and took up her hide pillow. She took out a handful of straw from within, setting it upon her lap and seeking out strands of a goodly length for her purpose.

Kerenza watched curiously for a while as she ran the comb through the honeyed strands of her hair with flowing motions. 'What are you doing?'

Kerra looked up, her eyes bright. 'Making a doll for Jacob. It will keep him company now that his brother has gone.'

Kerenza smiled as she regarded her daughter. She had always been a thoughtful child and she was gladdened that this trait showed no sign of abating as the years passed. 'I think I will come with you on the morrow and visit with him for a while.'

‘He would like that,’ nodded Kerra as she gathered the selected strands together and bent them at the centre, folding them onto themselves and fashioning the bend into the semblance of a head.

Holding the body of the doll, she took up a loose strand and attempted to secure it about the middle. The old straw snapped and she picked up another piece. Repeating the process half a dozen times, she found to her growing annoyance that none had the strength to be tied in place. The straw had been weakened by a touch of rot and constant buffeting during the months they had been within the hide pillow.

Kerenza rose and placed her head covering upon the stool. ‘Here,’ she said as she stepped over and crouched before her daughter.

She took a few strands of her hair from the lower row of teeth on the comb and twisted them together. ‘If you hold it, I shall tie it,’ she stated.

Kerra held up the straw and her mother tied the hair about the middle of the doll’s body. Taking more strands, she tied them at the neck so that the head retained its oval shape. ‘There,’ she said with a smile, ‘and there is more to tie the arms.’

‘My thanks,’ said Kerra, her expression brightening.

She took up some shorter lengths and collected them into a small bundle as her mother readied more of her hair. Holding the tiny sheaf across the body, Kerenza then tied it in place. Kerra watched the nimble movements of her fingers and a feeling of sadness came over her when she noted a growing laxity to the skin of her mother’s hands, age slowly drawing out the vitality from her body.

‘All done,’ stated Kerenza as she reclined.

She looked to her daughter's face, smile immediately replaced by a look of concern. 'What is wrong, Little Bird?'

Kerra simply shook her head, regarding her mother for a moment before leaning forward and kissing her on the cheek. 'I love you, Mamm.'

Kerenza studied her daughter's expression curiously. 'And I love you too,' she responded, unable to fathom the sudden change of mood.

She looked to the doll. 'I am sure Jacob will be pleased with the gift.'

Kerra turned her gaze to the straw figure in her hands. ''Tis little and he has lost much.'

A howl was carried on the wind from the north.

'A wolf!' exclaimed Kerenza, 'and 'tis close if I be any judge.'

'White Paw,' said Kerra.

She turned to her daughter questioningly.

'That is what Jacob calls her.'

'You know of this creature?' she responded in surprise.

'Aye,' replied Kerra with a nod. 'Jacob shares the food from his table with her, as he does with the other creatures of the vale.'

'It rests in the vale?'

'To the north of the croft.'

Another howl lifted into the night.

Kerenza looked to the door, fear in her eyes. 'There has ne'er been a wolf in these parts afore,' she whispered.

'I fed her only this morn.'

She looked to her daughter in shock. 'You went near the beast?'

'She is beautiful.'

'She is wild and dangerous,' responded Kerenza disapprovingly. 'You must promise not to venture close again.'

'But she offered no threat, only the awe of her presence.'

She took hold of her daughter's wrists as Kerra continued to hold the doll. 'Promise me,' she stated, holding her gaze.

Kerra hesitated, turning her eyes to the doll and gently rubbing the straw with her thumbs.

'Promise me,' repeated her mother, giving her arms a gentle shake so as to draw her attention.

'I promise,' said Kerra in eventual defeat, her frown deep.

'I only make you give your word because I worry for your safety,' said Kerenza softly, seeing the disappointment in her daughter's face as she continued to hold her wrists.

'I know, but if you had seen her…' Kerra's words trailed off and she sighed.

'I am sure she is a sight to behold, but you cannot trust such a beast. Wolves are a symbol of the wilderness and the hunt for good reason. They are also the subject of many a dark tale and I do not wish you to become a victim in the recounting of another.'

'Jacob was with me and I would not go near her without his company.'

'You will not go near with or without his company,' stipulated Kerenza. 'Now, we must to Mass or we will fall out of favour with the reverend.'

She released her daughter's arms and straightened. 'I only think of you, Little bird,' she reiterated, pausing before making her way back to the stool and picking up her hair covering.

45

Jacob lay on his side beneath the fleeces of his cot, Bess curled at his feet. Most of the interior was gathered into the darkness that had bloomed from the corners, the failing flames within the fire pit merely hinting at the presence of stools and table, flock and woodpile. Soon the pitch would overcome the flames and all would be swallowed by the black maw of night.

He shifted, the hound briefly raising her head with the disturbance. He had gone to his bed earlier than was his habit, finding naught to do and no will to sit alone by the pit. The absence of his brother was keenly felt, like warmth stolen by a chill gust of winter wind.

A howl arose to the north, echoing his loneliness and finding resonance in the emptiness he felt within. Bess looked up in alarm and Jacob reached to scratch the hound behind the ears, welcoming the distraction. Sleep would not come so early and his wakeful mind unceasingly picked over Joseph's departure.

Another howl lifted into the night. One of the sheep bleated in disturbance despite never having heard such a call, some primal instinct giving rise to fear in response to the sound.

'She announces her presence to those in Lannust,' he stated with a deepening frown as he continued to fuss the hound, concerned that the villagers would act out of fear.

Jacob swung his legs over the side of the cot and sat up, tightening the cord at the waist of his woollen robe, his feet bound in furs. Rising, he passed to the opposite side of the cottage and took some thin branches from the depleted firewood. He glanced at the hand axe leaning to the left and considered passing outside with a burning brand to collect more.

Shivering, he decided to remain indoors and took the timber to the meagre flames within the pit, seating himself on the nearest stool. He placed the branches on those which were almost spent and held his hands to the warmth. Nose pained by the chill, he rubbed it and waited for the wood to catch so as to bring greater heat and chase the darkness back into the corners.

His thoughts returned to White Paw and he was gripped by the certainty of cruel action to be undertaken by those of the settlement. 'Should I attempt chasing her away?' he asked the gloom as the flames began to catch and Bess clambered from the cot, making her way to his side.

Jacob was unsettled by the thought of the wolf coming to harm. She had done no wrong, but that would not stop a harsh sentence being metered out by those who judged her to be a danger. The stories of her kind and the possibility she may attack livestock would be enough to condemn her, of that he was sure.

He looked to the stool across the pit where his brother had often sat. 'Your words of advice are sorely missed.'

Bess let out a groan as she yawned and Jacob turned his attention to the dog. He reached down and stroked her head, glad for her companionship.

46

Breoc strode across the fields in the darkness, seeing the silhouette of Goose Back Farm on the rise ahead. Kilgoodh Ust reached into the ocean beyond, the land dipping and then rising again at the far end of the Cape, its rocky tor set again the grey sheen of the waters.

He approached the cottage and could see light through the gaps between the shuttered windows. Male voices that he recognised drifted out into the night, the wolf that had sounded its howl the topic of conversation.

He gave the secret knock, rapping his knuckles on the door twice and then three times in quick succession.

The door opened and Samuel stood beyond. ‘Good evening, Breoc,’ he greeted as he stepped back and the talk about the wild beast continued to fill the confines of the farm.

The trapper entered and closed the portal behind him. Turning to the scene, Breoc found most of the men of the village gathered within, about twenty in all. He regarded their faces as they sat and stood about the fire pit. The most noteworthy absentee was the reverend, his loyalty to king and country being stated with zeal on many an occasion in order to discourage such meetings as the one taking place.

‘I am glad to find ye could join us, Breoc,’ said Jeremiah with a touch of irritation as he sat on a stool to the right of the fire, a large fleece draped about the aging farmer’s wide shoulders, his brown beard shot through with grey.

Some of the others about the flames nodded their greetings, the rest still engaged in conversation. The trapper remained at the periphery of the group, noting the farmer's wife and three children seated upon a cot at the rear of the room. The shadows of the men on the far side of the pit were cast upon them as they sat in watchful silence.

'Enough!' exclaimed Jeremiah. 'I will hear no more of the wolf.'

'B…b…but 'tis a threat to my flock,' stammered Collen, a stocky farmer from the south of St Just.

'I care not for thy flock. This meeting has been called for more important reasons,' stated the thickset farmer.

'What is this news from Scotland?' asked Talvennor the cordwainer, a rangy man with a weasel-like face.

'This is not the only gathering to take place this night,' announced Jeremiah, looking at those assembled in his cottage meaningfully. 'Those sympathetic to an independent Cornwall meet in St Buryan, Pendeen and Zennor. Even in Marghas Byghan they gather in the hope that Kernow will be freed of England's yoke.'

Looks of surprise and intrigue passed around the fire. Never in all the years of meetings had there been such concordance between the communities of the far west and this leant the gathering greater import than any before.

Jeremiah placed his large and weathered hands upon his knees, leaning forward significantly and looking to the faces about the fire pit. 'Scotland has won a great victory,' he announced.

'What victory?' asked Talvennor in a voice hushed by expectancy.

'An army of Scots has defeated the English at Stirling Bridge.'

'Defeated the English,' whispered Samuel in shock.

‘Aye, their forces were crushed.’

‘W…w…when did this happen?’ asked Collen.

Jeremiah’s expression become somewhat sheepish and he looked to the flames. ‘Mid-September,’ he replied.

‘Mid-September!’ exclaimed Padern, a farmhand and the largest man in the village, his strength and size meaning his aid was much in demand. ‘But that is long past. We have just welcomed winter and the month of November.’

‘Such news oft travels in whispers for fear of accusations of treasonous dissent and suffering the hangman’s noose,’ replied Jeremiah, looking across the fire at the leather-clad farmhand. ‘We are far to the west and our isolation serves to make it travel all the slower.’

‘Our isolation,’ echoed Talvennor. ‘The full reach of the king falls short of our lands. Are we truly in need of freedom from England?’

All eyes turned to the sallow cordwainer, his wiry frame shrinking under the weight of the stares.

‘What of the taxes we must pay?’ asked Samuel with a hard tone. ‘And the price of non-payment be even higher than the taxes themselves, such are the punishments set out by the king. The nobles do as they please while the peasants do as best they can. The king’s reach is long, and this you should well know.’

‘But rebellion?’ Talvennor shook his head.

‘W…w…why do you join us here?’ asked Collen. ‘If you do not support a revolt against the English you have no p…p…place under this roof nor in this g…g…gathering. We are proud men of Kernow.’

‘As am I,’ responded the cordwainer.

‘You are a coward,’ stated Padern with force, causing Talvennor to take a step back from his looming presence.

'I am no such thing.'

'Come now, let us not become divided,' said Jeremiah with his hands raised. 'We must discuss what we are to do.'

'W…w…what do you suggest?' asked Collen.

'Is there news from east of the county, from Bodmin or Lostwithiel? Are there others with us?' asked Samuel.

Jeremiah sighed and once more turned his gaze to the fire. 'I have had no word.'

'You have had no word because there is nothing to receive word of,' stated Bideven, the portly carter who was seated before the fire pit with his back to the door. 'I have held my tongue while you have had your say, Jeremiah, as I have for nigh on twenty years, but now I shall speak.'

All those within the cottage turned to him, his rounded cheeks flushed by the heat of the fire. He licked his dry lips and scratched his balding crown, shifting awkwardly due to the size of his stomach, which was swelled beyond its normal excess by a bout of worms.

'Well?' asked Padern impatiently.

'Is a man not allowed time to compose his thoughts?'

'By the way you spoke, I thought there had been time enough,' responded the farmhand, raising an eyebrow.

'We wait,' stated Bideven flatly.

'What?' Jeremiah looked at him aghast. 'Now is the time to strike.'

'A ragged bunch of farmers and the like?' said Bideven with a dismissive shake of his head. 'We have no idea of the support that resides in the rest of the county. The fact that we have had no word of unrest or even dissatisfaction from eastern Kernow would seem to imply that either they seek no revolt or they wait to see what King Edward's response will be to the Scottish victory and what the Scots themselves will next do.'

‘Aye, in the king’s response we will discover our own fate should we rise up against him,’ said Talvennor.

‘Coward,’ stated Padern under his breath with a sideways glance at the cordwainer.

‘So we wait and gather our strength in readiness,’ said Bideven, with a silencing look to the large farmhand. ‘If naught comes of it, then naught is lost, but if this is indeed the time to fight for our independence, then all those who are willing will be ready to go to war.’

Silence ensued. The men looked at each other across the fire pit, their shadows afforded movement by the flickering flames, as if reflecting the disturbance of their thoughts.

‘Or not,’ said Bideven after a few moments, slapping his palms down upon his knees before struggling to his feet with a grunt of effort. ‘As for me, I go to my bed so that I may be rested and ready for the morrow.’

He stepped around his stool and Breoc moved aside to let him pass, the pair sharing a departing glance as the others about the fire bore expressions of confusion.

‘W…w…what is your meaning?’ asked Collen as the carter reached the door.

‘My meaning is that I am tired,’ he replied, turning to the rest of the gathering. ‘Not just from the day’s work, but of these meetings. All these years we have met and now that we are faced with something more than bird sign and omens there is indecision and hesitance.’

He shook his head and snorted derisively. ‘I am done with it,’ he said with a wave of his hand, as if swatting away a fly.

Bideven turned and took hold of the handle, exiting the cottage and slamming the door behind him. Jeremiah stared at the empty stool to his left, crestfallen and looking half the man he had seemed only shortly before. The carter was highly regarded by all in Lannust and without his support there was little likelihood of preparations being made for an uprising.

'I have something to say,' stated Breoc, breaking the hush and stepping forward into the light.

All eyes turned to him.

'We must set aside thought of revolt, for there is more than a wolf at our door,' he said, looking about the company of men.

'Be there a pack?' asked Collen worriedly.

The trapper shook his head. 'Worse,' he replied weightily. 'The howling you have all heard upon this night is not that of an ordinary wolf. 'Tis a changling demon and it abides with Estren Onan in the vale at our eastern border.'

'A demon you say?' Talvennor looked at him in concern.

'I had thought Estren Onan to dwell with spirits,' said Padern.

'As had I,' said Breoc, 'but with my own eyes I have seen the terrible truth of the demon at the croft, both in the semblance of a man and wolf.'

Worried looks passed between the men.

'What should we do?' asked Talvennor.

'We should pass into the croft this night and bring about the demon's end,' stated Breoc after allowing the cordwainer's question to hang in the air a moment. 'Let this meeting not be in vain, but let us strike a blow against the evil at our door,' he added with zeal, seeing the doubt in the eyes of some of the men.

'Aye,' said Padern with a nod. 'Such evil should not be allowed to linger.'

'But the demon roams and may not be in the vale,' said Talvennor.

'Then we kill the one that harbours it,' replied Breoc firmly.

‘We kill Estren Onan?’ The cornwainer looked at him with fearful eyes.

Breoc nodded. ‘He is its master.’

‘Are you sure of this?’ asked Padern.

‘You all know of my union with Kerenza,’ began the trapper.

There were a few nods of confirmation.

‘He directed the demon to enchant her and she is greatly changed. I saw her and her daughter go to the croft. She was entranced by magic, though the girl seemed in league with Estren Onan and has been visiting the vale against her mother’s express wishes,’ he said, making sure not to directly accuse Kerra of wrongdoing, allowing the men about the fire to draw their own conclusions.

‘Is this t…t…truly so?’ asked Collen.

‘Only yesterday we shared the promise of each others lips and yet today she breaks our union. There can be no other explanation.’

‘What of Kerenza? Have you enquired after her reasons?’ asked Talvennor.

‘She could give me none,’ he lied.

‘I say we do as Breoc suggests. We should rid ourselves of this corruption before its darkness spreads further,’ stated Padern.

‘It may be we should wait for the morning light,’ said Talvennor.

The farmhand snorted and shook his head. ‘I would guess that to be your response.’

‘Who is with us?’ asked Breoc before an argument could ensue, glad that he had the farmhand’s support and sure that his substantial presence would lend confidence to the other men.

Questioning looks passed about the fire and were followed by nods of agreement from all but Talvennor and Jeremiah.

'What of the revolt?' asked the old farmer, turning to Breoc.

'This is your chance to fight in the defence of St Just and our way of life,' he replied. 'Seize it,' he added firmly.

Jeremiah held his gaze and then nodded. 'Aye,' he said, rising to his feet with purpose.

47

Jeremiah led the knot of men down the slope of Nancherrow Hill. He had taken charge after agreeing to help rid the village of the demon, instructing his wife to wrap cloth about the sturdiest branches from the woodpile in order to make torches. The men had then made their way east, the old farmer feeling enlivened and imagining that he was heading a group of militia against the English.

The barking of a dog arose from the croft as he ponderously leapt the stream, the flames of his torch fluttering. The others followed as they turned north and headed for the gate fifty yards away, their eyes nervously casting about for any sign of the changling demon.

The door to the building opened and the dark shape of Estren Onan stepped out, the hound at his feet growling and barking at the oncoming party.

'Who approaches?' he asked, narrowing his eyes and trying to make out their faces, the torches held aloft by half of their number throwing shifting shadows onto the grassland about them.

'We have come to cleanse this place of the evil that abides here,' stated Jeremiah as he reached the gate, stopping before it.

'There is no evil here,' responded the shepherd.

'He lies,' said Breoc under his breath as he stood by the farmer's shoulder.

‘Ye will not sway us from our purpose.’ Jeremiah placed his hand on the top rung. ‘We will enter and flush out the beast with or without thy say so.’

‘Aye,’ called Padern. ‘The demon meets its end tonight.’

Jeremiah pushed he gate open, the solitary bell chiming to mark his entry. He kept a wary eye on the shepherd as he entered the garden, glancing at the dog as she bared her teeth and continued to growl.

‘On whose authority do you find me guilty of harbouring such a fiend?’ asked Jacob as he stood in the doorway to block their entry, Bess staying close at hand.

‘Move aside,’ demanded the farmer without seeing fit to answer his question.

‘I said, on whose authority…?’

Padern stepped forward and barged Jacob out of the way, the shepherd stumbling backward and almost falling into the fire pit, a few embers still glowing in its confines. The farmhand moved into the cottage and waved his torch from side to side, the flames phuttering as he tried to discern the whereabouts of the demon.

Bess barked and snapped at the air before him. Padern ignored her, looking to the flock gathered nervously by the door in the far left corner. He strode over as Jeremiah and Breoc entered, the rest of the group choosing to remain outside, pensively peering in and clearly disturbed by the possibility of confronting a demon.

The sheep and goats leapt away from Padern’s approach, a couple making for the door and then skipping away towards the cots when they found the exit blocked. A cup of water resting on the table was upset as one of the goats barged past the leg, the liquid running over the edge as the flock bleated and jostled by the beds on the opposite side of the room from the farmhand.

‘Bess,’ called Jacob, the hound moving to his side and her barking fading to occasional growls.

Padern opened the door to the enclosure, peering out with his torch before him. ‘Nothing,’ he said while closing it and turning back to the others.

‘There is no demon,’ said Jacob as he stood by the fire, his pulse made quick by the threat of the men’s presence.

‘Then why is there need for two cots?’ asked Breoc.

‘Aye, why indeed?’ added Jeremiah.

‘One is mine and the other was my brother’s,’ he replied, ‘but many years have passed since last it were used.’

He turned as he heard the bowls and other household items upon the table being disturbed, finding the farmhand looking amongst them. ‘What do you hope to find there?’ he enquired, the invasive actions of the man increasing his tension.

‘Evidence of the creature that abides with you,’ he replied flatly and without turning.

‘There be no such creature.’

‘Then what howled in the d…d…darkness this very night?’ asked Collen from the doorway.

Jacob turned to those gathered at the entrance with a look of confusion. ‘You mean the wolf?’

‘Aye, the changling demon that can take the shape of man or wolf,’ said Jeremiah.

Jacob shook his head. ‘There be no such demon. ‘Tis but a she-wolf residing in the woods.’

Jeremiah held his gaze suspiciously. ‘Ye have seen this wolf?’

‘While collecting wood for my fire,’ he replied with a nod, regretting the need to reveal White Paw’s presence, but knowing her howls had already done so in truth.

'You are Jeremiah of Goose Back Farm, are you not?' he asked.

The old farmer nodded. 'Aye, what of it?'

'You and my father were friends before my mother passed. Was he not a man of his word?'

Jeremiah nodded.

'I am my father's son, and I tell you all that upon my life there be no demon abiding here with me.'

There was a brief hush as the men stared at Jacob and assessed the honesty of both his statement and his eyes.

'I find no evidence to contradict his words,' stated Padern, moving to stand by the woodpile, his torch flickering as the wind reached into the cottage.

'What of the second cot?' asked Breoc, a touch of desperation in his tone as he felt the situation turning from the purpose he had intended. 'He is hiding something, of this I am certain.'

'Unless you can reveal it, you have no further business here,' challenged Jacob, his confidence growing as the confrontational mood of the men became one of uncertainty.

'Did we not say we would kill the demon's master?' asked Breoc, turning to the men standing beyond the threshold. 'Well, there he stands and I say we stay true to the course of action we all agreed upon,' he said, pointing at Jacob.

Jeremiah looked to the trapper. 'We did not all agree on such action, especially such action carried out with no proof to substantiate your accusations.'

The farmer turned back to Jacob. 'We will take our leave,' he stated with a slight bow of his head, which served as an apology for the disturbance.

'We cannot!' exclaimed Breoc in frustration. 'What about the spell he and the demon have cast on Kerenza?' he asked, holding his hands out pleadingly.

‘I will speak with her when time permits,’ stated Jeremiah. ‘As for tonight, we should all be to our beds.’

‘And the wolf?’ asked Padern.

The old farmer looked to the man looming by the firewood and thought for a moment. ‘We will meet at the Gathering Place at noon on the morrow and beat the woods to flush it out,’ he replied eventually. ‘Is that agreed?’ he asked, turning to the men beyond the doorway.

They nodded and Jeremiah made his way past Breoc, the men backing away from the door to allow his exit. Padern stepped over and drew to a halt beside the trapper.

‘Come,’ he said, laying a hand on Breoc’s shoulder. ‘We can share a cup of mead at my cottage. ‘Tis much needed.’

Breoc batted his hand away with force and stared up at the farmhand, who looked upon him in surprise. ‘I will not leave until we have done what we came to do,’ he seethed.

Turning sharply, he glared at the men outside. ‘Are you all spineless? Are you all willing to let this evil lurk unchecked at the edge of our village?’

‘There be no evil other than that loosed by your tongue,’ stated Jacob.

‘Quiet, villain!’ he snarled.

‘‘Tis plain for all to see.’

Breoc made to step over to Jacob, but Padern halted him by once more placing his hand upon his shoulder, this time with greater firmness.

‘Release me,’ he demanded.

Padern shook his head. ‘You are not yourself.’

Breoc laughed bitterly. ‘Not myself?’ he said with a shake of his head. ‘You are all fools and the Devil himself has deceived you.’

‘Aye, he brought you all here for naught but his own ends,’ stated Jacob.

‘One more word and it will be your last,’ he hissed as he turned his burning gaze to the shepherd.

‘Do not make this harder than it has to be. I have no wish to cause you harm,’ stated Padern.

Breoc sneered and suddenly tried to break free of the farmhand’s grip. Padern grasped his collar tightly, stepping between him and Jacob. The shepherd quickly retreated over the fire pit, the table banging against the rear wall as he backed into it with Bess at his feet.

Padern took hold of the trapper’s other shoulder and held him fast. ‘You will leave with us willingly or unwillingly. The choice is yours,’ he stated coolly.

Breoc looked to his face and then glanced back to the door. He saw the shocked expressions of the other men as they regarded him as if he were beyond recognition. There would be no persuading them to pursue the course of action that he so desired. His purpose was undone.

Checking his fury, he took a breath. ‘I will leave willingly,’ he conceded.

Remaining between Breoc and the shepherd, Padern released him, his stance showing his readiness to restrain the trapper once again if needed. Breoc glanced around the bulk of the farmhand before turning for the door, fixing the shepherd with a look that left him in no doubt that matters between them were far from over.

The men backed away as he approached, the anger apparent in the trapper’s expression causing a retreat beyond that which was necessary, as if the heat of his rage pushed them back. He made his way out into the night and passed between their nervous ranks, storming to the gate without a backward glance.

‘Let us away,’ said Jeremiah, leading off the rest of the group as Padern exited the croft, nodding to Jacob before shutting the door.

48

The wan dawn light crept beneath the door and Jacob looked to it with raw eyes. He had barely slept, instead finding himself tossing and turning, his body allowed no rest by the activity of his mind. The confrontation with the men of the village had disturbed him greatly, as had thoughts about his brother and concerns about White Paw. Bess had curled by his feet once again, but had soon abandoned her usual post due to his movements, going instead to the fireside.

Prior to going to his bed, Jacob had remained seated by the pit for many hours. He had stoked the fire for a third and final time before returning to the fleeces of his cot, hoping the warmth and illumination would help him settle, but finding himself staring at the flames while listening to the cracking and hissing demise of the timbers.

He yawned and stretched, a tear forced from the momentary closure of his eyes and making its way down his right cheek. He wiped it away with the back of his hand and then pushed himself up, the simple movement taking greater effort than usual as his tired muscles strained.

Sitting on the edge of the cot, Jacob reached down and slipped his thumbs into the top of the furs wrapped about his feet, loosening them a little in order to aid in circulation. He peered at the woodpile through the deep gloom that afforded only a vague hint of the few timbers that remained there.

He rose and took up his brown cloak from where it rested over the foot of the cot, seeking additional warmth. His thoughts turned to the wolf and he glanced at the leg of venison hanging from the wall by the table. His mind fumbled for a course of action, the lack of rest a muddling influence as he looked to the timber on the opposite side of the cottage.

'Two birds with one stone,' he mumbled to himself as he finally reached a decision on what he should do.

Jacob took down the meat and set it on the table, taking up a knife lying nearby. He stared at the leg a moment and held the knife at the ready, a thought slowly emerging in his lethargic mind. He realised he would be hard pushed to eat the venison before it reached a state beyond consumption, that due to his brother's departure there was one less stomach to fill and he could afford to be more generous with his portions.

With a nod, he began to cut large slices, expression blank and movements conducted as if in a trance. The blade tapping on the tabletop lulled him, his mind drifting and aimless.

Bess barked and Jacob was given a start. He looked down beside him and discovered the hound sitting expectantly on the earth, tail swishing from side to side.

'Here,' he stated, taking one of the slices and dropping it to her.

Bess eagerly snapped it out of the air and then settled upon her stomach. Holding the venison in place with a paw, she began to chew on the sustenance as he watched for a moment.

Returning his wavering attention to the leg, he looked at the slices already cut. There were more than enough for the wolf and so he took up another and set it before the dog.

Wrapping the rest in the stained piece of cloth he so often used, Jacob tucked the food parcel into the cord about his waist. He stepped over to where the axe leant again the wall and lifted it, resting the handle's length on his shoulder as he made his way to the door.

Bess looked up as she began to consume the second slice and her master took hold of the handle. He opened the door and left the croft without a backward glance, his mind blank and without thought of issuing the command to remain.

Jacob passed out of the garden gate, going left and walking around the corner of the boundary wall before heading north towards the woodland. His thoughts began to meander, banked by concerns for his brother's welfare and White Paw's safety.

Entering the trees, he spied the vague path which led to the fallen elm and veered to the right. The sounds of the woods seemed more vivid than usual as a gentle northerly passed through the few leaves that remained on the branches above. There was scant birdsong, the jubilance of spring and summer subdued by winter's coming.

The elm came into view in the gloom and he looked to the trunk, seeing no sign of the wolf. Passing through the tall grasses and between the whispering trees, the hollow beside the root bowl became visible.

Jacob slowed his approach, still unable to detect the wolf's presence. The hollow at the rear of the dell was hidden in shadow which the light of the new day had yet to penetrate and he narrowed his eyes as he stared beyond the hanging roots.

He drew up less than five yards from the dell and found that the wolf was absent. Glancing around, he sought any hint of her whereabouts, but much of the landscape was concealed in the gloom. Nearby strands of bracken were thick with shadow and a faint mist hung in the air as drizzle began to fall, caressing his skin with a cool touch.

His frown deepened. He had hoped to see her one last time before the men of the village set to beating the woods.

'May Dor Dama watch over you and see that you come to no harm,' he said softly.

With weary effort, he took the axe from his shoulder and moved towards what had once been the top of the elm, now hidden within long grasses. Selecting the thinnest branch, his body wearied by lack of sleep, he bent forward and swung the axe. He gritted his teeth against the strain in his shoulder as the blade bit into the wood with a regular rhythm.

Ripping the limb away to the sound of tearing timber when the chopping was done, he let it drop to the ground. With a deep breath, he began to cut the next, his efforts flagging.

Jacob stopped after hewing two more branches from the elm, his energy spent. He looked about the woodland, the day brightening slowly and the mizzle thickening the air. He decided to hunt for fallen timber, a task more time consuming, but less taxing upon his physical condition.

Resting the axe against the trunk, he gathered the few cut branches beside it, reminded of the food parcel at his hip when he bent and felt its bulk. Jacob pulled aside his cloak and removed it, making his way with heavy steps to the dell.

He passed around the root bowl and frowned, having hoped to find White Paw returned. Standing beside the indent, he unfolded the cloth and threw the venison to the damp earth.

He tucked the material back in place as he looked around, finding no movement other than the soft stirring of trees and undergrowth. With shoulders sagging, Jacob began to wander about the nearby trees, seeking out fallen branches with which to restock the woodpile.

49

Wynfred washed his feet in a shallow pool as he sat amidst the yellowing grasses of the moorland. The throb of the sores was easing, the cold waters numbing all sensation. Caspian sat nearby, watching the track and his coat glistening with the moisture that was carried on the air.

Their vantage point was high and the huntsman looked out over the rolling hills and valleys as he straightened, mist greying the scene and gathered in the folds. He left his feet in the water, hoping to deaden them further before setting out once again.

'The wolf lies low, but she is out there somewhere,' he stated, certain he had heard a distant howl in the hours of darkness, the sound at the edge of his hearing.

The wind rose in gentle gusts as he took out food purchased in Penzance. Setting down the bread and smoked mackerel, he tore off some of the former and took a bite, following it with a sliver of fish.

'Caspian,' he called through the mouthful of food before picking a bone from his teeth and flicking it to the side.

The wolfhound approached and Wynfred tore off the fish's head, tossing it over. Caspian lowered his snout and sniffed at the offering before taking it up, the crunch of the mackerel's skull following soon after.

As the huntsman ate, the mist began to clear on the westerly wind and he was thankful for the relative mildness of the weather that rode on its back. He chewed on the tough bread, regularly spitting or plucking bones from the mess of food in his mouth.

Finishing all he could stomach, he threw the last of the fish to his hound and then wiped his slick fingers upon the grass. He looked out over the landscape once again and his eyes widened when he caught sight of the ocean only a few miles to the north. Turning, he spied its waters on the western horizon and in the middle distance to the south. It was even visible to the east thanks to the arc of Mount's Bay.

'This land is almost an island,' he observed, not having realised the sea was so close at hand in every direction, the night and then the settling mist having hidden its presence.

'To the ends of the earth,' he said with a smile of amusement, remembering the vow he had made in pursuit of the wolf.

He turned to the wolfhound. 'We have journeyed far, my friend,' he said, looking beyond Caspian to the narrow passage of land that linked the last stretch of Cornwall to the rest of England.

The clop of hooves and grumble of wheels upon the rock-strewn track drew his attention down the slope of the hill. The road below ran east to west, another branching from it and heading north. Moving steadily towards the junction along the branch was a wagon, a pair of oxen in the yoke and two men seated on the bench at the front, an uneven and covered load behind them.

Wynfred quickly dried his feet as best he could, binding them in cloth and then putting on his boots. Taking up his spear from the grass beside him, he leant on its length for assistance, rising with a grimace.

'Come, Caspian,' he stated, beginning down the rocky slope.

The wolfhound walked beside him as they made their way to the junction in the morning light. He could hear the murmur of the men's voices, sure that they made comment upon his approach.

Jumping from the small bluff that edged the track, Wynfred moved to stand at the junction, spear held like a staff as Caspian stood beside him. 'Good morning, gentlemen,' he called as the cart drew near.

'Clear the way, there,' responded the man on the right, a brutish club held across his substantial lap, his smaller companion gripping the reins.

'I seek information,' said Wynfred as he remained in place.

'Clear the way or you will feel the weight of my club.' The man lifted the weapon and patted its knotted head against his palm.

The huntsman stood his ground, Caspian letting out a low growl. The driver gave the reins a tug and the oxen drew up ten yards from the junction, one snorting and bucking its head against the yoke.

'You best not delay us, stranger.'

'Then you best tell me what you know of a wolf in these parts,' replied Wynfred.

'A wolf!' scoffed the man with a smirking glance at the driver. 'I can tell from your accent and the ignorance of your words that you are not of Penwith. There are no wolves this far west.'

Wynfred noted the look on the driver's long face and fixed him with his gaze. 'You know of what I speak,' he said, nodding towards the man.

'Clear the way,' demanded the stocky guardsman. 'I will not ask again.'

'Then remain silent while I speak with your companion,' replied Wynfred sharply.

The man's expression darkened and he rose from the bench, beginning to clamber down to the side of the track. Caspian growled with loud fierceness as the guardsman leapt the last and turned to face the duo blocking the way. He blanched at the sound, his club raised more as an act of protection than threat.

'I only have to give the word and he will be upon you.'

'What manner of unnatural beast stands at your side?' asked the driver, staring at Caspian with wide eyes.

'An answer for an answer. What have you heard of the wolf?' replied Wynfred.

The driver and guardsman looked to each other, the latter giving a vague nod, wishing to avoid a closer confrontation with the beast and be on his way.

'I heard its cry last night,' admitted the driver, 'though until your enquiry I believed it to be only a conjuration of my mind.'

'From whence did it arise?'

The rakish man turned and pointed north-west. 'Between Pendeen and St Just, I thought,' he said, looking back to the huntsman. 'Take this road and you will find a track that follows the coast westward beyond the mines.'

Wynfred nodded. 'My thanks.'

'And your beast?' asked the guard from beside the cart.

'A hound only, but one bred for the purpose of hunting wolves.'

The man regarded Caspian. 'He is indeed fit for purpose.'

'Aye, and there is no other I would wish by my side,' responded Wynfred, moving to the edge of the track and the hound with him.

The guard continued to eye Caspian for a moment and then climbed onto the wagon, the timbers creaking with his weight. Seating himself, the driver gave the reins a snap and the oxen took the strain, setting off once again.

'What do you carry?' asked Wynfred as they slowly passed by.

'Copper and tin,' replied the guardsman, his club resting upon his lap. ''Tis for the boats at the Mount and then to be taken to London.'

Wynfred nodded. 'May your journey be a safe one.'

'And may yours end in the wolf's demise.'

Wynfred gave a nod as the cart reached the junction and headed east. He stepped onto the track and began towards Pendeen, limping slightly as the feeling returned to his feet. Caspian loped at his side, the sounds of the cart fading at their backs.

They passed over a rise and the northern coastline was revealed, ragged and wild. The sea beyond was blue, turning a steel grey beneath a bank of cloud near the horizon.

Wynfred looked to the cliff-tops set below their position, seeing a gathering of miner's cottages down to the left. Squat chimneys arose from the stretch of land between the modest dwellings and the sea. Trails of smoke drifted from their hollows and about them were mounds of tailings from the open-cast mines. It was as though a castle stood upon the cliffs, its turrets bearing dark banners that fluttered in the wind.

He turned to the west and stared along the coastline. A woodland began not more than a couple of miles away, a swathe of stumps before it where the trees had been cleared.

‘I will find you,’ he stated, a sneer upon his lips as he raised his free hand and touched the scars upon his cheeks. ‘There is nowhere left to run.’

50

Kerra crouched between the beds of plants in front of the cottage, taking cuttings before they naturally died back in the grip of winter. A basket rested beside her and brimmed with the sprigs she had already gathered. Her mother worked nearby, a cloth on the path next to her piled with stems.

The smell of the plants mingled with that of the earth as Kerra shifted to ease the growing pain in her knees, bending forward and trimming the mint before her. She lifted the first handful and took a deep breath, rubbing the leaves gently to encourage their scent.

A stray bee flew about the plants briefly, seeking out flowers that were no longer in evidence. She watched it with a melancholy smile, knowing that it was out of season and its search would likely prove fruitless.

The sound of a throat being cleared caused Kerra and her mother to turn to the gate. Tetker stood beyond, a fleece draped over her shoulders which she held tightly about her neck with withered hands.

'Tetker!' exclaimed Kerra in surprise.

'Good day to ye both,' said the old woman with a smile.

'Good day, Tetker,' responded Kerenza. 'Should you not be resting at home?'

'I have been a prisoner to those walls since Kalan-Gwav and was in need of a fresh air,' she replied. ''Tis a good day for it,' she added, looking up at the blue sky.

'Aye, and mild with it.'

'Indeed,' nodded Tetker. 'May I enter?'

'Of course.'

The old woman stepped through the gate. 'Can I be of help?'

'You can keep us company as we take the trimmings,' replied Kerenza.

'I could be of greater assistance if thee would but lend me a knife.'

Kerenza shook her head. 'I would not see you using your newfound strength only to find the cold returning. It would please me more for you to sit and conserve yourself.'

'I will fetch a stool,' said Kerra, placing the mint in the basket and rising.

'My thanks,' said Tetker as the girl hurried into the cottage. 'What news of Breoc?' she asked, turning to Kerenza.

'I have seen naught of him since cutting the bonds between us,' she said, bending forward and the knife slicing through a supple stem.

'And his reaction? Ye spoke little of it afore.' Tetker regarded her closely.

'As to be expected,' she replied without turning, the next cut made with a sharp movement.

'Here,' stated Kerra as she returned from the cottage with a stool in her hands. She moved to the old woman and set it down on the path. 'If you need more comfort I can bring my pillow on which to sit.'

Tetker shook her head. 'There be no need, though I thank thee for the kind offer,' she said with a smile.

'Will thee visit with Jacob on this day?' she asked while seating herself, the girl returning to her previous position before the mint.

'Aye, once we have finished the gathering.'

Tetker looked about the garden and to the beds on either side of the cottage. 'It may be ye will not visit with him for a week or two,' she commented in jest.

Kerra looked over at her and chuckled when she saw the expression on the old woman's face.

'She may leave when the basket is filled,' said Kerenza.

'Ah, then I can take her knife and help with the task.'

Kerenza laughed and shook her head. 'Then you may continue to watch as I gather,' she responded, 'otherwise I fear you will push yourself beyond the limits of your recovering health and I would be pained to make more curatives on your behalf. My prayers are that Dor Dama sees you through the winter without further suffering.'

'Well, my offer stands and I shall say no more on it,' stated Tetker.

'I have made the straw doll for Jacob,' said Kerra after a few moments of silence, glancing over her shoulder.

'Indeed,' nodded Tetker.

The girl turned her thoughtful gaze to the basket beside her and frowned. 'I thought it could keep him company, but it seems a poor offering with grand ambition beyond its means of fulfilling.'

'There is naught wrong with grand ambition that has arisen from thy heart,' said Tetker. 'Ye try to bring cheer in a time of sadness and that be a sign that ye care. Such a sign will bring comfort.'

'But it be a poor substitute for what has been lost.' Kerra looked to the old woman, her expression downcast.

'Do not give cold counsel to heartfelt deeds. They were set in motion by the warmth of thy affection towards Jacob and are pure.'

'What Tetker says is true,' stated her mother with an encouraging smile to her daughter.

Kerra looked to them both and then gave a nod, clearly not convinced as she returned to the trimming. She reached forward and then let out a gasp, dropping the knife as she raised her left hand and stared at the nick in her thumb, a line of blood blossoming along the cut.

'Pay heed to your task, Little Bird,' reprimanded her mother gently.

'Let me see thy wound,' said Tetker, holding her hand out to the girl.

Kerra rose and stepped over to the old woman, who took her wrist and studied the injury. 'It bleeds aplenty, but 'tis not a deep cut,' she stated.

'There is a balm on the table,' stated her mother. 'You will find it in a bowl covered with a blue cloth. Go rub some into the cut.'

Tetker released her and Kerra made her way into the cottage.

'I think she is done here for the day,' said Kerenza, moving over to where her daughter had dropped the knife and taking it up. She wiped a small smear of blood onto the trodden grass of the path and then tucked it into her jerkin.

'Ye guessed my intent,' said Tetker with a grin, having been about to rise and take the blade in order to help with the trimming.

Kerenza looked over to her. 'Aye,' she replied distractedly, glancing at the open front door.

'She will be fine. 'Tis but a nick.'

She nodded and moved back to where she had been cutting stems. 'I will take rest for a while. Will you join me inside?'

'Indeed.' Tetker rose with a groan. 'Should I bring the stool with me?'

‘There is no need,’ replied Kerenza over her shoulder as she walked to the cottage.

Kerra appeared in the doorway, nursing her thumb as it glistened with the ointment. ‘It stings,’ she commented.

‘Good. That means ‘tis working,’ responded her mother. ‘I think it time you went to the croft. ‘Tis almost midday already and Jacob will be wondering what has kept you.’

Kerra looked to the basket. ‘What about the rest of the plants?’

‘I will see to them. Go and give him your gift.’

She turned to peer into the gloom, spying the doll resting by the pillow of her cot. ‘It may be I should leave it for another time.’

‘Nonsense,’ said Tetker, moving past both of them and looking about the interior. Seeing the doll, she walked into the rear corner and picked it up.

‘But it be…’

‘I will hear no more of thy doubts,’ said Tetker, wagging a finger at the girl as she returned to the doorway.

‘Tis a fine gift,’ she stated, studying the doll. ‘I would be pleased to receive such and am certain Jacob will be gladdened by thy thoughtfulness.’

The old woman held the doll out to Kerra. She hesitated, staring at it with a deep frown before finally taking it and holding it limply at her side, her head bowed.

‘Promise me that ye will give it to him and not drop it in the woods as ye pass to the vale.’

Kerra looked up at her in surprise.

‘I guessed thy plan,’ responded Tetker with a bright smile. ‘Do not fret, Young Kerra, he will find this gift as I do; from the heart and with great charm.’

The girl gave a vague nod.

'So, do ye promise?'

'I promise.'

'Than be on thy way and enjoy thy time with him.'

'Be sure to return before nightfall,' stated Kerenza as her daughter leant forward and gave the old woman a hug of parting.

'I will,' she responded, stepping to her mum and briefly taking her into her arms.

Kerra set off, moving between the beds and passing around the side of the cottage as the two women watched.

'She is a dear child,' stated Tetker warmly as the girl passed from sight around the corner.

Kerenza turned to her. 'She is Dearest,' she said with a smile.

'Indeed,' chuckled the old woman as they turned and made their way inside.

51

Kerra made her way over the stream via the mossy trunk and headed towards the croft. There was no sign of Jacob or his flock in the sunny vale and she looked to the hole in the cottage's thatch. No smoke arose from its darkness, the door and window shutters closed on the mild day.

A bark arose from the eastern slope to her right and she was given a start, turning to the sound. Bess came bounding out of the woods on the upper reaches, her tail wagging fiercely and tongue lolling as she approached.

Kerra crouched, putting the straw doll safely on her lap before the hound came jumping and licking. She fussed her and smiled, looking up to the trees as Jacob came into sight with a bundle of firewood across his shoulders and his stick in hand.

'Good day, Kerra,' he called as he drew near. 'I see Bess gives her usual greeting,' he said with a smile as the hound licked the girl's cheek.

Kerra laughed as she wiped the saliva away with the back of her hand. 'Good day, Jacob,' she replied, taking the doll from her lap and holding it behind her as Bess sniffed at her shins. She looked to Jacob's face and noticed the brush of darkness beneath his eyes that hinted at his lack of sleep.

'What do you have there?' he asked as he came to a halt, glancing around her.

'Oh, just a gift I made for you. 'Tis not much.' She hesitantly revealed the doll, blushing slightly with embarrassment.

The shepherd's smile broadened. He reached out and took the gift, looking upon it with apparent fondness.

'Do you like it?' she asked, still unsure as to its value despite his expression.

'Aye,' he said, looking to her. ''Tis a fine doll and a wonderful gift.'

'I thought it may keep you company when I am not able,' she stated. 'Though Bess is likely better suited to that purpose.'

'It shall be welcome company in addition to hers,' he responded. 'It will also remind me of you and in so doing will ne'er fail to raise a smile and bring warmth in times when 'tis needed.'

Jacob noted the look upon her face and drew back his cloak, tucking the doll into the cord about his waist. Placing his hand upon her shoulder, he held it firmly. 'My thanks, Kerra,' he stated, his eyes communicating both his gratitude and affection.

'You truly like it?'

'Aye,' he replied with a nod. 'Come, let us to the croft so that I may stow the firewood and the flock can be brought out into the sunshine.' Jacob released her shoulder and they began towards the building, Bess taking the lead.

Opening the gate, the shepherd glanced at the bell, its solitary chime one of sadness. He crouched and moved the rock so as to secure the exit for the flock, Kerra having to take a step back to avoid the branches protruding from his shoulders.

'They must have taken you a long time to cut,' she commented, having seen the smile fade from his face at the sound of the bell.

'They were not cut,' he stated as he straightened. 'They were collected. I have not the energy to be chopping this day.'

‘Have you already visited with White Paw?’ she asked as they made their way to the door.

He nodded. ‘But she were not at the hollow.’

‘I heard her calling last night.’

‘Aye,’ he replied, taking hold of the handle. ‘I fear she announced her presence to all of Lannust.’

Jacob opened the door and Bess entered first. He stepped in and went over to the woodpile, taking the bundle of branches from his shoulders.

‘What do you think will happen?’ asked Kerra as she went inside, the sheep bleating in response to the disturbance and jostling for position by the door to the enclosure.

‘That I cannot say, though I fear the reaction of the village will not be a kindly one.’ He set the branches on those stacked against the wall, his morning spent gathering and restocking.

‘Do you think they will kill her?’ asked Kerra worriedly.

Jacob turned to her. ‘I think it more likely they drive her away,’ he replied before stepping past the fire pit and standing by his cot, taking the doll from his robes.

Leaning over the bed, he paced it in a crevice. ‘There,’ he said, ‘now it can watch over me as I sleep.’

Kerra looked to the doll as it rested in the shallow hollow, still feeling that it was a meagre gift. She frowned as Jacob bent to a pail resting by the foot of the cot, cupping his hands as if to gather water from its confines.

His fingers slipped beyond sight and she heard the faint sound of ripples. Lifting his hands back out of the pail, the sound of blowing drew her gaze and she discerned a large moth perched upon his palm, the edges of its wings dampened after it had become trapped upon the water’s surface.

Moving over to him as Jacob rose, she looked to the creature. A pale line divided its top wings, fading into soft grey towards the rear. The front portions were the colour of rabbit's fur and each sported a single white spot. The honey coloured hair about its head stirred as the shepherd continued to blow, the moth briefly fluttering its wings, but not deigning to leave the combined warmth of his breath and skin.

''Tis beautiful,' she commented quietly.

'Last night's fire must have stirred it into flight,' he commented. 'More oft than not 'tis wood lice that I save from the water.'

'You save wood lice?' She looked at him with nose wrinkled in mild disgust.

'Aye, they are no lesser than this moth.'

'Why do such a thing?'

'For want of drinking water free of bugs, for one,' he said with a smile, 'and because every life is sacred.'

'Surely there is little difference made in saving a wood louse?'

Jacob shook his head. 'To each creature that I save my actions make all the difference. They make the difference between life and death,' he stated.

'I have saved its life,' he said, looking to the moth. 'There is no greater deed I could have done in regards its existence.'

Kerra looked at the creature as it flexed its wings. 'What of killing for food?' she asked, turning to him curiously.

'That is out of need, not out of pleasure or a lack of consideration. In this time we must kill in order to live and should give our thanks to each life that is ended so ours may continue. In this way we show our appreciation and understanding of their sacrifice and of their new existence as part of us.'

The moth took to the wing and they watched its flight. It flitted first to the fleeces of the bed, settling for a moment before lifting back into the air. Making for the light spilling through the doorway, it passed out of the cottage and beyond their sight.

'If I had not saved it…' he said, letting the sentence go unfinished.

Kerra nodded her understanding, staring thoughtfully after the insect as she considered what he had said.

Jacob let out a low whistle and Bess moved to the rear of the cottage. The hound encouraged the flock from the corner, the sheep and goats moving to the door and bleating as they passed out into the sunshine.

'Let us enjoy the day while the light remains,' he said, patting her shoulder and then moving over to the door.

Taking his stick from beside the entrance, Jacob made his way out and Kerra followed. They passed along the path and out of the gate, which was left open for their return.

The flock were already fifty yards ahead, Bess keeping a close eye and ensuring they stayed bunched as they made their way down the vale. The low winter sun drew shadows out of the woods on Nancherrow Hill, ones which would lengthen to consume the valley as the day drew on.

'Mamm spoke of visiting with you today,' said Kerra, 'but has been taken by the task of gathering cuttings from the garden.'

''Tis a good day for it and an important undertaking before an prys a kosk truly takes hold.'

Kerra smiled at his description. 'The season of sleep,' she repeated.

Jacob glanced at her, his own smile rejuvenated by her bright expression. 'That is what my mother used to call it. 'Tis a shame the land must sleep in such a cold bed and that we must share it,' he said jokingly.

Kerra chuckled. 'Let us hope it does not come with a blanket of snow.'

'Aye,' laughed Jacob. 'That would indeed be a cold bed.'

She took hold of his free hand and they looked to each other in happiness as a small flock of gulls flew overhead. They turned their eyes upward, squinting as the birds passed to the west, rising on the breeze and vanishing from sight over the woodland atop the Nancherrow Hill.

'I ne'er had the opportunity to have children,' began Jacob, turning to the girl, 'but I love you like my own.'

Kerra did not know how to respond and Tetker's words of a similar nature were brought to mind. 'My thanks,' she stated, feeling the inadequacy of her reply. 'I love you like an uncle,' she added.

His expression tightened and was laced with regret. 'I…,' he began, words failing him and shaking his head.

'What is it?'

'Nothing,' he replied, head bowed.

She studied him as they walked, seeing an internal struggle within his eyes but unable to guess at its cause. 'You can share all with me,' she encouraged. 'I will not judge.'

'I would that were true, but fear otherwise,' he said, looking to the passage of his walking stick as it brushed through the grass and padded softly on the earth with a steady rhythm. 'Our minds are as blades of grass, swayed by the wind of our imaginings and misconceptions, a wind that can drown out the truth with the disturbance of its passage.'

Kerra looked at him in puzzlement, seeing the weight of what he kept within heavy upon his shoulders. ‘Of what do you speak?’

Jacob remained silent for a moment. ‘I will share it with you, but this is not the time.’

He looked to the crab apple tree as they drew near and let out a sharp whistle, Bess bringing the flock to a halt. Walking over to the tree, he glanced at Kerra with a haunted expression, but no words were forthcoming.

They seated themselves against the trunk and Jacob tucked his cloak beneath him as protection from the damp ground. They did not speak, but simply watched the flock as they grazed in the winter sunlight, Bess trotting over to lounge in the grass nearby as the afternoon drew on.

52

Tetker moved between the pair of cottages which rested before her own and spied a figure moving stealthily away from her door. It was a woman, her head bowed and covered in a cloth which was held at the neck to keep her identity concealed.

'Brecca?' she called, catching a glimpse of the woman's face as she made to depart.

The woman stopped dead in her tracks, given a start by the old woman's cry. Slowly turning, she revealed herself. Her face was long and pale, expression pensive as her eyes darted this way and that in nervousness.

Tetker hurried over to her. 'What are ye doing here?' she asked, 'and in such a secretive manner?'

Brecca looked over the old woman's shoulder towards the Gathering Place. 'We must speak,' she said in a whisper.

'Be there something wrong?'

'Not here,' breathed the woman, the hollows of her cheeks filled with shadow. 'Inside.'

Tetker looked to her grey eyes, seeing tightness about them and fear within. Turning, she led them to the door and ushered Brecca in with a wave once it was opened.

The woman entered in haste, moving to the concealment offered by the wall beside the entrance. Tetker closed the door and glanced out as she did so, seeing no sign of anything untoward.

'What have thee to say that warrants such behaviour?' she asked, the woman's disquiet proving infectious and causing her to feel tense.

Brecca pulled the cloth from her black hair and bent close. 'Breoc,' she stated.

'What of him?'

'He and Kerenza share a union that the village bore witness to at Kalan-Gwav. I have seen Kerra pass back and forth to your cottage and know you are friends with both the girl and her mother,' said Brecca, words almost tripping over themselves in their urgency to be spoken.

'You must warn Kerenza,' she stated firmly.

'Of what?' asked Tetker.

'Breoc is not a man with whom she should seek union.'

'What cause do you have to say such a thing?'

'When we were together I was punished for the slightest of mishaps and had the bruises to show for it. He is a man of ill temper, one who will brood and become savage after thinking on what has occurred.'

Brecca blanched at the sound of a cow lowing nearby, her tension visibly increasing. 'He warned me not to speak of it, but I must,' she stated.

'Ye need fret no longer. Kerenza brought their union to an end only yesterday,' said Tetker, placing her hand upon the woman's arm comfortingly. 'Come and sit.'

They moved to the fireside and Brecca seated herself.

'Then she must be warned to remain wary, for telling Breoc 'tis over and his acceptance of such are two different things,' she said as the old woman gathered a few sticks from the woodpile and added them to the weak flames in the pit. 'He is not a man to accept rejection with ease, but more likely with continuing attempts to keep the union alive or, worse, with vengeance.'

'Vengeance?' Tetker swallowed hard, her pulse rising as she straightened and turned to her unexpected guest.

'Tyra.' She bit back tears.

‘Thy dog, the one that used to follow wherever ye went?’

Brecca nodded. ‘He killed her.’

‘I thought she died of some illness,’ responded Tetker as she sat down.

‘That is the story I told for fear that to reveal the truth would be to suffer further at his hands.’ She sniffed and wiped her nose. ‘He snuck in one night and slit her throat as we slept, leaving her body where she lay upon the foot of my cot.’ A tremor ran through her as she recalled waking to the grizzly discovery in the dim morning light.

Tetker saw the distress in her expression and felt sickened by the thought of harm coming to either Kerenza or Kerra. ‘There be some brandy hereabouts. It will help settle the nerves,’ she stated, rising and seeking out an earthenware jug which she discovered tucked against the wall near the head of her cot.

‘Do not worry yourself. I will be fine with water.’

‘That may be so, but I will not,’ responded the old woman as she took up a couple of wooden cups and returned to her stool. ‘I am in need of this tonic after hearing thy words.’

She unstopped the jug and poured the warming liquid into one of the cups, passing it to Brecca. Filling the other, she set the jug down and proceeded to take a sip, nodding to herself as the branches upon the fire hissed with escaping steam.

Brecca drank from her cup and then cradled it upon her lap, the alcohol bringing heat to her cheeks. ‘If only I had found the courage to speak of what he had done at the time,’ she said, shaking her head. ‘I had hoped no other woman would take to him, but saw Kerenza by his side at the celebrations.’

‘At least ye have found the courage now.’ Tetker reached over and rested her hand upon the woman’s knee. ‘I will see to it that Kerenza is forewarned. All will be well.’

Brecca looked at her and sighed. ‘I hope your words prove true, but Breoc has not shown himself to be a reasonable man in times past.’

‘It may be he has changed. Age has a mellowing effect.’

Brecca’s expression was filled with doubt as she turned her eyes to the flames.

Tetker patted her knee and then removed her hand. She took a sip of brandy whilst hoping that her words would be born out. With a nod to herself, she set upon a plan. Once Brecca had departed she would visit with Kerenza again and give her a timely warning to be watchful.

53

Kerenza crouched between the beds to the right of the cottage, using the basket now that her daughter was no longer in need of it. The woods loomed nearby, the westerly wind whispering through the branches as the knife cut through stem after stem and she pushed the pain in her knees from her mind.

The scent of the plants filled her as she felt the warmth of the sun upon the side of her face. It was sinking towards the horizon, its journey shortened by its low winter position in the sky.

A large moth with white spots upon its forewings fluttered close to her face as it flew by. She watched as it briefly settled on the contents of the basket and then lifted into the air once again, making its way across the beds at the front of the house.

Her gaze was drawn by a shadow and she turned to find Breoc standing at the gate, feeling discomforted by his silent stillness. His face was unclear, the sun at his back transforming him into a mere silhouette.

The moth flitted towards him.

With sudden movement, he clapped his hands together and then brushed the remains from his palms.

'Good day, Breoc,' she greeted, made tense by his unnecessary and unkind action.

He remained wordless, his dark presence brooding.

'Is all well with you?' she asked, her grip on the knife tightening as she got to her feet and felt increasingly uneasy.

'Has your mind been freed?'

'My mind?'

'I know your heart, but does your mind still remain under the enchantment? Do you still believe that we are no longer to be together?'

'There is no enchantment, Breoc. We are ill-suited, is all,' she replied.

'And what of your love for your husband? I thought that to be the reason for our end,' he said coldly. 'It seems you do not know your own mind.'

'We are ill-suited due to that love,' she responded, trying to keep her voice level despite her trepidation.

'That is not as it seemed before your visit to the croft. Your lips upon mine said otherwise without need of words.'

She blushed. 'That was…'

'A mistake?' he finished darkly.

Kerenza shook her head. 'Hasty,' she replied.

'So, the spell still lingers.'

'Of what spell doest thou speak, Breoc?' asked a familiar voice.

The trapper turned to find Tetker approaching along the path from the Gathering Place. She drew to a halt a few yards away from him, feeling a warning within and keeping her distance.

'I do not speak of such to you, *old woman*,' he responded, the last words spoken with undisguised scorn. 'This is not your business.'

'Indeed. Then I suggest ye keep such words to the privacy of thy mind or a place more suitable.'

Breoc scowled at her. ''Tis said you are wise, so show this wisdom and pass on,' he said with a shooing gesture.

'Ye are not my master, Breoc, so do not suppose ye can give me instruction and I will follow. I have come to visit with Kerenza and until I have done so I shall remain.'

'I see your wisdom is but hollow talk.' He stepped up to Tetker and towered over her. 'Be gone,' he demanded.

'I will not,' she replied firmly, holding his gaze as her wispy hair moved in the breeze.

'You may both visit with me, if that be your wish,' stated Kerenza, hoping her words would come between them.

Breoc glanced over his shoulder and Tetker took the opportunity to quickly step around him. Going through the gate, she made a point of shutting it after her, gleaning a sense of satisfaction from the petty action and grinning at the trapper.

He glared at her and then made his way along the boundary fence at a brisk pace. Reaching its end, he strode alongside the beds that surrounded the cottage, making his way towards the woodland. Without so much as a glance, he passed into the trees, his dark cloak flapping at his heels.

'Good riddance,' stated Tetker under her breath.

'And what, may I ask, was that about?' Kerenza looked to the old woman.

'There are things I must tell thee in the privacy of thy home,' she replied.

Kerenza looked at her quizzically, Tetker's grave expression giving rise to concern. 'Is all well?'

She nodded. 'And I come here to ensure that it stays so.'

'I would have you tell me if there be some danger of which I should know.'

'I will be happy to do so inside.'

Kerenza paused, looking to the basket while considering whether to take it in with her. Leaving it in situ, she walked to the main path and led the way to the front door.

'If this be about the wolf, you need not worry yourself. I have already spoken with Kerra and she knows not to venture near the beast,' she said over her shoulder.

''Tis about a wolf of a different kind,' responded the old woman obliquely.

They entered the cottage and Tetker made sure to close the door behind her, glancing out as she did so. Kerenza went to the table and reached for a cup at the back, the cuttings gathered during the morning arrayed before her.

'I have no need of anything to drink,' said the old woman. 'I have just shared a cup of brandy with Brecca.'

'Does she fare well?' asked Kerenza.

'She was most perturbed,' replied Tetker as she moved to the fireside and warmed her hands. 'She had much to say in regards Breoc and their time together, much that was not easy to hear.'

Kerenza looked at her in puzzlement as she took one of the stools from beneath the table and placed it beside her guest. 'Please sit,' she stated.

Tetker rested herself with a slight groan of effort as Kerenza fetched another stool and positioned it opposite the old woman.

'She bade me warn thee of his character,' continued Tetker once Kerenza had taken her seat.

'Warn me?' She looked across in puzzlement.

'Indeed,' answered the old woman with a nod. 'She suffered at his hands, was beaten for little reason and oft with forethought.'

'Poor Brecca,' said Kerenza sadly, turning her gaze to the fire.

‘And poor Tyra.’

‘Tyra?’

‘Do ye recall the black hound that could always be found at Brecca’s heel?’

Kerenza nodded.

‘Breoc slit its throat one night as Brecca and the dog lay sleeping in her cottage.’

‘No!’ she gasped, looking to the old woman in shock.

‘It were the fulfilment of a threat he made to her when she brought their union to an end,’ said Tetker, holding Kerenza’s gaze meaningfully, ‘and brought to mind the threat he made to Kerra.’

‘You think she be telling the truth?’

‘I was not certain at first, but now…’ She let the sentence go unfinished.

Kerenza blanched at the thought. She felt guilt as having dismissed her daughter’s claims so easily and worried at her safety.

‘Does she still abide with Jacob?’ asked Tetker.

‘Aye, though she is due home before nightfall.’

‘It would be best to keep her close.’

Kerenza nodded. ‘If she visits with him again on the morrow, I shall accompany her.’

‘And for my part I will keep a watchful eye.’

Kerenza pondered a moment. ‘Do you truly think Brecca’s account to be true? It seems so…’ She shook her head as she sought the right word. ‘…Unreal. So opposed to the man I thought I knew.’

‘There was no lie in Brecca’s words or eyes,’ replied Tetker. ‘What she revealed to unto me was the truth and one which has tormented her for a long count of years. When she saw thee with Breoc at Kalan-Gwav, she knew it could not remain hidden any longer, that a warning must be given.’

‘I only wish it could have been given before I developed and expressed my feelings for him. He believes my heart is his and my mind lies under an enchantment cast by Jacob.’

‘Then Jacob must also be warned.’

Kerenza gave a nod as she fell into a contemplative silence. Tetker studied her features, seeing the strain evident and wishing she had not been the bearer of such ill tidings.

‘His feelings will pass in time,’ she said.

‘And then another will become the subject of his attentions,’ responded Kerenza as she stared at the flames.

‘It may be we can warn those of Lannust who are without husbands, thereby ensuring Breoc ne’er causes another to fear or suffer again. Out of the bad will come good,’ she said with a forced smile of reassurance.

‘I pray you are right.’

‘May Dor Dama see ‘tis so,’ responded Tetker with a nod.

54

Jeremiah looked to the path that led south out of the circle of cottages surrounding the Gathering Place, hoping to catch sight of Breoc. The trapper was the only man from the previous night's meeting to have not made an appearance, all the others already waiting and even a couple of their wives having joined the throng.

'The reverend,' stated Padern from beside him.

The old farmer turned in the opposite direction to see Reverend Catlin striding purposefully towards them from the direction of the church, his black vestments rippling in the breeze. 'Good day, Reverend,' he greeted.

'What transpires here?' asked Catlin with a furrowed expression, looking to the sticks and staffs carried by all who were present.

'We ready to go to the woods and flush out the wolf that lurks there.'

The reverend came to a halt before Jeremiah. 'Ah,' he said with a nod. 'I thought I heard the likes of such last night.'

'Indeed ye did,' replied the farmer, 'and upon this day we will see to it that there be no further disturbance.'

'This gathering is well done, Jeremiah. I commend you.'

'My thanks, Reverend.'

'I am glad to find that the will to be rid of the beast is so easily able to bring you together in purpose. If only the same could be said of your attendance of Mass,' he said with greater volume, a few of the men bowing their heads and averting their eyes.

‘‘Tis a distance to travel from the farm, especially during inclement weather,’ replied Jeremiah, being one of those guilty of not visiting the church daily.

‘You are not making the journey to me, but to God,’ reprimanded Catlin. ‘Surely you can endure a little wind and rain to praise Him? See it as a chance to show the Lord your strength of faith.’

Jeremiah nodded. ‘I shall do my best.’

‘I pray that be so.’ The reverend raised an eyebrow.

‘It shall be,’ responded the farmer, turning his gaze to the ground like a naughty child.

‘As for this venture,’ began Catlin, raising his voice once again, ‘I give it my blessing. May God see fit that you are successful.’ He crossed himself and bowed his head momentarily.

‘I will expect you all at Mass upon this eve in order to give thanks,’ he added, looking to each of those present in turn and receiving vague nods of response.

‘God shines His light upon you,’ he commented, looking to the sun. ‘Do not let it be in vain.’

‘Our thanks for the blessing,’ said Jeremiah. ‘With God’s grace we shall flush out the beast.’

‘You must bring about its end,’ stated the reverend. ‘Such a creature should not be permitted to live. ‘Tis a bringer of fear and death, and in this I see the hand of Satan.’

‘We will kill it if the chance arises,’ nodded the farmer.

‘Ah, here is another that chooses only to attend Mass when they see fit,’ said Catlin as he looked to his left.

Jeremiah followed his gaze and found the hunched form of Tetker coming along the western track. ‘If thee will excuse me Reverend, I will take my leave,’ he said with as much politeness as he could muster, setting off towards the old woman before Catlin had a chance to respond.

'Tetker, old friend, how goes it? I heard thee were unwell and am glad to see thee recovered,' he said in greeting.

The old woman smiled at him as they stopped before each other. 'Good day, Jeremiah. 'Tis a rare sight to see thee in the village.'

'We have gathered so as to flush out the wolf.'

She glanced past him and nodded. 'I heard its howls rising into the night.'

'Have ye been foraging in the woods?' he asked, glancing down the track along which she had come.

Tetker shook her head. 'I have been visiting with Kerenza.'

'Kerenza?' His expression tightened.

'Be there something amiss?'

'Does she seem…?' He hesitated, shifting awkwardly beneath her searching gaze. 'Does she seem enchanted?'

'Enchanted?' she said with a bemused look. 'Why would ye ask such a thing?'

'Breoc, he claims that Estren Onan is in league with a demon and they have cast a spell upon her. Further, he claims this is what has brought their union to an end.'

Tetker shook her head. 'The only demon hereabouts is Breoc himself.'

Jeremiah looked at her questioningly.

She frowned. 'I cannot say more, but know this, he is not a man to be trusted and Kerenza has made a wise choice in breaking their union.'

The farmer nodded.

'Heed my words. There is more than one wolf that is in need of flushing out.'

Jeremiah held her gaze. 'I have known ye all my life and know thy words to be true,' he responded.

There was a thoughtful pause as the men and women milled about the Gathering Place, the trapper still not in attendance.

'We did not have occasion to speak at Kalan-Gwav,' said Tetker. 'How goes it with Mary and the children? Are they in good health?'

'They are,' he replied with a nod. 'Thy dancing about the bonfire was a sight to behold,' he added with a smile.

'There be life in these old legs yet,' she grinned.

'Of that I am glad.' Jeremiah smiled in response. 'I should return to the men so we can set to the task at hand.'

'It has been a pleasure speaking with thee, Jeremiah. We must not leave it so long next time.'

'Aye. I shall make sure to call when next I am passing. Fare ye well, Tetker.' The farmer gave a nod of parting and turned, returning to the group that awaited him, the reverend still lingering.

''Tis time we were to the woods,' said Jeremiah as he came to a halt before the group and Tetker looked on.

'We will start at the Sacred Oak,' he stated, noting the reverend's expression tightening at the mention of the Pagan site. 'Then we shall move through the woods atop Nancherrow Hill and down into the vale north of the shepherd's croft.'

There were nods of agreement as the group readied their sticks.

'Ladies and gentlemen,' announced the reverend, raising his hands and waiting for all eyes to be upon him. 'I bid you good day and will see you all at church upon this eve. May God be with you and bring you success in this venture.'

'Let us set to it,' said Jeremiah, waving them forward as he turned towards the western track.

Tetker watched as the villagers exited the Gathering Place, the reverend left standing on his own. Setting off in the opposite direction before he could accost her, she felt pleased by the chance meeting with Jeremiah and the opportunity to reveal something of Breoc's true nature.

Smiling to herself, she made her way home and felt as though a weight had been lifted. 'All will be well,' she said to herself as she raised her face to the warmth of the sun.

55

They moved through the woods in a staggered line beating vine and fern, bush and bramble. Jeremiah was stationed in the centre, Padern using his staff to disturb the undergrowth ten yards to his left. They had passed through the arm of woodland upon the brow of Nancherrow Hill with no sign of the quarry and now walked down the slope into the head of the vale.

Jeremiah glanced to his side and spied the croft through the trees, recalling the events of the previous evening with shame. He had known Jacob's father well as a boy, had fought off many a goblin and battled Tewal-Tan with a stick for a sword shoulder to shoulder with Gorlas.

He shook his head and beat a strand of bracken with his staff, not truly expecting the wolf to be hiding amidst the browning leaves. His thoughts turned to what they would do if the beast were revealed. He would be satisfied with scaring it away, but he knew there were those that wanted its death.

'There!' exclaimed Padern.

Jeremiah turned to him and found the farmhand pointing into the trees ahead and to the left. Narrowing his eyes, he peered through the increasing density of the woodland, the trees seeming to huddle closer within the confines of the vale. Thirty yards away stood a large grey beast. It stared at the approaching beaters, its cold gaze unfaltering.

'That be no wolf,' he said in a whisper.

‘Could it be the demon Breoc spoke of?’ asked Padern as the line drew to a halt, everyone with their eyes fixed on the beast or craning to catch a glimpse beyond obscuring trunks.

‘I do not know,’ he conceded. ‘‘Tis of a likeness I have ne’er seen before.’

Jeremiah stared at the unnatural creature as a tremor ran through him. ‘Collen,’ he called softly, turning to his right.

The farmer looked over and Jeremiah made a sweeping motion with his arm. Collen nodded his response and began to lead those on the flank around to entrap the creature.

Turning, Jeremiah found the other flank echoing the movement and then glanced at Padern, nodding at the large farmhand. The two of them began to advance, holding their sticks like swords, the games of his youth brought to mind once again.

The old farmer set his gaze on the beast as it remained before them, showing no sign of concern despite the men encircling its position. Its apparent confidence gave rise to a feeling of unease, his pace slowing and his pulse beginning to rise.

‘It makes no attempt to flee,’ whispered Padern, also perturbed by the creature’s behaviour.

‘‘Tis an unnatural beast for sure,’ replied Jeremiah under his breath as they drew within twenty yards.

‘Gentlemen!’ A man carrying a spear and wearing a wolf-skin stepped into view from behind a large trunk beside the beast.

Jeremiah’s heart leapt at the sudden appearance and all those in the beating party drew to a halt, their faces drained of colour and expressions a mixture of surprise and confusion.

‘My apologies for not making myself known sooner, only you disturbed my need for relief,’ he said with a glance back to the foot of the elm.

‘Are ye in the company of this unnatural beast?’ asked the old farmer, noting the three parallel scars upon the man’s cheek.

‘Aye, that I am,’ he replied with a nod. ‘This *unnatural beast* is called Caspian.’

‘What manner of fiend is it?’

‘*He*,’ began the huntsman with emphasis, ‘is a wolfhound and was gifted to me for my services to the crown.’

‘The crown?’ Jeremiah shared a worried look with Padern as their thoughts turned to the meeting the previous night and their talk of revolt.

‘What business does a servant of the crown have here?’ asked Padern.

‘There seems a challenge in your tone,’ said the man with an amused smile as he regarded the large farmhand.

‘We would have ye tell us thy business,’ stated Jeremiah.

‘My name is Wynfred of Wales and my business is the hunt.’

‘The hunt for what?’ asked the old farmer with a touch of nervousness.

‘Wolves.’

‘Of what nature?’

Wynfred looked at Jeremiah quizzically. ‘That is a curious question to be asking,’ he commented. ‘To my knowledge there is only one kind of wolf, but it may be you know differently. Please, enlighten me?’ he replied, his eyes twinkling with mischief.

‘I…’ Jeremiah struggled to find an answer that would allay the huntsman’s obvious suspicions.

‘He refers to outlaws,’ said Padern.

'Indeed? Do you get many in these parts?' Wynfred raised an eyebrow as he regarded the farmhand.

Padern looked to Jeremiah for aid, but he could not think of a suitable response.

'Do not worry yourselves gentlemen… and ladies,' he said, giving a nod to the two women who stood upon the right flank. 'I only seek a single she-wolf that is said to be prowling these lands.'

Jeremiah felt a sense of relief, his demeanour sagging as the tension faded. 'We seek to flush out the beast and bring about its end,' he stated.

'I would have guessed at such,' said Wynfred with a nod. 'I would also guess you have seen no sign of the creature.'

'Aye, but we have yet to pass into the deepest woods of the vale.'

'I have made my way from the track to Pendeen and there is no wolf between here and there. If you will aid me in the hunt, I suggest we move north to the crook in the vale.'

Jeremiah nodded his consent.

'Will you give me your name by which to address you?'

'Jeremiah,' he replied simply.

'And you, good sir?' asked Wynfred, looking to the farmhand.

'Padern.'

''Tis indeed a pleasure to make your acquaintance. My hope is renewed now that I have your help in hunting the she-wolf. Good fortune has smiled upon me,' he said with a heavenward glance.

'Be there a reward f…f…for finding this creature?' asked Collen.

Wynfred turned to the stocky farmer. ‘A reward?’ he said, adopting the pretence of thoughtfulness and placing a finger to his lips as he pondered.

‘I know!’ he exclaimed with a click of his fingers. ‘Upon my return up-country, I will make no mention that there may be other wolves dwelling here,’ he replied, looking to Jeremiah knowingly. ‘Does that seem fair?’

The old farmer nodded weakly.

‘Good, then the deal is done. You will help me and in return I will hold my tongue.’ He patted Caspian’s shoulder.

‘You would be surprised how many wolves I come across in my travels that at first seem nothing of the kind,’ he said with false nonchalance, ‘but I only hunt those with four legs, for the time being at least,’ he added while rubbing the hound beneath his chin.

‘Come, let us depart and make good the hours of daylight that remain.’ Wynfred turned and began to walk away through the trees, Caspian following and moving to lope at his side.

Those with Jeremiah looked to him for guidance and saw a man deflated.

‘We follow Wynfred of Wales,’ he stated, waving them forward without enthusiasm.

56

‘Do you think Tewal-Tan is still alive and slumbering beneath the Mount?’ asked Kerra as they made their way to the croft, looking to the tumbledown enclosure at the far end and wishing to break the silence.

They had heard the beaters moving through the western woods while seated beneath the apple tree and Jacob had looked to Nancherrow Hill with melancholy eyes. He suffered at the sounds and she had noted his sullenness, believing him to be concerned for White Paw’s safety.

‘It may be so,’ he replied while watching Bess round the sheep towards the open gate, the vale filled with shadow now that the sun had passed behind the trees. ‘Dragons live a long life.’

‘So he may rise again?’

‘From what we have previously said, I would say you know the story as well as I,’ he replied. ‘Meloc cast a powerful spell which sealed the dragon within the cave beneath Carrack Looz en Cooz for all eternity and so even if he were to wake there would be no escape.’

Kerra thought on his words as they passed through the gate. Jacob crouched and moved the rock aside, the single bell chiming as it closed.

‘Wait here and I will open the door so the flock may enter,’ he instructed, walking towards the cottage as Bess kept the sheep and goats together by the widened stream to the left.

Jacob went to the door and took hold of the handle, pausing a moment before opening it. He peered inside, hoping to find his brother within even though there had been no smoke rising from the hole in the thatch, finding only stillness and shadow greeting him.

With a sigh, he moved back and let out a short whistle. Bess hurried the flock inside, one of the sheep leaping through the doorway after the hound blocked its attempt to make for the enclosure with a snap and snarl.

Jacob looked to Kerra as she stood by the gate. He knew he must tell her, had been able to think of nothing else since they had first approached the apple tree early in the afternoon. It could wait no longer.

He turned to Bess as she stood just inside the cottage. 'Triga,' he instructed before closing the door.

'I should be on my way. Night comes and I promised Mamm I would be home.'

'There is something I must show you first,' stated Jacob as he walked over to her.

'What is it?'

'Come.' He opened the gate and allowed her to pass through first.

Taking the lead, Jacob went south down the vale, moving towards the foot of the eastern slope once they had passed beyond the strip of rotting stubble. As he walked he tried to organise his thoughts, to find the right words by which to reveal the truth.

Kerra noted his pensive expression and wondered at the reason for his seriousness. An inexplicable touch of nerves churned her stomach as they made their way up the incline and into the trees, her gaze briefly settling on vague indents in the sparse grasses by the trunk of an elm, realising that it was the tree beneath which they had sort shelter the previous day.

They walked beyond and made their way through a strand of bracken which brushed and scraped at their clothes. Jacob drew them to a halt and she looked at the small clearing before them, the grass short and a pair of young trees growing at its centre, the one on the right five feet tall and the other barely half that height.

'Are they apple trees?' she asked, the churning of her stomach increasing.

Jacob nodded, his pulse elevated as he prepared to finally put voice to the words he so dreaded to speak to the girl. 'That,' he said with a nod to the taller tree, 'is where my father is buried.'

She swallowed hard. 'And the other?' she asked in a nervous whisper.

Jacob turned his sorrowful gaze to her. 'Your father lies beneath.'

Kerra stared at the shorter sapling for a moment as his words sank in. She slowly turned to him with a look of dismay. 'My father?' she said breathlessly.

He nodded. 'Though I did not know he was your father until you spoke of it.'

She stared at him with wide eyes.

'He happened upon Joseph and I in the mist,' revealed Jacob. 'Upon seeing my brother's face he let out a yell and ran towards the woods on Nancherrow Hill. I followed after him, wishing to stop him and tell him the truth of our existence. When I came upon him in the trees…'

'You killed my father,' she stated in horror, backing away from him as the first desolate tears fell upon her cheeks.

'No, I…'

Kerra spun on her heels and ran, careering through the bracken. Her sobs were carried on the westerly breeze as she made her way between the trunks, Jacob catching glimpses of her golden hair as she made haste down the slope towards the stream.

‘I did not kill him,’ he called, his voice filled with misery as he stared after her and recalled the sight of her father laying amidst the undergrowth clutching his chest, face red and perspiring as a great pain gripped him and took his life. Not knowing what else to do and worried that he would be accused of the man’s murder, he and Joseph had buried him beside their father and said prayers of safe passage.

‘I did not kill him,’ he repeated softly, his heart aching as the sounds of Kerra’s sorrow continued to drift to him.

57

Kerra broke free of the woods and ran down the grassy slope with body trembling, her cheeks streaked with tears. Her legs threatened to buckle as her speed overtook her ability to make such a hurried descent.

Stumbling as she reached the foot of the slope, she righted herself and rushed across the vale. She leapt the stream, the rush of adrenalin fuelling her need to return to the comfort of her mother's arms.

She made her way up Nancherrow Hill, veering left towards the trees beyond which her home rested. The chilling screech of a barn owl sounded overhead and she glanced up, spying the bird's pale shadow passing south down the valley as it embarked on the hunt for unsuspecting prey.

She ran into the trees, the deep shadows embracing her coldly. With throat burning, she pushed onward, crashing through ferns and stumbling over rocks. Her heart thumped against her ribcage with desperate exertion, her thoughts chaotic as they seethed like the ocean in the grip of a storm, one born of Jacob's terrible revelation.

The snap of a twig drew Kerra's attention to the right. She glanced over, vainly attempting to blink away the tears that blurred her vision.

She glimpsed a dark shape moving through the trees and her heart leapt. It slunk from sight after only an instant, but the sight had been enough to inform her that it followed her course.

Turning forward, Kerra was hit in the face by a branch. It whipped across the bridge of her nose and cut the flesh beneath her left eye as she raised her arm in a belated attempt to stop the strike.

Unbalanced, her feet slipped on a rock just beyond, the moss covering its cold form ripped away by her shoes. She let out a yell as she was sent sprawling in the tall grass, fingers sliding and then digging into the earth.

Kerra gasped for air, the wind knocked from her lungs by the force of her landing. She rose, pushing up from the ground and her legs aching with the effort of her flight.

Glancing around, she spied the Sacred Oak in the gloom and knew she was not far from home. She looked down at the front of her long woollen dress, seeing the stains of grass and earth left by the fall.

A sound at her back caused Kerra to turn sharply.

Her high scream filled the woods and then abruptly fell silent.

58

Kerenza stood at the table, the basket half empty as it rested on the floor beside her and she tied bundles of plants. Others were already hanging from the lower rafters, casting shifting shadows on the walls and the underside of the thatch as the fire blazed.

She glanced to the shutters and saw the last rays of sunlight through the cracks. Wishing that her daughter would soon return, she looked to the plants before her, the air heavy with the mingling scents of herbs, earth and smoke.

She gathered half a dozen nettle stems and held them in place against the tabletop while taking up one of the cut lengths of cord resting to her right. She carefully tied it about the plants and glanced about the interior for a convenient place to hang them.

Suddenly falling still, Kerenza's brow became furrowed. The hairs on her forearms tingled in response to the brief and distant sound she had detected at the edge of her hearing.

Head cocked to one side, she listened intently, but discerned nothing more. A shiver ran through her as she stepped over to the rear of the cottage and reached up. Tying the nettles in place, she returned to the table, an increasing feeling of unease growing within.

Staring at the array of plants for a moment, Kerenza then turned to the door. She walked over and opened it, seeing the partial sun sinking out of sight over the darkening village.

She made her way out of the cottage and walked barefooted along the paths between the beds. Passing around to the rear of the building, she drew to a halt ten yards from the woodland and stared at the trees. The front ranks were gilded with the sun's failing light, a small group of silver birch seeming aglow.

'Little Bird?' she called tentatively, looking to the shadows beneath the boughs.

There was no answer bar the quiet whispers of the stirring breeze and the cry of a fox to the north.

'Kerra?' she called with greater volume, yearning to see her daughter materialise from the woods as the trees darkened and the birch lost their lustre, the brightness fading from the world.

Kerenza looked over her shoulder to find that the sun had passed from the world, the glow that marked its passage illuminating the worry in her eyes. Pulling her jerkin close, she turned and walked back to the front of the cottage, entering and closing the door behind her.

She stood and stared at the fire, her stomach light and nausea rising. Something was amiss and she tried to root out the cause of the sensation as she took a deep breath, finding only the words of warning that Tetker had given earlier that day. The dark image of Breoc standing at her gate arose like a phantom in her mind as one of the branches on the fire snapped in the heat of consumption.

'Mamm.'

The word came whispering through the stones of the rear wall.

'Mamm.'

'Kerra!' she exclaimed, turning and making haste from the cottage.

She passed along the side and rushed around the rear corner. A white flash momentarily filled her vision as a fist crunched into the bridge of her nose.

Dizzy and with sight blurred, Kerenza could see naught but shadows as she wavered on weakening legs. Darkness drew in from the periphery and her eyes rolled back, mind slipping its moorings and passing into oblivion.

Breoc watched as she collapsed onto the plant bed beside her. He flexed his fingers, blood drawn from his knuckles by the strength of the impact, her momentum lending it greater weight.

Briefly rolling his shoulder, he stepped forward and took hold of her ankles. He dragged her from sight, glancing to the path beyond the front gate and finding no witnesses to his actions.

The trapper crouched beside her, taking some twine from his belt and binding her hands. Hefting her limp form over his shoulder, he gritted his teeth against a flare of pain, certain he had pulled a muscle.

'The enchantment ends this night,' he stated as he began towards the dark woods.

59

Jacob knelt before the young apple trees. He stared at their smooth bark, their slender trunks mottled with faint sunlight as rays pierced the woodland at his back. He had resisted the urge to follow Kerra despite the yearning of his heart to tell her what had happened, that he had not been responsible for her father's death. She needed time and when he felt it was right, he would visit with her and her mother in order to tell all that was to be told of that fateful morning.

A cry of distress arose from Nancherrow Hill. He looked over his shoulder and stared at the woods on the far side of the vale, their growing darkness visible through the leafless branches of the trees marching down the slope behind him. Brow furrowed, he listened closely, but heard nothing more.

'Most likely a fox,' he said to himself, remembering childhood evenings when he had been made fearful by the wailing of foxes in the woods.

He turned to the saplings as their trunks darkened, the vague golden light fading as the sun sank towards its rest. A thought crossed his mind and his expression tightened.

''Tis not the season,' he stated to himself, realising that such sounds only arose in spring.

A shiver caused him to tremble momentarily.

'Kerra,' he stated worriedly, rising to his feet and turning.

He stepped to the strand of bracken and went still, seeing movement beyond. White Paw slunk through the trees, coming from the north with her lower jaw darkly stained by a recent kill.

'You are alive,' he whispered with a sense of relief.

She stopped and sniffed the air. Turning her head, her golden eyes held him in their aspect.

He stood motionless as they looked at each other and he saw the raw wildness within her gaze. She yawned, tongue curling as her mouth opened. Letting out a faint groan, she licked the blood about her lips as she continued to regard him coldly.

She lingered a while longer, ears rotating to the chatter of starlings settling in the trees at the foot of the vale, their cacophony drowning out the sound of gulls that drifted from the coast. Then, with a slight nod of her head, White Paw continued southward through the strand of trees.

Jacob watched her silent passage until she could no longer be seen, feeling as though the nod had been one of thanks for the food he had delivered while she convalesced in the hollow. He pushed aside the first of the ferns and moved through the strand as quietly as possible, watching for any sign of her, but seeing no trace.

Reaching the other side of the strand, he walked down the slope towards the tree-line, passing the elm under which he and Kerra had sheltered as he looked across the vale to the woods on Nancherrow Hill. He was about to leave the shelter of the boughs when a dark figure drew out of the shadows on the far slope, moving towards the croft as it entered the grassland.

Jacob become still and narrowed his eyes as he tried to discern who it was. They were too large to be Kerra and seemed to be carrying something over their shoulder.

A look of confusion upon his face, Jacob stayed within the trees and moved north, glancing over to check the figure's progress through the gloom. Passing through another large strand of bracken, he drew level with the rear of the croft as the shadowy shape moved to where the stream had been widened on the far side and was hidden from view by the building.

Making haste, Jacob made his way across the grasses between the woods and the boundary wall. He lifted his robe and vaulted the stones, one of their number shifting beneath the weight of his palm. He hurried across the vegetable beds to the back of the cottage, his pulse elevated as he drew up to the corner and prepared to glance around.

'ESTREN ONAN!'

'Breoc,' he whispered, recognising the trapper's voice.

'ESTREN ONAN. REVEAL YOURSELF,' called the trapper as he stood on the bank of the stream, Kerenza's body laid at his feet.

Jacob took a breath and stepped from the rear of the croft, the trapper's gaze immediately drawn to the movement. 'I am here,' he stated, using the rhythm of his walking stick to try and calm his heart.

'Skulking in the shadows,' commented Breoc. 'Why am I not surprised?'

'What be your business here?' asked Jacob as Bess barked from within the cottage and he came to a halt five yards from the waters, glancing over to the door as the hound scratched at its base.

'Remove the enchantment,' demanded the trapper.

'There be no enchantment other than that conjured by your own mind,' he responded.

'I saw its effect upon her with my own eyes, just as I saw the demon that dwells with you.'

‘You are welcome to search my home again if the evidence of last night be not enough.’ Jacob held his hand out towards the door.

‘What I witnessed *is* enough,’ responded Breoc forcefully.

‘My actions against her will be forgiven once the spell is lifted and she is returned to her own mind,’ he said, looking down at Kerenza as she lay motionless before him. ‘She will give testament as to your foul ways and the offering you have left at the Sacred Oak will seal your fate.’

‘I have made no such offering of late.’

‘I have done so for you,’ replied Breoc through the half-light of dusk, ‘and ‘tis one which will earn you the hangman’s noose. Now, release her from the enchantment or suffer the consequences.’

There was a moment of silent inaction as they stared at each other across the stream.

‘Ah-ha, your demon shows itself now that you are threatened,’ stated Breoc, pointing to the eastern slope.

Jacob looked over his shoulder and saw White Paw standing at the tree-line a hundred yards away. An idea came to mind and he turned back to the trapper. ‘Aye, and if you do not leave I shall call it down upon you.’

Breoc dropped to his knees, drawing Kerenza onto his lap and cradling her head. He drew his knife and placed the blade to her neck as he held the shepherd’s gaze. ‘And I shall slit her throat and call the village down upon you,’ he countered, the words filled with conviction.

‘You would kill the woman you profess to have feelings for?’ said Jacob in bewilderment.

‘As long as your spell remains our union will be undone,’ he said, ‘so if you will not free her from the spell then I shall free her from her life, one stolen by the enchantment.’

‘This is madness,’ said Jacob with a shake of his head.

‘I will not ask again,’ stated Breoc, knife pressing to her throat.

Kerenza groaned and began to come round. The trapper looked down at her as Bess continued to growl and bark from the confines of the croft.

‘Where am I?’ she asked groggily.

‘You are soon to be freed,’ stated Breoc before looking across the stream. ‘What will it be?’

Jacob stared at him dumbfounded for a moment and then released his walking stick, which fell to the grass as he spread his arms wide. ‘Take me instead,’ he stated. ‘The enchantment you imagine will be ended with my passing.’

‘And your changling demon?’ Breoc glanced at the wolf.

‘It will not interfere,’ replied Jacob as he stepped up to the bank. ‘My life for hers, that is the bargain I strike with you.’ He climbed into the stream and stood waist deep in the waters, raising his arms once again.

‘Come no closer,’ stated the trapper as he considered the offer.

Kerenza stared fearfully up at him and felt the touch of his blade against her throat, swallowing hard and her chest heaving as her heart pounded.

‘So be it,’ he responded after a few moments, removing the knife and placing her on the grass before him.

A shadow drawing from the northern woods caught Jacob’s eye as he stood in the stream’s cold embrace. He turned to the right and found a beast the likes of which he had never seen before prowling into the grassland twenty yards from the trapper. Its gaze was set on Breoc as it steadily approached him and the trapper rose to his feet.

Breoc followed his gaze and blanched, moving to face the oncoming beast.

'So, there be more than one demon that abides with you, and this more unnatural than the other,' he stated as it continued to bear down on him. 'Give your command so that it will halt its advance.'

'I can command no such thing for 'tis not mine to control,' responded Jacob.

'This is my last warning.'

'Indeed it is,' said a man clothed in a wolf-skin and holding a spear as he stepped from beneath the boughs to the rear of the strange beast.

Jacob and Breoc both looked to him in surprise as the creature halted, its gaze remaining fixed on the trapper.

'You have no business here, stranger,' stated the trapper threateningly.

'Ah, but I do,' he replied with a rye grin, 'but do not take my word for it. Ask these men who stand with me, ones who I am sure you will recognise.'

Jeremiah and Padern materialised from the shadows of the woods to either side of the man. The other beaters stepped into sight staggered along the tree-line, half a dozen on the croft side of the stream beyond the boundary wall.

Breoc looked to them in alarm as Kerenza strained against the bonds about her wrists, unable to gain her freedom.

'Release her, Breoc,' instructed Jeremiah. 'Whatever this is,' he said with a nod towards Kerenza's bound form, ''tis done.'

'No,' he replied with force, ''tis not done until he releases her from the enchantment.'

'There be no enchantment,' said Kerenza.

The trapper glanced down at her and then looked to the old farmer. 'Do you not see the demon that stands before you all?' he asked.

'That is no demon,' replied Jeremiah. ''Tis a hound bred for the purpose of hunting wolves.'

Breoc turned his gaze to the creature, finding it regarding him with back legs trembling in readiness to leap.

'We flushed out the wolf near Kenijack and were on its trail when we heard voices in the hush, thy voices,' said Jeremiah pointedly, Jacob glancing to the eastern slope and gratefully finding no trace of White Paw.

'We heard everything you said,' stated Wynfred, accusation carried in his tone as he moved closer, coming to a stop within ten yards of the trapper, his hound a few steps ahead.

Breoc glanced at Kerenza as he considered his course of action, Caspian taking the opportunity to draw closer to his position. 'Keep your beast to heel,' he stated, raising the knife.

'He hunts a wolf,' responded Wynfred, the implication of his words not lost on the trapper.

Breoc quickly crouched and gathered Kerenza to him, his knife once more resting at her throat.

'No!' called Jacob, wading forward as the trapper began to back away from the wolfhound.

Kerenza jabbed her elbow backward with panicked force, striking Breoc in the side. Taken by surprise, his grip loosened and she pulled away from him, the blade cutting the side of her neck as she came free of his hold.

Wynfred acted quickly, raising the spear and throwing it in a fluid movement. The weapon pieced the air, its point flashing through the dusk.

There was a gasp and a brief cry as it buried itself in Breoc's chest. The trapper looked down at the dark shaft protruding from his body, his eyes wide and mouth hanging open as the knife fell from his hand.

Turning his gaze to those arrayed before him, his mouth moved as if he were trying to speak. Only a pained gurgle issued forth as blood began to drip from his lips, his face becoming ghostly pale.

Legs collapsing beneath him, Breoc fell to the ground and came to rest on his back. His gaze was set to the first stars as they revealed themselves in the darkening sky, the trapper's life vacating his body beneath their cold and distant light.

The beaters stood in shock and stared at Breoc's still form. The sound of gulls drifted from the coast as the last remnants of the day were chased west by the cloak of night.

Jeremiah walked stiffly over and crouched by the trapper. Kerenza dropped to her knees a few yards away, bruising darkening her eyes and her nose swollen by the unexpected blow she had received as she rushed to the rear of her cottage.

The old farmer placed his hand to Breoc's neck for a few moments and then looked over his shoulder. 'He is dead,' he announced regretfully.

'It seems I have killed a wolf after all,' commented Wynfred as he went to the corpse, putting his boot to its stomach before yanking out the spear.

'Had thee need to take his life?' asked Jeremiah as Jacob made his way to the bank and drew out of the stream, seeing Kerenza's distress and wishing to bring her comfort as the other beaters were held in place by their dismay.

'The spear is not a weapon by which you can easily wound alone. 'Tis a weapon of death and thus my weapon of choice. Had I tried to pierce only an arm or a leg, you may have found your village deprived of one of its women,' he replied, glancing at Kerenza.

Jacob made his way to her side. He crouched before her, purposefully blocking the view of Breoc's body as best he could. Reaching forward, he began to undo the bonds about her wrists.

'Jacob,' she said softly, staring at his face with a haunted look.

''Tis me,' he replied, the cord coming loose and then falling from skin made sore by its rub.

'Am I dreaming?' she asked, holding his gaze.

The shepherd shook his head. 'I fear not, unless it be a dream we all share.'

Padern walked over to the body as Jeremiah straightened by its side, rubbing the small of his back and shaking his head. The other members of the party began to make their way over, those beyond the boundary wall of the croft jumping over the stream where it became narrow once more.

'Look!' cried Samuel, pointing up the slope of Nancherrow Hill. 'A spirit comes.'

Jacob's eyes widened when he spied the pale figure which had emerged from the woodland further down the vale.

''Tis not a spirit, but a leper,' stated Wynfred as he leant upon his spear, 'one that I met upon the road from Penzance only yesterday, if I am not mistaken.'

Jacob narrowed his eyes as he noted a dark shape being cradled by his brother, a hint of soft gold trailing over his right arm. His brow furrowed as he tried to discern what Joseph was carrying, his pulse beginning to rise.

Realisation struck him with fearful force, its impact causing him to swoon momentarily.

‘NO!’ wailed Kerenza, her voice filled with despair as she stared at her daughter’s motionless form.

She rose upon unsteady legs and desperately made her way to Joseph. Stopping before him, she brought him to a halt and stared at the body cradled in his arms..

‘Little Bird,’ she whispered, face wrung by torment as she looked upon her daughter’s restful countenance. ‘Open your eyes.’

Jacob went to her side and noted the dark stain of blood upon the wool at the girl’s chest. He looked to his brother’s face as Joseph lifted his head, seeing the regret and sorrow in his eyes.

‘I heard a scream as I approached the foot of the vale and found her lying beneath the Sacred Oak,’ he said softly.

Kerenza gathered her daughter into her arms. She sank to the ground and held the body close, hand to the back of Kerra’s head. ‘Wake up,’ she pleaded into the girl’s ear as she began to rock back and forth. ‘Please wake up.’

Jacob’s eyes welled with tears and he looked upon the sad embrace, Kerra’s arms limp and unable to respond in kind to her mother’s need. His imagination conjured the image of the girl lying before the trunk of the Sacred Oak and he thought of the offerings of flowers he sometimes left there, their wilted remains discovered upon his return.

‘Please do not leave me,’ moaned Kerenza, tears beginning to stream down her cheeks as the beaters looked on with forlorn expressions.

She clutched a hand to her chest, her heart feeling as though it were being rent apart by her anguish. Struggling for breath, she closed her eyes tightly, feeling Kerra’s cold cheek against hers and yearning for the warmth to return.

‘He has killed the girl,’ stated Padern, pointing at Joseph. ‘We must enact swift justice upon this foul creature and bring about his end.’

The large farmhand walked towards Joseph with purpose and his stick held at the ready. The other beaters moved forward in the gathering gloom, their expressions hard as they drew near and Joseph began to back away.

‘Wait!’ called Wynfred, bending to pick up Breoc’s knife before examining it closely. ‘There is fresh blood upon the hilt of this blade.’

He crouched and rolled the corpse onto its side as the beaters turned to him. ‘And there is the stain of blood wiped upon his leggings,’ he added, letting the body fall back. ‘I say this man is guilty of the girl’s death.’

Jeremiah looked down at Breoc’s pained expression, the trapper’s lifeless eyes still set to the stars. ‘‘Tis a sad day indeed,’ he murmured with a shake of his head as those who had been rounding on Joseph lowered their sticks.

Jacob moved to Kerenza’s side and tentatively placed an arm about her shoulders. ‘May Dor Dama watch over her,’ he said quietly as she leant into the comfort of his presence, retaining a tight hold on Kerra’s body as her own trembled with the release of her agony.

60

Jacob hurriedly cleared the cups, bowls and cutlery from the table. He threw them upon his cot as Bess leapt at his legs, finding herself ignored. Standing aside once the task was done, his brother stepped forward and rested Kerra's body down, her mother moving to her side and taking her limp hand in hers as she continued to cry.

Jeremiah and Padern stood just inside the doorway with the huntsman, the rest of the beaters gathered outside. They eyed Joseph nervously as he stepped over to the woodpile in his bloodied robes and collected a few branches, fearful of catching his horrific disease.

'Who are you, stranger?' asked Padern.

Joseph bent to place the timber upon the flames in the fire pit so as to bring warmth for his brother, whose robes were still wet and dripping. Straightening, he turned to the men at the door, keeping his head bowed so that his face remained concealed. 'I am Joseph, brother to Jacob and son of Gorlas,' he replied as Bess moved to stand beside him.

'Ye are Joseph?!' exclaimed Jeremiah in surprise.

He nodded. 'Aye, and 'tis I that has abided here with Jacob, not spirits, as many have believed.'

The men and women beyond the threshold shared a few glances in response to his words as Jacob placed his arm about Kerenza's shoulders to comfort her.

'Why did ye not make thy presence known to us?' asked the farmer.

'We feared persecution, the likes of which I would not have my brother endure and which is oft the accompaniment of my condition.'

Jeremiah regarded him for a moment and then looked to Padern. 'What say ye to Joseph abiding at the croft?'

The farmhand looked at Joseph. 'I say you are welcome here, as any son of the village should be,' he responded.

'Ye have our word,' stated Jeremiah loudly in order that all those gathered at the croft would hear. 'Naught of malice will be done unto thee.'

Joseph gave a nod beneath his hood. 'You have my thanks.'

'It seems you knew of the wolf after all,' commented Wynfred, glancing over his shoulder towards Breoc's body as it lay in the darkness on the far side of the stream.

'Of which wolf do you speak?' he responded. 'Man or beast?'

'It may be you knew of both.'

'It may be I did,' conceded Joseph, raising his head so as to regard the huntsman, the other men flinching, but Wynfred showing no sign of disturbance in sight of his face.

A hush descended, one filled with the sounds of the fire and Kerenza's gentle sobs. She leant her head on Jacob's shoulder as they looked upon her daughter.

Jeremiah turned to those gathered outside. With ushering motions, he moved them back and stepped from the croft. ''Tis time we returned to our homes and left them to mourn,' he stated quietly as Padern moved to his side.

'I will take my leave of your company,' stated Wynfred as he exited behind them and began towards the gate, Caspian waiting patiently beyond the boundary wall as the beaters allowed the huntsman through their throng.

'There is still another wolf that has yet to taste the tip of my spear,' he said over his shoulder.

'Fare ye well, Wynfred of Wales,' called Samuel after him as he passed through the gate.

The huntsman raised a hand in the air as he headed south, the wolfhound moving to his side.

Jeremiah looked over to the far side of the stream. 'Samuel. Collen. Ye carry Breoc's body,' he instructed.

'I will aid them,' said Padern, the two men who had been assigned the duty showing their relief at the offer of help from the large farmhand.

The beaters moved out of the croft enclosure, the single bell upon the gate's top rung marking their departure. They moved through the night, a faint light in the west hinting at the recent passing of the day. Joseph watched as they made their way over the stream and then turned to his brother and Kerenza. They stood with their backs to him, holding each other close as the girl rested in stillness before them.

He slipped from the building, patting his legs to encourage Bess outside. Quietly closing the door, he left them to their mournful peace and began towards the pair of apple trees upon the eastern slope as the villagers carried the trapper's body up Nancherrow Hill.

61

The sound of Kerenza's weeping mingled with the whisper of the trees as she knelt at the graveside in the small clearing. Her eyes were raw and desolate as she looked upon the fresh earth, the saplings of the apple trees on the far side. Jacob and Joseph stood behind her, the latter's face hidden beneath his hood. Tetker lingered by the strand of bracken that bordered the foot of the clearing, clutching a fleece about her neck and Jeremiah at her side as they bowed their heads in silent prayer.

'Dearest,' mumbled Tetker, tears glittering upon her wrinkled cheeks.

Stepping forward, Jacob took the straw doll from his robes and bent to place it upon the grave. 'May she rest peacefully in winter's sleep,' he said softly, straightening and resting a hand upon Kerenza's shoulder before returning to his brother.

She began to hum the Lay of Ailla and Jacob wept in response to the tune, recalling Kerra's light rendition and seeing her dimpled smile. He covered his face with his hands and succumbed to the sorrow that welled within, releasing it in a flood of tears.

'I miss you, Little Bird,' said Kerenza when the tune came to an end, her voice cracking and face contorting.

There was a long silence punctuated by Jacob's distress.

'May the Lord welcome her through the gates of Heaven,' stated Jeremiah before slowly turning away.

He moved through the bracken and began to make his way down the slope through the trees. Tetker looked to the grave one last time, shaking her head before following after her childhood friend.

Trying to hold his sorrow in check, Jacob stepped to Kerenza and knelt beside her. He placed his arm about her shoulders and they sat together in silence, their eyes resting upon the straw doll. She leant against him, made weary by her grief and grateful for his company.

Joseph looked upon them for a moment and then made his way from the clearing, his robe brushing against the bracken as he passed down into the vale.

'We will plant an apple tree upon the grave and in years to come we will taste its fruit,' stated Jacob softly as she looked into his eyes and saw her own sorrow reflected in their depths. 'Upon that day she will become part of us, just as she will be part of the vale and beyond.'

'She will take to the wing with the birds and the bees,' said Kerenza, blinking tears from her eyes as a group of gulls called overhead as if to say farewell.

Jacob turned his gaze to the cold blue sky. 'Aye, she will take to the wing,' he responded with a sad smile.

Epilogue 1

Wynfred crouched in the cold morning light and studied the fresh paw prints in the mud before him. Turning his gaze to the promontory of land reaching into the ocean ahead, he sensed that the journey was reaching its conclusion.

The land dipped as it drew out to sea and then rose again to a high and rocky hill. The waves crashed far below, frothing and seething as they were driven by the wind that toyed with the huntsman's dark hair.

'There is nowhere left to run,' he stated, hunting for the she-wolf with his eyes, but seeing no sign of her amidst the crags.

He stood and turned to Caspian as the wolfhound waited by his side. 'She is ours,' he said, patting his companion on the shoulder.

Holding his spear at the ready, Wynfred began down the slope, boots slipping on the mud and wet grasses. Caspian equalled his pace as they moved towards the outcrop, both looking for any sign of the wolf's whereabouts.

Reaching the lowest point, the sea embracing their position, they started up the far side. Spray was torn from the waves and drawn up the cliffs on the wind. It settled on the huntsman's cheeks, its touch enlivening as he anticipated the beast's demise.

His grip upon the spear became tighter as they moved around boulders rising from the earth, patches of grey and yellow lichen growing on their permanence. The grass came to an end and they halted before the tor of weathered crags.

'Wait here,' he stated to his hound, holding up his hand to underline the instruction.

Moving to the right as Caspian watched, the huntsman sidled into a narrow fissure. The rough stones behind him pulled at the wolf-skin and scraped at the hide cloak beneath as he slunk into the dank confines. The sounds of his awkward passage were accentuated by the looming sides and he looked up with brow furrowed, hoping to escape the constriction and spying sunlight on the rocks five feet above his head.

Seeing a crevice that would act as a suitable handhold, he began to climb up. His right hand slipped on the slick surface as he tried to retain his grip on the spear while making the ascent. The weapon was loosed from his grasp and fell clattering below, the sounds making him tense and accompanied by the scitter of small stones.

Wynfred stared down at the spear for a moment as he thought about collecting it. Deciding to leave it until his return, he continued up the steep cliff, finding the going much easier without the weapon in hand.

Upon reaching the top, he straightened and looked about the outcrop. His vantage point was obscured by towers of rock and he could see numerous crags in which the wolf could be hidden.

The huntsman glanced back, having to stretch his neck in order to see Caspian's head, the hound remaining watchful at the edge of the tor below. Grinning to himself, he felt satisfied that the wolf would not find escape even if it tried to flee whilst he clambered amidst the rocks. He drew the knife from his belt, the sunlight flashing on its blade as he set off in search of her.

Passing around a large boulder, he came across a cleft too wide to jump. Placing the blade between his teeth, Wynfred made the descent into the small ravine and heard the wind softly howling between the rocks.

'Where are you?' he whispered, following the shadowy passage with his knife at the ready.

He ducked under a stone that lay across the cleft and moved out onto a slab of flat rock, finding himself at the southernmost point of the outcrop. Stepping to the edge, he peered down as gulls called out and their cries were taken by the wind. The ocean frothed on the spill of boulders and bed of rock that rested at the foot of the promontory forty feet below. A boom resounded as a wave crashed against a dark spine of stone rising from the waters to the left, bursting upward and sending a mist of spray into the air.

A faint scrabbling sound caused Wynfred to turn on his heels. The wolf stood upon the rocks above his position, framed against the blue sky and her pale fur bathed in sunshine. She held him in her golden gaze, a snarl upon her lips.

'A merry dance you have led me, but we come to its end at last,' he said with a grin, adjusting the grip on his knife in readiness, expecting the beast to flee and the final chase to ensue.

The wolf sprang as another boom lifted into the air. Wynfred stared in surprise as she bore down upon him, claws reaching out and jaw open.

She ploughed into the huntsman, his knife burying in her chest as they tumbled over the edge of the rock. He turned away as the wolf snapped at his face, her teeth sinking into the side of his head as they fell through the air.

'A merry dance,' murmured Wynfred through the pain as the shore rushed up to meet them.

They crunched into the bed of rock and were embraced by frothy lips. The body of the wolf toppled from the huntsman, the hilt of his blade protruding from her fur as the retreating waters drew her away from him.

Overcome by the pain of his broken body and sight blurred by seawater stained with blood, Wynfred took his last breath. His arms twitched in final release of life as the waves boomed once again.

Epilogue 2

The desiccated corpse of a dwarf sat cross-legged upon the remains of a grass mat, the thatch above black and fallen in places, the cloudy sky visible through the holes. Its right hand rested upon its knee, skin leathered and sunken onto bone. A selection of teeth lay upon the open palm, their decay echoed by the ragged and rotting furs in which the figure was clothed.

Windblown ash coated the furs draped over its legs, the fire pit before the dwarf long since grown cold. Marsh grass grew at its side, slowly claiming the figure in its concealment.

The door hung loose where its upper hinge had torn free of the frame's rotting wood, the entrance choked with swaying grass as two skulls stared sightlessly from the lintel above. The breeze reached into the hut and the pale webs of the dwarf's hair stirred with borrowed life.

A robin flitted in, landing upon the damp earth beyond the grasses intruding through the doorway. It looked about curiously and hopped closer to the figure, warily regarding it with beady eyes.

Taking brief flight, it settled upon the dwarf's shoulder. There was the soft sound of tearing and the upper arm came loose, suddenly dropping until the furs in which it was confined cradled the fall.

The robin let out a tweet of alarm and flew out of the hut as the dwarf's head shifted, leaning to the side as if listening. Its hand slipped from its knee, the teeth spilling and chattering as they fell to the ground. They spoke of legends of a beast neither wolf nor hound lurking in the woods far to the west. They whispered of the first spring blossom opening on a small apple tree in a clearing, a butterfly of pure white flitting to its promise before taking flight with the dusting of another's life upon its fragile wings.

The teeth fell still and silence followed. The last of the tale had been told.

Afterward

The first draft of *The Shepherd of St Just* took six weeks and four days to write, the longest it has ever taken me to write a novel. As with most of my novels, I began with a situation and a couple of the major characters. From that starting point, I simply let the story unfold, allowing the characters to act of their own accord, remaining true to themselves rather than being forced along a particular path by me. Unlike authors who plan their novels and rigidly stick to these plans despite their characters sometimes wishing to deviate from them, I am not akin to a dictator, but I am more like a god in that I allow my characters free will.

Writing this way means that unforeseen events will occur and new characters will unexpectedly arrive as the story unfolds. This is an organic way of creating fiction and lends an additional sense of flow to a narrative and also makes the writing process one of discovery. The characters live and breathe, acting of their own accord and sometimes surprising me, though always remaining true to who they are.

The Shepherd of St Just is the last book in what I loosely term as my 'Outcast Trilogy.' Though the books can be read in any order and the links between them are minor, they create a set of three novels all focussing on the existence of outcasts in the late 13th Century.

They also present stories that could have led to beliefs in the supernatural and to the creation of myths and legends. In this novel the myths relate to the existence of spirits and demons. In this way *Where Seagulls Fly*,

Song of the Sea and *The Shepherd of St Just* create bridges between reality and myth.

Also like the previous two historical novels set in western Cornwall, there is deeper meaning, and in *The Shepherd of St Just* this relates to how we interact with the natural world. Jacob is unselfish. He takes only what he needs and shares with nature. His view of life is one of harmonious existence with the world rather than discord, and this a view modern society could well learn from. At this time the stability of the environment that sustains us hangs on a thread. It is vital we start to live in harmony with our planet and recognise that we are an integral part of it, that our actions will effect the world and will therefore also have an impact on us.

The story also relates to death and the fact that the energy of which you consist is redistributed when you die. Each of us is just a passing form of constantly changing energy, like a current in an ocean. The energy itself is immortal and when we pass on it moves on to become part of other currents within the ocean.

There are a number of factual details woven into the narrative that I would now like to leave you with. These follow below and I hope that you will find them interesting. It may also be of note to those that have yet to read it, that the complete Lay of Ailla appears in *Song of the Sea*.

Time is the most important thing you have, your life is measured by it, and so I thank you for taking the time to read this novel and hope it has left a mark in some way.

1. During his reign, King Edward ordered the extermination of all wolves in his kingdom. He personally employed a man named Peter Corbet, who was instructed to eradicate wolves in the

Welsh border counties of Gloucestershire, Herefordshire, Shropshire, Staffordshire and Worcestershire, where the creatures were most common at the time. By the end of Edward's reign in 1307 the attempt at exterminating wolves had not been successful and they are not thought to have become extinct in England until the reign of Henry VII (1485 and 1509).

2. The festival called Kalan-Gwav in Cornish is known as Samhain throughout the rest of Britain. It takes place from sunset on the 31st October until sunset on the 1st November and is one of the four main festivals on the Gaelic calendar. It marks the end of harvest and the beginning of winter. Bonfires would be lit and it was traditionally the time when livestock to be slaughtered for the winter would be selected.
3. The Plen-an-Gwary proposed to be built at the Gathering Place in the narrative was actually constructed in St Just sometime in the early 14th century. The name is Cornish for 'playing place' or 'place of the play.' Though many were created during the late Middle Ages 'the Plen,' as it is called locally, is now only one of two examples of these early theatres to still exist in Cornwall. It can be found in the heart of the village and there is a society dedicated to the preservation of this scheduled ancient monument.
4. The Cornish name for St Just can be spelt either as 'Lannust' or 'Lanust.'
5. The word 'gwynsek,' which is used during the story in the name 'Gwynsek Farm,' is Cornish for 'windy.'

6. The Cornish name for Cape Cornwall is Kilgoodh Ust, which means 'goose back of St Just.'
7. Leprosy was commonplace at the time this novel is set and between the end of the 11th century and 1350 at least 320 houses and hospitals were established for the care of lepers. These were known as leper or 'lazar' houses and two were known to be located in Cornwall, one in St Keverne and the other at Veryan. All leper houses were religious and concentrated on a life devoted to praising God. Attitudes to leprosy were divided. Some thought it was punishment for sin whereas others thought it was akin to the suffering of Christ and that lepers would go straight to heaven as they had already suffered purgatory during their life on earth. Those who made charitable donations to leper houses or to individual lepers begging for alms thought they were reducing their own time in purgatory by doing so.
8. The Battle of Stirling Bridge took place on 11th September 1297 and was a battle in the First War of Scottish Independence. The forces of Andrew Moray and William Wallace defeated those of John de Warenne, 6th Earl of Surrey, and Hugh de Cressingham. This occurred at a bridge over the River Forth near the settlement of Stirling and their victory was largely afforded by the narrowness of this bridge. The Cornish did not revolt at the time, but did attempt to do so in 1497, during the reign of Henry VII. However, this rebellion was put down at The Battle of Deptford Bridge when a 15,000 strong Cornish army led by a blacksmith named An Gof was

defeated by a superior and better equipped royal force.

If you enjoyed *The Shepherd of St Just* then try *Where Seagulls Fly*, *Song of the Sea* or *The Hanging Tree*. For a contemporary story by the same author, try *Quiddity* or *Synergy*. All these books and more by Edwin Page are available in paperback and Kindle formats.

16090062R00201

Printed in Great Britain
by Amazon